THE WOMAN IN THE LOBBY

PRAISE FOR LEE TULLOCH'S NOVELS

FABULOUS NOBODIES

'(A) lighthearted yet devastatingly accurate and witty social satire . . . Tulloch's cutting humor suffuses every detail'
Publisher's Weekly

'Ms Tulloch's voice is sharp, affectionate and hilarious'
New York Times Book Review

'One of my all-time favourite books. I adore it . . . Tulloch was ahead of her time' *Marian Keyes*

'A riot of a story . . . This is a book that makes you laugh and wince at the same time, it's so awful, so funny, so right'
Cosmopolitan

WRAITH

' . . . full of searing insights into the business of being beautiful, and drips with caustic, cosmopolitan humour. Tulloch has a real understanding of fashion's international 'cool crowd'
Harper's Bazaar

'Stiletto sharp' *The Australian*

'As blockbuster entertainment, it fits the bill perfectly' *The Age*

TWO SHANES

'Genuinely funny . . . a good-hearted romp' *Bulletin*

'Tulloch has always shared Armistead Maupin's skill for writing quirky characters' *Sydney Morning Herald*

'This is a Manhattan cocktail made with the merest hint of Martin Amis strained over early Jay McInerney; stirred with Vegemite jokes, Crocodile Dundee stereotypes and a suspicion of Bazza McKenzie' *Weekend Australian*

LEE TULLOCH

THE WOMAN IN THE LOBBY

VIKING
an imprint of
PENGUIN BOOKS

VIKING

Published by the Penguin Group
Penguin Group (Australia)
250 Camberwell Road, Camberwell, Victoria 3124, Australia
(a division of Pearson Australia Group Pty Ltd)
Penguin Group (USA) Inc.
375 Hudson Street, New York, New York 10014, USA
Penguin Group (Canada)
90 Eglinton Avenue East, Suite 700, Toronto, Canada ON M4P 2Y3
(a division of Pearson Penguin Canada Inc.)
Penguin Books Ltd
80 Strand, London WC2R 0RL, England
Penguin Ireland
25 St Stephen's Green, Dublin 2, Ireland
(a division of Penguin Books Ltd)
Penguin Books India Pvt Ltd
11 Community Centre, Panchsheel Park, New Delhi – 110 017, India
Penguin Group (NZ)
67 Apollo Drive, Rosedale, North Shore 0632, New Zealand
(a division of Pearson New Zealand Ltd)
Penguin Books (South Africa) (Pty) Ltd
24 Sturdee Avenue, Rosebank, Johannesburg 2196, South Africa

Penguin Books Ltd, Registered Offices: 80 Strand, London, WC2R 0RL, England

First published by Penguin Group (Australia), 2008

1 3 5 7 9 10 8 6 4 2

Cover design by Allison Colpoys © Penguin Group (Australia)
Text design by Anne-Marie Reeves © Penguin Group (Australia)
Cover photograph shot on location at the Hotel de Crillon, Paris, by Carla Coulson and styled by Arno Ferrie, with special thanks to Tessa Taittinger
Author photograph by Tony Amos
Typeset in 12/16.5 pt Fairfield Light by Post Pre-press Group, Brisbane, Queensland
Printed and bound in Australia by McPherson's Printing Group, Maryborough, Victoria

National Library of Australia
Cataloguing-in-Publication data:

Tulloch, Lee.
The woman in the lobby.
ISBN 978 0 670 04295 1 (pbk).
I.Title.
A823.3

penguin.com.au

FOR RAMONA

Part One

Violetta and Violet

HOTEL METROPOLITAIN

Avenue de Friedland, Paris, France

The marble and gilt lobby of the Hotel Metropolitain is full of aimless souls looking for a little diversion. It's the devil's hour, cocktail hour, when gentlemen are known to stray from their intended paths.

Sooner or later, one of them will stray my way.

I am sitting on a sofa by an arrangement of lilies, a respectable young woman waiting . . . for an assignation, perhaps? No, it's a little late for *cinq à sept*, unless one is very quick, so perhaps I am waiting for my husband for an anniversary drink? A meal in the hotel's overpriced dining room followed by a night of rekindled passion amid the Frette sheets? Or else I am meeting a woman friend – or two – whereupon we will retire to the bar for a night of character assassination (husbands, bosses, other girlfriends, Olivier Martinez) and some harmless flirting.

Waiting is what I am doing – and tonight I may not have to wait so long. The lobby is full of prospects. It is check-in time for businessmen who have caught the afternoon flights from London, Brussels, Frankfurt, Milan, Dubai . . . places that have the sound of money to them. Some of them are busy with porters, others yell into phones. A few lug thick briefcases to the elevator banks, eager for the mini bar. Some will shower and come back to the lobby, the musk of their anticipation even stronger than the citrus of their over-applied cologne.

I hope one of them will be mine.

I have arranged myself so that my skirts are smoothed around me, my back propped against a firm cushion so that I don't sink into the fat sofa and disappear. I am beautifully groomed but very lightly made up. This distinguishes me from the independent contractors, a pack of €300-an-hour hyenas in tight skirts and deep slashes of blush who lurk behind the flower arrangements, ready to pounce. I am a class act. I have an elegant crocodile vanity case at my feet, suggesting I am also a traveller, in transition, that if you blink you may find me gone. On the cushion beside me there is a very large handbag of excellent quality that gentlemen connoisseurs, who have bought for their mistresses similar bags, would know is valued at upwards of €10,000. If the wait proves long – and it often does – I will extract from it a hardback copy of Ayn Rand's *The Fountainhead*, which I found at a *bouquiniste* along the Seine. It is the favoured read of the connoisseur. It has started conversations, saved me many times when there's nothing to say. This book, the vanity case and its contents, the handbag with my journal and a few euros tucked inside, my dress and jacket, my good shoes, a gold panther bracelet, a Cartier watch and a modest emerald ring, are all I possess in the world.

But *he* isn't to know that. He who is to take me away from all of this.

A handsome young Japanese nods as he walks past, but he is followed by two porters, a jumble of expensive luggage and, depressingly, a wife clutching what might be either a fluffy dog or an amusing handbag. A redhead in a pinstripe suit casts a lingering glance but his porter leads him away from me to the far bank of elevators. A black man in a nylon anorak emblazoned with slogans catches my eye but he is joined by other men in other anoraks and they go to the bar. A pair of independent contractors arise from their seats and slink after them. Bless their mercenary souls, I think, they have saved me from the football players.

A manager in a black suit is standing by a vase of delphiniums. He has been watching me for some time, as if I might be a *risque pour la sécurité*, as ladies who sit alone in hotels sometimes are. (He knows all the independent contractors; I am suspicious because I am new.) He strolls over to the reception desk and engages the girl in conversation. I let my eyes catch hers and smile. Don't worry, dear, I think, I won't be here much longer. No need this time to book a room and skip through in the early hours of the morning. This last thing I have done, and done, and gotten away with, or not, as the circumstances might be. I may even have done it in this hotel but all hotels meld into one stone edifice with marble floors and men in black suits and porters wielding gilded trolleys and polished tables aching with oriental lilies. (If I have skipped out on this hotel before I'd better be quick.)

The man who is approaching me now would not be my first choice. He's short, rotund, walking as if on tiptoes, his medicine ball of a stomach leading the way. He looks as if he might tumble forward at any moment, onto his face or into my arms. He is not attractive. But I have had enough of handsome men. And I have learnt not to set my heart on anyone. Not least when I'm hungry.

As he approaches, I make a show of holding out my wrist to check the time, tap the face of my watch in a display of frustration. I catch his eye immediately, a sign he is on the prowl. 'May I bother you for the time, sir? *Quelle heur est-il?*'

I know my pronunciation is clumsy but the old gentleman stops nevertheless, consults a handsome lump of gold and glass on a thick glossy strap, and tells me it is *dix-neuf heures moins cinq*.

'Oh, it's that late already?' The prettiest flush I can muster stains my cheeks. '*Je regrette* . . . oh, damn, I don't know how to say it in French.'

He nods and says, in English, that he is sure my French is very good.

'You're very kind, but my accent is appalling. Will you forgive me if we speak English? I've only been in Paris a day and six years of school French doesn't get a girl very far.'

Well, that was the first lie. I've been in Paris so long I feel like the Eiffel Tower.

The gentleman continues to lean towards me, in a half bow. He tells me it is a lovely accent. Am I from London?

'Oh, I am from much further away than that!' I say enigmatically. 'Hours and hours of flying and I couldn't get a wink of sleep last night.'

I am from far away – only, not recently. And I didn't get a wink of sleep last night – I was out on the tiles . . . I remember lots of tiles.

He asks me if I will be in Paris for long.

'Well, I don't know, really,' I say. 'It's difficult to get suitable accommodation. I arrived yesterday and hoped to spend the week at the Hotel de Charme. You know it? Oh, I see you are familiar with hotels of quality! But it wasn't to my taste, not at all. Yes, *exact*. You can't swing a *chat*. Not even room to put my shoes under my bed.'

Half true. I'd been to the Hotel de Charme a year ago. The room cost €400 a night and you couldn't swing a mouse. It *is* charming, though. When my gentleman flew off to Kinshasa they let me have the room for the whole day before they turfed me out.

The old fox dips his head and says that under my bed must be a hotly contested place. Or something like that. His English syntax isn't all that good.

I run with it anyway. 'Well, thank you, but aren't you flirting with me? Just a little? I'm not in the habit of putting the shoes of strange men under my bed.'

He chuckles at that. Am I intending to stay here at the Metropolitain?

'Yes,' I say. (I am, but I expect someone else to pay for it. Like *you*, monsieur.) 'But I'm still waiting for my room. The manager promises it won't be long.'

The gentleman says he recommends this hotel. It is *discret*.

'I certainly hope so! I prefer big hotels for that reason, don't you? I do love an elegant lobby. And this one isn't bad, although the location seems a bit dull.'

Ah, but the Lido is only a short walk away, he smiles.

'Really? That close? I should check it out then. I'm looking for a diversion.'

In that case, the gentleman says, I must buy you a drink.

Bingo.

The gentleman sits so that his body is a proper distance from mine. But his sharp knees in pinstriped cloth form >< with mine across an expanse of cherubic tapestry.

'Shall I call the waiter?' I ask. 'You don't have to be anywhere special? That's very sweet of you. I don't suppose a drink will take long and then my room will be ready and I can slip out of this rumpled dress. I absolutely agree! When you're sitting in a hotel lobby you must drink champagne, it doesn't matter what time of day it is. Just a glass, a bottle's too much.'

No, no. He insists on a bottle.

'That's very agreeable of you.'

An attendant is called, a very nice champagne is ordered.

'You know your champagnes, *monsieur*. Is that so? Then I'm speaking to an expert! Don't be modest. Here am I, sitting in the lobby of a big, glamorous Paris hotel, being offered champagne by a man who owns a wine distribution company! I'm starting to think 2005 is going to be a very good year.'

He shrugs, waves a jewelled finger in the air.

'But tell me, your accent, now that I hear it, isn't French at all, is it? I'm not very good with accents, but I'm sure it's – Belgian! Like Hercule Poirot! Plastic Bertrand! Jacques Brel! I've played that game, you know. Name ten famous Belgians. No one ever gets past five . . .'

. . . All the while my mind is off somewhere else, a small café in a more intriguing part of town, perhaps, sucking a Gauloise and sipping on a *crème*.

The gentleman – this fine, rather elderly, gentleman with a yellow silk handkerchief in his pocket, who wears on his pinkie a bolt of gold stuck with a red stone the size of a drawing pin – this substantial gentleman has told me he is on his way back to his room to collect his papers for a conference of *Le Comité Interprofessionel du vin de Bordeaux* or something like that. But he has a moment for me. It might turn into an hour or two, now or later, and then, perhaps, a day or a week. He doesn't know that yet, but I can see the signs, those beautiful signs so full of possibility. I don't even have to hold his eyes in mine to know that he is watching the way I watch his lips. (The bottom one is moist and slightly loose, as if a hinge has broken.) When I catch his look I see his eyeballs are rheumy but his expression is remote. It's just an act. His right hand is hovering over his thigh, now so close to mine I can feel its nervous vibration. The hairs in his nostrils are vibrating, too, as he takes in the scent of the world's most expensive perfume wafting from unseen wads of tissue folded into my bra. He has noticed my good bag and the hand-embroidered lace of my underskirts as they froth about me. I make sure he notices my excellent shoes, too, by stretching out a leg and jiggling the foot a little. When his eyes come back to me they alight on my hands, the way my sugar-tipped fingers are twining themselves around the cool stem of my misty champagne flute. He is not listening to the words.

My fine gentleman says he is *désolé* but he must go to his room now and prepare. He hopes that I might be shown to my own room very soon. The delay is unconscionable. He stands stiffly and holds my right hand between his dry ones as if thinking about kissing it. I wait. Of course, he adds, if I find myself unexpectedly free tonight – which is unimaginable, a beautiful young woman like myself – would I consider accompanying him to dinner? He has a reservation at the Carré de Feuillants, which has two Michelin stars but deserves three. (A reservation for two no doubt, the sly old dog.) I would be delighted, I say, but it all depends . . . Naturally, he says. Shall I meet you here in *une demi-heure*?

And so it begins. As always, I don't know where it will lead. It may start in Paris but end in Lisbon. Santiago. Cape Town. Places I am yet to go. (Where do wine merchants travel? Timbuctu?) Or it may stop right here in this lobby. There are negotiations. He might be shocked. He might be intrigued. He may have *complications*, which he can't speak of: a wife who checks all his credit card bills, a (very) old mother living at home, a temporary liquidity problem, a leaky bladder. Or he may be a widower, the children long gone, a fortune sitting in the bank waiting to be lavished upon a young(ish) woman in Leslie Caron petticoats like me. I don't know and I want to enjoy not knowing, at least for a while, until this bottle of champagne is finished and the rumble of my empty stomach makes a commitment from this gentleman – or another – a necessity.

THE HOTEL LORD MELBOURNE

Collins Street, Melbourne, Australia

The doormen at the Hotel Lord Melbourne wear long green worsted topcoats with gold-braided epaulettes, beefeater's hats and cotton gloves, even in a heatwave. This evening the outside thermometer has not yet dropped below a marshmallowy twenty-seven degrees Celsius and yet the doormen betray no ill effects as they dash from torpid kerbside to ice-cold lobby, ushering guests and luggage through the heavy revolving doors and directing street traffic – exhausted tourists, belligerent drunks, groups of teenagers with fake IDs – away from the hotel's daunting Victorian edifice.

Inside, the ceiling fans revolve at an alarming clip but they are only for show. The hotel is cooled by battalions of industrial airconditioners, which ruffle the tops of the potted kentia palms and make women reach for their jackets as soon as they're several paces inside the front door. It's Friday night and the usual rabble of office workers heading for the Raj Bar's Happy Hour-and-a-half (5:30–7p.m.) push through a throng of impatient hotel guests waiting to check in. The guests are a sporty lot, the women with cotton sweaters tied around their shoulders, the men in navy jackets or open-collared striped shirts. They've come from Sydney, Adelaide, Auckland, Hong Kong for the finals of the Australian Open tennis championships, which will be held this weekend. They will invade the city's finest restaurants and bars, exhaust its supply of hire cars, and complain, frequently and loudly, about the temperature of their rooms, and the rather unfortunate problem of the TV remote control in certain suites interfering with neighbouring airconditioning thermostats. For a five-star hotel this is a serious flaw but it cannot be fixed until March. (The wide corridors are already full of porters dispatching complimentary tropical fruit baskets.)

But downstairs, in the lobby, in a corner of the long room that is forever Victorian Britain, Violet Armengard stands on jewelled heels by a faux marble column, staring fixedly at the entrance to the hotel and barely registers the melee behind her. Her arms are firmly tucked into the sleeves of a white Chinese cardigan, which is embroidered with starbursts of creamy pearls. Underneath, she is wearing a clinging lemon yellow dress with an uneven hemline. Her hands twist the straps of a pink satin handbag embroidered with black flowers. She is cold, she is tired, she is overdressed and she is nervous.

There is a small frisson in the lobby when a famous American tennis player enters with his teenage girlfriend, a minion walking a few paces behind them with a clutch of beribboned shopping bags. But Violet doesn't notice them. She knows nothing about tennis but even if she did, she would hardly care tonight. One or two of the gentlemen in navy blazers look her up and down, note her beauty but, deciding that no hooker would look so anxious, so uncomfortable, pass on. Violet doesn't notice them, either, or the elderly lady with immaculate silver hair who looks at her yellow spindles of skirt with distaste. It's just as well because Violet knows the dress is wrong and is trying not to think about that. She bought it last Saturday in a panic and she bought the yellow rather than the more fashionable black, this being 1997 – simply because the yellow was on sale. (Well, of course it was on sale, it's yellow, a voice in her head, which she is trying to suppress, is saying.) Changing into the dress in the staff toilets at work, she'd accidentally dipped the hem in the cistern and had to dry it off with the hot air of the automatic hand dryer. She is not usually this clumsy but she has things on her mind. One of the systems analysts whistled as she trotted down the corridor, less in approval, she thinks, than surprise at seeing her in those fluoro-lit hallways in anything other than a neat black suit.

She wants to be sunny and upbeat and sexy. The white cardigan is ruining the effect. She fears she looks like a fried egg. Since thirteen, she has adopted a defensive stance when she is nervous – arms folded across her chest, hugging her body like a swimmer shivering by a pool – but she is resisting now and is wringing the straps of her bag in a conscious effort to keep her elbows away from her body. Even so, occasionally one hand seeks out the opposite arm and picks at the white wool.

In her little bag is a pink vinyl purse containing toothbrush, lip gloss, nail scissors, eyelash curler, a palette of four brown eye shadows, mascara, powder, a black pencil, roll-on deodorant, a sample vial of Calvin Klein One and a packet of contraceptive pills with the 'Friday' yet to be punched out. Elsewhere in the bag are a clean pair of lace knickers, folded small, a comb, a snap-shut coin purse, two sets of house keys and the key card to room 503 (superior room with king-size bed).

He is not late: she is early. She planned it this way, wanting to check in before he arrived, a *fait accompli*. The woman on reception had taken an imprint of her credit card and suggested she make a reservation for brunch in the dining room. *It's very popular on Saturdays.* Violet shakes her head, imagining a tray on rumpled white sheets and crumbs of toast in the bed. *Check out is 11 a.m.* She nods obediently: she doesn't want to think that far ahead.

The transaction happened too quickly – she now has eleven minutes to spare. Should she go to the powder room and wait him out there? Appear in twelve minutes looking casual and sounding nonchalant – *oh, you're here already?* Or should she stroll over to the far wall and pretend to be fascinated by a display case of the city's genteel history, women playing croquet in leg-o-mutton sleeves and men at the crease in cricket whites? Either might be preferable to standing here by this column with her face screwed like a light bulb into an unnatural smile.

She tries the powder room, which is busy with lipstick and comb activity. She sits on the toilet, her bowels twist and ache, but nothing comes. In the mirror, a face stares back at her bug-eyed with fright. She's wearing too much make-up. Even in the candy pink light of this vanitorium her skin is as chalky as lime-wash. She gets out the blusher and makes a clown face, then rubs it off with a tissue. The woman at the basin next to her says, 'Big night out, ay?' Violet slams the blusher in her bag and backs off like a spooked rabbit.

Bloody hell, she thinks in the corridor, I can't do it. I'll just go home and make a cup of tea and let life fall where it may.

But she's not ready to do that yet.

Patrick is standing in the lobby, in almost the same place she deserted, guided there by silent radar or unseen pheromones or simply the desire to be as far away from the thronging tennis fans as possible. He wears his prickliness like tinsel on a Christmas tree, royally pissed-off to be there. He is checking his watch ostentatiously, a man who is programmed to be always on time. She lurks behind a palm, risking his ire. The white corpuscles chase the red corpuscles through her veins like a fox after a chicken. The heat rises under her thick mask of make-up, the skin beneath her cardigan begins to crawl. She is losing her nerve. She fiddles with her wedding ring, as if to magic something up or away.

What she magics is him. He looks up, spots her, and frowns.

She almost turns and runs away. Another day, another day, she thinks, when I don't look like an elongated egg and he hasn't got a Princess on Monday.

But she can't help herself. As she moves towards him she feels like she's wading into an unfinished painting, with Patrick as the dark centre and everyone else around them firefly smudges of charcoal and lead, darting about without definition or meaning. And what she knows is that the painter is still working, that she might need some definition herself, and that the risk is that she'll come out of the frame filthy and blackened or, worse, done in with an eraser.

But, really, that's her brain having one of its convoluted fancies.

She just wants him back.

She moves her cheek towards his mouth for a kiss. Instead, he snaps his Motorola StarTAC to his ear and holds up a sharp finger. *Stop. I've got to take this.* It's a gesture so familiar she feels warm tears welling up. He turns his back and bends into the phone, then paces away. It's a good seven minutes before he paces back. In this time, a camera crew follow a tennis star around the room and have him pose with a bust of Queen Victoria. But she's used to this. Patrick's clients would intrude on his every waking minute if he let them. Which he sometimes – often – does. With the Princess coming she's lucky he's got an hour, or so he told her each time she called to confirm. But it's just bravado, he's on tenterhooks like she is. She can tell because he runs a nervous finger between his bespoke collar and neck as his other hand slides the phone into his suit pocket.

The cheek kiss is awkward. Her lips brush him rather than the other way around. He smells of something new, the bitter skin of oranges.

'So, where do you want to go?' He looks over her head and nods at someone, then back at her, unsmiling. 'It's a bunfight in here.'

Not the room, not yet. 'What about the lounge? I think they serve drinks.'

'All right, then.' He paces ahead of her, his hand hovering over the phone in his hip pocket like a gunslinger – a gunslinger in a dark grey Italian suit and impeccable cuffs. He whispers to the maître d and he leads them to the curtained window and a pair of high-backed chairs at a small table. The maître d whisks the *reserved* sign into his pocket and pulls out her chair. Before she is even seated Patrick has his phone out and is pressing buttons.

'Don't.'

He looks through her like she's a busboy cleaning the table.

'Patrick, *please*. They can wait for once.'

'Look, I've got – '

'The Princess coming, I know. But it has to be morning in Europe now and she's probably out riding her ponies.'

'All right.' He shrugs, fiddles with the phone, places it on the lace tablecloth. He squares her up. 'So, Violet, I'm all yours for forty-five minutes.'

She is about to say something sexy – *I think we're going to need more than forty-five minutes* – when a waitress interrupts. Patrick orders champagne for both of them. Not because it's a special occasion but because he has the account for this particular drop and he's always careful to be seen drinking it.

The waitress sashays away. Her sway has become more pronounced on the outward trip. Patrick has that affect. He is having that effect on Violet. She wants to reach across the table and unpick the buttons of his shirt, take up where they left off nine weeks ago. Sixty-six calendar days slashed through with black pen – and this one, Friday, marked with a dozen red exclamations.

!!!!!!!!!!!

He is still her husband.

She gazes at him as he tugs at his collar, runs a palm up the side of his head to make sure there are no strands of black hair straying from his sleek ponytail. She is not the only one at this table who thinks he is gorgeous. But she can live with this, admires it even, the complete confidence in the male self which as a woman she has never learnt.

She wants him to want her the way he did when they first met, when he was so hungry for her he would pull into alcoves or toilet stalls, and allow her to bite his hand so she wouldn't make a noise. At times this was deeply embarrassing to her and she was relieved when the marriage bed put an end to it – but now she frets, after all that has happened, that it wasn't her he wanted after all. It was the thrill.

But she has read all the magazines: she can put the thrill back. She has a key to a hotel room in her bag. A key to a new start in life.

'Patrick?'

He studies her with calm grey eyes. 'Why are we here, Violet?'

His look unnerves her. 'Let's have our drink first.'

'Suit yourself.'

She has to remember that she is the one who kicked him out. She tells herself he's distant with her because he is still hurting.

They don't speak until the champagne comes. He pushes his chair back, crosses his legs and gazes at her. He won't make it easy.

She stares at his hands. 'You're not wearing your wedding ring.'

'Should I be?'

'We're not divorced, Patrick.'

'Technically.' He takes a sip of champagne, a careful little mouth sip and raises his eyebrows as if he's assessing a new client.

'There's nothing . . .' she was going to say *technical about it* but she knows his response. *Technically you threw me out so you have no say in it.*

'Nothing what?'

'There's nothing . . . much going on at work.' God, how stupid. They're not here to talk about work.

'How *is* the baby selling business?'

Violet devises fund-raising strategies for an international charity. She has had a comfortable life: she likes to give 'something back'. But he considers it all a futile pursuit. Especially since he lost the PR account.

'World Care matches needy children to sponsors,' she says for the millionth time. She holds his eyes. 'Louvenx and Eliniphao are doing well, thank you for asking.'

Patrick says what he always says. 'They're not our children. They're faces on a card.'

'They depend on us.'

He's never comfortable with this subject. He has made it clear he doesn't want children. She's not clear about what she wants. But she has always thought children, from her own body, might be a step too far. Too far into what she doesn't know.

But she's only thirty, she doesn't have to think about it yet.

Patrick changes the subject. 'Where did you get that dress?' he asks.

'Chapel Street.'

'It doesn't go with your hair. You should wear a different colour lipstick if you *have* to wear yellow.'

'I don't need your fashion advice.'

His look says, *don't you?*

She has tried so hard to please him. Clothes. Conversation. Sex. She had been doing so well, she thought. She still can't see where she went wrong.

She pulls her cardigan tightly across her chest.

'Don't do that.'

'Why not?'

'You're disappointing every man in this room.'

'I'm not interested in them. I'm only interested in you.'

'A bit late, isn't it?' He downs the last of his champagne – too quickly, she observes.

'Well, that's what I've been thinking—'

He cuts her off. 'Violet, I've seen a lawyer.'

'Oh.'

'You should too.'

She feels her chin tremble. She is losing the illusion she has any control. 'Why?' she asks stubbornly.

'You know why.' He considers her for a minute. 'We're not going anywhere with this.'

This? It's a two-year marriage, not a proposal for a sportscar campaign, she wants to say. But the words don't come. She fiddles with the stem of her glass.

'You haven't touched your drink,' he observes. There is the usual criticism in his voice.

She gulps it down. 'Happy now?'

He holds his empty glass up and catches the waitress's eye, which in truth hasn't roamed very far from his. 'You can get me another, too,' she says.

'Another two?'

'No, another *one*.'

He puts up two fingers and then he pulls his chair closer to the table, places both his hands on the cloth. The moons of his manicured fingernails are like an army rallying against her. 'Violet . . .'

'I'm sorry,' she blurts out.

He's irritated with her cutting in. He has a speech to make. 'Sorry about *what*?'

'Sorry about . . .' *Throwing you out.* But she can't say it. ' . . . what happened.'

'It was your choice. I would have stayed. I told you.'

So there *is* hope. She was right. 'At the time . . . at the time I thought it was the right thing. But, I've been thinking—'

'I didn't mean it to turn out this way, you know.'

She makes a gesture of exasperation. 'It's not *turning out*. Nothing's *turning out* yet.'

'You can't expect to make me leave and suffer no consequences.'

'*I'm* the one to be punished? You were the one who was unfaithful.'

'I wasn't unfaithful. I paid for a few blowjobs.'

'A few?' she asks weakly. She'd thrown him out over one.

'It's not even sex. It means nothing.'

'So, all those times we were together—'

'I don't mean *us*.'

'Were they better than mine?'

He sighs. 'No, they weren't *better* than yours. Why do you always put yourself down?'

The question, so unexpected, is thrown like a blanket over her sense of outrage. She feels her mouth flapping, but no words come out.

The waitress brings a tray with two fresh glasses. Puts them down and exits swiftly, sensitive to the vibe.

'Look,' he says, exasperated. 'I thought you'd be okay with it. I should have realised you'd be upset.'

Upset? 'So the only thing you regret is being caught? If I hadn't have found that business card you'd still be doing it?'

He looks at her. 'I'm admitting I'm in the wrong in this. But you have to take a little bit of blame.'

'For what?'

'For being so fucking . . . *good.*'

'I'm not good!'

'You don't think so? You're beautiful and smart and kind.'

'Thank you. You make me sound like I should be in a commercial for washing powder.' She can't even imagine what he's talking about. Is it something sexual she didn't do that hookers do? She thought they'd done most things. She never said no. And she told him he was wonderful every time. 'So, I was boring, is that it?' she asks angrily.

'For God's sake. Stop asking questions. I don't want to hurt you.'

A bit late for that, she almost says. But she pulls herself together. 'If I get arrested, does that mean we can get back with each other?'

'You don't get it, do you?'

'No, I don't. I thought we were happy.'

He grimaces at the word. 'What's *happy*, Violet?'

She can't answer that.

But he has his speech to make. 'Grow up, Violet. Just because you're content with one person, it doesn't mean the rest of us are. I can't live with someone I know I'm going to wound every time I do something that's *normal.* A wedding band is not a pair of handcuffs. For you *or* me. I can turn a blind eye to you flirting with that Daniel guy.'

'Daniel?' Violet keeps her voice low. This is shocking to her. Daniel is a volunteer in her office, a friend who's a little bit in love with her, perhaps. Well, she's sure he is, but, still, does she flirt with him? It's absurd. 'How could you think that?'

He throws his hands up, shrugs. 'All right. I got it wrong.'

'I never flirted with him,' she repeats mournfully.

'Did you think we were going to live together for thirty years and only sleep with each other?'

I did, she thinks. *What's wrong with that?* Instead she says, angrily, 'I thought you'd wait more than thirty minutes.'

He shakes his head and then she feels him disconnecting, like he usually does. Old throw-in-a-grenade-and-disappear Patrick. 'Look, I have to go,' he says suddenly. 'I've got to drop in on the Bradley launch. I'm sorry, but you know how it is.' He puts his hand on his phone.

She is not going to let him go. Lab technicians can control life in a Petri dish: why can't she control *him*? 'You haven't finished your drink.'

He shrugs. 'I have that stuff running out of my ears. I'll take care of the bill. Order more, sit here as long as you like.'

'That's kind of you.'

'It's no use getting twisted about it, Violet. I left when you asked. I haven't made a fuss.' He puts his phone in his pocket and stands.

'Is there someone else?' She cringes inwardly as she asks it. 'Apart from the girls with the business cards?'

'What do you think?'

There is. Of course. *Well, good luck to her,* she thinks. *She won't be alone.* 'Patrick —'

He stands, all business now. 'We don't have to be cut off from each other. We can be friends. But it's no use prolonging the agony. Look . . .' His hand is still on his phone, his fingers searching for the ON button. 'You know I adore you. You're fucking *gorgeous*. Look around you, every man in this room has his eyes on you. Inside, I'm raging with jealousy. I *want* you, Violet. That's never going to change. But there's nothing *dangerous* about it . . . I like a bit of edge, you know. And you can't give it to me . . . Look, don't cry.'

'I'm not crying.'

'I'm not good for you but that doesn't mean I don't want you . . . I've got a hard on right now, in fact.'

Violet is not that slow off the mark. She seizes the opportunity. 'Then prove it.'

'What?'

She thuds her right hand on the table and opens it. The key card to Room 503 lies across her palm.

Patrick looks at it and then into her eyes. She thinks he's smiling. 'So *that's* what you want.'

His phone goes off.

He takes it. 'Patrick Armengard.'

HOTEL METROPOLITAIN
Avenue de Friedland, Paris, France

Ah, I can see there is a problem.

The manager in the black suit has gone off his shift but not before he has engaged the next manager, also in a black suit, in conversation about me. The new manager has been busy greeting guests but he is idle now and in need of a little ego boost. At this moment, no hapless porter or housekeeper in sight, I am the lowest creature on the food chain. I have been wined if not dined by a valued guest, but he has disappeared to his room and ninety-three minutes have passed since he promised to take me to dinner.

It's a fiction that I am waiting to be checked in, of course. There are no bags. There will be 'lost' bags eventually, bags and contents that will need to be 'replaced' by kindly gentlemen. M. Vatin, for that is my wine merchant's name, would be outraged to know I am still sitting here and if he returned this moment he would feel obliged to take it upon himself to complain on my behalf.

But he has not called. Perhaps he has taken a *sieste*. Perhaps he has died. It has happened. He's old, he drinks too much, maybe he has business worries. More likely, he has called his wife and has been stricken with an attack of conscience. This has happened too, all too frequently.

From experience, I would not expect M. Vatin to be adventurous. He's rather provincial. It's only the connoisseur who plays the game. The oil man. The diamond merchant. The high roller. The media mogul. The sports star. If M. Vatin falters at the starting block now, it's not all that desperate, even though I need someone to take me to dinner. It saves time. And it keeps me in circulation. The connoisseur might be arriving at the entrance to this hotel at this very moment and if I am seated opposite M. Vatin listening to him drone on about inventory – even if it is at Carré de Feuillants which deserves three Michelin stars – I run the chance of missing my true destiny. If I still believed any such thing.

But I'm hungry – *starving* – and the manager has now resolved to toy with me. As he makes a beeline across the red marble floor, which looks like blood stirred in milk, I think that perhaps I should have called the gentleman's room and prompted him. But that is against the rules and I'm a stickler for them, unless I'm really desperate, as in life-and-death. It is M. Vatin who has taken the bait and yet I am the one twisting on the hook.

I smell the manager's woody aroma before he reaches me. He's squeaky clean, shining brown hair, a spray of *muguet* in his lapel because it's the *fête du travail,* May Day. In fact, not bad looking at all. But he is forbidden.

'Bonsoir, mademoiselle.' He clicks his heels. The curl of his lip suggests he's mocking me.

He's about my one thousandth hotel manger. *'Bonsoir, monsieur.'*

He knows from my lousy accent I speak English. 'Perhaps I can be of assistance? Do you need directions?'

Usually the hotels don't mind the classy working girls. The guests like them. It's a service the hotel doesn't need to outsource – the girls *in*source themselves willingly. If they're pretty enough and well-groomed enough and make themselves scarce, they are tolerated. (More so if they give the concierge a cut.) The French hotels, in particular, are sanguine about them. *Ooof! What is the fuss! They are just doing their jobs. And besides their ankles are nice.*

I am not like them. But I should have made myself scarce. There is a limit and it's usually, by my calculation, one hour and forty-five minutes. My glass is long empty and I have been here a total of two hours and fifty-three minutes. It is clear I have nowhere to go. I try it on anyway. 'Thank you for your concern but I am waiting for M. Vatin. He is making some calls and refreshing himself before he escorts me to dinner.' Hmmm. Escort . . . maybe the wrong word. 'In fact, I am a little worried about him, perhaps I will call.'

The manager gives me a weaselly smile. 'But M.Vatin has already left for dinner, *mademoiselle.* We have his key.'

I don't believe it. 'But I have been here all along.'

'I think you will find that there is an exit on the Rue Beaujon. He left his key at the desk there.'

The old bastard. He's had a bit of tease and it's only cost him the price of a good bottle of champagne.

Only one thing to do. Lie. 'But I don't understand. I brought him a message from his daughter. She's an old friend of mine. He invited me to dinner. Surely there's some mistake.'

'I'm sorry, *mademoiselle*. Perhaps he had another urgent engagement.'

This lobby has been contaminated for now. There is nothing left to do but find another. No use asking for a room and then sneaking out in the morning. I've played my hand. It's a pity because it's the kind of hotel I like. Expensive. Busy. Impersonal. Connoisseurs prefer impersonal.

'Of course,' I say. 'I'll leave him a message and then I must go home.' Home, suggesting I have one. 'If you'll oblige me with a pen?'

He nods and takes a sliver of silver from his pocket. I have a little notebook tucked away in the inside pocket of my handbag. I scribble something, tear it out, fold it twice. 'Oh, just a minute,' I say, before handing it over. I take a €20 note – one of my last half dozen – out of my purse and enfold the note in it. I smile sweetly and give it to him. 'Please make sure M.Vatin gets this.'

He is pleased with the money, even though, as far as I am concerned, the gratuity turns the tables on him. I pay *him*. He clicks his heels again and says, 'Certainly, *mademoiselle.*'

I've learnt about greasing palms the hard way.

I watch him snake back to reception. Yes, there it is, he busies himself behind the desk but he's really reading the note. He looks up at me and then down again sharply. He might even be blushing.

Better luck next time, I've written. He thinks it's meant for him.

But it's for me.

THE HOTEL LORD MELBOURNE

Collins Street, Melbourne, Australia

Violet sits on the edge of the king-size bed, swinging her legs. She's more than a little tipsy. Patrick has left her with an open tab and she has taken advantage of it, swilling glass after glass of champagne until the sour-faced waitress smugly suggests she might find a taxi home.

Fuck her. *Fuck* him! She's paid for the room and she's not going home. What's home anyway? A little cottage in South Yarra that's been ransacked of all their furniture? ('You don't care about this Arne Jacobsen table,' Patrick had said. '*I* chose this Imants Tillers painting. I'm taking it.')

She kicks one leg and a shoe thuds off. She starts to nod, her head whips back. The truth about Patrick is . . . It's all her fault. She can see now. She thought the bedroom was enough, she thought he was busy and tired, she thought he'd grown up, got lazy, preoccupied and content. Was she really that boring? She hadn't thought she was. She wore sexy underwear, she did all the clever things with her mouth. She was *beautiful,* they all said – she never understood it – but wasn't that usually enough?

It was all her bloody fault. She should have made him jealous. She was never short of offers. There was even a visiting Italian baritone, one of Patrick's clients. And then, of course, there is

Daniel. He has Irish green eyes and makes her tea every day when she arrives at work. He buys her presents to cheer her up and once rode all the way home with her on the tram to make sure she was safe, even though he lives twenty kilometres away in the opposite direction. Everyone knows he is in love with her . . . but she cannot lead him on. *I am getting back with my husband,* she had to tell him, kindly, at the World Care Christmas party. He nodded solemnly and went out the door, never to return to the office, his paper party hat still on his head . . . Dear, darling, Daniel with his wire glasses and delicate hands, it's her fault he can't take it any more and is moving to Mozambique. It's all her bloody fault.

She thinks about calling him, inviting him up to the room, knowing that bed and skin would be enough for him if that skin was hers, but the act of finding her phone and then turning it on and then pressing buttons . . . and if she's getting back with Patrick it would be a cruel thing without a future and she couldn't in all conscience be so *irresponsible.*

Responsible, reasonable – she carries these words like a dowager's hump. And fucking Patrick, he *liked* her that way, balancing the accounts, managing the house, dressing to please him, joining in knowledgeably with dinner party talk of this internet thing, O.J Simpson and how appalling the Spice Girls are.

She fiddles with the hem of her dress. So, she doesn't look good in yellow, or so Patrick says. She swings around to find her bag and upends it on the mattress. Her pink plastic toiletries bag thuds out. In there, if she can only find them, are her nail scissors.

Aha! They tumble out with her eyelash curler and she pries them apart. She's none too steady but she's not doing brain surgery. She manages to get her fingers through the loops. With her other hand she holds up the uneven hemline and attacks it. *Snip, snip.* Fabric comes away. She hoists the dress around her hips so that she can hack the rest of it. The hem is still none too even. She gets herself vertical and wobbles on one heel to the bathroom mirror, floor-to-ceiling, woozy her. She hacks the dress some more until the whole hem is roughly – *very* roughly – above her knees. *Better*, she thinks.

She staggers sideways and looks at what her mother calls her *figure*. Yes, it is nice, spectacular even. But she has had no control over it. Her breasts are alien growths. Fuck Patrick's obsession with them. They don't need *him*. The nipples are doing perfectly well by themselves, thank you, hardening in the cold controlled air. If she wasn't tipsy she'd be alarmed at the way each little pucker is clearly visible through the yellow fabric, you can almost see the pink of them . . . but she *is* tipsy and she doesn't care.

She spends a few minutes finding her other shoe, another few minutes putting it on. The room's too cold, she'll rescue her cardigan, a little nightcap in the bar . . . but she needs the bathroom first.

Before she knows it, the door has closed behind her and she's standing in the hall.

The elevator opens and a young giant blinks back at her. Maybe he's not a giant but he's very tall. She gives him a faint smile then turns her back to him. She looks at the control panel and prods a button. The doors close.

Before they've gone half a floor – it's a *very* slow mechanism – she feels a hand on her hip. She reaches behind her to brush it away and glares at him over her shoulder. He grins at her, raises his huge hands in the air in a gesture of innocence.

'I'm sorry, but your dress was tucked into your underwear. It's no good for you to be seen in public like that.'

She blushes crimson and faces him, tugging at the back of her skirt. 'I'm sorry.'

'Don't be sorry. Are you in a hurry to meet someone for dinner?'

'Me? No. I'm locked out of my room.'

'And there's no one waiting inside it for you?'

It's only now she realises his English is inflected with an accent of some kind. She peers at his face more closely. He's brown-skinned, flat-cheekboned, hair a loose tangle of curly black. But his eyes are pale as Bombay gin.

'You recognise me,' he says.

'No. Who are you?' She doesn't have a clue. 'And why are you speaking to me in that accent?'

She swears his laugh shakes the elevator. 'And who are you? And why are you in this hotel with hardly any clothes on?'

She puts one arm across her chest.

He gently takes it away. 'Don't do that.'

The old elevator might be travelling at a crawl but she is dropping like the brakes have gone.

'You're cold,' he says.

'You're tall.'

'One metre ninety-six.'

'I've never had' It's the wrong word but she goes on, 'a man who's one metre ninety-six before.'

'Would you like to?'

The elevator shifts sideways, drops, groans and the doors open. The portly man who steps inside grunts a 'good evening.' His wife looks flustered and nudges her husband in his rotund side. But Violet doesn't notice this.

The elevator thumps to the ground floor. The doors shudder open. The older couple exit. There are three people waiting to get in. The giant does not seem perturbed. He bends towards her and cups one paw under her chin. 'Go to the bar. Order what you like. I have to meet someone. Then I'll come.'

As they separate, Violet hears the people getting in the lift say things like 'great match' and 'bad luck' and 'you were robbed'.

How she finds the bar she doesn't know because she has no legs.

At the bar she climbs on to a high stool. Her companions are a plaster blackamoor holding a small potted palm and a bony-backed girl who moves her stool closer to her standing boyfriend as soon as Violet appears. It's an unnecessary gesture – there are plenty of men to go round. And that's what Violet's head is doing. Going round.

She orders a mineral water. The barman makes a face of mock disappointment and suggests a special cocktail made from Cointreau and several other ingredients her brain can't process. Unable to argue, she agrees to both drinks. It takes about thirty seconds before a booze-fuelled male approaches, intent on offering her advice on what sort of man she needs in her life and what she should be doing with him right then and there. She deflects him but more keep coming, until she has to turn her back to the room and pretend to be interested in the disinfectant-like colour of her Calcutta Iced Tea.

She might have been there fifteen minutes, an hour, two, she doesn't really know, except that there seems to be a fresh cocktail in front of her and there is a different person sitting on the stool beside her every time she looks up. The barman slides her another glass of water and begins to say something when he suddenly stops mid-sentence. His eyes are fixed on something a metre above her head. She swivels around on her stool and almost falls off into the arms of the giant.

A moment later finds herself seated in the middle of a leather sofa with the giant occupying a club chair to the left of her and a ferrety man wearing a shirt covered in kangaroos occupying the one to the right. An ice bucket sits in the centre of a low table carved with elephants and a white-coated waiter is pouring them champagne. They are obscured from most of the room by palms but she still has the crawly feeling of eyes on her.

'This is Vladimir,' the giant is saying. The ferrety man nods but does not smile. All she can think of are Vladimir and Estragon, the endangered baboons in the zoo that she supports.

'And you, beautiful creature who has been locked out of her room?' he asks, taking a champagne.

'What?'

'Do you have a name?'

'Sorry,' she says. 'It's Violet.'

'Ah, that's a pretty name.'

Vladimir makes a face.

'Vladimir is not happy about girls.'

'Why?'

'They are very distracting.'

'Oh.' She can't think of any witty repartee. She knows she's out of her depth even though the depth she's in isn't very deep. 'Am I distracting too?'

'That is to be seen,' he smiles. He is slouched in the low chair with his long, ungainly legs hinged open. He's wearing khaki pants and red sneakers and a polo shirt with a pouncing cat embroidered over the chest pocket. The veins along his thick, tanned arms seem to be writhing. Although, when she looks down, the carpet seems to be writhing too.

'You are not well?' he asks, leaning forward.

'I am perfectly all right,' she manages to say in the hesitant style of a child struggling with a reading test.

'Vladimir, get some ice,' the giant commands. Vladimir looks put out but gets up from his chair.

'Who's Vladimir, anyway?' she asks.

'My coach.'

'Coach of what?'

'Well, he is *one* of my coaches. The least important of my coaches, but don't tell Vladimir that. He has been with me since I was thirteen.'

'Why do you need a coach? Oh—' The alcohol is making her stupid but not *that* stupid. 'You're one of those tennis players.'

'You are disappointed.'

'I don't know anything about tennis.'

'No! In a crazy place like this where everyone is mad about sport?'

'I've seen it on the news. When' She can't even think of the player's name. ' . . . when the Australians play.'

'And you have never seen me play?'

'I've never seen you.' She shakes her head – not a good move – as Vladimir returns with a glass of ice cubes.

'We have to be with sponsors at two.' Vladimir nods curtly to Violet. 'Good evening.'

'I don't think Vladimir likes me,' she observes after he's gone.

'Forget about him. He thinks women ruin my concentration.'

'You're playing tomorrow?'

'No. I lost today.'

'Oh, I'm sorry.'

He shrugs. 'I smashed a few racquets and now I'm good.' She doesn't know if he's joking or not. 'Besides, if I had to play tomorrow,

I couldn't be with you tonight.' He pours himself another champagne, grasping the bottle by the neck. 'I couldn't be drinking. I couldn't be having sex.' He eyes her champagne, which is untouched. He sighs, and puts the bottle back in the ice bucket. 'You must eat your ice.'

She stares at the ice on the table. How do you eat ice? She can feel her eyes lolling in her head.

'Here.' He leans forward and scoops up the glass. He unfolds himself from his chair and sits beside her. He takes a piece of ice and holds it in front of her mouth, like a father offering a spoon to a toddler. 'Open.' He places it on her tongue. She crunches down on it. 'No,' he says. 'Suck. It will make you feel better.'

He's so close she's tempted to run her tongue along the rough stubble on his jaw. He must see this thought in her eyes because he blows gently on her lips, sour, warm air, soft as sifted cornflour. The fingers that have held the ice slip under her top, brushing her nipple. His groin grinds into her thigh. She begins to slide under his pressure until she is almost lying flat. He moves with her lightly, slipping his hands around her back to support her. He smells like camphor and chewing gum as he bears down. Her brain keeps trying to assert itself over her body but it lost the battle a few gins ago. His mouth on her throat is like a sea cucumber. She feels she is going to fall through the floor to Istanbul.

Suddenly he pulls back. 'You know what?'

'What?' She is talking to the ceiling.

'I am not very comfortable.'

At the very moment he says this, a girl in jeans appears from around a pot plant, points a camera, which flashes, juts her hip boldly and is off again. Violet registers nothing of it but she feels him sit up. He whispers into ear. 'Did you get your key?'

'My key?'

'To your room.'

'My room.' She barely knows where she is. Why is that ceiling fan going round and round?

His laugh is the laugh you give an enchanting child. 'We can't very well go to mine.'

HOTEL CHARDONNE

Avenue George V, Paris, France

I crave a modest little restaurant and a plate of stewed gigot, with a glass of Bouzet, perhaps. But my fortunes won't change in a restaurant. The night is hurtling towards me. I need to find another lobby and sit on a drink and some nuts, or maybe an overpriced club sandwich, which might last me an hour or so if I pick off little bites of lettuce with my fingers, as the French women do.

The Hotel Chardonne is close enough to the Hotel Metropolitain to walk it comfortably, even in flimsy heels, but I don't roam streets. I need to arrive in a taxi. I need an excuse to give the doorman another of my dwindling supply of notes so that he will tolerate me.

The doorman's smile is broad but his eyes are flat as he palms the note and lopes ahead of me to open the heavy glass door.

Bonsoir, mademoiselle.

Good. If he recognises me he does not show it.

I hesitate for a moment before stepping inside. They have very long memories in hotels, which is why I am here rather than at the grander George V down the road. I have done my dash at the George V. I had to do a runner, leave my luggage behind. When was that? I don't know – the years stretch out like a faded carpet. I suppose I could have sold the luggage and paid the hotel bill. Many women sell off the things that men have given them but I am not one of them. It would be too much like payment. Besides which, there is always someone to buy me new things. Eventually.

The doorman holds open the door, his face neutral. It's as if he's opened the door on the first time I was here. I am not the only one who cannot forget it. 31 August 1977. The waiters served drinks with tears in their eyes. Right there, in the middle of the lobby, a woman stood, head bowed, sobbing, like someone who had been sentenced to the gallows. I sat in the lounge, drinking Armagnac with my . . . well, I don't need to think about him. He was everybody's, never mine.

I don't think I like this hotel.

Mademoiselle?

The doorman is now impatient, missing the chance of other tips. I nod my thanks and am sucked inside. A porter asks if I have luggage but I wave him away. The atmosphere is chilly, the airconditioners blasting away, an over-reaction to the slightly balmy air outside. Everything seems embalmed, the waxy-faced porters, the stiff lilies in huge Chinese vases, the spindly old couples drinking *fine* in the lounge. The furniture, the wall sconces, the fittings of the ponderous chandeliers, even the rims of the plates and glasses are laid thick with gold. I walk slowly to consider my options. If I head for the bar I only find drunks. But there's a very real chance that at this time of the evening I will only find drunks anyway. If I sit in the lobby and the only other people are the bunch of stuffed shirts there now I'm in more trouble. I can't ask for a room and risk the black card. It will no longer work. If there's one thing I know it is that the black card will no longer work.

I step off marble on to plush carpet. So far, so good. Everyone is smiling the normal affected smile. Well, I can't sit at the little circular banquette in the middle of the room. It's already occupied by an independent contractor. She's as expensively dressed as me and she's tapping on a Blackberry with a gold pen, as if it's business hours and there's a stockbroker at the end of an email waiting for her command to sell NRMX buy ACAP. I suppose it *is* business hours for her. The affectation of red-framed reading glasses works but the way the ankle cuffs on her black stilettos are fastened with diamond-encrusted gold locks perhaps does not. But what do I know? These days secretaries carry crocodile handbags from Hermès and it's the doctors' wives who carry the fakes. The domestic slave gets her lingerie from Agent Provocateur and the call girls shop at Liberty.

But I'm in luck. An old crone bent double with osteoporosis and wearing a Pacific Ocean's worth of cultured pearls is lifted to her feet by a handsome young man who effusively kisses her twice on each cheek and then carries her away on his arm like a broken umbrella. Without appearing to hurry I nevertheless dash to the chair. It's one of those annoying leather club chairs that you sink right into, your arms raised so high you feel like you're being frisked. I rearrange the back cushion so that I am sitting on it, which raises me two inches higher and allows me to lean on one elbow and prettily toy with a strand of hair. A roving drink waiter pounces immediately and I am forced to order a Lillet.

Think positively: someone will come and pay for it.

Sitting on a couch across a square of Aubusson are two women sharing a bottle of Heidseick. One has bobbed black hair, dark vermilion lips and an arrangement of black garments that cry fashion maven. The other could be her sister but her hair is pulled back tightly and her clothes are more conventional, lots of gold buttons and a shawl thrown over one shoulder as if it were still January. But I suppose it is perpetually January in European lobbies.

The women scrutinise me and then the black one whispers in the shawled one's ear. They smile at me. I smile back, then deliberately turn my head away. I don't do women if I can help it. You get a very bad outcome with a woman.

The waiter brings my drink, on a silver tray with a glass of water and a small bowl with five ice cubes in it, and tucks the check under the ice. I smile sweetly. I drop three cubes of ice into the Lillet with silver tongs and then notice he didn't bring nuts. The women opposite have nuts. My stomach makes a grinding sound. The waiter has disappeared.

I'm starting to regret this choice. There are only women and couples here. And, damn, that tart on the banquette has snagged the attention of the only possible connoisseur. On his way to his room she has managed to divert him. He waves the porter ahead. The transaction is so quick he might have sneezed and she'd said *Gesundheit*. She smiles to herself as he leaves and snaps the handheld into her bag. In ten minutes she'll be gone. Back in an hour or contracted for the night? The latter, I dearly hope. I want her out of the way. Connoisseurs are easily distracted. They will take it fast and easy if they can, while I am slow and complicated.

I sip the Lillet like I'm in the middle of the Sahara with my camel dead and water skin almost empty. Maybe, in a way, I am.

The waiter, on his next round, drops a bowl of nuts in front of me. Thank God for small mercies. *Very* small mercies. I ransack the bowl for thick cashews but mostly it contains tiny, hard hazelnuts. I inhale them anyway. They drop to the bottom of my stomach, little bones into deep acid.

I am suddenly aware the women are still watching me, noting the way I have emptied the bowl like a street urchin. It's a slip I must rectify. I raise my hand for the waiter who, damn him, appears on call. (Why is *this* one so efficient, now?) I make a show of reading the little appetiser card and ordering *croque madame*, which I specify should be cut into six small pieces (to stop me from wolfing it down). Nineteen euros, a scandal for something that costs six at any *bar tabac*.

The Lillet is almost finished. I slide the last two slushy ice cubes into the glass and jingle the glass thoughtfully. Ice in glass is my meditation where others have gurus and mandalas.

When I look up, the lesbians have been joined by a man. And not just any man, I can assure you. This one looks like castles in Spain or at least a stable of thoroughbreds in Ireland. He is tall and dressed in the sort of casual that would have taken a team of butlers to press and lay out. His white hair probably has a butler all of its own.

The gentleman is possibly seventy years old but still with the waxy tan skin of yachtsmen. He bows and kisses the women's hands and they shuffle close so that he can occupy one half of the couch. He protests that he is creating discomfort but only mildly. It is clear he expects them to sit on top of each other. His accent may be Italian, Greek, Hungarian, Polish. It has something of the Count about it. A *real* Count I hope. I have had enough of phoney ones.

He takes up his position, crossing his khaki legs, opening his navy jacket, loosening his silk cravat and adjusting his black eye patch. He leans against the leather arm, a picture of confident elegance. But his one good eye is looking away from me.

I am very glad the hooker has gone, for this is a man to do business with. A true connoisseur. I sincerely hope he is not married to one of these witches. But, then again, when did marriage ever matter?

To me or anyone in this world?

And so, it happens as it is meant to.

In turn the waiter, a concierge and a manager appear and pay tribute to the gentleman. More champagne is called for and poured. The women whisper to each other and him. My sandwich arrives, cut into six pieces.

He never once looks in my direction and yet, after forty-seven minutes of this charade, the black-clad woman rises from her seat and comes to me.

The gentleman would be very pleased if I could join them for dinner. And then, perhaps, if we are getting on agreeably, and if my agenda will allow, I might accompany them in the morning to Naples and then to Monrifi, his private island. It is very small, *signorina,* but in this place there is not a care in the world.

I'm willing to believe her.

THE HOTEL LORD MELBOURNE

Collins Street, Melbourne, Australia

When Violet answers her door there are no preliminaries. As soon as she closes it behind her he has her forced up against it, his big hands cupping her face and his mouth sucking the air out of her lungs. After a moment of that, he wraps his arms around her hips, hoists her up his body so that she has to grapple her legs around his thighs, arms around his neck, and pins her to the panelled wood, so hard she feels the ridges of timber sharp against her spine. She has an uneasy feeling in her gut but there's no time to indulge it because the tennis-playing giant has his fingers inside her, testing her for size, heat, wetness, and with barely a moment's fumbling his cock follows, not getting the angle right at first, but then ploughing into her like a batsman whacking home a tricky pitch . . . but that's the wrong analogy, she should think of something to do with tennis . . . grand slam . . . ace serve . . . but she's too intent on keeping her reproductive system from being pulped and her skull from being cracked against the door . . . So this, she thinks as her teeth rattle, her breasts quake, is what being banged senseless means.

She reaches backwards and pushes her hand against the wall to free her head and the thrust of her hips has a seismic effect on him. He gives an almighty groan, which can probably be heard five floors down at the bar, certainly in the corridor outside, and pulls her down on him hard. She hangs on for grim life while he unloads . . . the sting is sharper than with Patrick, whose ejaculate merely tickles.

It has lasted less than three minutes, but he's not apologetic. He puts his mouth on her neck and his voice is hoarse. 'I wish to get you wet first.'

First?

His belt buckle stabs her inner thigh. He must be very adept at this, not dropping his pants. Without saying anything more, he lifts her away from the door and delivers her to the bed, which, this being a 'superior' (therefore standard) room, is only a few steps from the door. He lays her down and stands over her for a moment, smiling. Then he puts one foot at a time on the bed and unlaces his shoes. Shakily, she props herself up on her elbows and watches him as the pants and shirt are peeled off. Naked, except for the gold ropes and charms around his neck, he goes into the bathroom and returns rubbing his genitals with a towel. She reaches up to take the towel from him but he shakes his head. 'No. I want you like that.'

She looks down. The remnants of her underpants are hooked around one knee. The hem of her dress lies damp across her belly. The halter neck is skewed around one breast. Her coppery pubic hair is glistening. She raises her knees and opens her legs for him.

He drops the towel and goes to the mini-bar. Disappointed, she studies the muscles on his back, his shapely calves, the strong, pale bum (so he doesn't sunbake in the nude?) and the dark mystery of his crack. Patrick – why does she have to think of him? – is smoother, solarium-tanned, his muscles gym-cut and mean. Even his prick looks polished. This man is bigger and rougher, rawboned, the bruises from recent injuries shadowing his skin. But he has the grace of a cougar while Patrick has all the coiled tension of a Siamese cat.

He closes the fridge door and returns drinking from a small glass bottle of Coca-Cola. Tattooed along his pelvis is a line of Chinese characters. Because she is well-mannered she tries not to look at his prick. But it is already showing definite signs of revival.

He sits on the bed and nudges her thighs open. A finger traces the sticky trails down her leg. She moves so that he can fit between her legs. She expects a tongue and closes her eyes.

He presses the cold Coke bottle against her instead.

She opens her eyes.

'Does that feel good?' he asks.

Surprised, she nods. It does. In fact, she's now the one who's erect.

'And this?'

He gently slides the neck of the bottle between her lips.

God.

'It's your turn now,' he says. 'What would you like?'

Violet learns his name when she's flicking through the cable channels at 2 a.m.

Luka Uyanik.

She's never heard of him. According to the television he played for the Ukraine in the 1996 Olympics, he's twenty-five years old and the world ranking number eight. That's all she can glean, except that he lost yesterday's semi-final and his temper over a bad line call. There's a few seconds of video of him arguing with the umpire, throwing down his racket and sulking to the sidelines, then a couple of clips of him losing points to his opponent, an American, and one dizzying volley where he runs right across the court to lob the ball just over the net. He is, says a commentator, 'the most naturally talented player in the competition' but 'erratic,' 'moody' and fighting a groin injury. (She has seen no evidence of *this.*)

She feels unjustifiably proud. Or perhaps justifiably, given that she has just done two things with him that she has never done with Patrick and so feels bound by a guilty intimacy. While she has no doubt he has done all these things many times before she also believes him when he says she excels in at least one of them.

'And your husband didn't ask you to do this?' Luka had questioned her. 'Or *this*?'

'No,' she giggled.

'He didn't want to do this . . . or *that*?'

'Never.'

'I don't believe it! Is he a homosexual?'

She smiles as she remembers reminding him that what they had just done was what homosexuals do.

She clicks the remote control and the TV goes blue. She rolls over and lies on her back on the bed, knees bent, arms abandoned. I'm *wallowing* in it, she thinks. I'm filthy with the scent of a stranger. I'm covered in his sweat and spunk, filled with his DNA. If I died now, what a treat I'd be for the medical examiner. His skin under my nails, his saliva on my neck, his pubic hair caught in my throat. Guilty, Mr Uyanik, tennis star.

So, she's done it. She's had sex with another man while married to Patrick. And not the clumsy, furtive sex she always feared, sex that makes you cry with longing for the man you miss. No, this sex is dirty and energetic and . . . funny. And so what if he's spoiled and dominating and treats her like a new toy at Christmas, she likes it because he's also beautiful and sweet and has legs that crush the juice out of her.

It's not so difficult after all. In fact, it is a revelation. She has opened more than her thighs. What she feared would be a Pandora's Box is a cave of treasures that lies glittering before her. She feels a rush of greed for more of it. And she is full of wonder at the discovery that she is capable of allowing her body to function independently from her mind. With Patrick she is always thinking about keeping him happy but with Luka, the thoughts have just flown out of her head. For a few blissful moments, the wind of pure eroticism inflates her sails and cuts her loose, floating, exquisitely weightless, above herself, above the earthly limitations of guilt, expectation and marriage vows.

But soon she is grounded by creeping insecurities. Luka has gone to his room to call Monte Carlo, where he lives. She wonders if there's a family there, a girlfriend. But don't tennis champions' girlfriends travel with them? She's seen them in magazines, tossing their long hair, snapping their white teeth, clapping wildly from the stands. Maybe his girlfriend is a movie starlet on location elsewhere but sending love down the wires . . . she fights to banish the unexpected jab of jealousy the thought brings her. If only her mind would stay out of this! But there it wanders again, like a skein of wool, rolling down unclear paths, snagging and tangling on obstacles as it goes.

Luka said he'd make the call and be back in an hour. She has no reason not to believe him. He took her key card. And he took her dress. 'Now you can't go anywhere.'

She is flattered that he thinks she has somewhere more interesting to go.

HOTEL BELLISSIMA

Monrifi, Mediterranean Sea, Italy

Lucrezia is the name of the black-clad witch and she is procurer and translator for her brother Ettore, who speaks very little English or French or even much Italian from what I can observe. Of course, you don't need to say anything when you're rich. The third member of their jolly little group is Carla, who is either their sister or their lover and the editor of a magazine about textiles. Which makes it very cosy for Ettore, who owns fabric mills, and for Lucrezia who has a chain of expensive clothing boutiques in Milan, Rome, Florence and Venice.

The only other guests on the island are two English girls who would be barely the age of consent in Swaziland. They are the house models for Lucrezia. Or they are to *become* the house models for Lucrezia, once they've shown themselves amenable to certain tasks quite commonly practised in the fashion business.

I overheard them weighing up the consequences in the loggia yesterday afternoon.

'You only have to stick your finger up her bum or somefing,' said the more articulate of the pair.

'Give me a fag, will ya,' replied Thing B, unperturbed.

When we arrived two days ago, by motor launch from Crotone, we disembarked at a jetty, where a caravan of donkeys was loaded with our luggage and set off up a steep incline to the hotel's splintered gates. We were ferried in two black Mercedes, garaged at the bottom solely for the purpose of the two-minute trip up the hill. The models seemed so uninterested I thought they might have been here before, but when I questioned one of them she shrugged and said, 'It's just a rock, innit?'

Monrifi does indeed appear to be nothing more than a small rock, a volcanic hairball spewed up and spat out by Etna centuries ago. There are no other buildings that I can see. The hotel hangs precariously off the face of it like broken shingles off a wall. One earthquake and the whole edifice might go sliding into the sea – or, at least, that's how it looks to a land-hugger like me.

This much I have learnt from Lucrezia – the hotel was once a monastery, built by enterprising monks on the site of a Roman ruin. There is a crypt, which is barred, and a sacristy holding the bones of bona-fide saints. Some frescos remain and chalky Roman faces with huge brown eyes follow you through room after room of failing grandeur, as if to say *see, it has come to this.*

Although we are the only guests, the Bellissima is in every way a working hotel. There are maids and porters and, I discovered, beauticians in a subterranean cave who drop their fashion magazines when you stumble on them and rather despondently try to drum up business. The halls are filled with vases of fresh olive branches, the sheets are changed when you're not looking, there is satellite television and a wonky internet connection and intercom telephones to summon hash, toothpicks, *langoustine*. Downstairs, grey flagstoned rooms open up to more grey flagstoned rooms, hung with washed-out tapestries and iron chandeliers whose candles drip grimy frozen wax. The limestone hearths are all swept clean, and appear unused, the charcoal stains probably dating back to Copernicus. It is bone cold inside but no one seems to know about fire.

It is Ettore's personal hotel and Lucrezia acts like the chatelaine, but I'm still not sure where Carla fits into this. Since we arrived here two days ago she has retired to a turret and has only been seen once at dinner where she performed the elaborate ritual of serving up several beautifully composed plates of food – figs, *pasticcio* of pheasant, *sardine fresche* with celery hearts, braised quail, *torta di funghi*, veal roasted in anchovy sauce, cinnamon cannoli with candied peel – and then placing them on the floor, in a line, so that her dachshund, Peppe, could lap it all up with his precise little tongue.

There are more dogs than people. Ettore has two Chinese crested pups that look like plucked bantam hens. He carries them in the pockets of his towelling robe and feeds them by chewing their food first and spitting it into their throats. (Lucrezia has a famous Great Dane that is dressed by Romeo Gigli but is in Milan this week having a hysterectomy.) The models have bought their silky terriers in twin zip-up Vuitton bags.

Everything I might need is in the hotel. Lucrezia is wardrobe mistress to rooms of clothing, some of it antique, some of it very new. There are furs and corsets, gowns and sailor pants and no doubt a collection of nurses' outfits hanging in the back somewhere. In my room, so large it might once have been a gynaecium for a Roman Empress, I have drawers full of flimsy underwear and shelves stacked with every available skin potion and pharmaceutical, including Zoloft and several kinds of Temazapan. Many combinations could be fatal, if you were so inclined. The bras and ribbony thongs are all approximately my size, except for the occasional, optimistic D-cup. A few of them are soiled. Either these have escaped Lucrezia's attention, or they have been placed there as a bass note in the perfumed landscape of the room.

Last night Lucrezia dressed me for dinner. She tried this and that – a silk dress slipped over my head, a tower of ebony bangles up my arm, a lace-up corset and then a sarong, a white mink coat, low shoes, high shoes, a neck brace, sheer pink *peignoir* with nothing underneath and then with frilly pants, a wide-legged palazzo jumpsuit with a gold mesh belt – all the while tut-tutting and sighing and standing back with her hand on her chin and then pouncing to pull at a seam, readjust my cleavage or insert a finger between elastic and thigh. I was unnerved by this at first, having never been anyone's mannequin, but abandoned myself to her touch once it was apparent it was not me she was stroking or whispering to, but the fabrics and gowns. *Molto carino . . . tesorino . . . diavoletto!* None of this was for me. I might have been made of plaster or fibreglass. In the end, she settled on black dress, flat shoes, diamond earrings, hair fastened by a diamond clip. I watched as she taped the bottom of the shoes so I would not scrape them and then halted my exit down to dinner so that she could pin the back of my slightly loose dress.

I sat stiffly at the head of the banquet table, pricked by little pins if I leaned back. The models came down in skin-tight, shimmering jumpsuits that made them look like a pair of cobras.

While Carla fed a feast to Peppe, we were served Prosecco, cold grey risotto and pomegranates, whose red seeds popped from their skins like ejected fetuses. Ettore sat at a sort of card table, away from the rest of us, in his white robe, while a houseboy pulled the claws off crabs and fed him the flesh. (The dogs, in turn, got most of it.) Then we all retired to the screening room, where we watched Ettore's favourite film, *Now Voyager,* while Lucrezia, Ettore and the models chain-smoked black cigarettes, the miasma of nicotine cloud reaching impenetrability by the *Don't let's ask for the moon, we have the stars* scene.

Dessert was cocaine and Turkish delight and Turkish delight coated with cocaine. Lucrezia kept jumping out of her club chair to push more pins into my flesh. I was at the point of intolerance when she suddenly took them all out and stuck them in her chair arm. The models danced with their dogs while images from *Casablanca* ran across their snaky bodies. Ettore arose to take his two little bantams for a walk.

Lucrezia told me that I should now go to bed. She instructed me to hang up the dress. I should have a bath and then wear nothing while I slept.

I did all this dutifully. It's her fantasy.

The bath had already been drawn when I came back to my room. I stripped, hung up my clothes and lowered myself into the oval tub, which was set into the rough stone floor and filled to the rim with water, blood warm and slippery with oil. The scent of lime blossom rose up around me but I couldn't relax in the tepid water. The old wooden shutters on the windows had been thrown open and the tide seemed to ebb and flow with my heart. A cool breeze tickled the flames on the dozens of thick stubbs of wax the maid had placed around the room and chilled the dampness of my neck. She'd done her job well and I wasn't so *annoiata* that

I didn't appreciate the beauty of my surroundings. But the starless sky over the water was like a black bandage around my soul.

Enveloped in musty velvet covers, I couldn't sleep, wired from sugar and cocaine and the expectation of a visitor, male or female. But none came and I eventually fell into unconsciousness, under a canopy of muslin edged in ivory baby's teeth.

It seems I may get off lightly. Ettore has not come to lay a finger on my flesh. Perhaps, we are only here to be dressmaker's dummies for Lucrezia after all.

THE HOTEL LORD MELBOURNE

Collins Street, Melbourne, Australia

On Sunday night Violet is still in the hotel, although now in a corner suite provided by Luka. In other rooms, on different floors, are scattered Luka's people, a fitness trainer, an assistant, two coaches, a masseur, a racquet stringer and someone called Eduardo. In the course of the weekend he has disappeared for hours at a time, leaving her with the two television sets, a Bose stereo system, and an on-call butler for amusement. Luka keeps a continual flow of things arriving at her door when he's out – gardenias, champagne, chocolate, cake, crayfish sandwiches, fresh towels, a pillow selection, maids to pour a bubble bath, one of the hotel's masseuses, someone to wash her hair, an ugly necklace of gold and silver bought from the hotel boutique – and chides her when he comes back to find she hasn't ordered anything herself.

'I'm worth a million dollars for every birthday,' he boasts. 'And the year has just begun.'

He still has the dress. He won't let her go.

'But I have to go to work tomorrow,' she protests, knowing as it comes out, how dreary that sounds. He has not yet asked her about work, has been incurious about her life, even when she's offered details.

'No, you don't. I am leaving on Tuesday and I'm going a long way away.' He says this with a smile, as he yanks off his tie and throws it on a chair. He has just come back from a sponsor's dinner and it's the first time she has seen him in a suit. It's ill fitting on his lanky frame, the sleeves of the jacket pushed up, eighties-style. He should stick to tennis clothes, she thinks, and then chastises herself. That's the kind of thing Patrick would say.

She is perched on the end of the bed like a bird, bent over her feet, freshly bathed and naked under the enormous white bathrobe pooling around her. She has refused the turndown service, so the curtains are still pulled open. The hotel might once have overlooked parks and rivers but now it is hemmed in by high-rise. Not all the floors in the office building opposite are dark. The offices are so close she can see files piled high on desks, photographs pinned to partitions and one tinselly helium balloon in the shape of Tweetie Bird tied to a chair . . . the world she'll return to when Luka goes. (The deflated red heart Daniel sent her last birthday still droops from the back of her office chair.)

Luka kicks off his shoes and turns on the radio, cruising through the static of TLC, 'NSync and U2 until he finds an angst-ridden Natalie Imbruglia. He moves to the window and draws the curtains. 'I hate those buildings. They remind me of Monte Carlo. Rich people living on top of each other, all avoiding tax.'

'Isn't it beautiful?'

'It has no soul.'

'Do you have to live there?'

'I don't live.' He takes off his jacket and throws it on top of the tie. 'I am incorporated. I have an apartment, but it's nothing to me. I have a house in Barcelona and one near Odessa where my parents live. I'm going to be in Monaco on Wednesday but only for a day and then I go to Delray Beach, Buenos Aires, Rotterdam, Odessa, and then Paris, Moscow . . . Indian Wells.'

Buenos Aires, Odessa, Paris . . . She has only ever been to Bali, once, and Fiji, on her honeymoon. She often sits at her desk and scans the faces of the tiny brown children, dreaming of Mozambique, Tanzania and Bangladesh, and wondering if she would ever have the courage to go. If she were Daniel, who has a man's ability to follow his urges, to go off into the world, even foolishly, like men once went to war, she might have done it long ago.

'I wish I had your life,' she says.

He comes over to her and kisses her on the forehead. 'You think that because you only have the ocean around you. But these cities are all very . . . boring after a while. I have lived all over the world since I was thirteen so no place means anything to me.' He grips her arms. 'Come on, have some champagne. I did not drink during dinner, thinking of you.'

She pads after him to the second room. He takes an opened bottle out of a tub of ice and looks at the level. 'You haven't been drinking much.'

'Do I have to be drunk?'

He hands her a glass and tips her chin. 'You are funny drunk. Like a child.'

As he's pouring one for himself she says, 'I'm not a child. I'm older than you, Luka. I'm thirty.'

He puts the bottle down. 'Yes? I never know how old women are. I spend too much time with tennis coaches.'

'You expect me to believe *that?*'

He laughs and downs his champagne. He fills the glass again. 'All I know is I have spent too much time with them tonight.' He moves towards her and slides his free hand down the front of her robe.

Something he has said about being thirteen is bothering her. She remembers all too clearly when she was thirteen. She likes him, she lusts after him and now she *feels* for him, the little boy with no home, being carted from tournament to tournament. She is afraid of these feelings. In one weekend she has been rejected by her husband, made a falling-down-drunk spectacle of herself in the city's poshest hotel, and has had unprotected sex multiple times with a god in tennis shoes who, presumably, has a contingent of twenty-nine teenagers waiting to take her place. No wonder she is scared of going beyond lust.

'Why do you like me, Luka?' she asks. Not a good question. Too needy. She'll regret it later, when she goes over and over the scene in her mind. She should have said, *Tell me what you like about me.* Or nothing at all. But she is used to being devalued. She has no confidence in herself. She has contempt for her own beauty.

'I like you because I like you. I do not know why.' He bends into her and slips his hand between her thighs. 'Or maybe I do.'

'But you don't know anything about me.'

'I know everything there is to know. You're pretty. You're enthusiastic.' He uses his hand like a violinist fine-tuning a string. 'And very, very wet.'

'But you don't know where I was born, what I think about.'

'Tell me then.' Humouring her. He throws his glass on the floor and drops to his knees.

But she can't tell him, of course. How do you make an

ordinary life sound anything but dull? Especially to a man who has his tongue in your navel.

'Good,' he says. 'You can stop talking now. It is hard work speaking English.'

'You can speak Russian if you like.'

'No. I only speak in tongues.'

'Then you're very articulate.' She closes her eyes. But somehow her body has lost the connection. She can't stop herself from thinking about Patrick standing like this, with a hooker on her knees in front of him.

'Luka?' She touches his ear with her hand. 'Have you ever paid for sex?'

He looks up and grins at her. 'Still you talk?'

'I'm just wondering what it's like.'

'To pay for it? Or to be paid?'

'I don't know. Both.'

He laughs. 'I think there are many ways we can pay for sex that have nothing to do with money.'

'Would you pay for me?'

'Are you thinking of joining the profession?'

'I was just wondering how much.'

'You are worth?'

Now she's embarrassed. 'Yes.'

'I will tell you one thing. The more beautiful a woman is, the more money she needs. Is that an answer?'

But it isn't. 'I don't need anything from you.'

His eyes are full of mischief. 'Then you will think I am taking advantage of you. But perhaps it is you who is taking advantage of me. For a woman as beautiful as you I might do anything.'

'There are a lot of beautiful women.'

'But you are the only one in this room with me now. So enjoy.'

'You've been very generous.'

'Huh! You make me sound like an uncle giving out *strela* at parties.'

She touches his hair. 'Well, you're no uncle.'

'And who is to say you haven't been generous? You have been *very* generous.' His fingers find her deep pink and he brushes it with his tongue, so lightly it might have only been the thought of it. 'So let's show each other how generous we can be.'

HOTEL BELLISSIMA

Monrifi, Mediterranean Sea, Italy.

This afternoon I arise at two, my room so quiet I might have been sealed in a tomb. My dress and shoes had been whisked away, and a bathing costume, robe and silver sandals laid out. I dress and go downstairs in search of the pool. There are out-of-season figs, rounds of goat cheese wrapped in oiled paper, sugar pastries and jugs of blood orange juice arranged on a table in the lobby. I pick up a fig and wander out into the loggia. A white-coated boy drops his cigarette and takes me to the pool, through a colonnade of cypress trees and a terrace paved with pink slabs the shape of coffins. Some of them jut unevenly and the occasional weed darts like a poison green tongue. The pool is lined with dark slate and gleams like an oil slick. The boy finds some cushions and arranges a lounge chair for me. He asks me if I need anything. I shake my head and hold up the fig.

A cloud sits over the sun. I'm glad it's a tea-weak Mediterranean orb rather than the furnace I was born into.

The models are wearing nothing at all today and that includes body hair. They arrive together, giggling from some kind of chemical high, throw themselves on a pair of sun lounges and don't move for an hour, glossed, legs open to the Mediterranean, the square black sunglasses across their eyes giving them the appearance of mutated flies.

Lucrezia is wrapped like a nori roll in something black-green, with laced espadrilles that wind up her leg and a large straw hat to protect her unnaturally smooth sixty-year-old skin. She is flipping through fashion magazines with minimal interest, snorting as she tosses each on the ground when she is finished. A white-coated boy hovers to collect her discards and spirit them away to the place where dead magazines go. (The subterranean beauty parlour?)

Ettore is reading the *Milano Finanza* with a magnifying glass. The most I have been able to find out about him is that his principal villa is in Como and he is estranged from his children. Whether he has divorced his wife or not I do not know – there is a ring on his wedding finger but it is a coiled nugget of gold, not a band. Silver hairs spring from his chest where the towelling gapes but his stringy brown legs are unexpectedly smooth and hair-free. I think about having sex with him and don't mind, as long as the dogs aren't involved.

Right now, as we're all sunning ourselves on the terrace to the sounds of Vangelis, the four pampered pooches are hoisted under the arms of two white-coated pool boys and taken to the mineral spa for a spot of hydrotherapy.

Beyond a low flagstone wall the Mediterranean crawls away towards Libya as if this island was a mollusc on a whale's back. I have the sensation of moving, riding on a ship towed from harbour, across an ocean and then off the edge of a flat earth.

I am already bored by these Italians and their rituals and hope the days don't stretch on like this. But how life has changed!

I have gone from being boring to being bored. It seems like a lifetime but it is only a few long years.

I wave at a pool boy and he hurries to my side. He's far and away the best-looking thing here, a long-haired Naples street kid in a white coat. *'Panino al prosciutto, grazie?'* I ask in a terrible accent. He smiles and nods. *'Subito!'* I command in echo of my hosts.

Before he can scurry off, Lucrezia lowers her glasses and yells at him. I'm not sure what she's saying but it involves elaborate instructions, something about an *insalada,* a *noce* and a *barbabietola.* Thing A puts up her hand and orders a Coke. The boy can hardly tear his eyes away from her crotch. She makes it even more difficult for him by flopping a leg wider so that her bruised pinkness is open to him.

I wonder if she's set any rules. I suspect not. There has probably been no spoken arrangement. She and Thing B probably think they're on an endless gravy train of free drugs, free clothes and free suntanning. Their stupidity is mind-boggling. As, of course, is their lack of morality. Opening your legs to a pool boy in front of your hosts is the height of rudeness. Unless they have specifically asked you to do it.

When my food comes, it is not the ham sandwich I asked for, but a plate of beetroot and walnuts. I stick my fork into a crimson globe. I feel eyes all over my back. Is it Lucrezia watching my figure like a proprietorial governess? While I'm chewing – the beet is sweet, drizzled with honey – I hear a rustle of papers and Ettore gets up from his lounge.

He's gone for only a few minutes when Lucrezia calls the gypsy-handsome pool boy over and gestures at me. He is to show me to the *suite matrimoniale.*

At last I am being summoned.

The pool boy leads me along hallways that are cold and gloomy as a crypt. He looks over his shoulder occasionally to give me a conspiratorial smile. I know that I need only wink at him and we'd be in one of the curtained alcoves with our mouths all over each other. He's up for it, I can tell. As I walk I open up to the possibilities of his breath on my neck, his rough hands on my breasts, his arrogant teenage prick against my belly. It's not going to happen, but what's the harm in fantasising? I need some help here, some visual stimuli. I am about to have sex, or something like it, with an old man who spits food into the mouths of dogs.

The boy raps on Ettore's door and leaves me there, but not before the cheeky bastard gives me a little nudge on the buttocks. I'm trembling by now, a combination of mind-fucking young Romeo and trepidation about what lies behind this massive iron-studded door. I've been on this threshold more times than I can count but still I dread the step over it. You can drink a man's champagne and eat his food and sleep next to him on his private jet but until he has you alone in his room you don't know anything about him. Once he has had you, or you him, however you see it, you know *everything* about him. In the meantime you are in a suspended state between fantasy and reality, desire and repulsion. I like the meantime. I'd rather stay suspended forever.

No such luck. The dogs have started yapping and throwing themselves against the inside of the door. A maid in a black dress and white apron opens the door and exits as I enter. She looks so perfectly maid-like in her starched collar and cap I suspect she may be another of Lucrezia's mannequins. The hotel is a little dusty. I think of the dirty lingerie in my drawers. Maybe none of the maids are expected to clean.

The door closes behind me. The dogs quit yapping and sniff my toes obsessively. They're still damp from their spa. I find myself in a kind of ante-chamber, sparsely furnished, with the remnants of trompe l'oeil cypress trees and rolling hills fading from the walls. Through an archway I see the edge of a desk and two wicker dog baskets side by side. Ettore's foot in its monogrammed leather slipper.

He is sitting at the desk, still in his towelling robe, his back to me. I can see now why he doesn't turn around – he has his elbows planted on the desk, his fingers tented in front of him, with one of those iPod things plugged into his ears. The little silver machine looks incongruous resting on ink-stained vellum blotting paper on wood that probably has Galileo's schoolboy initials carved into it. I am contemplating sneaking up on him and jerking the earphones out, when one of the dogs does the job for me, jumping up into his master's lap and getting his paws tangled in the wires.

Ettore turns to pat the second dog and sees me. 'Ah, *bene.*' Like I'm a servant who has just brought him his afternoon *ristretto.*

He picks up the dog, tosses it on the floor, where it slides across the polished stone and collides with the other with a yelp. As he rises, his robe falls apart and I glance at his swimming trunks. Surprisingly, unless his penis is the size of a hazelnut, there's no waving projectile. Unlike many European gentlemen he seems not to have discovered, or chosen to use, that sexual aid beginning with V.

I am his sexual aide beginning with V.

Ettore speaks very little English.

In the bedroom you don't need words.

He likes that I'm shivering a little. It makes it easier for him to pretend that I am virginal, if that's what he wants. But I still have no idea what he wants. Nothing would surprise me. These

Europeans disguise their sex in silly little games, as if they're so weary of doing it for centuries that they need a parallel diversion.

Ettore takes me by the hand and leads me to the side of the bed. He gestures for me to drop my gown. Conventional enough. He nods for me to untie the halter of my bathing costume and pull it down over my breasts, my hips. I step out of it and lean down to unbuckle my silver sandals but his *'Non!'* is explosive. Okay, I'll leave them on. Foot fetish, is it?

I stand up straight and stare out at the flat sea through a window swagged in ancient red velvet and tattered gold. When I look back at him, his one eye is scanning my body hungrily. It's the first spark of anything I've seen. He's been the debonair gentleman in a 1950s cigarette advertisement until now.

'Ettore,' I whisper, as if Sophia Loren were calling his name.

That works. He puts his hands on my shoulders and manoeuvres me to the bed. I sit on the edge and he beside me. One hand moves to my left breast and he has his mouth on the nipple in a moment, gentle at first but soon pulling on it with his teeth like a dog at a rope. It hurts. I ease him off a little. He starts sucking like a piglet, making popping noises. The nipple is going to look like a banana before he's finished.

He moves to the other breast and clamps on it. I make suitable noises and shut my eyes tight, willing a response. It's not working. Every pop and graze distracts me from the mood. I can hear the dogs scratching around. I'm still hoping they're not in the scenario. They're getting more excited, the little voyeurs. Now they're yapping. The noise seems to make Ettore more aroused. His sucking becomes frenzied. Just as I think I'm about to call it quits my thighs are yanked apart and a snaky thing, a tongue, slides its way deep into my cunt.

Two mouths?

I open my eyes and I feel Ettore roll away from me. Down below there's someone else toiling. I raise my head from the bed.

Pool Boy.

This is a turn-up for the books.

He stands and hoists my legs over his shoulders, pulling me roughly down the bed towards him. My toes are skeleton bones in their silver sandals. His giant cock points at my mouth like a signpost. But he has somewhere else to put it. And he does.

It's *amazing*. He's big enough to go in my cunt and out my mouth. I'm a tunnel that he's driving a truck through. I am just a spinal system to process the electrical shocks. His hands tear at my waist, his hipbones slap against my thighs. And all the while Ettore sits on the edge of the bed masturbating.

Well, not really.

I lie.

Ettore is sitting on the edge of the bed masturbating but Pool Boy is nowhere to be found. I need some kind of fantasy to help me through. Ettore's technique is to force his rubbery cock between my thighs and make like he is starting a fire with kindling before waving it over my body to my mouth for a bit of reciprocal sucking.

He finishes himself off away from me. It's a hiccup rather than an eruption. He seems pleased with himself as he wipes the residue away with a sheet. I'm still lying flat on my back on the bed, my toes touching the floor. He puts a hand on my thigh.

'*Bene.*' He pats me. '*Senza bambini.*'

Even I know what that means. No children.

It wouldn't matter anyway.

No children for me either.

No one is pretending there is love here. A man like Ettore has had enough of love. Over the years, it has cost him money and property and an unhealthy level of hypertension. When he was young, he fell for every beautiful woman who walked by. There was emotion as well as lust. He was far from the cold fish he is now. He would kiss them from their pretty toes to their nebulous hair. He would lavish them with gifts. He would love that he made them fall in love with him. It made him feel more than a walking bank vault, it made him feel invincible. He was a rogue, he was a roué, but never heartless. He slept with waitresses and princesses. He adored them all! Eventually, there was pressure from his family to procreate, so he chose a wife who was sexy and fertile and smart. She bore him children. He was besotted by them. He became less besotted with his wife once she'd been weighed down with sables and jewels and the responsibilities of servants. She reminded him of his mortality. He longed for girls who were fresher, more naïve. He liked having a brace of them hanging off his shoulders, beautiful, young, captivating pheasants. And what was the fault in that? He travelled, he had great wealth, he got bored and restless and lonely. Women set their sights on him. They'd do anything. He couldn't believe it! They were like puppies doing tricks for boners. And he was performing too – the great lover, the bestower of riches. But the occasional fling proved indiscreet and expensive. His wife found out, demanded significant financial concessions each time. The children became teenagers and developed costly habits. And one day he said to himself, *Basta*! Enough! These women are driving me crazy. I'm tired. I need someone who won't make demands. Someone I don't need to perform for. Someone who won't milk me dry. An arrangement.

I am his arrangement. I am his companion. If Ettore simply wanted sex, he could have picked up one of those €300-an-hour independent contractors in the lobby of the Hotel Chardonne. Or, like Lucrezia, convinced two stupid models he is good for their careers. But young girls are dangerously fertile. Call girls are avaricious. Ettore is prepared to be generous but he hates to be reminded the clock is ticking, the cash register ringing. And he's less interested in sex than he used to be. Besides, anyone can buy sex, anyone can seduce silly teenagers with dollar signs in their eyes. Leave that to the Russians, who scoop up women like loose change.

No one is pretending love but I try to provide a reasonable facsimile of it. Otherwise, what is the point? Chance – with just a little bit of prompting – has brought us together in that hotel lobby. We might never have met. But since we have, and I'm caught up in his slipstream, there's nothing to do but swim along with him. He's *my* fate and it's foolish to stroke against him. Eventually the rip will bring me where I'm meant to be.

Another hotel lobby. Another man.

THE HOTEL LORD MELBOURNE

Collins Street, Melbourne, Australia

Violet wears her beauty reluctantly, as if it were the skin of another creature. It sits on her conscience uneasily, like a mink coat on the back of an animal lover, something that is stroked and admired by others but uncomfortable for its wearer, eagerly shrugged off.

Because she was an odd-looking child, beauty took her unawares. It didn't sneak up like it might on other girls. Rather, it threw a sack over her head and ran off with her. There was Before Beauty and After Beauty and hardly a week in between.

At school they called her Close Encounters for her rice noodle-white skin that sometimes showed the veins, her ginger eyelashes, her big, unblinking violet eyes, the long neck and small head and the flame-coloured hair clipped into an unfeminine hedge to keep it neat. It didn't help that her mother, knowing pretty wasn't possible, tried relentlessly to make her daughter 'cute'. In a photograph taken when she was eleven, Violet is wearing lavender overalls and a purple-striped sweater and stripy socks over skinny ankles that emerge from clogs. But Violet is not cute. Her head is bowed, she does not smile. A true Shrinking Violet, she looks as if she wishes the earth that pushed her out would swallow her up again.

There was no one to tell her that pretty girls are pretty ordinary all their lives but great beauties always start out plain. There hadn't been a beauty in her family for generations, as far as anyone could see. Her colouring came from her father, a high-ranking police official nicknamed Big Red, not only for his ginger hair but his public rages over criminal acts, such as cigarette butts tossed out of moving cars and teenagers avoiding fares. Her mother was a bottle blonde, without the face to match. Beauty was something belonging to unearthly angels and biblical temptresses. It was to be looked upon with suspicion. In some of its forms, such as the poster of Farah Fawcett on her brother Andrew's wall, it could be positively terrifying.

The summer Violet turned thirteen, her body rearranged itself as smoothly as a morphing reflection in a funfair crazy mirror. Then her face gained cheekbones and her lips pillowed out and her hair rambled to her shoulders in fetching curves. She was entirely unprepared. She didn't have the practice pretty girls had with compliments and head patting and chucking under the chin.

At first she thought she had done something wrong. There were sideways glances and public-transport oglings and whisperings she could never quite decipher. One day she overheard one of her mother's friends say, 'You're going to have trouble with that one.' It was bewildering.

She had tried hard not to disappoint her parents and had always done what she was told, unlike Andrew, who was a 'handful' and at fourteen 'broke his mother's heart' when she discovered *Penthouse* in his underwear drawer. Violet's ambition was to be her parents' one good child, to make up for Andrew's juvenile perversions with perfect grades at school and impeccable good manners and a high-minded character that fitted exactly with her parents' view of the world. She joined what she was supposed to and stayed clear of what she was not. She won prizes for science projects and for a sketch of a bunny in the municipal art show. She was always the first chosen by teachers to take on responsible tasks, such as art-room monitor, a coveted position she held three years in a row. Although she was too reserved to win the popularity contests at school, she was not without friends. She attached herself to girls who were also well-behaved and played competition basketball on Saturdays and could be trusted to go on unescorted excursions to see *Grease*. When they scrawled hearts in their diaries it was around the names of ponies, not boys.

Everything went smoothly for Violet, living her parents' life. But now, at thirteen, she was 'trouble', a label cruelly undeserved.

When she started high school the consequences of beauty became clear. She felt all wrong from the start, as if the Violet who might have fitted in, the good, well-behaved Violet who flew under the radar and didn't make waves, had been painted purple and set with carnival lights. The three hundred potential new girlfriends looked on her with disdain. She thought it was her uniform, which wouldn't sit correctly over her new curves, or her lilywhite legs, which she slathered with fake tan. When that didn't work, she stayed back in class to avoid being snubbed in the hallways. In those first wretched weeks, the only students who showed any interest in her were the lads from the neighbouring boy's school, who would squirt her with their drink bottles on the tram and sometimes follow her home, whistling and throwing things.

And then one day, in the breezeway near the toilets at school, a group of fourth-form girls surrounded her and called her a slut. It seemed that one of the girl's boyfriends had fallen in love with her. Violet didn't even know who he was. The unfairness of it was crushing. She walked around for a while with her head down and her arms across her chest. But as she sat alone in the tram, surrounded by boys trying to attract her attention, her embarrassment grew into a sense of wonder that she could have this effect on someone. And as she became more curious, she started to feel the power of what she could do. One afternoon she smiled directly at a boy and was amazed to see that he blushed more deeply than she ever had.

It was terrifying.

The English teacher's name was Robert Pilsen. He wore spidery black mohair sweaters and looked like the lead singer of Simple Minds. All the second-form girls were in love with him, even the ones who feared they might be lesbians. Violet knew this because his was the one class where she was not the only one who stayed back.

They were studying *Tess of the D'Urbervilles,* on the curriculum as a cautionary tale against following your natural urges, but it proved a dangerous choice for the only male teacher under fifty-five in a progressive all-girls' school. As Tess swooned her way through the novel, so did the girls in Violet's class swoon through their English lessons, divided amongst themselves whether Mr Pilsen was more like Alec Durberville or Angel Clare.

If he had been a nervous, stammering type, it might have been different. But he wrote lyrics for a punk band, played the keyboard with the school orchestra at a first-year dance and took a group of fifth-form girls to see *Equus* at the local cinema. (He asked them to call him 'Rob'.) Many girls imagined him to be their boyfriend and he could not have been oblivious to the fact, but he continued to smile on each of them equally, and accept the confidences they gave him and talk to them as if they were women of the world. The school principal assured parents he was a 'positive male role model' but the girls joked that she was in love with him too, even though he was young enough to be her own son.

He was twenty-six, twice Violet's age. She thought this was significant.

Violet knew she was special, the way he looked at her. He always praised her questions in class. He wrote more words in the margins of her essays than in those of the other girls and he drew little stars next to the grades he gave her. The only time she got less than an 'A' he waved his finger at her and said, 'You can do better.'

This new power she had was an astonishing thing. Outside school, she would plug into the schoolboys' lust like a battery taking a charge. By the time she got to English class she was practically levitating from the static. She would sit in the front row and *emanate* sex, or what she thought was sex. She expected that any day now Mr Pilsen, 'Rob', would ask her out on a date, a real date, alone.

And so it happened, sort of. The English class had gone to see an amateur production of *Antony and Cleopatra* one night. Afterwards, Rob waited with them as the parents collected each girl. Violet's parents didn't come. (And why would they? She had told them she would get a lift.) And inevitably, instead of putting her on a tram, Rob drove her home in his old Valiant with squeaky red vinyl seats. She sat so close beside him their thighs touched. When he pulled up where she instructed, a few doors down from her house, she kept him talking about the play, all the while waiting for him to make his move. All her nerve ends seemed to be bunching in her stomach. Her lips tingled and, quite strangely, she felt as if her breasts would burst out of their sensible cotton bra.

When he yawned and said, 'Well, I guess it's past your bedtime,' she took it as her cue. She put a hand on his knee and whispered 'You're the one that I want', which was the sexiest line from *Grease*. She could smell his sweat as she offered her face for a kiss. He physically recoiled and said, quite flustered, 'Look, Violet, you're a fucking policeman's daughter' and turned the key in the ignition. As she stood on the pavement and watched him drive away she wondered, *if I weren't a fucking policeman's daughter would he have done it with me?* She thought probably, certainly, yes. And she got another charge from the way he said 'fucking' in front of her. It meant that he saw her as a grown up woman and not a child in class.

But after that he was different with her. She was amazed to realise that he was scared. He no longer looked her straight in the eye in English lessons or called her first to read. The other girls noticed this too. The last girl to be collected by her parents after the play told everyone she'd seen Rob put his arm around Violet's waist. It was decided that they had 'done it' and Violet's ostracism was complete. In the way of the world, it only served to enhance the male's mystique.

As the days went on Violet knew she had lost her preferred status. She didn't know how she could get it back. When she stayed behind in class Rob was terse with her and made sure they were never alone. She began to invent illnesses to keep her from school. And then one day she was called into the principal's office. Her father was there, in his uniform, looking grim. Had 'anything happened' with Mr Pilsen, she was asked. 'No,' she answered in a very small voice. The principal looked at her father and her father glared at the principal. And her beloved Rob was no longer there.

She had the power to make boys love her and men lose their jobs. Another girl might have been thrilled by this, but she was ashamed. Her moral compass had been the innocent Sandy from *Grease* but now she discovered she had been the bad girl Rizzo all along. Her mother apparently thought this too – she gave Violet a stern talk about 'leading men on'. But *on to what*, Violet asked herself. She decided she no longer wanted to know.

Like Tess of the D'Urbervilles, her beauty was not a fact of nature but a character flaw. There was something about being beautiful that upset the order of the world. Everyone was quick to make a judgement about her, as if everything was her fault. And she supposed it was. She could make herself unbeautiful by slashing her skin or getting hugely fat or stopping eating like other girls did. But while she did nothing about it she had to bear the blame.

She retreated back into shyness and walking hunched-over, blushing crimson whenever anyone gave her an appreciative glance. And later, when sex with boys became unavoidable, she let them make the choices and make the moves and expend all the emotion because then the shame of it – and the thrill – was borne equally.

No one could say she asked for it.

HOTEL BELLISSIMA

Monrifi, Mediterranean Sea, Italy

It has been light for a few hours but the energy required to get out of bed has eluded me today. I'm enervated by days and days of luxury. Another glass of champagne, another snoutful of coke, another morsel of foie gras, another plate of honey figs, another table setting of antique silver, another pretty dress to try, another beautiful nightgown laid out on the bed, another pedicure, another manicure, another fragrant elixir massaged into my skin, another tortoiseshell comb through my hair, another blossom-scented bath drawn by unseen hands, another afternoon basking in a hazy sun, another servant grovelling as I walk by, another sly look from Pool Boy. We all have a pleasure quotient and I might have just reached mine.

I have been lingering in bed with a dog-eared copy of a Harold Robbins novel, the only book in English I can find. Many of the pages are faded and stuck together and cigarette ashes fall when I open it. Its presence amongst the magazines in one of the sitting rooms suggests that 1) a very long time ago someone who spoke English was a guest here and 2) no one who reads English has visited since. If all the visitors have shared the intellectual capacity of Things A and B that's not a big leap. The book inspires visions of bare-chested men in velvet pants and girls in white boots and see-through blouses. I imagine Ettore rolling naked on a tiger-skin rug and Lucrezia doing a striptease with seven black veils. But were they ever that amusing? Or have they always existed in this state of mummified decadence, as if they've been wrapped in reindeer skin and buried under a glacier for a millennia, then unearthed to stagger wearily through the world laden with old jewels.

I find myself chuckling, for the first time in – God, how long? – when we are thrown into chaos.

There is shrieking in the corridor and raised voices drifting up from the sea.

I jump off the bed, not so languid after all. I snatch up my robe and pull the heavy bedroom door open. The heart-rending sobs are coming from the staircase, the cries from further below as maids, kitchen hands, pool boys and the two British dolly birds come up to see what is happening.

Lucrezia has thrown herself on the steps, pounding at the marble with her fists, her velvet dressing gown flowing behind her. She looks like a prostrate Scarlett O'Hara pleading for the return of Rhett. Carla stands over her, frozen like a Pompeiian citizen immortalised in solid lava. Her little dog, Peppe, has the lace trim of Lucrezia's hem in his teeth, but Carla doesn't move to stop him. The servants look on helplessly. Pool Boy's face is lifted towards me wearing an enormous grin.

Lucrezia kicks her legs and her cries are feral, guttural, more like a hound than a woman. I don't understand her Italian but there's a name I can distinguish amongst the bellowing. *Beatrice. Beatrice.*

Carla shoos the servants away and I go back into my room and run the bath.

I'm dressing when a maid comes to the door. '*Per favore*, madam, you are to leave.'

'Leave the room?'

'*Non*. The hotel. *Tutti partendo*. There is a death.'

I'm shaken by this. *Il Dottore?* I ask. Ettore?

She shakes her head. '*La cagna.*' The bitch.

On the speedboat to Crotone I learn that it's Lucrezia's Great Dane, Beatrice, who has died. She developed an infection after her hysterectomy and expired in the arms of the veterinary surgeon. Lucrezia is demented with guilt that she trusted someone called Video with the dog's care. The whole way to Crotone she sobs in Carla's embrace. She rails against God, she rails against the Pope, she points a gnarly finger at Thing A and cries '*Strega*!' Thing A takes it fairly well considering but Thing B is agitated. 'What did we do? What did we do?'

From Crotone we are driven in a caravan of limos to Napoli. Ettore takes me in his car but sleeps the whole way with a satin mask over his eyepatch. At Napoli airport the driver picks up my suitcase and looks at me questioningly. Ettore fires some rapid commands in Italian. I hear him say 'Parigi'. No, I tell the driver, 'Nice.' I've been thinking about this all along. I don't want Paris. I'm tired of it. It's tired of me. Besides, the film festival is about to begin in Cannes. It's open season on the connoisseurs who come into port on obscene yachts, hunting for starlets. The competition is fierce but there are plenty of gentlemen to go round. And the hotels are very tolerant. They have to be – the lobbies are teeming with women who might be whores, porn stars, heiresses or Hollywood ingénues with breast enhancements. Most of the wily old concierges know the difference but few of their male patrons do. The terrace at the Carlton, the lounge at the Majestic, the bar on the beach at the Martinez, the pool at Eden Roc, the Black Jack table at the Casino – these places are among the crème de la crème of pick-up joints when the season is in full swing.

Which is now.

The driver takes us to the ticketing office where a seat on a commercial flight to Nice is purchased for me. Ettore doesn't mind where I go as long as I don't follow him to Milan and make complications. He kisses me dryly on the hand when his private jet is ready for departure. There are no offers of another assignation, no small, extravagant gift pressed into my palm. But that's fine by me. I'm not looking for gifts.

I have, however, swapped my old clothes for a selection of Lucrezia's better ones. Lucrezia hasn't noticed any of this through her vale of tears. And possibly she wouldn't care, as long as I haven't stolen one of her darlings. I'm now wearing something more suitable for the Riviera – wide striped pants, a navy linen jacket with silk camisole underneath, espadrilles, a white cashmere sweater tied over my shoulders, a floppy hat. I've loaded on as much as I can wear without being obvious. I feel only slightly guilty that it's all Valentino. Besides this, I've stashed a slithery satin gown, some expensive lingerie, a bathing suit and a pair of silver sandals in my vanity case. I've emptied my makeup into the sink and replaced it with new products. I've snatched a bottle of Joy. This, really, is all I need for the life I lead.

'Ta-ta!' Thing A calls over her shoulder to me as I watch the group stagger towards the departure gate. She's unsteady on high wedges, trailing a foxtail stole and sloshing a bottle of Billecart-Salmon. I feel a momentary pang that I didn't get to know her, get to hear about her childhood in the slums of Yorkshire, or wherever, or her first kiss or what her mother made her for breakfast. Things I don't want to remember about myself.

But none of us are whole people. We don't have pasts. We only come alive when we intersect with fractions of other people. In hotel lobbies. In airports. In casino gaming rooms. Even then, 'alive' is a bit of a stretch. We're episodes. Episodes in other people's books, sketchy at best, faded with time, half-memories captured between sticky pages, a cascade of old cigarette ash on someone's lap, triggering fleeting recall.

Ettore doesn't look back.
But I can't help it.

Part Two
Violet

HOTEL ROYAL PARC

Boulevard Murat, Paris, France

Hello Violet!

Most beautiful of muses. I am a knight carrying the flower of your body close to my heart. Your scent is still on me and it brings me great good fortune. I have beaten the world number one at Delray Beach and Buenos Aires. This is a shock to some but not to me, as I think of you. Today I am in the quarter-final at Rotterdam against your compatriot Patrick Rafter where I will again be victorious. I must see you, you must watch me play, Davis Cup, Paris. Come March 4. Hotel Royal Parc, Boulevard Murat. I will be waiting.

I kiss you now across the many thousands of miles that separate us.

–Your friend, Luka

On the Paris Métro, late at night, gliding from spectral station to spectral station, Violet turns Luka's letter over in her hands, trying to find the words underneath the words. She is still not entirely convinced that it isn't a figment of her imagination. But the paper is heavy and yellow, and the creases made from repeated readings have texture when she runs her fingers along them. She cannot quite believe the truth of the letter, just as she cannot quite believe she is in Paris, as if for the past twenty-five hours she has been merely sitting in a comfortable chair in her Melbourne house while scenes of airports and airplane interiors and Métro stations have been projected behind her onto the wall. She feels like a child reaching to stroke a phantom lion that leaps off screen at an Imax cinema. She can't connect with anything. The strangers who step in and out of the carriage, or huddle on the platforms, tired and weighed down by winter clothes, the snorting drunk who leans, uncomfortably close, against the window of an adjacent seat, the old man who strings a puppet theatre between poles, performs, then gets off at the next stop – they might be characters in a pageant that is screening in her mind. There is a *here* here but she isn't in it yet. She won't be in it until Luka's touch earths the crackling current of her excitement, her hope . . . her anxiety.

Violet is afraid, in her heart, that things might have changed between them, that five weeks might as well be a century if someone has moved on, especially if that someone is moving all the time, from airport to airport, hotel to hotel, tennis court to tennis court, woman to woman. He might be disappointed when he takes another look at her; he might regret his hasty invitation. Or she might have misunderstood his intention – he is her 'friend' and nothing else. This is what the sensible Violet fears, feared before she left Australia, but sensible Violet is like a tiny person down a deep well trying to be heard.

Another Violet has brought her there, a Violet who is as skittish and off-centre as a kitten in the wind. A Violet who would resign from her job, leaving her colleagues bewildered, close the door of her house behind her, without even cancelling the newspapers, and hop on a flight to Paris with her modest savings – minus the funds for Eliniphao and Louvenx – converted to traveller's cheques, all on the strength of a note, hastily scrawled on paper torn from a stenographer's notebook, folded into a buff envelope and addressed in a secretary's hand.

And there is the matter of the first-class ticket enclosed.

Well, who *wouldn't* go?

This is what she's asking herself as the train pulls into the Métro station Porte d'Auteuil and she disembarks onto an empty platform lit with a liverish fluorescence. She gathers her courage and warily follows the underground tunnels to the street, the wheels of her small suitcase clacking on the tiles. She feels like a target in her silver parka and black high-heeled boots and almost becomes one when a trio of punks rounds a corner swilling clear liquid from a bottle and clashing chains. They slide to a stop, dance around her for a moment (*ooh, baise-moi, baise-moi*) and then flee, screeching, the scent of aniseed drifting behind them. She can hear their amplified cackling down the tunnel and quickens her pace in case the empty platform fails to amuse them. (She doesn't know that their *coiffures* are too carefully arranged to be any kind of threat.)

Up on the boulevard, the cars cruise by, streaks of neon. The cold is a shock, it bites at her ears. Fortunately she can see the hotel's circular driveway and flagged colonnade from where she stands. She slows down for a moment, wishing she could find a place to fix her make-up, tame her hair. On reflection she is glad Luka didn't meet her at the airport, as she expected, really quite glad. She has needed this time to compose herself.

But she is not composed, with her lipstick chewed off and her clothes awry. And just a few metres away he is waiting for her, standing in the lobby with a bunch of flowers, expecting her to be perfect.

The unwelcome return of insecurity drains the confidence from her like a silk slip from her shoulders. She suddenly feels her emotional nakedness exposed. Up ahead, the beige-coated doorman spots her hesitation, starts to stride towards her, smiling. But her feet cannot go forward. While she was in motion she was exhilarated, but now she has stopped she is gripped with terror.

Her journey has been more than a flight across continents, it's a giant leap of faith. Only a few tiny baby steps to go, but they are more difficult than gymnastics. She suddenly realises the immense folly of what she's doing. Does she really believe she belongs in Luka's world? She has taken to reading the sports pages, but still she knows little about it. What will he expect from her, besides the opening of legs?

The doorman reaches her, tips his hat. *'Pourrais-je vous aider, mademoiselle?'* He clicks his fingers and a porter dashes over, takes the handle of her suitcase and wheels it away before she can protest.

But why should she protest? She's a guest after all. She makes a conscious effort to raise her chin, pull her shoulders back and look the doorman in the eye as he holds the heavy glass doors open for her.

There's nothing for it but to go in.

Gold. Everything inside is gold. Yellow marble, brass fixtures, mustard-coloured leather banquettes, the beige and gold coats of the staff. It's a new hotel, huge, impersonal, buzzing, even at this hour. She feels like she's walked into a sickly-sweet honeycomb.

But Luka is not standing there with a bouquet of flowers.

She is not altogether surprised. He will be in the suite with the champagne on ice and candles erupting over every surface, Natalie Imbruglia singing *Torn* in the background.

She follows the porter to the front desk. The receptionist beams at her.

'Guy will assist,' says the porter, beaming just as brightly. Violet feels like the meat in a very courteous sandwich. 'Is there anything else you need?' he asks, rubbing his hands together.

'No, thank you,' she says, oblivious to what *he* requires, a gratuity for service.

The porter waits another beat, then bows his head and backs off, the brightness dimming from his smile. *Another guest with shallow pockets.*

'The name, please, *mademoiselle?*' Guy asks.

'Oh, it's not my name. I'm visiting a friend.'

Guy raises his eyebrow precisely enough to suggest he is curious without being dubious. 'Your friend's name, then?'

'Uyanik.' She swallows it.

'Pardon?'

'Uyanik,' she says more clearly. 'Luka.' She swears the woman receptionist at the counter next to Guy looks at her with interest. But maybe she is being paranoid.

'Can you spell that?'

She does. Guy sighs at his screen. 'No. I'm sorry, *mademoiselle,*' he says. 'The Mr Uyanik we have has checked out.'

In the cavern of the lobby, someone drops a glass. It shatters on the hard floor and drags her heart with it. She has fretted about many possibilities, but not this one. 'It must be a mistake.'

'No, it is not a mistake. I remember now myself.'

'He might have gone to another hotel,' she tries.

Guy is offended. 'I doubt that, *mademoiselle.*'

'But he left a message for me?'

'Your name?' He taps it into the computer. 'No, *mademoiselle.*'

It doesn't make sense. 'But he's playing in the Davis Cup tomorrow.'

The woman receptionist looks up. 'Excuse me, *mademoiselle*, but Mr Uyanik is not playing. He hurt his knee at practice.' Violet imagines a smirk under what she says.

'When was that?'

'Oof,' shrugs the woman. 'I think two days ago.'

Two days ago! Just as she was leaving home. There would not

have been time to get a message to her. She feels a little more hopeful.

'Do you know where he went?'

'I'm sorry, but we do not keep that information.'

'But you must have a forwarding address.'

'That we cannot disclose.' She goes back to staring at her terminal.

'But I've come all the way from Australia to see him!'

Guy examines her dispassionately. 'Perhaps *mademoiselle* would like a taxi?' he suggests.

'Back to Australia?'

Guy gives her a pitying look. She can see now they don't believe her, they think she's some kind of fan, a stalker. Suddenly it's imperative to show them the letter. Flustered, she unzips her backpack and starts hunting through it. She hauls out her scrunched-up travelling clothes, the sexy underwear she has brought with her, a hairbrush, some guide books, her travel journal. Guy pulls an agonised face as she slams a lacy bra on the marble counter in front of him. 'I've got a letter here somewhere,' she explains.

But she hasn't. It isn't anywhere. She goes through the pockets of her jacket, unzips the front compartment of her case. While she is doing this, Guy has called another porter. '*Mademoiselle,* the porter will help you.' He says something in French to the young attendant, which Violet doesn't understand, but has the tone of *Get her out of here, stop her making a mess, she's a lunatic*. The porter starts collecting her things in his arms.

'Look, you don't have a cancellation, do you?'

'I'm sorry, we are fully committed because of the tennis.'

'Any kind of room will do.'

'There is a very nice little hotel a street away, *mademoiselle,* which is probably not so busy. Shall I call it for you?'

She suddenly feels like a parcel being handed from porter to receptionist to porter, getting shabbier and shabbier with each transaction. She doesn't want to go anywhere else. She doesn't have the energy. 'I'm not feeling well,' she says. 'I've just got off the plane and I haven't slept for two days. Can I sit for a moment?'

'Of course,' Guy says coolly.

'I *do* have somewhere else to go,' she lies. 'I just need to—'

'Excellent,' says Guy, dismissing her.

The porter carries her things to a banquette, which is about as far away from the reception desk as you can get and facing a bank of elevators. There is a sign on a stand, the plastic letters spelling out BIENVENUE UTF FÉDÉRATION FRANÇAISE DE TENNIS. Although her heart jumps with every ping of the opening doors – she still imagines Luka is hiding out here somewhere – she's glad to be away from Guy's scrutiny. If she can just compose herself for a few moments.

'*Mademoiselle.*' The porter is still standing before her, slightly bowed.

'Thank you for your help,' she says.

He's not expecting a tip. He has something else on his mind.

'Yes?' she asks. She looks at him more closely. He's only a teenager, eighteen at the most. Black wiry hair, the blueness of stubble coming through, front teeth snaggled – he's not pretty but he's got the eyes of an adoring hound.

'There is a *chambre*,' he says.

She doesn't understand.

'There is a room I know, here, in this hotel. A room you can have for tonight.'

'How—'

'It is *la chambre de bonne,* the maid's room, as you say. It is always vacant. But it is very clean. I have the key.'

'Oh, I don't want to get you into trouble.'

He looks offended. 'It's no trouble. No one will know.'

'That's very kind of you.'

'You will have to wait here. It may be some time. But I will come back. Okay?'

'Yes, thanks,' she says. 'What's your name?'

'Patric, *mademoiselle.*'

'Patrick. That's my husband's name.'

He beams at her.

Patrick. She feels even sicker now that she is reminded of him. Sick, because she told him about Luka. She couldn't help it, her little moment of triumph, when she called Patrick to tell him she was going away. Indefinitely she had said. His 'Oh, why?' was so offhand she'd felt the urge to king hit him with something. Luka was that thing. It had worked – Patrick went silent for seconds. Then he'd said, 'Don't be ridiculous, Violet.' And she didn't know what he meant. Ridiculous to make such a thing up? Or ridiculous to contemplate going? So she told him about the first-class ticket and the Davis Cup and the life she was going to have following Luka on the circuit. Barcelona, Odessa, Rome, New York, Moscow, Patrick. The more she could feel him fuming at the other end of the phone, the more she cranked it up. He kept me in a hotel room for four days. He wouldn't let me go. He took my dress away – the one you didn't like. You should read his letters, they're so poetic. He's only twenty-five but he's so . . . dominating. Don't expect me to come back any time soon. We're still friends, though, aren't we, Patrick? You're happy for me?

Bitch, she thought. I've never been a bitch before, but it felt good. Patrick had responded by coming around with gerberas, magnanimously offering to take care of the house (which is half his after all), snooping through her mail while she made him a cup of coffee, promising to forward the monthly payments to Eliniphao and Louvenx, and then pressing her against the dishwasher in an attempt to establish that his newly desirable wife would throw over the tennis star the minute her husband reasserted himself in her life.

And when that didn't work, three paragraphs naming her and Patrick and Luka and a blurry photo taken in the Raj Bar appeared in the gossip pages of *The Age* as if they were some kind of *ménage à trois*. At first she didn't attribute the leak to Patrick – why would he out himself as a cuckold? – but then she realised it had to be him. Because having a wife who was in the bed of a celebrity was almost as good as, in fact, *better* than, having that wife in your own bed. It granted him a certain status. Patrick would dine out on this for months – he was probably regaling dinner guests and clients about it right now, as she sat trembling and abandoned in this cavernous, jaundiced lobby.

Her parents had made it clear they were *disappointed* in her. This tennis player was a *bad lot* – a sportsman, a playboy, a foreigner, a Communist. They wouldn't even drive her to the airport in case it looked like they approved. 'Oh, well, if you must go, send me a postcard,' her mother said. Violet knew, even then, she wouldn't be sending many cards.

And her friends? She had few confidantes and never bonded with anyone for long. She was cautious with her affections and slow to respond. She thought it unwise to speak frankly about herself and unkind to gossip about others, remembering too clearly the cruel judgements of school. But this made her an oddity in the world of women, who demanded reciprocity in the confession of intimacies and secrets. She didn't have any small talk to honey the sharp edges of the defensive wit she'd learnt from her hard cop dad. She was inept at the blithe ripples of conversation that filled the vacuum where content should be. So she came off as morally superior. At work, where she was generally liked, there was still a pocket of female volunteers who thought she was *up herself*. She didn't struggle against the misapprehension. Women demanded too much out of friendships anyway. It was like joining a cult, drawing blood with a blade across your wrist and then never being allowed to leave. In the end it was easier to pretend Patrick's female colleagues and friends were her own. But when she kicked him out, they disappeared too.

Daniel had been her only friend and she had hurt him.

As she boarded the plane in Melbourne, so full of hope, she had joked to herself, *Oh well, I've made my bed now. I can't come back, not any time soon.*

The porter stands back while Violet walks ahead of him into the room.

'It's okay?' he asks. 'Very quiet.'

It's quiet, all right. It's not a bedroom at all, but a windowless storeroom with a narrow bed along one wall. The bed is made up, with a thin cotton blanket and two pillows, one of which bears the impression of a head. 'Does someone sleep here?'

'No, no. It is for the *malade*.'

'A sick room?'

'Yes. But no one is sick. You will not be *dérangé*.'

Patric places her suitcase on the bed. She shrugs off her backpack. 'Thank you,' she says. The room is unbearably stuffy. She begins to unbutton her parka. Patric is looking at his feet. 'Is there a bathroom somewhere?' she asks.

'I take you.'

She follows him down the corridor. They're in the bowels of the hotel, the twilight zone beyond the kitchen, the health club, the staff changing-rooms, the cave of engines. The door Patrick opens gives immediately on to a toilet and washbasin. She enters and locks it. She avoids looking in the mirror over the basin, fearing what she might see.

Back in the storeroom, she sits on the bed.

Patric points to the wall of folded linen. 'If you are cold.'

'No, I'm warm, thank you.'

'No one will come,' he says. *'Bonne nuit.'*

'Bonne nuit,' she repeats and smiles.

Patric shuffles backwards out of the room, looking at his feet.

She gets up and turns the catch on the door, locking herself in. She takes off her dress and pulls on the first thing she can find in her suitcase, a T-shirt. She switches off the bright overhead light and feels her way to the bed. The sheets are crunchy as she crawls between them.

Her sleep is not quite dreamless. Somewhere, deep in the black of it is a little tumour of anxiety, fuelled by Patrick's mouth, Luka's lucky charms and Daniel's deflated balloon. While she's asleep it stays there, a hard, small, itchy thing. But her subconscious is keeping the lid on it, knowing that when she awakes the tumour will metastise into bitter self-recrimination, moral confusion and monstrous humiliation.

Let her sleep . . .

But someone isn't going to.

There's a click. A disturbance in the air, a rustling.

Her skin feels the lift of the sheet and something hard and cold like a slab of beef pushing against her. She reacts by turning toward it and flinging an arm across it. From the depths comes a memory of a one-night stand at university, which involved a filthy futon, an engineering student with foot fungus and an erection that would not go down. That erection is insinuating its way between her thighs right now . . . the warm breath of sour cherries, like cough mixture, covers her nose.

She opens her eyes in shock. The room is black, ebony black, but she catches the shine of his eyes. She pulls away but now there is a bony chest lying across hers and a sharp knee digging into her thigh. She flails out with her arms. 'Get off!'

'Calme-toi, calme-toi. C'est Patric.'

'What?' She wriggles from under him, backs away into the corner of the cot.

He makes another lunge at her, his spidery fingers clawing at her arms. 'Do not be shy, *chérie*.'

She's angry and frightened but something in the way he says *chérie*, like a third-rate matinée idol, drags an unexpected guffaw out of her, a bubble rising in a bottle neck. She puts a hand over her mouth to suppress the eruption of more laughter but it's too late. The giggles glug out like decanting wine.

Patric is offended. 'You do not want me?'

And suddenly she's outside herself, not skittish Violet any more but sensible Violet, Violet with a streak of purple cynicism, hard-nosed Violet who peels herself away from the bed and is now observing the scene from the top shelf of the linen cupboard. One day this Violet is going to find her own identity but now she's not so defined, she's like the crunchy skin off the cicada, whole but hollow, leaving her soft self behind.

From this height she can see in the dark, see herself pressed into the corner of the bed, T-shirt stretched defensively over her knees, giggling dementedly. Look at you, you idiot, sensible Violet is saying, you're so naïve you'd trust any man who smiles at you, even a clammy teenage lothario with a Maurice Chevalier complex. *I* could see this coming a mile off, as I could see it with Patrick and his vanity and that Russian with his phoney philosophies.

Ukrainian, says Violet, sobering up. *And his letter was beautiful.*

It's not so beautiful now. You don't even have it. And that's all you *ever* had of him.

He was injured. He had to go home.

He couldn't wait a day or two?

Maybe he couldn't. There's another letter for me somewhere. Those bastards haven't given it to me yet.

So, you're going to conduct an investigation? Hang around here until the next Davis Cup? Follow him to Monte Carlo?

I could.

Go home, Violet. Buy yourself something nice, visit the Louvre and go home.

I'm not going home!

'Bien! Bien!'

Violet slams back into her body, focuses on the shape before her who has jumped from the bed and is hopping on one foot trying to put his jeans back on.

'*Bien!* You can stay. Okay?' The force of Violet's conversation with herself has alarmed her seducer, who thinks that perhaps this one might be *perturbée* enough to report him to the front desk. She had smiled so sweetly and gone with him so willingly and compared him to her husband – surely this was an invitation to bed? But what is it he has heard about the English? They say one thing and mean another. They are all *fous.* He must make a note of it in the journal he will one day sell to Gallimard.

Now she is throwing a pillow at him. 'Get out of here! Or I'll scream!'

No one will hear her if she does but he knows it's not wise to point this out. 'You can stay. I go.'

'You bloody well better,' she says but he can hear the conviction fading from her voice. He buttons up his fly, picks up his shoes and finds the door handle. The minute he closes the door behind him, he hears the lock inside click.

Violet presses her body against the door in case he decides to come back. She has no idea of the time but she can't sleep here now. She struggles into her dress, shoves her T-shirt into the backpack, pulls on her boots, bundles her parka under her arm and carries her luggage guardedly into the hall. It's deserted.

In the lobby, there's morning activity. A porter pushes a trolley of newspapers, a few guests are checking out at reception. It's light outside, a clinical, grey light without any humour in it. No one pays much attention. Fortunately, the staff has changed over. Even the doorman is different.

Violet doesn't know it yet, but when one door closes, another generally opens.

HOTEL QUELQUECHOSE

Rue Mazarine, Paris, France

Violet sits in a warm corner of the Café du Bois counting her traveller's cheques. If she were thrifty she could find a cheap hotel and make it last several weeks, months perhaps. She could wait until the French Open, when surely he must return. Or she could take a flight to Monte Carlo and . . . what? There's no point. Luka has hurt his knee. His luck has run out. And so has the luck of his lucky charm. All those talismans he wears around his neck – she realises now she has been just one of them.

She wants to find a hotel room, curl up and sleep for a week but she can't bring herself to get up from the table. She thinks this is misery but she doesn't know anything yet. She's warm, she has money, she has her dignity back, sitting here amongst strangers who give her curious and interested glances. The café is steamy and lacquered with the scent of burnt butter, coffee and nicotine. It's how she knew Paris would smell, and she wonders at it. Perhaps she has past lives layered on top of one another like the leaves of the pastry she has left half-eaten on her plate. From the moment the airport taxi took her inside the *périphérique* she has fought the feeling that there is something immeasurably sad about this place. Has she lived here before? Has she been abandoned before, in a café just like this? There's something there, a whisper of familiarity. Her brain scratches at the surface of her soul, trying to capture it. But it would take an excavation to dig it out. No, it's just an empty case of *déjà vu*, a feeling that goes with the territory. They spray you with it the minute you get off the plane at Charles de Gaulle.

Although she's trying to be philosophical, tears fill her eyes and slide down her cheeks. She wipes a hand across her face to dry it.

'Permit me, *mademoiselle.*' The man beside her on the banquette offers her a handkerchief. The little tables are close-packed and she hasn't paid much attention to him before this. When she doesn't immediately respond, he says, 'It's clean but not pressed, I'm sad to say.'

There's nothing to do but accept it. She dabs her eyes. 'Thank you.'

'Please keep it.' He drops a sugar cube into a tiny cup and stirs it. Then he looks back at her calmly. 'He is late?'

At first she's startled. 'How —?'

He laughs. 'Beautiful women don't sit alone in cafés with tears in their eyes because they don't like the taste of their *chausson aux pommes*.' He points his spoon at her half-eaten apple pastry. 'There must be a reason you've lost your appetite.'

His probing flusters her. 'It's a misunderstanding.'

'Ah Ha.' He sips his coffee. Embarrassed, she counts some francs into the small saucer in front of her. She puts her hand on her backpack.

He doesn't look up. 'Don't leave.'

She scrutinises him more closely now. He looks decent enough in his brown tweed jacket and beige scarf tucked like a cravat into his lapels. He is fiftyish, with a youth's long hair, a prominent bridge to his nose and a round mole like a beauty mark high on the cheek facing her. A ratty kind of handsomeness like the actor in those Truffaut movies they played at the university cinema. He seems harmless, but she's not in the mood to trust any man. 'I'm sorry. I've got things to do.' It comes out more curtly than she means it to.

He gives her a look of mock astonishment. 'It's only *huit heures*. What is there to do at 8 a.m.?'

'I have to find a hotel.'

'I see. Have you just arrived from Australia? Sydney perhaps?' He pronounces it *Sidenny.*

'How do you know I'm Australian?'

'Oh, I know many Australians.' He offers her his hand. 'Clotaire Litvak.'

'Violet,' she says, taking it.

'Well, Violet, what brings you in Paris?'

'Holiday,' she lies.

'Your first time?'

'Yes.'

'I envy you. The first time is always the best. This man who has stood you up, he's from Paris?'

'No, he's Ukrainian.'

'Ah, those Russians are all gangsters. Not to be trusted.'

'He's not a gangster.'

'No, of course not. Can you find him? Do you know where he is staying?'

'No.'

'And you don't have a hotel?'

'They . . . lost my reservation.'

'That's very unfortunate. Do you wish to stay in this *arrondissement*?'

'I don't suppose so.'

'Good. *Le seizième* is rather dull. I have lived here for thirty-five years. You would be more amused by *le sixième* or la marais. If you would permit me, I know a hotel that's very popular with Australians. It's near Le Pont des Arts. You can walk across the Seine to the museum. It's very inexpensive.'

She might as well accept his suggestion. 'Thank you. What's the address?'

'No. I shall take you.'

She doesn't want this and says so.

'Don't protest. My office is very near there.' He picks up her check, counts the money she has laid out and adds an extra note. Then he collects her backpack and takes the handle of her rolling suitcase. *'On y va.'*

There's nothing to do but follow him.

Violet finds herself in a tiny hotel lobby down a street so narrow the taxi has had to drive along the pavement. Clotaire seems to know the *patronne*, a jolly woman with a necklace of heavy keys. He negotiates a room for 200 francs a night, which he insists proudly is 'very cheap for this arrondissement'. She watches as money that's not her own changes hands. While they are waiting in the ancient foyer for the room to be prepared, she tries to pay him back. He refuses.

'I'm pleased to rescue a damsel in distress. The opportunity does not arise too often.'

He orders coffee from the *patronne*. 'If you want café with milk, you must ask for *un crème,* okay? Would you like a little *goûter*, something to eat?'

'I'm not hungry, thanks.'

'This is Paris, you have to eat.'

'Really.'

'All right, but this afternoon I'm going to take you to Ladurée for the macaroons.'

'You don't need to.'

'I insist. I am attached to *le Ministère de la Culture* and it is my task to show foreign journalists around Paris. They always love the macaroons. Do you prefer *pistache* or *vanille*?'

'Clotaire . . .' She doesn't know what to say next. She wants him to stop making assumptions that she's alone and helpless, even if that is the case. His enthusiasm, his focus on her pleasure, makes her uneasy. 'Don't you need to get to work?'

He makes a gesture of indifference. 'I have a delegation from *la Chine* this afternoon, that is all. You can accompany us to Ladurée and several monuments. I have arranged for a tour with *le Chef du département conservation-restauration* at the Louvre. It will be very fascinating.'

'Thanks, but I need to get some sleep.'

'But I'm afraid you will go to your room and cry all day.'

'I'm not going to cry.'

'There are many other men, Violet. There will be men who will want to take care of you.'

'I don't need them.'

'Maybe not. But you might grow to like the idea.'

The coffees arrive and they sip them in silence.

If she thinks he has given up on her, she's wrong. 'So, you will not come on my media tour?'

'Sorry, I'm just too tired.'

'Then we will have dinner later.'

'No! There's no need. I can look after myself.'

'Are you nervous?' he asks.

'Nervous of what?'

'Of me? I'm really a very good lover.'

She's shocked at this development. 'Clotaire, what are you talking about?'

'We don't need to rush, of course. You are tired. But we can have dinner tomorrow night and make the arrangements. I can't see you until seven because of *les Chinois*, but other days it will be different. You won't be bored, I will keep you amused.' He reaches over and puts a hand reassuringly on her knee.

She stands up quickly. 'I have to go.'

He raises an eyebrow. 'I don't think you have had a French lover before.'

'Clotaire, I'm married.'

'Is that so? To the Russian?'

'No.'

'Then I don't think you're as married as you say you are. But what does it matter?' He stands and puts his hand on her shoulders. She recoils but he does nothing more than kiss her lightly on both cheeks. 'I'll be at your door at *dix-neuf* tomorrow night. I know a little bistrot that is very romantic.'

'I'm not ready for this, Clotaire.'

He waves his hand in the air. 'Nonsense. I've never seen a young woman who is *so* ready.'

PAVILLON DE LA PAIX

Rue de la Paix, Paris, France.

Violet awakes from her nap, knowing she cannot stay. She doesn't want to be anywhere Clotaire can find her. His attentions embarrass her, she is repulsed by the idea of becoming his mistress. Besides, his presumption is astounding. As if she would make an arrangement like that after knowing him a couple of hours!

She stands in front of the bathroom mirror and studies her reflection. There is a crease down one cheek from her tussle with a twisted pillow. Her hair is matted, sleeplessness bruises the delicate skin under her eyes. *What do men see in me?* she asks herself. But she is not naïve; she knows very well. She has been capable of amping it up for Luka. What she doesn't know is how to turn it off.

Her misery is deepened when she steps into the sexy lingerie she has bought for Luka. The lace feels prickly, as if it's annoyed with her that there is no man to seduce. She dresses carelessly, pulls a knitted beanie down low over her head to hide her hair, puts her *Plan de Paris*, passport and wallet in her backpack, slings it over her silver parka and tentatively steps onto the rue Mazarine, scanning the street for any signs of Clotaire. She needs to find another hotel, as far away from here as possible.

She crosses the Pont des Arts, from the left to right banks.

The river is the colour of mercury, the afternoon sun weak behind leaden clouds that look like they've been laid on by a painter's trowel. She inhales misty droplets of air, scented with diesel oil. This is the first time she has any sense of where she is, away from claustrophobic streets and the little hotel room window that looks up at a handkerchief-size patch of sky. The Seine stretches out in one direction like a wide, straight canal and in the other it divides around the leafy point of an island. She stands in the middle of the bridge and does a 360-degree turn, then does it again, taking in the barges ploughing down the river, the tip of a distant Eiffel Tower, the stone bridges, the slate roofs with their shuttered attic windows. At last she feels that she is in a landscape rather than an emotional prison of her own making. The students with their arms full of books, the tourists taking photos of each other, the African woman laying out amber beads on a sarong – all these people exist independently of her. At last, a group of people she's not responsible for! It's a sensation just as liberating as taking off her wedding ring.

I could begin all over again, she thinks. I can put Patrick in his box and shut the lid tight. I can do the same with Luka (a pang, but she lets it go), and Clotaire. They're just false starts. I am in a place where no one knows me, where I can be anyone I want. I can be *bad* if I want to. And who would know?

Cheered a little by the thought, she sets off towards the Louvre, but veers away from it at the last moment. She avoids the tourist haunts and takes the back streets. On one corner of the rue St Honoré, she stops at a café and orders *un crème*, as Clotaire has instructed. The woman at the table beside her sits so close she blows cigarette ash into Violet's china cup.

On the Faubourg St-Honoré her heart sinks again as she takes in the windows of the famous shops. If she were honest with herself, she'd admit she imagined looking in windows of shops like these with Luka and trying on dresses for him and watching him sign for them while teams of assistants wrapped her purchases in tissue and gold ribbon. She tucks the longing for Luka away, like a handkerchief in a pocket.

But maybe she can afford a scarf? A pair of earrings? She summons up her courage and goes into a corner boutique. The sales assistants are pleasant enough when she tells them she is just looking. Now she feels like she has wandered into a cocktail party populated by store dummies, some of whom are swinging off the chandeliers, others spreadeagled on the floor as if they've had one absinthe too many. She stoops to pick up a shoe that has fallen off a dummy's foot but before her hand touches it she realises it's part of the display, that all the mannequins are choreographed in distress, like characters in a Hitchcock movie.

The sales assistant who has been subtly following her around asks if she'd like to try on the shoe. Violet pretends this is what she meant all along.

The shoe is satin with lots of straps and a heel that must be ten centimetres high. The salesgirl goes back to the storeroom twice to find the right fitting. Then there is a discussion of colour – would *mademoiselle* prefer the fuchsia, the gold, the black? There is also a dark green that may look *très coquet*. In the end, after so much attention, Violet feels obliged to buy the shoes and buy them in the colour the salesgirl suggests. She signs away enough traveller's cheques to keep her at the Hotel Quelquechose for another week. But she enjoys a little shiver of enjoyment from her extravagance.

The fix doesn't last long. It's only a few more steps down the Faubourg before she feels like an idiot. To be talked into shoes she doesn't need, like an impressionable teenager! She consults her watch. She doesn't want to go back to the hotel to collect her things until it's so late Clotaire would have given up on her. She needs to work out where she can find a cheap hotel.

But she gets distracted looking at expensive bed linen, lacy corsets and creams for maintaining the elasticity of the bust. She wanders through the windswept Palais Royal and stares in wonderment at the antique shops. In a crowded café she discovers an abandoned cigarette in a crumpled packet in her ashtray and decides to smoke it. She takes small puffs, careful not to let the smoke down into her lungs, and feels wonderfully risqué. *There, I'm being bad.*

At six o'clock she finds herself at the Place de l'Opéra. It's dark, it's rush hour and not a soul is walking in an ordered direction. She slips away from the square into the quieter Place Vendôme. She thinks it might be nice to sit in a bar and nurse a drink for an hour or so. But she regrets that she's not dressed for a place as posh as the Ritz. When she passes a pretty little hotel with a blue and gold awning, she decides to duck in there instead.

The Pavillon de la Paix looks modest from the outside but in fact it is one of the city's finest hotels, established one month after the Ritz in 1898. Inside, it looks like a courtesan's jewel box, the walls padded in pale blue silk and the ceiling cupolas painted with frolicking shepherdesses and nymphs in tender pinks, blues and peaches. Gilded branches of trees sprout from the walls, shimmering lights budding from their leaves. A chandelier the size of an open parachute sparkles with thousands of prisms of cut crystal.

Violet realises her error but before she can turn around and walk out, a grey-suited young man attaches himself to her. 'I see *mademoiselle* has been shopping today.' He sounds impressed by the heavy card shopping bag she is carrying. 'Can I be of assistance?'

'No . . . thank you, I'm just . . .'

'It's a very beautiful room, yes?'

'Very beautiful.'

'Perhaps you are tired from shopping? You would like a drink in our bar?'

The truth is, she would. 'Yes, I would like that, thank you.'

He leads her through another door to a small bar, with white and gold chairs set around low tables inlaid with mother-of -pearl in floral patterns. 'I'll call for a waiter. Would you like me to take your parcels? Your coat?'

Ashamed of the shabbiness of her backpack, Violet declines. She sits on the chair that is offered.

'Have a pleasant evening,' the young man says before disappearing. He seems to want something but she doesn't know what.

There are several people in the room, all rather old and conservative. She is relieved that no one pays much attention to her. It's not long before a waiter arrives. Bereft of ideas, she settles on champagne. '*French* champagne,' she specifies. The waiter looks at her oddly and exits.

She takes off her parka and beanie and bundles them on the chair beside her. She wishes she were dressed as well as the other people in the bar. Her sneakers, in particular, are a disgrace. She contemplates the shopping bag and the box inside.

In the ladies' room, she buckles on her new shoes, squashing her sneakers into the box. The heels are ridiculously high and perhaps a bit odd worn with jeans but at least they look expensive. She can walk on them if she takes it very slowly. She's glad she painted her toenails apricot for Luka.

Back in the bar, her champagne has arrived and it stands on the table with a little silver dish of pink macaroons. She can't imagine what the champagne has cost but she'll sit on it for an hour or so. She takes out her *Plan de Paris* and flips through it to look occupied.

Without intending to, she drinks the first glass quickly. Another one takes its place even though she hadn't ordered it. When the third one arrives, she tells the waiter she doesn't want it.

'But the gentleman says you must have what you like. I have opened a bottle specifically for you.'

'What gentleman?' she asks, stunned. She casts her eyes quickly around the room. She can see only one man sitting alone and he's at the bar, his back to her.

'If you would like him to join you I will tell him. Otherwise, he has instructed me to allow you to enjoy your drink in peace.'

'No, ask him over.' She surprises herself at her boldness. But what's there to lose? She's bored with scrutinising her guidebook. Right now, she'd be happy if the little gold Marie-Antoinette on her drink napkin had something to say.

'Eugen Mozer,' he says, holding out his hand.

She takes it. It's firm and cold from nursing a whisky. 'Violet Armengard.'

'How extraordinary. Your eyes are the colour of tanzanite, which is an exquisite purple-blue stone. Is that why you're named Violet?'

'My mother thought they were purple when I was born. But it's just the light.'

'Nevertheless, it's a most unusual colour. I'd like to see them in the daylight.'

'They're just ordinary old blue then.'

'I don't think so.' He smiles at her and releases her hand. He is not, after all, the man who is sitting at the bar – that man is still there, hunched over his drink. Wherever he was sitting, she didn't notice him. Then again, he's not very noticeable in his plain, dark suit and grey silk tie. He's average in height, tanned, not bad looking but a little fleshy, especially around the jaw. One of his eyes has a squint, which makes him appear as if he's permanently winking. He could be forty-five or fifty-five, she can't tell.

'May I sit down?'

'Yes, of course.'

He crosses his legs and exposes socks with little golden fleur-de-lis on them. He holds his glass of whisky in his left hand. On his ring finger flashes an enormous deep pink stone.

'That's a beautiful ring,' she says.

'Yes, it is.'

'Is it a ruby?'

'No, it's a diamond.'

'A *real* diamond?'

'Yes,' he says. 'A real one.'

'I didn't know they came in pink.'

'Only one tenth of one per cent of diamonds from the Argyle mine is classified as pink. They're very rare. On the current retail market, they fetch about one million dollars a carat. Yes, this is about three carats. But rest assured, I didn't buy it. It was a gift.'

'A very nice gift.'

'I deserved it.'

It's her turn to say something but her mind is churning through the ways one might deserve a three-million-dollar gift. At World Care they spoke about 'conflict diamonds' often. But how conflicted would you need to be to accept one like this? Not very, she decides.

'I noticed you changed your shoes,' he observes.

She looks at her feet, crosses her ankles modestly. 'I've been walking all day.'

'They're very elegant shoes. But, if you'll permit me.'

She looks on quizzically as he bends down and examines the sole of each shoe. When he sits upright again he has two little stickers on his palm. 'You needn't tell everyone your shoe size. Although I have taken note.'

She looks at the stickers and blushes. 'Oh dear. What an idiot.'

'Not at all. The saleswoman should have removed them. You like this designer?'

'Just about everything in the shop.'

'This label is very popular in Tel Aviv. I have two daughters who are always asking me for it.'

'That's where you're from, Tel Aviv?'

'Yes. But I spend almost all my time away from there. I have just been in Angola and in two days' time I'll be in Vienna. Then I go to Antwerp.'

'Really? What do you do?'

'I'm a diamond broker. And you?'

'Oh, nothing so exciting. I'm a strategy research analyst for World Care. You might have heard of it. We raise sponsorships for children, in Africa mostly, in countries that are poor or torn by civil war.'

'That sounds very impressive. Africa has brought us together. I work in Africa too.'

She shrugs. 'It's an office job. Basically, I'm a fund raiser.'

'Perhaps you would like a cheque from me?' He is looking at her in a peculiar way.

'The children could always do with the money,' she says carefully.

'I sense you are bored with this job? Looking for new adventures?'

'I think so.'

'You *think* so?'

'Yes, I am.'

'Good. ' His smile is mischievous. 'Do you like diamonds?'

'I suppose.'

'That's not very passionate.'

'Isn't everyone supposed to like diamonds? The girl's best friend?'

'That's just marketing. Personally, I don't care for them so much. They're overvalued. But I've made a very handsome living from overvaluing them, so I can't complain.'

'I've never met a diamond broker before. What do you do?'

'I trade mostly in rough diamonds. Those are the diamonds before they are cut. I liaise between the mines and the cutting factories. It's not that interesting. Everybody knows everybody. There are only a certain number of players.'

'Do you have any diamonds with you?'

He laughs. 'In a briefcase in my room like a jewel thief? No. Although that is one of the advantages of diamonds. One can fit a whole month's production of gem-quality diamonds in an attaché case. Not that anyone does that any more. They are required to be sent in certified containers but, like everything, there are exceptions.' He shrugs. 'Would you like something more to drink?' He waves the waiter over. 'You look like you need to unwind. How do you find the hotel?'

'Oh, I'm not staying here. I'm in a small hotel on the Left Bank.'

'That's unfortunate. The suites here are excellent. I'll show you mine, if you like. If you don't mind the mess of a few thousand diamonds strewn about, that is.'

She must look worried because he adds, 'I'm only joking about the diamonds.'

The waiter arrives and pours another champagne. This is where she should get up and say she has another appointment. She looks at her watch. It's only seven o'clock. Clotaire will be at the Quelquechose, waiting for her.

'You are meeting someone?'

'No. I'm in Paris alone.'

So there it is. Violet chooses. No matter how she looks at it later, it is a choice. And in choosing to stay she knows she will get herself in deeper with him. She'll accept the offer of a meal, which will be delicious and expensive, and they will go to a subterranean nightclub, where a private booth is waiting. She will allow him to put his arm around her shoulders and she won't protest when he instructs the limousine driver to take them directly back to his hotel. She will feel an obligation to sleep with a man she doesn't find attractive because . . . why? She is lonely? He is kind to her? He has spent so much money on her? She feels guilty for leading him on? She hasn't felt any obligation to Clotaire for the 200-franc-a-night hotel room. But Clotaire has disturbed her by wanting all of her, whereas Eugen Mozer has made it clear he requires only the smallest part.

The part she will discover she can give away.

'So, would you like to have dinner with me and maybe visit a nightclub?' he asks. 'I think there's a lot more life in the night yet.' He reaches across the low table and offers his hand.

When she puts her palm over it, the pink diamond briefly pricks her conscience.

GRAND HOTEL RIVIERA
Boulevard de la Croisette, Cannes, France

The lobby of the Riviera is as busy as a train station. But I'm happy to be here: it feels like home. Or, at least, one of my homes, the definition of which is a place where they won't turf me out onto the streets.

It seems like I was here only yesterday, as if a wind has caught the pages of my life and rifled through them, skipping chapters. Nothing ever changes in this lobby. The deep blue velvet chairs still show the imprint of warm bodies. The chandeliers still look perilous, as if they'll pull the heaven-blue ceiling down with the weight of thousands of crystals. The enormous marble pillars still look like they'd keep it up. The windows facing on to the terrace bar are still swagged with the same gold silk, yellow roses still grace the carpets, the curious little table-lamps with their red bobbles still brighten the lounge. The potted palms are still glossy and luxuriant – and I swear it is the same attendant who is lovingly polishing the leaves with oil. There are newer, younger waiters and porters but they all still wear the same green uniforms with navy epaulettes.

People come, people go. I look at them and think: we're no different from each other. Here, in the neutral space of the lobby, we're all in some kind of transition, between outside and inside, public and private, exposed and secluded, guest and interloper, servant and master. Between one arrangement and the next.

Hervé, the concierge, knows me from better times. 'Hervé,' I whisper discreetly, slipping him a few of the notes Ettore's driver has folded into my passport. 'I am waiting for an associate. Do you think it might be possible for me to freshen up and for my luggage to be stored?' To my relief, Hervé greets me like a long-lost friend. 'Of course, *ma petite,*' he says smoothly, taking both my hands in his. *Il est trés charmant à vous recontrer.'*

Hervé organises my luggage and arranges for a porter to show me to a lounge chair and a waiter to bring me a glass of champagne. I feel safe here, composed, and after three or four glasses of Deutz, unperturbed by the prospect of running into any of the smirking ghosts from my past. In any case, they're probably all dead, bankrupt or reduced to a vegetative state from the over-ingestion of illegal substances. I do see a couple of film people I have met in passing but they stare right past me as if I'm part of the furniture. Good. They are not surprised to see me here, which means I haven't been away too long.

After a while, a waiter suggests I move to the terrace bar where most of Cannes is meeting for pre-screening drinks. I catch Hervé's eye and he nods. He is looking after me, buying me more lobby time, a roof over my head, a place to sit and wait for the next man, the next experience, the next life. Perhaps he is being kind to me. Perhaps he is anticipating another a roll of notes. I don't care to dissect his motives too closely. He is the closest thing to a friend I have.

I do not have to wait long.

I assume a pose at the end of the bed, my legs apart, hands on hips. The Helmut Newton, I call it. I'd met the wily old photographer at the Chateau Marmont in Los Angeles. He'd asked me to pose for him but I'd refused, thinking he was a pervert. When his identity was pointed out to me, I combed bookstores for his photos and made a study of him. The images have come in very handy. The swimsuit with one breast exposed. The cigarette cupped in a palm like a man. The skimpy bra and tight skirt, cross-legged on the bed. They work for most men and they work for me.

Sayyid is no different. He lies on the bed cockily, his arms stretched out, embracing the pillows as if they were plump, acquiescent hookers. He makes appreciative noises. He is expecting a show.

I am surprised at what I expect from him. He is not my type at all. Too young, too beautiful and his financial reliability is in question, although he says he is the son of an Omani government minister, related somewhere along a very convoluted family tree to the Sultan. But he is handsome and exotic and even I am weak sometimes.

I feel the stir again, so long repressed in me. I am afraid of it. And I get pleasure from my fear.

He reaches down and unzips his fly. When he flops his prick out it is soft and serpentine, meandering like a dusky road. He smiles benevolently and strokes it like a favoured pet.

My heart is already pounding through the liquid silver of my gown. I am a bunch of tangled nerve-ends on high heels and not too steady on them at that. It isn't sex I am after, but the long swoon that sometimes goes with it. You have to remember I have only been with old men and ugly men for years and, while one or two of them were rather frisky, I am starved, *starved,* for the sensation of smooth skin against my belly and muscles that are hard under my hands and breath on my body that is warm with sweet pheromones, not foul with medicine and decay. I am so starved for it that I choose to ignore the one truth I have learned the most painful way.

In this life, there are many dangers, but none as dangerous as a handsome young man.

I hoist my gown over my head. Sayyid's brown eyes are focused between my legs like a drunk trying to concentrate on walking a chalk-drawn line. As I crawl on to the bed and over him he lifts his hand from his groin and pushes it under my bra. When his arm falls limply to the bed again, I can tell that he isn't quite as focused on me as I'd thought.

The suite is testament to the good time we have had. Chemicals of various kinds have been ingested indiscreetly, washed down by gobs of Crystal. Sayyid's partying cousins have come and gone, tagging the room with the stench of cigars and a patchwork of bottles on the floor. The top of the television set is covered in drifts of powder and there's a wet patch on a chair where Sayyid shook a champagne bottle so hard it erupted over my face.

It may be the only thing that erupts tonight.

I hold his cock in my hand, warm, tender, unresponsive, and ponder it regretfully. Regret for all the young men who are lost to me, the waiters and ski instructors and music teachers and mechanics. I had only wanted to spoil myself a little, just a little, and I have been denied even that.

I should have known what would happen next.

Nothing.

No matter what I do: nothing.

Suddenly he pulls away from me. He says something in Arabic, which sounds like a curse.

I understand he is humiliated. I say the usual soothing things women always say, suggest we could lie together and explore each other more when we awoke.

'No,' he says coldly, turning away from my kiss. 'You are too old.'

I mishear. 'Then let's get a blanket.'

His look is contemptuous. 'I have changed my mind. I never go with women your age.'

I am shocked. 'What, you like schoolgirls?' I spit back.

'Your bosoms show the effect of gravity. They are not firm.'

'I could say the same for your penis.'

'He is simply not aroused by you.'

'Maybe it's something to do with the drugs.'

'Sayyid can fuck through a storm of drugs.' He zips up his fly with a jerk that makes me wince, gets up and staggers around the room until he finds his jacket. He pulls out a wad of euros and waves them at me drunkenly. 'There. Go.'

'No.'

'Take the money. It's yours.'

'I'm not a whore.'

'You want more?'

'No. I don't want any of it.'

'Two thousand? Three thousand? It makes no difference to me. I have more.'

'I'm sure you do.' I move away from him to the sofa, where I'd left my bag.

He follows me, unsteadily. 'I said for you to take the money.'

'And I said I'm leaving.'

He lunges at me and grasped my arm, thrusting the wad of euros into my left hand and closing my palm over it. I yank away and the notes shuffle to the floor. We both look at the money. He doesn't care about it and I could use it. But I don't take money for sex. Travelling money and shopping money and powder room money, yes. But not cash for sex. It would make me something else.

I pick up my bag. He glowers at me. Somehow my refusal of the money is even more offensive than my failure to arouse him. 'You think there is something wrong with it? It's dirty money?'

'I told you, I can't be bought.'

'You are not going until I have paid what I owe. I always pay. It is a point of honour.

'Pick up the money.'

'I won't.'

We look at each other. He is very unstable. His burst of agitation has exhausted him. He turns his back, fumbles in his trouser pocket and shells out several tiny glassine envelopes. While he is busy self-administering, I pick my way through the bottles and walk slowly to the door.

In the elevator, I can't avoid myself. The three walls are mirrored and the brass doors are polished to such a shine that I am captured in every facet.

The face of a woman who turned her back on two thousand euros.

My lipstick needs attention. My hair is mussed. My eyes are puffy. But the truth is that most men find a little debasement a very big thrill. I examine myself critically and decide I am holding up. Even after a few hours of partying, the worst you could say about me is that I look a little strained. The things that I am prized for are still in place. The auburn hair, the lily-white skin, the lapis lazuli eyes, the hourglass shape.

Sayyid says I am too old for him. I am – I grit my teeth to even think it – on the downhill slope to forty. I could be his mother. A teenage mother, certainly, but *still* . . . I try not to think of these things but the thought escapes and crawls over me like a bad rash.

Luckily, the elevator ride from third floor to lobby is rapid and my introspection is cut short.

The doors open and a breeze shuffles the pages of my life backwards a few chapters.

HOTEL PRINZ EUGEN

Kärntner Ring, Vienna, Austria

Violet can't sleep. She hasn't slept well since they arrived in Vienna, three days ago.

She lies curled in a fetal position on one side of the king-size bed, as close to the edge of the bed as she can manage. It's not that she is repulsed by Eugen. He is good company, he is fastidiously clean, his demands on her are not excessive. Even on that first night, at his Paris hotel, when the sex was listless, he politely asked her forgiveness for drinking too much wine, when in fact it was she who was nervous and unresponsive. And he's thoughtful. He brings her gifts, chosen with some care. This afternoon he returned after the Bourse with a gift of boots. Gucci, her exact fitting. Yesterday it was a new coat. Armani, pale blue cashmere. The day before, a quilted bag from Christian Dior. In Paris, it was a crystal flask of perfume, the fragrance of violets crushed in grass. 'Believe me, this gives me more pleasure than it does you,' he tells her. But she knows that's not true.

She lies with her eyes open, unsettled, scanning the dark. A light from the hallway casts a faint light across the parquetry flooring and illuminates the painted legs of chairs, the garlanded roses edging a carpet, the tapestry cushions she has thrown off the bed. She is cocooned in the luxury of white linen sheets, puffy eiderdowns, monogrammed pillowcases, the scent of a single gardenia candle flickering away on the nightstand. She likes the feeling of cool sheets on her skin and plush oriental carpet under her bare feet. She likes it when the room-service trolley comes rattling in, laden with bone-china cups, heavy silver cutlery and tiers of torte and strudel. She likes the way the maids fold her clothing and pick up towels. She likes the way her bath is drawn and a glass of champagne is left beside it. She likes the heavy embossed writing paper in the secretaire and the button on the phone that summons a porter to post the cryptic note she has written to her mother. She likes the peacocks on the curtains and the gold-framed prints of various Habsburgs on the walls. She likes the sitting room, with its antique sofas and huge urns of roses and the television hidden in an oak cupboard, which shows movies at the flick of a switch. And she likes the way her underwear is returned from the cleaner like gifts in cardboard boxes lined with tissue.

Yes, she likes all this, all right. She likes it more than she likes Eugen. Despite the intimacy of lying in bed with him, she cannot make herself like him enough to calm her conscience. She doesn't find him sexy. He is very correct, fastidious. He hangs up his clothing before he gets into bed at night. He carefully wraps the used condom in a napkin when they are finished. He mops his brow with a linen handkerchief and then folds it three times before placing it back in his pocket. He is precise about change and consults his watch frequently. He opens doors for her and lights her cigarettes. (She has taken up smoking, now that she's a scarlet woman.) But he is charming in a way that seems rehearsed, as if there is a rulebook for charm and he is following it to the letter. Even the way the gifts are tailored to her taste suggests he is a man sophisticated in the arts of keeping a mistress. And there is vanity in him – he struts around the hotel room like a little prince with a soft, plump body. Prinz Eugen, he points out. He stays in this hotel because of the name.

Violet turns onto her back, careful not to disturb Eugen's

sleep. Luckily he's a heavy sleeper. If he has a fault she can see, it's that he drinks too much red wine. Never enough to be drunk but enough to make sex unlikely after dinner. He prefers it before they go out, for obvious reasons. So far, the ritual has been the same. The unwrapping of the gift. A glass of champagne. The unhitching of her bra. Eugen is precise, making certain he gives her the same number of minutes she gives him. His skin smells fragrant, like lavender water, and his hands are soft. It's not so bad.

Two days in Paris, three in Vienna. Five days in the bed of a man she's doesn't find arousing. And yet, somehow, it doesn't seem to matter as much as she thought. It's no different than those short-lived liaisons she had at university. You couldn't call them affairs. Stand-offs, more like it. And what did she get out of them? Bruises on her neck. Rashes inside her thighs. Thrush. Pneumonia, once, from sneaking out of a ski lodge in the middle of the night half-naked. Not love and rarely even affection. Just the unsettling knowledge that if any one of them had asked her to do it again, she would have. Why? Because it would have been rude to refuse. Because she knew men were fragile about their sexual performance. Because she didn't want to hurt anyone's feelings, even if she suspected there were no feelings there.

In all those afterminutes of all those sexual encounters she would find herself wanting. *I should have shown more enthusiasm. I should have shown less enthusiasm.* You should have shown them the door, says sensible Violet, making her regular nocturnal appearance. Because you are sexually attracted to men who are pricks and who would sacrifice you on the altar of their own egos. And you keep trying to make yourself right when it is they who are wrong. Here lies a nice, rather inscrutable man who has been generous with you and is not unpleasant in bed and you question the morality of being with him. But you wouldn't question the morality of being in bed with bastards like Patrick or Luka.

It's not like that.

With Patrick or Luka you put too much value on sexual attraction. And look where that gets you, dear. A headlong rush into disaster. What else do you get out of great sex but misery?

It's not like that.

Her mind is a locust plague of teeming thoughts. If she could find Eugen sexy she would sleep peacefully. She has often wondered about call girls, how they do it, how they feign amorousness on an hourly or nightly basis. Did the prostitutes who went with Patrick think themselves lucky they were with such an attractive man? Or did it not matter to them? Was it only about the money? She supposes the prospect of money, lots of it, might be arousing in itself. There are those stories of rich Arabs picking up female tourists in airports and paying them tens of thousands of dollars for the night. How much money would you need to make sex with a fat, ugly Saudi prince okay? Twenty thousand dollars? Fifty? A million? And if one million dollars is enough, then that means there is a price on what she's doing . . . and she has given herself to Eugen for much less – a bag, a coat and a nice pair of boots, which she could so easily hand back.

Maybe she should give them back.

She slips a leg out of the covers and carefully sits up, sliding her feet on to the carpet. Eugen doesn't stir. She creeps into the bathroom and closes the door. Then she turns on the light. She reaches for a bathrobe to cover up her body, which looks sick, her white skin absorbing the jaundiced colours of the caramel marble, the golden fittings. She sits on the toilet and then washes her hands. She runs a comb through her hair and wipes the remains of mascara from under her eyes. She's wide awake. Wired. Now what is she going to do?

The digital clock in the bathroom reads 12:16. It's Friday night. There are people in Vienna still dining at this hour, coffee houses packed, bars jumping. She's already sick of dining at stuffy restaurants, being tucked up in bed by midnight. Whenever they have strolled past bars and clubs oozing with people her age Eugen takes her arm as if to protect her. As if they were contaminants! Despair rises in her. She feels like she has said goodbye to her youth in the single act of taking an older lover. A *married* older lover, with two daughters.

He doesn't speak about the wife, except in the most oblique of terms – 'we' have a holiday apartment on the Dead Sea; 'we' resisted pressure to have a son; 'our' favourite restaurant in Paris is L'Arpège. He doesn't pretend the marriage is unhappy. There's no talk of marital disharmony. It suggests the wife is tolerant of his affairs, that they have an arrangement. (He's too smooth with her for Violet to be the first.) She accepts that scenario. It makes her presence in his bed easier. She doesn't want to break another woman's heart.

But she'll never sleep, now that she's thought about the wife.

She was a wife once.

She sneaks into the adjoining dressing room where the maids have hung up her few clothes. She pulls on her black dress, the new boots, her new coat, leather gloves. She retrieves her new bag from the table in the hall and closes the door quietly behind her.

The lobby of the hotel is surprisingly busy, couples in evening dress – most of them twice her age – filtering back from a night at the opera. The pianist at the bar is hammering away at the keyboard, the notes crashing off the amber marble walls like someone throwing china in a fit of temper. No one seems to object to the racket. In fact, the contrary – a man in a dinner jacket gets up from his table and leaves a large tip.

The doorman clicks his heels as she exits, his face showing no hint of surprise that she chooses to go out into the cold air at this hour. A porter gestures for a taxi but she shakes her head.

She heads for the Kärtnerstrasse, the pedestrian shopping street that leads to the Stephansplatz cathedral, near Fabio's restaurant where Eugen has taken her for dinner. The old part of the city is circular, confusing, narrow streets with no visible landmarks, but she knows she won't get lost here. (And if she does get lost, so what? She won't be any worse off than she'll be when Eugen leaves for Antwerp tomorrow.) The promenade is washed in the pale artificial light of the shops but even though the night is frosty, people linger in front of the windows, gather in ragged groups around buskers or line up at kiosks for fat, greasy hotdogs and mustard. There's more traffic than she expected at this hour and, even though everything is unfamiliar, she feels easy with the city, as if the streetscape were a comfortable coat wrapped around her. Yet she walks along the pedestrian street aware there are shadows in doorways and they are watching her. She catches the occasional flare of a cigarette in the dark and the unmistakable shapes of people sleeping rough.

She's not sure where she is going – she just wants to feel she's part of something, a world with people in it, and not hermetically sealed in a hotel room. She pulls up the collar of her coat and wishes she had brought a hat. After a few blocks, she begins to realise a small boy has been following her. He looks about six, scrawny, thinly dressed, his head shorn and crusty with scabs. He trots beside her with his little hand out. His eyes never leave her face, imploring. *Bitte, bitte.* She holds her handbag tight under her arm. But she feels mean. He's only a child. *Bitte, Fräulein.* She stops and unzips her bag. As she does so the child looks back over his shoulder, his eyes connecting with a figure in a doorway. Suddenly she is surrounded by children, tugging at her sleeve, pulling the hem of her coat, stationing themselves in front of her, grubby palms extended. She clasps her bag tightly and tries to move away but they move with her like flies swarming on cake. An elderly couple passing by looks at her anxiously and the woman shakes her head in warning. *Be careful.* But Violet can't disentangle herself from the children without pushing or shoving them. She stands there helplessly. 'Please go away,' she says weakly.

Behind her a male voice speaks sharply in words she can't understand. The children scatter. She feels a firm hand on her elbow. She pulls away but the grasp is strong as a vice.

'Forgive me, I didn't mean to hurt you.' He releases her arm. Her rescuer is a young man, enveloped in a long dark coat with a muffler covering his chin. 'But I wanted to get you away from those gypsies. They're little animals, not children.'

Something in his haughty tone annoys her. 'They're not animals, they're human beings,' she says, rubbing her elbow.

'Believe me, they are not,' he smiles. 'I know.'

'What makes you so judgemental?'

'Because I am a gypsy too.'

He plunges both hands deeply into the pockets of his expensive-looking coat and shrugs his shoulders to keep warm. The scarf wrapped around his neck is soft and pale blue. He has tanned skin, strands of tawny hair falling across his eyes and remarkably shiny teeth. As he talks, his breath crystallises in front of him and dissipates like diamond dust.

'You don't look like a gypsy,' she says.

'I don't?' He smiles at her and takes a gloved hand out of his pocket. In it is a tortoiseshell cigarette case. He clicks it open with the one hand and offers her one of the short, rough cigarettes inside. 'They're Romanian. Stronger than Gauloises and unfiltered, I'm afraid. But if you're game?'

'No, thank you.'

'Why don't I look like a gypsy?' he asks, taking a cigarette with his teeth. He puts the case back in his pocket and pulls out a gold lighter. 'Because I don't have a horse cart with me?'

He's teasing her. This makes her wary. 'Look,' she says, 'thanks for helping me but—'

'But you are running late for something. Or someone.' He gives her a wry look. *I dare you to make up a satisfactory excuse.*

'I'm on my way back to my hotel.'

'So am I. Perhaps we are staying at the same one?' He lights the cigarette.

She hesitates but not telling him feels churlish. 'The Prinz Eugen.'

'Ah! Very nice. I've stayed there once or twice. I prefer the Palais Schwarzenberg these days.' A curl of cigarette smoke undulates between them like a provocatively crooked finger. 'The Prinz Eugen is in the opposite direction, by the way. Permit me to walk you back.'

'No thank you,' she says again.

'Is it because I'm a stranger or a gypsy?' He takes her hand and kisses it. 'If it's the first, allow me to introduce myself. Florin Esterházy de Bathory. If it's the second, I'm afraid I can't do anything about it.'

He's appeared from nowhere, ridiculously good-looking, well-heeled and smart-mouthed, at least one hyphenation too many. A very good reason to mistrust him.

'Violet Armengard,' she offers reluctantly.

'Pleased to make your acquaintance. But you don't look so pleased to make mine. I suppose a dozen men like me have asked to buy you a drink tonight. But I don't mind being the thirteenth. Have you been to the Loos American Bar? They make a very good dirty martini. It's just around the corner.'

'Thanks . . . I'd rather not.'

He takes both hands out of his pockets. She looks at the tan leather gloves, which have heavy gold chains across the wrists. 'I'm not carrying a gun. I assure you I don't need to rob you.'

'I feel like being alone.'

'You can be alone with me. I can talk or not talk, as you wish. I'm happy just to look at you.'

'Really. Thanks anyway.'

His confidence deflates. 'Oh. I now I see. You're very much in love with whoever is waiting at your hotel.'

'I'm not in love with anyone.'

He puts a hand on her arm, gently. 'Then there's no harm in a drink. If you're not in love with him he can wait a little longer.'

He's an intriguing man offering her some company. She doesn't have to go to bed with him, for God's sake. 'All right,' she says, decided. 'You better show me what a dirty martini is.'

It's gin and olive juice with a green olive on a toothpick. 'Nurok,' he says, raising his glass. 'To new friends.' He watches her take a sip. 'How is it?'

'Strong.'

'Good.'

They've hung up their coats. She is glad she put on her good dress. He is wearing a creamy cashmere sweater. She feels its softness next to her skin as they squeeze together on a tiny leather banquette. The bar is miniscule, caravan-size, with three or four banquette tables and a long bar occupied with drinkers sitting on high stools, their backs to them.

'It's like being in this cigarette case, no?' he observes, offering her another cigarette. She notices he only uses the one hand. 'I admire the tortoiseshell marble and the mahogany panelling. It's very fine. The bar was built in 1902 and restored only recently. That's a portrait of the architect, Adolph Loos, hanging over your head.'

She accepts a cigarette this time. 'He looks a bit stern.'

'The Viennese are all this way. Haven't you noticed?'

'Not really.'

'They don't know how to make small talk.'

'Unlike you.'

He smiles at her and lights her cigarette. 'Very good. The martini is doing its work.' His left hand lies on the table, unmoving. He watches her observe it.'You're wondering about my hand.'

'Have you hurt it?'

'A riding accident when I was five. I fell off my pony and it crushed the wrist. They mended the bones but the nerve endings couldn't be fixed.'

'How awful.'

'I give it therapy so that the muscles don't atrophy. See?' He uses his right hand to move the fingers of his left back and forth. 'You only need one hand anyway.' His smile is mischievous.

'Are you really a gypsy?'

'I'm one-quarter Roma, one-quarter Hungarian, one-quarter Italian, one-quarter Turkish, one-quarter Transylvanian.'

'That's five quarters.'

'So it is. I'm complicated.'

'What quarter is gypsy?'

'My mother's mother was a Romany queen. So I really am one. But this is boring. Where are you from? When did you get here? *How* did you get here? Did you have a pony as a little girl? A rabbit? I want to know everything.'

'I'm from Melbourne. Australia.'

'Ah! That's the one place I haven't been.'

'Only the one?'

'Well, I haven't been to New Zealand, either. Or Panama. There are more.'

'What do you do for a living?' she asks.

'Oh, I have a few fingers in a few pies. What about you?'

There is no way to make what she does sound interesting. 'Strategy analysis.'

He misunderstands her. 'Ah, a growing field this weapons business. Then you are related to the Armengards in Berne?'

'No. At least I don't think so.'

'It's your husband's name?'

'Yes. But I'm divorced.' It's no longer a lie – she feels divorced from Patrick in every way.

'Recently?'

'Yes.'

'And you're doing the grand tour of Europe, now that you're a free woman?'

'I suppose you could say that. I'm just following my nose.'

'And a perfect nose it is too.'

'Please!'

'You don't like being complimented?'

'I like it. But I'm not fishing.'

'I didn't think you were. You don't need to.' He looks at her glass. 'Drink up.'

'If you give me my hand back.'

He laughs and releases it but not before turning the palm up and pondering it for a while. 'I can see from your palm you're unencumbered. Excellent.'

'Why is it excellent?'

'Because you don't have a schedule. The doors of life have all opened for you.'

'I suppose so.' Until the money runs out next week, she thinks.

'Money doesn't matter to me,' he says, as if reading her mind. 'Life is about experience, isn't it?'

'Yes?'

'It helps to have money, of course. I, for instance, have developed an addiction to hotel bed linen. I can't sleep between anything else but hotel sheets. Porthault, preferably.'

'Don't you have a home?'

'No. I live in hotels.'

'By choice?'

'Of course! We have a family castle near Ecsed in northern Hungary. But a cousin I dislike is in residence. The rest of my family is scattered, mostly in Romania, Hungary, Germany. I was brought up in Bṛasov. In the Carpathian mountains.'

'Your English is perfect.'

'Thank you. But it's really not my doing. I was sent – kicking and screaming – to boarding school in England. How is another story. I speak eight languages and a few more dialects pretty well. Nine, if you count Romany.'

'I'm envious.'

'But you're from the new world. I'm envious of that.'

'Why?'

'Because you're free. There aren't any preconceptions.' He

rubs the butt of his cigarette into the ashtray and immediately searches for another. 'You don't hate the Hungarians, do you?'

'No?'

'You see? And you don't hate the Turks? And I can see from the way you defended that little street rat you have no reason to hate the gypsies. If you lived here in Europe, you'd be carrying the dead weight of history around with you. The Hungarians hate the Romanians and the Turks and the Austrians, and the Romanians say there are no good neighbours but the Black Sea, and everyone hates the Roma – can you imagine what it is like to be me, with all my quarters hating each other? I'm genetically predisposed to hate everyone in this bar. Except for you.'

'In that case I think you need another drink.'

He laughs and orders more martinis. As he jokes with the waiter who brings them, Violet has a chance to observe him closely. It's difficult to attach an age to him but she suspects he's close to hers. His hair is brown but it has gilded streaks, as if he's spent the winter in the sun. His eyes, she has decided, are the colour of walnuts, under dark eyebrows that slope downwards, giving him an earnest countenance. It's an imperfect beauty. His nose is excessively strong and he has a small gap between his front teeth. One of these teeth is slightly chipped. He opens his mouth and she can see that all his teeth, from the eye tooth backwards, top and bottom, are gold. When he talks, the hand that holds the cigarette loops and dives as if he were conducting himself. His fingernails, she has already noted when he took her hand, are translucent as pearls. This is a man who does not do manual labour.

He turns back to her when the waiter has gone. 'It's surprising, but he's from Romania as well. We're all mongrels around here.' He suddenly looks serious and takes her hand again. 'You know, you have the most beautiful hair and eyes. And I like the way you're not wearing any make-up. You should never wear lipstick. Your lips are a natural rose. It would be a pity to cover that up.'

Patrick used to tell her what lipstick to wear. Suddenly she feels queasy. He leans slightly towards her and she thinks for a moment he is going to kiss her. She flinches.

He smiles at her reaction. 'Tell me, why were you roaming the streets of Vienna alone tonight?'

'I couldn't sleep.'

'And you are with someone?'

'Yes.'

'He's waiting for you?'

'He doesn't know I'm gone.'

'Is this your travelling companion?'

'No, just an acquaintance.'

'So you often go to bed with acquaintances?'

'I didn't say I went to bed with him.'

'There's no need to be offended. Everyone is a stranger before they know each other in that way.' He looks at her palm again. 'I can see that this man is not going to last long.'

'Where can you see?'

He traces the line for her. The nerve endings on her palm jump at his touch. 'You see your heart line. It's long and chained. Many, many islands mean many, many men. This big island here? You see?' He holds her hand closer to the table light.

'I think so.'

'That big island is me.'

She feels as if someone has injected her with hot ink. His ardour is making her claustrophobic. She has heard the expression that a man 'presses his suit' on a woman when he wishes to make love to her. *Pressing* is what she is feeling. Weight. She can hardly bear it. She only wanted a bit of harmless flirting. (But when was flirting ever harmless?) She changes the subject. 'How old are you?' She has been wondering this but now she's embarrassed that she's put it into words.

'That's very direct. I wouldn't ask it of you.'

'I don't mind if you do. I'm thirty.'

'Then so am I.' She's not sure whether he's joking or not. He could be thirty. 'Am I too young for you? Do you like older men? You think I'm frivolous.' He looks at her in mock despondency. 'Someone has broken your heart?'

She pretends she hasn't heard the question. 'How long are you staying in Vienna?'

'I don't know. How long are *you* staying in Vienna?'

'I'm not sure.' She doesn't know why she doesn't tell him she's leaving the next day.

'And where are you going after this?'

'Back to Paris.'

'And then?'

'I don't know. What about you?'

'I have a few invitations. I'm thinking of going to Como but it's cold. I'd like some sun. There's a hotel in Tenerife I'm rather fond of but it's the wrong season. There's always Barbados, I suppose. But I'm thinking of somewhere more exotic. Madagascar? Have you been there?'

She shakes her head.

'I know a hotel in the jungle where you sleep under lemur-skin canopies.'

'That sounds revolting.'

'But the sheets are Porthault.'

She doesn't know whether he's teasing her or not.

'We could go to the Palazzo Vendramin in Venezia if you don't mind the damp. Or the Capidoche in Central Turkey. It's carved out of rock. But there are earthquakes to be considered. What about the Chèvre d'Or in Eze? No, it's too bleak this time of the year. We'll have to wait until May. The Casa di Carmona in Seville? Too quiet—'

'They sound wonderful but I'm going back to Paris.'

'Well, where will you stay there?'

'The Pavilion de la Paix,' she lies.

'Perfect! I adore that hotel. We can stay a few nights there and then I will take you down to Périgord where-' He breaks off. 'I am doing it again.' He says nothing for a while. They sip their drinks. A woman armed with dozens of roses makes her way from table to table. 'Would you like some?' he asks her.

'It's all right.' She shakes her head.

'No, it's not. You must have roses.' He negotiates with the woman in German. The bunch he hands her is extravagant, two dozen pale roses, their buds like the faces of tiny birds.

When she puts her nose in them, they have no fragrance. 'I'll need a truck to take these back to my hotel,' she says.

'You have me.' When she says nothing, he adds, 'This acquaintance, can you get rid of him tonight?'

She shakes her head.

'Tomorrow?'

'Maybe.'

She thinks *maybe* is dissembling: he sees it as an invitation. 'Well, it's better, then,' he says, frowning. 'It's better if we wait a little. We can think of each other all night.' He puts his cigarette case in his pocket and gestures to the waiter. 'Finish your drink. I'll walk you back to your hotel.'

He stands abruptly, all business now. The waiter brings the check and he dexterously pulls a few notes out of a gold money clip shaped into a filigree 'F'. They walk into the street. They say very little until they reach her hotel. She didn't want him to seduce her. It would have been ridiculous, two men in one night. But now she feels hurt. She was expecting him to try harder to take her to bed. And even though she didn't want to be seduced, she would have accepted him. That's how it works with Violet, the advantage of beauty. She doesn't need to pursue but she will follow. When someone else decides, whatever happens subsequently cannot be her fault.

Outside her hotel, he asks, 'When can I call on you tomorrow?' He's formal, casting a glance at the doorman and porter who are standing sentinel.

'I don't know,' she says.

'You haven't got cold feet?' He looks wistful. And then he smiles. 'You can't possibly have cold feet in those sexy boots.'

'Two o'clock?'

'Excellent. We can find somewhere to eat cakes and have other adventures.' He clicks his feet and kisses her hand. 'Until then.'

'Until then,' she replies, conflicted. She is due to be on a plane to Paris by then.

He places the roses in her arms. And then, as if he has had a sudden change of heart, he pulls her firmly against him and kisses her hard upon the lips. She feels as if a wild bird is trapped and fluttering in her gut. Her common sense flies off with the rest of the flock. To hell with the doorman, Eugen, Vienna, everything. There is no moral dilemma to a kiss like this. It's all instinct, a flood of warm sensation filling the emptiness inside her to the high-water mark, threatening to brim over.

As the roses crush against her breast the petals finally emit a fragrance, of bruised grass.

Eventually he withdraws his mouth from hers. It feels as if she has been plucked from a respirator. He runs a gloved finger over her eyebrow and looks at her tenderly. 'Tomorrow. I think we might skip the cakes,' he whispers.

Eugen orders a large breakfast and reads the International Herald Tribune while he's eating. Violet lies next to him, a down bolster over her head, pretending to be asleep. There's only a few more hours until he catches his plane for Antwerp and she goes to Paris and she wants to spend as little as possible of them with him. He appears repulsive to her now in the light of last night's gypsy kiss.

She sneaks a look at Eugen wiping the egg off his lips and draws the bolster over her face again. If she could find an excuse to get him to go to the airport without her, she could skip her flight and keep her rendezvous with Florin. It seems wicked to be moving from one man's bed to another's. She is not sure she has the courage for it. Florin might be an illusion: not a physical illusion, to be sure – she can still feel his arms around her – but an emotional illusion, someone she has conjured up to fill the void when Eugen leaves. But it's too early in the morning for her to wonder why she feels an emptiness whenever she is without a man, even a passionless one like Eugen.

She hears the tray rattle and feels Eugen get out of the bed. He's in the bathroom for a while. She hopes he's getting dressed. She dozes and is awoken by his weight on the edge of the bed. She feels him considering her. He puts a hand on her shoulder and takes the bolster away. 'Violet.'

She opens an eye. The diamond-crusted Star of David nestled in his chest hairs winks at her.

'I have something for you.'

She sits up slowly, feigning extreme tiredness. She doesn't want anything. She makes a muffled attempt at saying so.

He chuckles. 'I like this about you. You're not greedy.' (An Armani coat, Gucci boots, Lady Dior bag, perfume, first-class airfares, room service, expensive wines – she feels greedy enough. She wonders what other women ask of him.) 'Well,' he continues, 'you are greedy for *some* things. But more of that later.'

She clutches the sheet over her breasts. 'More of that later' is not what she wants.

He puts an oblong velvet box on her lap. She looks at it unhappily.

'Go on, open it.'

It's a bracelet. Mauve slivers of rock strung with tiny pearls. Ugly.

'I asked a jeweller to find you some tanzanite. Luckily he has excellent resources.' He takes her wrist and fastens the clasp around it. 'Do you like it?'

'It's beautiful. But you shouldn't.'

'It's simply a memento. You must accept it.'

'Thank you, then.'

He pats her on the knee. 'I'm sorry I can't take you to Antwerp but I will be working day and night. You would be bored.'

'I understand. You've been kind to show me Vienna.'

He raises the hand and waves it. 'No, not at all. But I would like to see you again. Sadly, I'm not going to be in Paris for a few weeks. But I will be in London next month. Perhaps you can come to London?'

'I'm not sure. I don't know where I'll be.'

'It makes no difference. I'm going to leave you a card with a number on it. You call it when you get to Paris and leave your details. My secretary will make the arrangements.'

'That will be lovely,' she lies. He makes her feel more like a line in an appointment book than a woman. She needs to get away from him. She yawns and makes a move to slip out of the other side of the bed.

He reaches over and puts a heavy hand on her thigh. 'Where are you going?'

'To have a shower. We should pack.'

'We have two hours.' Then he does what she's dreading and pulls aside his bathrobe roughly to reveal a Napoleon-sized erection, squat and cannon-shaped. 'I want to say goodbye properly.'

She can't disguise her dismay. 'I'm sorry, I'm feeling a bit unwell.'

'You are?'

'It must have been . . .'

'The fish? The dessert? The wine?' His expression is black. 'I did not think you had such a delicate constitution, Violet.'

'Please let me go to the bathroom...'

When he places his hand back on her thigh it is like a claw this time. 'Perhaps you are not so different after all. I should have given you the bracelet *afterwards.*'

Violet can't move her neck. She feels like she has the weight of an anvil on her head but it's only a pillow. Her eyes won't open. Inside her brain there's a buzzing like the broadcast space between radio stations. She drifts in and out of a grinding sleep, as if she's gone to bed under a printing press. Her mouth feels like she's eaten the whole pillow – goose down, duck feathers and four hundred percent Egyptian cotton coverlet and all. Her arm is trapped under her ribs but her body keeps bearing down on it, unable to move.

There is knocking on the door . . . hammering. *Go away.* She sleeps. A staccato buzzing noise. Her ears? The phone? She is sinking under the weight of tons of folded cardboard, like a homeless person in a Viennese doorway . . .

In her dreams a swarm of gypsies surround her, peeling back the cardboard piece by piece. She tries to cover herself. They're poking at her with sticks. A little boy picks up a chunk of violet-blue rock and aims. The blow strikes her arm.

'Violet?' She is being shaken. She crawls further under the covers. The pillow comes off her head. The light stings her eyeballs through the lids. 'Violet, are you all right?'

She hears herself grunt and manages to unstick her eyes. She's able, after all, to turn slightly to see who's there. The room is bright, light streaming through the open curtains. The gypsy is kneeling on the bed, hand on her shoulders, peering at her intently. She focuses on a woman in a maid's uniform, who is hovering behind him.

'Can you speak?' he asks.

'You,' she croaks, remembering. 'What are you doing here?' She's more confused than frightened.

Florin says something to the maid in German. He palms her a folded note. *'Danke.'* The maid leaves the bedside. The door closes softly behind her. 'Are you sick?' he asks. 'Can you sit up?'

She tries to drag her body upright, grasping the sheets so as not to reveal her nakedness, which seems suddenly shameful. 'Not really.'

He finds two pillows and puts them behind her back. 'Let me help you.'

'I think my arm's gone to sleep.'

He helps her sit up against the pillows, taking care she is covered, and examines her arm. 'It's bruised.' He runs a finger lightly from the shoulder to the soft underarm, just grazing her breast. Despite what has happened with Eugen she feels a tug of pleasure at her core – and also an invasion. She pulls away from Florin. 'What happened?' he asks.

She looks at her arm and shuts her eyes. She's humiliated that he's seeing her like this. 'Nothing,' she lies. 'I slept in, that's all. What time is it?'

'About three o'clock.'

'Oh, God. My flight to Paris!'

'Don't worry about that. You can always get another. Wait a moment while I get you some water.' He bounds off the bed, returns with a champagne glass of sparkling water and helps her to drink it.

'I'm okay, really,' she protests.

He takes the glass away from her lips. 'The front desk said the gentleman left three hours ago. He asked them to give you a wakeup call. But you didn't answer.' He looks uncomfortable sitting on the bed in his heavy coat. He has shadows under his eyes and there are pinched little lines between his eyebrows. He, too, hasn't slept much last night.

'But how did you know I was in this room? How did they let you in?'

'Money is usually convincing. Besides, they were worried about you. And they want to prepare the room for the next guest. I told them I was a friend who had come to take you to the airport. They believed me, of course.' He offers her another sip. 'You didn't tell me you were leaving.' He looks hurt. 'I came earlier as arranged but you didn't answer the house phone.'

She doesn't say anything.

'Who is this 'gentleman'?'

'I don't want to talk about him,' she says.

'Has he taken advantage of you? Hurt you?'

'Of course not.' She feels an overwhelming sense of shame. She feels raw and disgusting and angry with herself. Florin is looking at her so intently, she's alarmed. 'Is there something wrong with my face?' She touches a cheekbone delicately.

'He's careful, this one. He left the face alone.'

'It wasn't like that.' She struggles to pull her legs up. 'I have to get dressed.'

'You need to rest.'

'I'm fine. I have to check out of this room.'

'Don't worry, I'll take care of things.'

'No, please.'

'Stay there. Leave it to me.' He jumps off the bed again and goes into the other room. She hears him talking on the phone but she can't make sense of it. When he comes back, the coat is off, and he's all business. 'It is fixed.'

'What's fixed?'

'You don't need to leave. The concierge can rearrange your flights if you like.'

'But – ' She doesn't have the budget for a luxury hotel room. But she doesn't want to tell him that.

He studies her. 'Let me run you a bath. I'll be back in a minute.' He disappears into the bathroom. Taps are turned on. She can hear him opening and closing drawers in the dressing room. He comes back with a bathrobe. The serious expression on his face has been replaced by something more ironic. 'Put this on and I'll help you into the bath.'

She takes her arms from beneath the covers and he eyes her bracelet. 'Did *he* give this to you?'

'Is there something wrong with that?' She unclasps it. 'Anyway, I'm throwing it away.'

'Let me see.' He fingers the pearls. 'Yes, you're right. It's not good enough.'

'What do you mean?'

'They're seed pearls. And some chips of semi-precious stone.'

'Tanzanite. It's the colour of my eyes.'

'What else did he give you?'

His probing is making her uncomfortable. 'Nothing.'

'Don't be so defensive. I suppose he gave you that coat and those sexy boots.'

'So what if he did?'

'You're new to this, I can see now.'

'New to what?'

He tosses the bathrobe on her lap. 'You're going to get in the bath and I'm going to pour us a glass of champagne, of a standard we deserve. And then maybe I'll order some food. A good deal of food. I'm *starving*. You gave me quite a fright.'

'Florin – the truth is, I can't . . .'

'Yes, you can. *He* owes it to you.' He smiles at her encouragingly. 'Cheer up, they won't throw us out tonight. One night should be enough.'

One night. She thinks he means one night of romance. And she discovers she still wants it. She opens her lips slightly, ready for a kiss.

Instead, he reaches across to the bedside table and picks up the phone. 'Really, things have worked out very well,' he says, more to himself than her. '*Zimmerservice?*'

Violet lies in the bath until the bubbles turn to milky scum. She wants every forensic trace of Eugen washed away. How could she have known that he had access to some experimental virility-enhancing chemical and wanted to try it out on her? She's had no experience with such things. He could not be satisfied. And it turned him into a monster, all gentleness, all consideration gone. He'd only left her alone when the concierge called up to say his car was waiting.

He had kissed her on the cheek before he left.

She hoists herself out of the bath and wraps herself tenderly in a bath sheet. She avoids looking in the mirror. There are repulsive little traces of Eugen everywhere – a pubic hair in the bidet, rolled-up, semen-encrusted tissues in the waste basket, nail-clippings in the basin, the gritty remains of antacid in a glass on the marble vanity, a smear of blood on a towel. She pats her skin dry carefully and puts on the bathrobe. She doesn't have the energy to get dressed.

Florin is reclining on a chaise talking into the phone. He puts it down and stands when she walks into the room. 'You know, I think I stayed in this exact suite once,' he said. 'But they have redecorated since then.' He pulls a bottle of champagne out of an ice bucket on the low table in front of him and pours the straw-coloured mousse into a glass. 'Will the Krug do?' he asks, looking, she thinks, extremely pleased with himself. 'I could get an earlier vintage sent up.'

She refuses the glass but sits down beside him. 'Florin, I don't think we should be doing this.'

'Why not? Your gentleman won't care too much. He'll be glad he got off lightly.'

'I don't know what you think I am.'

'I'm not sure what I think.' He raises an eyebrow.

She folds her arms in front of her, offended. 'Meaning?'

'Well, at first it seems to me that this is a beautiful young woman, a little distant, a little shy, a little naïve perhaps, a young woman who has divorced her husband and made a nice settlement and who is looking for some pleasant companionship on her travels. She tells me that there is another man and he's in her room, but I sense that this man is the wrong man. From her body language, it's clear that she can be persuaded to rid herself of this encumbrance. And you know, Violet, this is extremely convenient because I am looking for a woman exactly like her – footloose and fancy free, as they say, a woman who needs to be protected.'

'But—'

He holds up a finger to silence her. 'So I arrange to meet her today in her hotel. But she isn't in the lobby and she doesn't answer her phone and I'm bored with waiting. So I ask a few questions of a very plain and malleable girl at the desk and she tells me that a Mr Moser is paying for the room and that he is a regular guest. The young lady thinks he has something to do with diamonds. So I think – aha! I understand now. This young woman is quite different from what I thought. I have a little laugh at my own expense. But then the girl at the desk tells me that Mr. Moser has in fact already left the hotel but his young lady has not and the room needs to be vacated for cleaning but she doesn't answer the phone. So I tell the girl that I am a very dear friend. Well, you know the rest.'

'You thought I was some kind of gold-digger?'

'Is that what you call it in Australia? I call it something else.'

'*Prostitute* then?'

He grimaces. 'Of course not. That's not a word I ever use. I thought you had negotiated an arrangement with this diamond merchant and I was worried for you. Sometimes these men go back on their word. I thought he'd killed you at first.'

'I didn't have any sort of arrangement with him. I met him in Paris at a bar.'

'And he asked you to Vienna. He gave you a couple of trinkets. Once I realised you didn't even get a diamond out of him—'

'You've been snooping through my things!'

'You travel very lightly for a wealthy woman. One or two inferior jewels, a couple of pairs of decent shoes, a nasty little suitcase, a collection of shabby clothing. I expected you to be a woman who brought trunks.'

'I'm sorry to disappoint you.'

'It's hardly your fault. I should have known. All I can say in my own defence is that I've never had a relationship with an Australian woman. You confused me.' He presses the glass of champagne on her again. 'Come on, the champagne is excellent.'

Although she is appalled he has mistaken her for another kind of woman, she is glad to have set him straight. She doesn't want him to think she's after *his* money. She takes the glass and swallows half of it in one gulp.

'You're nervous?' he asks.

'I just don't think we should be doing this, here. What about your hotel? Could I stay there?'

'Are you propositioning me?'

'You did say we could skip the cakes.'

His smile is impenetrable. 'In fact, I'm suddenly hungry. Why don't we go out? You need some food in you.' He leans towards her to place his glass on the table. But rather than standing to leave, he pulls his sweater over his head, dexterously using one hand, and tosses it on the arm of the chair. So he will make love to her first? She watches him curiously, knowing she won't refuse him, desiring deeply that his kisses cover the bruises Eugen has left, healing them as if by magic.

'You haven't been to bed,' she says, realising he is wearing the same clothes from the night before.

'When I left you, I ran into an old schoolfriend outside the Imperial Hotel. We had a few drinks. There was a party. And a group of very boring people, who insisted I stay through the night while they played some dismal hands of poker. And then the casino, of course.' He shrugs. 'I lost some money.'

'"Some" sounds like a lot.'

'It would be of no concern except that I'm still waiting for my allowance.' He now removes his T-shirt with the same effective grace. She stares frankly at the contours of his lean body, the torso that is endearingly paler than the tan of his arms and neck, and the chest that is smooth as anything she has seen in a gallery, except for a smattering of hairs like cross-stitches or kisses.

Words come out to fill the charged space between thought and seduction. 'When do you usually get your allowance?'

'Whenever some exceptionally charming woman decides to give it to me.'

He holds her eyes and smiles. Something clicks in her mind, like an electric calendar shuffling to a new date. *Now* she sees it. 'You thought *I* was one of those women?'

'We all make mistakes.'

Hope sinks in her like a barge. 'But I don't have much money left, not enough for a life like this. I can't help you at all.'

'That's where you're wrong. You found Mr Moser. He will provide the wherewithal. For tonight at least.'

'And then?'

'Something will come up.'

'You sound very sure about it.'

'Something always comes up for people like us.'

'But I'm not like you.'

He doesn't respond except to stand and unbuckle his belt. She still wants him, despite everything that has just been said. To put herself in his hands, in more ways than the physical . . . the notion seems exquisitely appealing. He will know things about love that she has never known.

She slips her robe off her shoulders and reaches out to him.

He gives her a bemused look. 'They are magnificent breasts,

Violet. But I'm not making love to you. I'm merely going to have a shower.'

Taken aback, she says, with a hint of bitterness that surprises her, 'I'm not rich enough?'

He pulls out his belt and throws it on the chair. 'Unfortunately, no.'

'Tell me the truth about you,' Violet demands as she and Florin share *Palatschinken* in a shabby little coffee house in the Jewish quarter. 'You obviously don't have a hotel room. Or any luggage that I can see.'

She is angry and hurt by his rejection of her. She has only come with him to the café because she doesn't know what else to do. Or, at least, that is what she tells herself.

Florin doesn't answer. He is attacking the plate of pancakes with his fork like a duellist fighting for his life.

'You *eat* like a gypsy,' she observes.

'You don't know how gypsies eat,' he responds, dipping his fork in a bowl of stewed plums and trailing the dark syrup across the tablecloth. 'Besides, good manners are only for the bourgeoisie. I once kept company with a billionairess who smuggled leftovers out of a restaurant in her handbag. The restaurant was Guy Savoy. The handbag was Hermès. She just opened her bag and shovelled the scraps in. When she arrived home she handed the bag to her servant and never used it again. She did it at every meal I ate with her . . . and there were many of them.'

'Where do you find these women?'

'I don't find them. They find me.'

'That's not true. You came up to me.'

'But that was different. You were in trouble.'

'Not much trouble.'

'You're very naïve. They would have taken your handbag in a second if I hadn't intervened.'

'Being a gypsy you know this of course.'

He picks up the cynicism in her voice. 'I'll tell you something I haven't told anyone. Look at my bad hand.' He raises it off the table. 'See how the knuckles are distorted? I didn't break it in a horse-riding accident. My father broke it for me. He held it down on a table and smashed it with a mallet.'

She is horrified. 'Why would he do that?'

'Because then I would have a disability. I'd be worth more money on the streets.'

'He was going to *sell* you?'

'In a way. It was the family business. Career poverty. Cute young children earn more money begging if they're crippled. Until a certain age, of course.' He sounds as if he's talking about someone else. 'Don't look so shocked. I was lucky. He needed me to have strong legs and one good hand to help him carry and store things. Stolen goods. My baby sister was so infested with lice they ate into her retina and she lost her eyesight.'

'God, that's horrible.'

'Not for my father. She made more money than all the rest of us combined. Until my uncle convinced my father that she'd make even more if she walked in between the traffic with her stick. She was killed by a taxi on the Calea Victoriei when she was nine.'

His mouth is set like mortar. She doesn't know what to say. She has never met anyone with such an extraordinary story. She forgets that she is angry with him. 'How many brothers and sisters do you have?' she asks eventually.

'There were seven of us. I am the eldest. But, really, I don't know what happened to them. Not all of them were employed begging. Only the pretty ones. The others, they were sent to raise pigs, work in the fields. I do not know. '

'You don't see them?'

'I haven't for years. I told you, I got away. I was partly educated in Britain.'

'How did a gypsy father manage that?'

He gestures towards the empty plate. 'Let's order some more. With apricot next time, I think.'

'Don't change the subject.'

'Let me just say the People's Revolution was very convenient, Eight years ago the whole world wanted to help Romanians, adopt our orphans. Of course, they've forgotten about them now as they forget about everything that's not on the television. But in those days it was fashionable. I was a young man. There was money donated for schools, university. A few of us were quick enough to take advantage of it.'

'But you had no education.'

'Who said I didn't? I learnt how to speak English when I was fourteen. There are always people willing to teach young boys English.'

'In return for sex?'

'May I say you have sex on the brain, Violet? In any case, a UNICEF official sponsored me. She arranged for me to have a scholarship. I was twenty, but I pretended to be eighteen. In any case, they didn't care if I stretched the truth. It suited them all very well. It made them feel that they were 'doing something.''

'If the revolution was eight years ago, that makes you twenty-eight.'

'Does it?'

'So, what did you study? Surely it was difficult.'

'Because I was an unschooled peasant? It wasn't difficult at all. I studied *them*. No one knew anything about Romanians. I was exotic. So I got away with everything.'

'What about your mother, what did she do when your father was hurting you? She didn't approve?'

'I don't remember. I haven't seen her since I was eleven.'

'She left you?'

'I don't know. My father beat her. He might have killed her. Women disappeared all the time in those days.' He scowls at his empty coffee cup and calls for a waiter. She declines another coffee but he makes a complicated order in German. When the waiter has gone, he asks, like a child, 'Don't you think those were the best pancakes you have ever had? Hunger is an exquisite thing.'

She hasn't finished with her questions. 'So it's not true about the castle in Hungary?'

'There's enough truth in it to make it true. I am, for instance, descended from Elizabeth Báthory, the infamous 'blood countess'. She was a sixteenth-century Hungarian noblewoman, a great beauty they say, but very vain. She murdered and drank the blood of six hundred female virgins because she believed it would bring her eternal youth.'

'Do you believe that?'

'Of course! It's in the history books. And to tell you the truth, I've met a few vain women in my time who would do precisely the same thing today if they could.'

'You don't seem to have much respect for women.'

'There, my dear Violet, you are wrong.'

'But you live off them.'

'That's not the case at all.'

'You do,' she insists. 'You've admitted as much. You take advantage of rich women. You trade sex for money.'

'You are entirely wrong. And confused, I must say. If I trade sex for money, which I do not, that would be an entirely commercial arrangement and no one would be taking advantage of anyone.'

'But you do have sex with these women.'

'If they want it.'

'I bet they always want it.' She can feel the colour coming to her face.

He doesn't appear to have noticed. 'That's very flattering, Violet, but not always the case. They want companionship first and foremost. I'm an excellent companion.'

'And they fall in love with you?'

'Very rarely. They know what the arrangement is. There is the occasional delusional woman but when I recognise the signs I extricate myself.'

'That sounds very cold blooded.'

'I do it for *her* sake, not mine. Quite often the arrangement is very comfortable and I'm sorry to see it end. But there's always another opportunity.'

'While you're twenty-eight and handsome.'

He looks pained. 'I am named in the wills of at least two of my friends. I'll be looked after.'

'Then how come you're wandering around Vienna without a hotel room and no change of clothes?'

'My clothes are temporarily unavailable to me. If you must know, I was skiing Zürs and the situation suddenly changed. I'm not going to say anymore about it.' He acknowledges the waiter's arrival. 'Good. Here's my *mélange*.'

He puts his spoon in the coffee and eats the whipped cream first. When the second round of pancakes arrives, he empties the bowl of warm apricots on top and doesn't look up until the plate is clean.

'I think this gigolo life is a bit risky,' she says, not entirely kindly.

Now he looks up. 'If I'm a gigolo, you're a gigolette. What happened with your Mr Moser is no different than what happens with me. Except I'm honest about it.'

'And more materialistic.'

'I didn't notice you giving that coat back.'

'I will then.'

'Don't be stupid. Your diamond merchant won't lose a second of sleep over it. It is *nothing* to him, don't you understand? He has his value from you. Next time you meet him you could obtain a decent diamond or two. You don't even have to be very cunning about it.'

'There's no way I'm seeing him again. He's repulsive.'

'More fool you. Although you could do better than him by a long way. He's only a merchant. And a cheap one at that. You could set your sights higher.'

'I told you. I'm not like you.'

'Because you think you have a conscience and I do not?'

'No. Because I have my own life. I don't want to be someone else's plaything.'

'May I ask what kind of life you do have? Working in some office somewhere, if that's what you do? In some place at the end of the world where no one goes? Travelling once every few years when you've saved up enough money? Going to bed with men who don't deserve you because you find them attractive after a few drinks? I don't know anything about your ex-husband but I'll tell you now that you've wasted enough time on men like that. Even though you act younger than you say you are, you haven't many years left. You could do very well for yourself and be no one's plaything.'

'You're just saying all this because you want to justify your own existence.'

'I'm saying this because you are missing your calling. Your white skin, your strawberry hair, that natural rose of your lips and nipples – which no doubt is replicated in your pussy – your perfect bosom, your grace, your intelligence. You have class. There are a lot of very beautiful women out there, Violet, but they're peasants. Some of them learn fast, I'll give you that, but it takes years to learn discretion. It's a valuable commodity and you've got it.'

Violet looks down at her water glass, enraged. How can he speak about her like she is some piece of meat to be traded?

'You see, that blush of yours sets you apart. You shouldn't be embarrassed by your own beauty. It will give a lot of men pleasure. Don't you want to be covered in diamonds?'

'I don't care about diamonds.'

'You would if you had them. They're addictive.'

She is silent. She can see all too well how certain things can be addictive. But she is in no mood to agree with him about anything.

'Oh well,' he says casually. 'If you don't see it, more's the pity. I have myself to look after.' He gestures for the check and, when it arrives, hands it to her.

'Why are you so keen to have me live like you live?' she asks as she counts out some schillings.

'It's simple,' he says, reaching for his coat and scarf. 'Amateurs like you ruin everything for the rest of us.'

Florin is broody on the way back to the hotel, chain-smoking and flicking the butts carelessly on to the pavement. If a dog crosses his path, he will kick it, Violet thinks. He is angrier with her than she is with him but she doesn't understand why. What does it matter to him what she does with her life?

The streetlamps are illuminated. Tiny snowflakes touch her face and melt on contact. On the Graben a Japanese woman in a light evening gown plays a grand piano, oblivious to the cold. Sales assistants are turning their signs to *geschlossen*. Every second store it seems is selling chocolates wrapped in red and gold tinsel emblazoned with portraits of Mozart. In the doorway of a shuttered shop a hooker in an electric blue fur stubs out a cigarette. They pass a casino, its doors open onto the pedestrian mall. Even at this early hour there are people in evening dress sitting inside playing garish poker machines. Two heavyweights in dinner jackets stand scanning the street for trouble.

Florin suddenly stops. 'We need some resources, Violet. I don't want to be stuck in that hotel all night.'

She feels as if she has been struck across the face. 'I'm sorry I'm so boring to you.'

He reaches out and brushes a strand of hair from her brow. 'That's not what I mean. You're charming to me. But it will do neither of us any good to sleep with one other.'

'Because we can't make any money from each other?' she asks tartly.

'Because there is no future in it. Unless one of us becomes very wealthy, of course.'

'What makes you think I'm going to invite you back, anyway?'

'Without me you'd be sitting at the airport right now trying to get on a flight to nowhere.'

'Maybe that's what I should be doing.'

He puts a hand on her shoulder and gives her his earnest face. 'Why are you resisting me? I'm only trying to help you.'

'What, into a life of sin?'

'No. Into a life that's sometimes a little risky, it's true. But it's a *life.*'

Despite all her protests, her clear arguments, the brain that has ascendance over her heart, she wants to go along with him. She doesn't want to sit in an airport lounge with her cheap case. She doesn't want to go back to Melbourne and grey office chairs and white people and numbing conversations about real estate and football and pre-school waiting lists. She wants to sleep under lemur-skin tents in Madagascar, in hotels carved out of rock in Turkey or Venetian palaces shrouded in mist. Maybe she'll go to Mozambique and look up Eliniphao.

'What kind of resources?'

GRAND HOTEL RIVIERA

Boulevard de la Croisette, Cannes, France

I exit the elevator as Charles Nathan is getting in.

He takes a step backwards into the corridor and allows the elevator doors to close behind us.

Neither of us says anything for a few beats.

'Charles – you sly old dog,' I say at last.

He holds out his arms and I fall into them, surprised at the affection I feel. 'What are you doing up at this early hour?'

'I'm afraid I am yet to go to bed,' he says in that husky, barbed voice that always gets its hooks into me.

'Yet to go to *your* bed,' I tease.

'I might say the same for you.' He runs his eyes from my

dishevelled hair to my fire-engine-red-painted toes. 'Who are you with? Anyone I know?'

'I've only just arrived,' I lie.

'I see,' he says. 'Then let's have breakfast, shall we?'

'I don't want to interfere with your sleep.'

'I'll sleep long enough when I'm dead.'

I must admit, I did thought he might have been dead already. The last time I saw him, from a distance, must have been two years ago. He was in a wheelchair being pushed into the Savoy Grill, tartan rug tucked across his knees. There was a problem with the door and he was growing red with anger and frustration, chastising the maître d and brandishing a stick, like an old codger in a nursing home. I thought at the time, it's a degenerative disease. Suitable for a degenerate.

But look at him now. Far from dead. A small man, he looks positively sprightly in his dinner suit and hand-tied pink bow tie. His eyes are brown marbles of mischief. His famous eyebrows, manic tufts, are still black with shocks of grey wire like lightning strikes. While the face has fallen and a ruffle of jowls decorates the top of his stiff collar, his skin is still that beautiful, golden, tea-stain colour, sprinkled with age spots like spilled tea leaves in the bottom of a cup.

I am so in need of a friend, I could forgive him anything right now.

'I'll be dead before you are,' I say.

'My darling,' he says, linking his arm in mine. 'I'm happy to take your wager on it. But I warn you, I'm eighty this year.'

'I don't believe it.'

'Yes, you do. You were in Berlin with me when I turned seventy-four. Surely you haven't forgotten?'

I squeeze his hand, gently. It has the texture of crumpled paper. 'I haven't forgotten any *minute* with you.'

'A charming lie, but I will accept it. Now, the terrace or my room? Your choice.'

'Do you have to ask?'

Charles is in residence in his usual suite, which wraps around a corner of the top floor, and faces the Palais, where the films in competition are screened. When the porter brings my suitcase up, Charles directs him to a bedroom. There are three of them and Charles keeps them to himself, only when he feels like it doling out invitations to guests to stay.

'Sammy's coming across from London the day after next,' he explains. This is his eldest daughter, a costume designer like her mother and, I remember with a pang, older than me. 'But for now, I'm all alone. Would you like to freshen up?'

You bet I would.

'The night hasn't been very kind to you,' he observes, shrewd as always.

Warm water on skin, the simplest thing, is a great luxury. I stand under the shower way too long, remembering standing just like this on many mornings in the two seasons I came with Charles to Cannes. I have written over this chapter of my life with other stories and yet the streams of water running down my skin, the steam in my hair, releases the memories of those days like heat brings to life invisible words scratched out in lemon juice.

The words are appearing selectively. The Belgravia house with its rooms of books. The four-poster bed in the Cotswolds 'cottage.' Dinner with Michael Caine. Lunch with Julie Christie. Red dresses and red carpets. Venice in October. Berlin in July. Good times. Nothing bad.

I was with him for two years after his last wife died. But

what is two years in the life of a man like Charles? His eight decades teemed with incident – wives and mistresses, children and bastards, conflict and ecstasy, anonymity and celebrity, piety and carnality, scandal and repentance, grinding poverty and great wealth . . . I could write his obituary myself and yet I knew less than half of it.

I remember fragments . . . the son of a tailor from Warsaw, Charles was always something of a rogue: three years in a cell block after the war for black marketeering; a chance meeting with Orson Welles, which led to a construction job on the set of *The Third Man*; his career taking off like a rocket in the fifties after he directed *The Princess Ransom*; a marriage to an Italian star and a quick divorce; two children to a costume designer and a longer divorce; falling for the great love of his life, Lily, a cousin of the Queen; her slow death from multiple sclerosis and his years spent championing medical research; the famous Vietnam-era Academy Award speech which began, 'Members of the Academy, I must remind you that within the word "award" lies another, more brutal, word, "war"'; a retirement, a comeback . . . and somewhere lurking in there, in what order I'm not sure, a devastating fire and a bankruptcy.

All these lives were enough for any man. But Charles was not content with that. He was always collecting other lives and mine was one of them. It wasn't much of a life – just a network of randomly-firing nerves. My heart had stopped in Bucharest and no kind of charge could get it thudding again. Charles sensed the damage in me and homed right in. He found me in the lobby of the Connaught and took me home that very night. And I was very lost . . . and very grateful.

As I am now.

I turn off the shower and dry myself. I replace my make-up,

dab my wrists and the back of my knees with Joy and pull on my day clothes. I look like someone to be collected again, not something the cat dragged in.

Charles is in the drawing room waiting for me, changed into faded jeans, which are very *branché* for a man his age, and a dark shirt with a Chinese collar. He's thinner than when I last was with him – the waist on his jeans is pulled in like a paper bag. He gestures to an armchair. 'Sit down, my dear. I've ordered breakfast.'

Barefoot, I sit with my legs tucked up under me. He takes the facing chair. 'I asked them to redecorate the room. I couldn't stand all that Louis Quinze. Do you like it?'

'It's much more masculine,' I say, taking in the beige colour scheme and the slimline modern sofas.

'I try,' he smiles. He looks at me carefully. 'You thought I was dead, I suppose.'

It's no use lying to him. 'Yes. I saw you once from a distance in a wheelchair.'

'I merely broke my leg.'

'I can see there's a lot more kick in you yet.'

'Don't be fooled by appearances. I'm a very old man.'

'Only in years.'

He seems to approve of that. 'You say you saw me from a distance? Yet you didn't come and say hello.'

'I thought it might be awkward.'

'For you or me?'

I think about it. 'For me.'

He nods. The past hangs between us like old washing that has faded on the line. He obviously feels it's time to take it down. 'I thought you wanted to go with Jeremy to Spain,' he says, suddenly. 'I could see you liked him.'

'Not to the exclusion of you.'

'My mistake then. I was merely facilitating.'

'Facilitating me out of your life.'

'You're still in my life.'

I look at him, trying to gauge what he means. 'It was all right in the end. I had a *wonderful* time.'

He knows I'm lying. 'I've heard Jeremy is a very good lover.'

'Do you want a blow-by-blow description?'

'I always like to know what the competition is doing.'

'Competition?'

'And I want to know that he looked after you. I'm responsible.'

'*I'm* responsible for me. I travelled with him for a couple of months. It ended. That's it.'

'And then?'

'I'm not going to fill you in on five years.'

'I'd like to know that you were all right.'

'Don't I look all right?'

'You look magnificent. But this is not your best year, perhaps?'

This is a subject to be avoided. 'I've been on Monrifi, at the Hotel Bellissima,' I say, putting a spin on it. 'Do you know it?'

'Can't say I do.'

'Well, it's superb. I might have stayed there all summer, except that there was a death.'

'You weren't involved, I hope.'

'It was a dog that died.'

'That's unfortunate. I've never met a dog I wanted dead. People on the other hand . . . When did you get here?'

'I've only just arrived. I have a few invitations.'

He doesn't insult me by believing this. 'Well, my dear, I'd be delighted if you'd have a private dinner with me tonight and tomorrow there's a party in Haute Cannes – that is, of course, if it doesn't interfere with your other plans. As it turns out, I haven't anyone to accompany me. You'd be doing me a great favour.'

He's as surprised as I am to see the tears tumble down my face. It has been a while since someone has been kind, actually *kind*, to me. And from Charles, it's unexpected. 'I'm sorry. I've had a stressful few hours.' I wipe my face with the back of my hand. My fresh mascara streaks a knuckle.

'Who is it? Anyone whose career we can ruin?'

I smile and the salty droplets run into my mouth. 'A cokehead Omani who is quite capable of ruining his own.'

'Just as well. I'm not in the mood for a hatchet job. Having you here with me has put me in extremely good spirits. Let's not spoil them.'

The manservant – an unfamiliar one – chooses this moment to bring in my tea and Charles' 'morning medicine' in a brandy snifter.

'I still need a kick-start,' he says, holding up the glass. 'Cheers.'

'Which reminds me, I haven't asked you where *you* were last night.'

'Yacht hopping. You lose track of time at my age.'

'As if I'd believe that.'

'I'm not up to much these days, my darling.'

'Even more unbelievable!'

He laughs. 'What would you like to do for the rest of the morning?'

'I don't know,' I say carefully. 'What would you like to do?'

He contemplates me quietly. 'Something for old times' sake?'

I know what he means. 'I'm not sure we should be starting this up again in the circumstances.' This is true, but I'm delivering my message with a coquettish smile, letting him know I'm not an entirely closed book.

'Which circumstances are those?'

'Five years of circumstances.'

'Forget about the circumstances.'

'You can't blame me if I don't. I have my rules after all.' The rules I have just broken with Sayyid.

'And what would those be this time?'

'I need to be looked after.'

'I think we can take care of that.'

'I am not just talking about material things.'

'I see.' He doesn't take his eyes from mine. 'You've changed, my dear.'

I deserve that. 'I haven't changed at all.'

Neither of us will say what we really need. I want to be drawn back into the security of his life. What he wants from me is more fundamental. But I will accept this bargain. My humiliation at the touch, or lack of it, from a young man has prepared me for Charles. As it did once before. I will be walking into his arms nicely tenderised.

I stretch out a foot and examine my red toenails idly. I remember his fetishes very well. 'It's funny, isn't it? I could have gone anywhere in the world but I chose to come here.'

'I almost didn't come myself,' he says, admiring the arch of my foot. 'It no longer serves much purpose.'

'Is this what they mean by "fate"?' I ask him.

But Charles has little time for philosophy. He leans forward in his chair, hands digging into the arms. The old mischief plays in his eyes. 'Would you do an old man a favour and take off your blouse, my dear?'

I look dispassionately at Charles sitting there in his chair, mouth open, a spittle of drool hanging from the corner of his lips.

An extraordinary man, reduced to an infant by the promise of an unbuttoned blouse.

I know what he wants.

He wants me to strip naked and lie on the carpet facing him, one leg raised and nestling in his crotch. He wants me to pleasure him with my toes while I pleasure myself with my hands. This is one of a few variations he requires.

And in return for this simple act of lying supine before him on the floor and feigning pleasure, and for the intellectual services I provide, I am rewarded with his patronage and the company of his impressive friends, I am housed in many residences and fed delicious food, I am given spending money and accounts at Knightsbridge stores, I travel at the front end of the plane and on the back seat of his chauffeur-driven Bentley, I attend film premieres and West End plays and play cards, into the night, with ministers of the realm.

Disproportionate perhaps.

I look at Charles, the saliva on his lip, his watery eyes, his scrawny neck, his gnarly tense hands and think, given all the hurts in this world, what hurt is there in this?

HOTEL STADPARK

Johannesgasse, Vienna, Austria

Look at Violet. Take a hard look. You won't be the only one.

More than a few sets of curious eyes flicker over her as she sits alone in the lobby bar of the Hotel Stadpark. She is the only woman without a companion and, what's more, she is sitting in the most public part of the baroque salon, where Florin has placed her. In a room of dark furs and sombre dinner suits, her pale skin and white dress make her as luminous as a lily on a grave.

White dress?

Florin has managed, without any funds, to relieve the expensive clothing boutique in the arcade of the Prinz Eugen of a slinky new dress for Violet and, for himself, a few shirts, a pale yellow cashmere sweater and a pair of cuffed trousers. He has done this by strolling into the shop as the saleswoman closes up for the night and spinning a tale of woe involving a suitcase delayed by an airline strike and an imminent dinner at the Hotel Bristol with – here he drops the names of people Violet has never heard of. Not surprisingly, the crusty saleswoman melts under his playful barrage of German, English, French and other, unrecognisable, languages (Romanian? Bulgarian? Czech?) She is the one to suggest, as Florin is about to dash to their suite to retrieve an imaginary wallet, that she send the clothes up now with a porter and he finalises the transaction on Monday morning.

Violet, who has always paid for her share of everything, is appalled. 'How did you get away with *that?*' she asks in the elevator to her room.

'Always go shopping at closing time. *Les vendeuses* are in a hurry to go home.'

'She's sending all those clothes to the room without us paying?'

'Why not? We're staying in a $2000-a-night suite. It's not as if she's sending them to a backpacker's hostel. Never underestimate the power of appearance. She knows the hotel has our details if we were to skip off without paying.'

'Eugen's details.'

'Why are you always worrying about paying for things? We all pay sooner or later.' He gives her a wicked smile. 'Me, I prefer it to be later.'

'Well, I feel bad about it.'

'So return the dress.'

She intends to, she tells herself, as she sits in the lobby with a bottle of champagne pointing at her accusingly from its ice bucket. Her mouth is aching from being constantly pressed into a half-smile. When people look at her, she glances away.

She can't disguise her discomfort. Florin has been gone a very long time. She has no watch but she knows it is almost an hour. She is four glasses into the bottle of Louis Roederer he has ordered and abandoned. A bottle that will have to be paid for, with nonexistent funds, for Florin has all her money, the traveller's cheques cashed in at the hotel reception for a disadvantageous rate. She doesn't even have enough for a taxi fare back to her hotel, which *might* be walking distance if she wasn't wearing heels. All she has is her Lady Dior bag with her passport and the hotel's complimentary hairbrush in it.

Just as she's thinking the worst of him, he slips into the club chair beside her. 'Good, there's some left,' he says, reaching for the champagne bottle and pouring a glass.

'Thanks for leaving me.'

He looks exasperated. 'Can't you sit here by yourself even for a few minutes?'

'It was more like an hour.'

'Anything can happen in an hour.'

'Yes, I can drink too much of this champagne we can't afford and fall asleep.'

'So – did anyone speak to you?' His eyes are sparking as he looks around the room.

'Why should they?'

'Because you're a beautiful woman alone. Don't the possibilities excite you?'

'Oh, I see what you're up to.'

'I'm not up to anything. I was in the gentlemen's room, if you want to know.'

'For an hour?'

'I got into an argument with an Albanian.'

'What about?'

'What a mess they are in. Surely you have been watching CNN in that big suite of yours?'

'I haven't had time between feeding you pancakes and stealing dresses.'

He ignores the jibe. 'The whole country invested in a pyramid scheme that failed and they're blaming their government. President Berisha has declared a state of emergency. The noble citizens are flooding into the streets with their guns like it's the Wild West. I'm not surprised – they're all gangsters and criminals.'

'That's rich, coming from a Romanian.'

'You know nothing about Romania. We're a very cultured people. Bucharest is the Paris of the East. These Albanians have always been primitive.'

'While the Romanians send their blind children out to beg in the traffic?'

'You feel superior to me?'

'No, I do not. But I resent you thinking I come from a place that's *backward*. We don't run into the streets with guns whenever anything upsets us.'

'Upsets us? Losing everything is a bit more than upsetting.'

'Well, I just mean that we're a more rational society.'

'And that's a good thing?'

'It is when the world is such a dangerous place.'

'It's only dangerous if you're in Tirana right now. Does Vienna feel dangerous? Did Paris? Really, Violet, I don't know much about that country you come from, but you are too protected. The world is less dangerous now than it has ever been. We're less than three years away from the twenty-first century. The Cold War is over. The Communist criminals have been banished. Sadaam Hussein and Gaddafi have been put in their places. Sarajevo has been liberated. Global prosperity will mean the end of conflict. Everyone wants to trade with each other, not fight. Trust me, there will be no more wars, only skirmishes. And, in the case of the Bosnians and the Albanians, there is always President Clinton to save them. With only one superpower, Violet, everyone is safe. On every level we are safer. What about this new technology, which will connect us to one another, making a nonsense of nations? And the advances in medical science? Science has conquered Nature, money has conquered evil – in all, a perfect time for you and me to be alive. To take advantage of all these newly rich people in optimistic moods.'

'That's quite a speech.'

'Don't make a face. It's not very pretty. You and I, we are *entitled*, Violet. Our beauty makes us valuable commodities in this world. It might come as a surprise to you, but there are rich people who actually like spending money. Just as there are people who like it being spent on them. The world is out of balance when there's a shortage of either one.'

'So you're doing your civic duty.'

'Precisely what I have been telling you for twelve hours. But it's more than that. I am protecting the women who support me from less scrupulous individuals, from unhappy liaisons. Look around the room. Do you see any women alone?'

'No.'

He sighs. 'The answer is *yes*, Violet. There's a woman in a long velvet skirt. Closer to the entrance. You see her?'

'She's not alone. She's with a man.'

'I assure you she is alone. He might be her husband, he might not be. But she needs rescuing. If only from a headlong plunge into old age. I can break her fall.'

'Good for you.'

He doesn't seem to register her sarcasm. 'I think it is. And it's good for you too.'

'So – I just sit here all night and a man will come along for me? A rich man, not one of those travelling salesmen over there.' She nods in the direction of a group of suits sitting around a low table with a brick-like portable computer.

'Not necessarily. You are rather inexperienced. You might need a procurer.'

'A *what?*'

'The person who makes your arrangements.'

'You mean, a pimp.'

'No, I do *not* mean a pimp, Violet. You are really very *sauvage*. I'm talking about a civilised practice that has been going on for centuries. Let us say a man of status, who has certain domestic entanglements, wishes to find a companion for pursuits beyond the confines of his home, which may include travel or even an alternative domestic situation in his own city. He can't go to an introduction agency, can he? And a whore is out of the question. It is a matter of taste as well as respectability. He doesn't have time to meet women socially and, besides, in these circumstances there is always the possibility of the woman getting emotionally involved. So he needs someone who he can trust, someone who is part of his world, to make the connection for him. There is no question of money changing hands, *per se*.'

'What do you mean, *per se?*'

'For the woman it's given that there are certain compensations. The best food, the best wine, the best hotels, the best transportation. There will be expenses and most certainly clothing and jewellery. If the relationship is long term, there may be property and other material assets. But in the first place she is looking for experience, luxury, the chance to travel the world in exceptional circumstances.'

'And the procurer? What does he get out of it? A commission?'

'Not at all. He – or she – simply gets the pleasure of seeing two people happily connected.'

'I don't believe that.'

'Well, for some people, there is also the appeal of being useful to a powerful man. Or woman. It works the other way, of course.'

'You mean wealthy women hire procurers too?'

'Not *hire*, Violet. You are not listening.'

'Yes I am. You're saying that if I used one of these procurers to make arrangements with Eugen, I'd have got a big diamond out of him. But I would have still had the bruises.'

He makes an irritated grunt. 'That is not what I said. Your Mr Moser is small fry. You are good enough for the big league. The serious money. The serious status.'

'Are these *serious* men going to be any nicer to me than Eugen was?'

'That is why you, at this stage of your career, need a procurer.'

'Career! Why do I think that person is you?'

'Me? Not at all. But perhaps there are other procurers in this city tonight, perhaps even here in this hotel.'

'You've spotted one, haven't you?' She looks around. 'What do they look like? How do you recognise them?'

He shows his gold teeth. 'Good. You're showing some interest at last.'

'I didn't say I was interested.'

'There is no danger, Violet.'

'Isn't there?' She can think of a few.

'Because you have already – how do they say? *Dived in head first.*'

'What do you mean?'

'Your Mr Moser. You took a risk with him.'

'And look where it got me.'

'Vienna. New clothes. Some excellent meals. Drinking good champagne in a fine hotel lobby with a very handsome young man. Don't be afraid of your own life.'

'I'm not.'

'*We must be willing to get rid of the life we planned, so as to have the life that is waiting for us:* that is what Joseph Campbell says. You've already taken your risk. It's time to take your reward.'

'I don't . . .' But she's wavering.

'Do you trust me?'

'No.'

'Do you trust me?'

'Maybe.'

'Then, goodnight, Violet.' He stands abruptly and kisses her hand.

And then he is gone, too quickly for her to stop him.

Violet deflects the waiter when he removes the empty champagne bottle and asks if she would like another. The result of this is that he returns with the bill on a little silver plate and leaves it on the small table beside her. She looks at it morosely.

Florin isn't coming back. She's never going to see him again. Gone, with her money and cards. She doesn't know what game he has been playing but she knows she has been played. She berates herself for not leaping out of her chair and following him. But she was too worried about causing a scene. And, yet, this is ridiculous: what kind of scene would she cause? Florin would have had to stop and take her arm and pay for the champagne. She doesn't know much about these things but she's already gathered that a breech of etiquette here in Vienna might very well reverberate in Paris, London or Budapest.

Being nice has done her in again. Florin has just demonstrated to her how naïve she really is. She is hopelessly out of place in this world of sophisticated games. And she curses him for showing her this. She went along with him to please him but she is like a child who has been shown a room full of toys and then had the door slammed shut on her fingers.

She needs, desperately, to make an escape, although where she might escape to is not clear. There is the matter of the unpaid check. If she just gets up and walks out, what will happen? Maybe if she slips the check into her handbag, her waiter will think that one of the other waiters has taken care of it. They are all exceedingly busy. And her waiter has temporarily disappeared.

It's an idea. She picks up the bill nervously and subtly unzips her bag.

'Oh, *please*, let me take care of that.'

Startled, guilty, Violet drops the paper and it flutters to the floor. The man who addressed her bends down and collects it, scoops it into his pocket. As he straightens, she's fascinated by the strict white part that cuts regimentally across his black hair. Erect, he smiles at her with teeth that shine like bathroom tiles. His eyes blaze radioactive blue out of skin that is tanned terracotta. He is anywhere from thirty-five to fifty-five but there are no wrinkles when he smiles, just a slight stretching of the skin at the corner of his eyes, which gives them a pixyish lift. His nose is disproportionately small in a wide face. As he offers his hand, Violet has a moment to take in the loden green jacket, edged in braid, over a T-shirt that appears to have fluffy sheep on it, and the black leather trousers, which are smooth as molten plastic. He looks like the spawn of a Hitler Youth and a Las Vegas lion tamer. She would not be surprised if the hand pressed behind his back has a whip in it.

When he takes her hand, his is soft and slightly damp. She waits for a Teutonic click of heels but instead there's just the introduction, 'Carl Schwamberg.'

She replies with her name and his fingers loosen but stay connected to the tips of hers. 'My friends would like to know if you'd join us for a drink,' he says in a voice like warm chewing gum, a North American accent that is a clip short of a drawl. He tips his head towards of a group of people occupying a banquette across the room.

When she doesn't immediately respond he adds, 'That includes any friends you may have here, of course.'

He must have observed Florin's exit. 'No, I'm alone.'

'Well, we can't have *that*, my kitten.'

She is smart enough to know that he is not just proposing a drink. She wonders for a moment if Florin has set her up. And she thinks, if he has, then I hope he is watching. I'll show him that I can be better at this than he expects. She squeezes Carl Schwamberg's hand. 'I suppose we can't,' she replies with a smile.

'Then may I?' He helps her to her feet. 'You'll find one or two of us a lot of fun.'

Carl Schwamberg does not consider himself, by any stretch of the imagination, a mere procurer. He is just one of those clever people who can multi-task, a new buzzword he likes to use often. While his business card reads art appraiser by appointment he can also turn his hand to party planning, fashion consulting, screenwriting, film production, interior decorating, crisis management, make-up artistry, hairdressing, dog-sitting, celebrity wrangling, tarot card reading, disc-jockeying, personal training, short-order cooking, golf caddying, chauffeuring, travel guiding, limited kinds of bodyguarding and the facilitating of various pleasurable activities including the consumption of illegal pharmaceuticals and high-priced, prime quality flesh. In brief, he has made himself useful to wealthy clients (although not, he has found out, necessarily indispensable). He sees himself as consigliere, confidant and collaborator; others within the wide international circles he operates view him less kindly as flunky, parasite and bumboy. He is tolerated because he knows where to obtain things and doesn't mind – in fact enjoys – the depths to which he sometimes has to go to secure them. If he has to scrub the barnacles on the dinghy to take his place on the yacht, then so be it. Besides, there are many planets, meteorites, rocks and fragments of space junk orbiting around every star, all with some purpose, even if it is to collide with one another to keep the star unscathed. He is not unaware: he knows that some people view him as debris, even, unfortunately, the occasional client for whom he 'consults'. But for most of the hours in the day he can convince himself that spending someone else's money is even better than having his own.

Right now, in March 1997, he is spending Lyle Huntington's money, *the* Lyle Huntington, as he likes to point out to anyone under the misapprehension it was a lesser Lyle Huntington. *The* Lyle Huntington is founder, CEO and *raison d'etre* of a major

American television network; significant contributor to the Democratic National Congress; close friend of Warren Beatty, Michael Ovitz and Mikhail Gorbachev; one-time lover, it is rumoured, of Barbra Streisand and Anouk Aimee; philanthropist; serious collector of early twentieth century European art; holder of round-the-world solo sailing record; enthusiastic falconer; husband of the formidable Bibi Carlsson, Scandinavian furniture heiress and his third wife; father of three children, Lyle Jnr, 27, Amelia, 25, William, 22, and step-father of Amando, 15; brain cancer survivor; devotee of an obscure bodywork pioneer called Joseph Pilates. Lyle Huntington seems happy enough for Carl to spend his money, as long as Carl is able to identify, from time to time, those highly desirable collectables that fly under the radar of the legitimate art world. They have been in Vienna to evaluate a little-seen Egon Schiele self-portrait from 1913 and, satisfied, they have made a pre-emptive offer, which is likely to be accepted. Carl has paid his dues for another several months and could probably sit back tonight, enjoy his champagne and start planning his summer season on the *Amelia*, Huntington's 279-foot yacht. But he's always a little edgy, always a little insecure, always looking for new opportunities to ingratiate himself.

Violet could be one of them.

Carl has come to Lyle by way of his wife, Bibi. Familiar with being passed around from capitalist to capitalist like a treasured nanny whose charges keep growing up, he has met Bibi through *her* friend Sissy Allen, who recommended him as an excellent shopping companion with an amusingly wicked tongue. Carl's loyalty to Bibi waxes and wanes. He buys the anniversary and birthday presents on behalf of Lyle and makes sure they are obscenely extravagant and *precisely* what she wants. (She gives him the list.) On the other hand, his first loyalty is now to Lyle, who pays his bills, and when Lyle looks lasciviously at another woman and tells Carl to 'get' her for him, he can hardly cite Bibi and refuse. In fact, there is a tiny little niggle of pleasure in doing it because it gives him a kind of power over Bibi, who loves her husband, despite her many complaints. Carl has never been happy in love (his taste for feckless deck hands may account for it) and it is rewarding to know that Swedish heiresses who have appeared in *Vanity Fair* aren't either.

So when he sees Lyle looking longingly at the redhead in the clinging white dress, Carl knows he has another opportunity to win the billionaire's favour.

Violet is introduced to five people, four of whom seem happy to meet her. There's an elderly Viennese couple, Josef and Marlene, she quiet and mouse-like in her enveloping fur, he pompous in his high collar and monogrammed bow tie; two American men, Lyle and Reed, both in their sixties, both relaxed and tanned; and a stringy, fiftyish woman, Misha, who may be the wife of either Lyle or Reed. It's Misha, perhaps predictably, who seems less than impressed by a rival's appearance. She raises her hand so limply that Violet is forced to make an awkward step over Reed's outstretched legs to reach it. Misha's smile is fleeting and she turns her head away from Violet to continue a monologue directed at the colourless Marlene, something about Bibi who apparently has the most marvellous taste.

Violet suppresses an instant dislike. Perhaps the woman is just being European.

Carl shows Violet a vacant club chair and sits on the arm of it, his leather pants squeaking as they come into contact with another flayed animal hide. He calls up a waiter to pour her champagne, even though the bucket and glass is at his elbow. Six sets of eyes observe Violet take her first sip and then the questions begin. Where is she from? Is she travelling alone? How did she find herself in Vienna? (She censors this response.) Has she had time to visit the *MuseumsQuartier*?

'No,' Violet says, 'I have only had time to eat cakes.'

The men laugh appreciatively.

'Lucky you,' scowls Misha, whose accent is educated British tinged with something fragrant, Egyptian perhaps by the shape of her eyes. 'Not having to worry about your figure. But you young women have such remarkable metabolisms. Isn't that right, Lyle?'

Lyle's smile is inscrutable.

'Oh, lay off, Misha,' Carl interjects. 'You of all people should know better than to raise the subject of *metabolism*.' His mouth puckers in a self-congratulatory smirk. Violet notices that every third or fourth word has a European inflection, as if he only occasionally remembers that he is trying to appear continental.

Misha fiddles with the neckline of her jewelled cardigan. 'Spoken by a man who virtually owns Afghanistan, he's invested so heavily in their agricultural products.'

Carl now looks peeved. 'Self-preservation, honey.'

'It's obviously not very cost-effective, my darling.'

The others laugh, even Marlene, who seems not to understand the joke. Lyle is amused but he issues a warning. 'Children. Please don't include us in your sniping. What will our guest think?'

Misha stretches her arms across the back of the sofa casually. 'Yes, what *does* she think of us? I'm all ears.'

Violet opens her mouth, about to compose something polite, when Lyle holds up a hand. 'Enough, Misha. You can't come to dinner if you keep this up.'

'Well, that won't be too much of a disappointment,' interjects Carl. 'Seeing as she's on a liquid diet.'

'Where *are* we going for dinner anyway?' Reed is slouched so that the folds of his neck rest in the V of his unbuttoned Lacoste golfing shirt. He looks like he is wearing a coat of loose, freckled flesh, overstitched with thick forearm hairs of a tarnished gold. 'Can we be American for once and eat before midnight?'

Misha, eyes still on Violet, ignores him. 'It's a pretty name, Violet. Old-fashioned. Surely it can't be real?'

Violet tells them the story of how her mother mistook her eyes for purple at birth.

'How convenient,' Misha says, 'to have your mother give you the name of a whore.'

Someone sucks in air sharply. Violet feels her face flood with blood. Carl quickly intervenes, touching her arm. 'Don't mind her, honey, she's in the last stages of bitchdom before death.'

Lyle, affable until now, is extremely displeased. He makes this known by tapping on the arm of his chair. 'All right, Misha. Reed's hungry. Take him somewhere.'

Whatever muscles have held up Misha's smirk now collapse. Her mouth twitches and the dark red lipstick suddenly appears to bleed into the corners, as if someone has shot her. Violet notices, for the first time, that the hand at her neck has a tremor in it. '*I'm* not hungry,' Misha says like a child trying to wheedle out of punishment.

'*Now.*'

Reed seems oblivious to the tension. He pushes himself upright in his chair. 'Good-o. Let's go to that place above the cathedral. Are you coming later, Lyle?'

'I've changed my mind. I might have something in my room.'

'You bet he will,' mutters Misha, who is now standing, smoothing down her dress. A waiter appears and helps her into a coat that might be made from a patchwork of the skins of tiny, silky fieldmice. Another waiter hands Reed a dark coat and scarf. They shake hands with Marlene and Joseph.

'Still up for a jog at 6 a.m.?' Reed asks Lyle.

'Of course.'

Misha flaps a limp hand at Violet. This time Violet doesn't reach for it. 'Enjoy your evening, *Scarlet*.' Misha's smile is back. She turns to Lyle. 'Oh, Lyle, when I call Bibi later, is there anything you want me to pass on?'

'Nothing, Misha. I spoke to her myself an hour ago.'

'But there have been so many developments since then.'

The comment remains unacknowledged. Lyle quite deliberately turns away from Misha and asks Joseph, 'So Professor, what's your estimation of Striechen's collection?'

Reed is anxious to get out of there. He takes Misha's arm. 'Bye all.'

'Enjoy your schnitzel,' says Carl in a way that suggests he's talking about more than meat.

Violet watches Misha and Reed career around low tables and chairs towards the entrance. Two dark-coated men follow them out.

'There goes one of the lesser concubines,' says Carl.

Violet is confused. 'I thought she was Reed's wife.'

'Who said she isn't?'

'So who's Bibi?' she whispers, although she has a fairly good idea.

'Oh, don't worry about her,' Carl says, casting a surreptitious look in Lyle's direction. 'She'll get a *major* jewel out of this.'

WHITE CLOUD PALACE

Wángfujing Dajie, Beijing, People's Republic of China

When Lyle Huntington has sex, he likes to gaze upon beautiful things. The woman he is having sex with, although invariably beautiful, is never enough: his eyes tend to wander from her face, her breasts, her buttocks to the walls, the headboard of the bed, the table lamps and the carpet, none of which will satisfy his exacting aesthetic standards. The Imperial Suite of the White Cloud Palace hotel has burnished gold walls, rosewood headboards copied from the Empress's divan at the Forbidden Palace, table lamps in the style of porcelain Ming vases and silk rugs hand-embroidered with a pattern of rising phoenix, but none of this is especially to his taste. He finds the chinoiserie cloying and distracting, forcing his mind to stray, mid-thrust, to thoughts of obtuse Communist Party officials, obstructionist foreign media ownership laws and unfathomable business rituals, all of which he would prefer to keep outside the bedroom.

He is sixty-two now, preternaturally vigorous, but he has noticed lately that his sexual equipment, as he likes to call it, sometimes will not operate *fully* unless his mind is completely engaged. The looming images of Chairman Mao and Jiang Zemin (or John Major or Jacques Chirac) have no place in his erotic scenarios. He prefers prettier, more voluptuous, estrogen-charged muses. And so, he demands that the collection of small paintings he travels with are hung on any wall where his eyes may drift during the act of intercourse – including, just in case, the walls of each toilet and built-in closet. Even though his stay in any given hotel may be as brief as one night, the collection of twelve works, which includes an Anders Zorn nude from 1910, a Marc Chagall bride dated 1915 and a miniature of a Tahitian maiden with tiare flowers painted by Paul Gauguin in 1903, are unpacked and hung and then re-crated at every pitstop. This endeavour involves two guards just for the paintings, which are valued in excess of fifty million US dollars, and a special container in the hold of Huntington's private jet, a converted 737-500 bought six months ago from Balkan Airlines.

Lyle's eyes are on the poignant Modigliani study of Jeanne Hébuterne, the artist's girlfriend, who committed suicide after his death from tuberculosis in 1920. The angular nude is one of Lyle's more recent acquisitions and he is not yet sure whether he likes it or not. There's something depressing in the way her head flops onto her shoulder, something half-dead about her, which is slightly off-putting, especially as he is now working himself up to the exquisite point of release with a very live woman underneath him. But even Jeanne is more aesthetically stimulating than mind's-eye visions of the apparatchiks from China Central Television with their doughy faces and dark suits and phlegmy way of coughing whenever an aspect of his presentation displeases. Or pleases – who the hell would know what this interchangeable trio of pork buns think? Seven meetings in two years and millions of dollars spent in lawyers, interpreters and cultural go-betweens and he hasn't cracked the code yet. That majority stake he took in Hong Kong T-Vision is looking more and more like a dud deal, particularly with Deng dead and Hong Kong's smooth transition in July less than assured. His rivals are snapping at his heels. It makes his blood boil.

. . . And his oldfella wilt. Fuck it. He's going to relegate that Modigliani to the bathroom. Or get Carl to exchange it for something lustier . . . a little Diego Rivera perhaps.

Violet, sensing this, shifts her ass slightly and he feels the roundness of her cheeks press into his groin. He slides his hands from her waist down to the fold of her thigh at the hip and back again . . . so strong, so soft! He sighs and his own softness telescopes to fill the welcoming space.

He's happy with *this* at least. He's a little bit in love with this beautiful woman. She's not like the others, not grasping, not twittering, not full of tricks and tics and manufactured pleasure. She's like a fresh green shoot miraculously sprouting on a very gnarled old vine, the deadwood of the sexual tree on which he finds himself hanging. He once delighted in women who came on strong – flight attendants who pulled him into first-class toilets and galley alcoves, starlets who slipped off their shoes and massaged his balls with their toes under the cover of the banquet table, associate's wives who took him in the Jacuzzi as the party wound down. There is still no shortage of these but in recent years Lyle has begun to abhor what he can have so easily. He remains an attractive man, his skin still tight on his bones, his teeth capped and perfectly white, his hair thick around his face. Even the old pecker, always respectable, seems to hang longer with the effects of gravity. He runs every day, has regular massages, facials and manicures, has the silver in his hair subtly painted on.

Sometimes he catches his face in a mirror and he thinks it looks like a brown paper bag that has been scrunched up then flattened out again, but he is disdainful of the eye lifts and chin tucks many of his colleagues seem compelled to endure. A bit of wisdom on a man's face is a sexy thing, he always says. And countless women seem to agree. Of course, he knows that what they *really* find sexy is his money. This is the sticking point for him and it has become stickier over the years. He makes no moral judgement. In his younger days he even enjoyed the power of it.

But more and more he finds himself outside the act when making love, watching obsessively for any signs of artifice, any hint that the groans and sighs and adoration at the temple of his body is little more than lip service.

But this one – she says she has not had many men. He actually believes it. She's a little bit tentative, a little bit nervous. She even seemed, at first, reluctant to go with him. How unexpectedly exciting that was! He was forced to woo her, to find a tenderness he hasn't called on for many years.

She doesn't treat sex like a shopping list of sexual positions. The Camel's Hump. Tick! The Frog's Posture. Tick! The Archimedean Screw. Tick! There's something delicate about her, like a blue bruise on pale skin. She's light as a breeze. But her laugh is earthy like a sailor.

She reaches under her belly and holds his balls.

Ahh. Forget the Diego Rivera.

He may keep this woman instead.

Lyle is both the oldest and the richest man Violet has slept with. A week into being his 'travelling companion', she is mesmerised by him, although she is not quite in love with him. But love is not such a big bridge to cross. For someone who isn't particularly large, Lyle fills any room he enters. He sucks the ions out of the air, leaving few for anyone else. Violet thinks of the word for women: ravishing. Or the word for men: commanding. She understands now how all those ancient generals could control thousands of troops, battalions of elephants and seraglios of slave girls with a wave of a hand.

In Vienna, Lyle took command without her even realising it. The casual invitation to Steirereck for dinner, as part of a group, the peeling off from the dull Viennese couple to have a nightcap in the red room at the Sacher, the losing of Carl to some subterranean nightclub named for a porn film, a last glass of champagne in a corner of his hotel's dark bar – she fell into step so naturally with his agenda she might have been a sleepwalker led by a hypnotist. It was only when the time came for him to ask her to his room that she pre-empted him with a yawn and a little speech she had rehearsed in her mind all night, one about being tired and not at her best and needing a good night's sleep above all else. Even then, she sensed he expected her to make this excuse, for he made no attempt to change her mind and sent his bodyguard with her back to the Prinz Eugen but only after extracting a promise from her to spend Sunday with him.

And on Sunday morning, at a respectable time, after she'd tossed and turned all night wanting Florin to appear, which he did not, a man arrived to take her and her luggage to the Hotel Stadpark, where she was checked into a suite a discreet two doors down from Lyle's. (She later discovered the suite between was reserved for Lyle's personal fax machine, which he loathes to hear click and whirr in the night.) There was no suggestion that she might protest the assumption. And she gave no thought to protesting it. She expected she would be required to respond in kind (she didn't know yet how she felt about that) but she had no desire to make a humiliating call to Patrick to send her the ticket home.

Her suite was full of lilies, which made her sneeze. This noted by a butler, they were immediately replaced by out-of-season roses with no scent, which reminded her of the roses Florin bought her two nights before. On a side table was a glossy box and in it, a pale green satin nightgown and robe, trimmed with exquisite lace, and a pair of slippers. In the bathroom, the vanity was covered with cosmetics and potions. The cupboards were so full of women's clothing that she thought she had stepped into another woman's room until she saw that each garment still had a tag hanging on it.

On a pillow lay a small, satin-lined box containing a pair of drop earrings with blue stones so large she hoped they were glass. Holding them up against her face in a mirror she thought of Eugen's ugly bracelet and Florin's comment, *You can do better than him by a long way.* It seemed she could.

But if this was a silent transaction, she was nervous that she wouldn't be good value. When she was brought to Lyle's room, she had handed him back the sapphires. He looked perturbed at first. Then he laughed and said, 'Very good,' as if congratulating her on something. Later he asked her to wear them for him, 'Just for today'. And she did.

They had lunch with a dozen other people at the American Embassy, galloped through the Egon Schiele collection at the Leopold (which put Lyle in a bit of a mood, 'because he can't stand not owning it all,' confided Carl) and inspected the Lippizzaner horses in their stables, before retiring to the hotel to freshen for dinner.

At dinner, alone in his room, Violet couldn't help feeling she was the main course. When she was served up by the butler, Lyle admired her black dress and asked if it were one of the ones he'd had sent up. When she said no he looked a little edgy. 'Why not?' he asked. 'Don't you like them? We could send for some others. It's Sunday but I can get any shop in this city to open for me.' She said she liked some of them very much and would choose one the next day. 'One?' he said. 'Jesus Christ, you can have the lot!'

'I don't need the lot,' she said.

In the bedroom, she admired his Chagall and this seemed to have as positive effect as admiring his penis, for he groaned with pleasure and commandeered her then and there, without removing her dress.

She was grateful for not having to make decisions, for his fundamental approach. It was fast, her underwear tugged aside and she pulled on to his lap. If she was not left tingling with pleasure at the end, she liked it. What she liked most was watching him liking her.

The only awkwardness came when her teeth banged against his perfect set as he came. His crowns were strangely inflexible, like wooden pegs.

But she could do this.

The next morning, she tried on the clothes hanging in her wardrobe. She looked like another woman in most of them. She decided she did, after all, need more than one dress.

She did not return the earrings.

When Lyle returns from his morning jog up to Tiananmen Square and around Mao's tomb, Violet is curled up in bed reading the *China Daily News*. Lyle's bodyguard, Su'a, a Tongan with upper arms as large and sleek as a seal, follows him into the bedroom. Not for the first time, Violet feels like a French queen with all the courtiers gathered around the nuptial bed. There is little privacy – Lyle sometimes takes his morning briefings while she is under the sheets beside him. On one occasion a delegation in dark suits stood impassively as Lyle lay naked on the massage table. On another, Violet walked into one of the bathrooms to find Lyle, shorts down, sitting on the toilet giving instructions to a young Chinese assistant. Violet has been caught in nothing more than a bath towel twice.

Lyle says, 'What's the problem? Privacy is not a concept that billions of Chinamen understand.'

So Violet is wrapped in a thick white robe, knowing the risks of being naked at this hour of the morning. Su'a nods at her, unsmiling, and takes the sweat towel from around Lyle's neck. She has never seen him smile, not once, as if he's been given the role of grumpy genie and won't relax until the director says 'Cut'. He has densely striped tattoos around his arms, which are repeated around his thighs. (When Lyle goes into a pool or hot tub, Su'a goes too.) The Tongan now walks from room to room, turning on every television in the suite. There are nine. Lyle likes the sound of televisions. He says they help him to focus his mind. The screen in a cabinet in the bedroom is showing the face of a decorated soldier, a general perhaps, who is explaining something to his audience in the deadpan drone of a station guard.

'Okay, boss?' Su'a asks when he returns.

Lyle gives him a distracted wave as he flips through the stash of newspapers on the sideboard and extracts *The South China Morning Post.* Su'a backs down the hallway and into the private gym, where he will lift weights until Lyle needs him again. Even there, ten metres away, he will leave the door open.

The tips of Lyle's ears and nose are bright pink from the cold. Sweat forms a damp V on the grey cotton of his chest. According to his usual habit, he has already been awake for three hours trouble-shooting the New York afternoon. And he will trouble-shoot LA for the next few before moving on to Asia. He spends most of his days like this, in virtual afternoons and virtual office complexes, even though in reality he is never far from a luxurious hotel room, the inside of a limo, plane, gym, pool, restaurant or a masseur's touch.

The butler hovers. He is a young man with the austere face of a Tibetan monk. 'Run me a shower, thanks, Jun.' Lyle peruses the headlines and then throws the paper down. Only now does he acknowledge Violet. 'Two guys are coming up to give me a massage soon. Do you want to join in?'

'I've been kneaded and pummelled every day. I feel like a loaf of bread that won't rise.'

'So ask for a gentler treatment. It's good for you. Gets the juices flowing.'

'You haven't forgotten you're taking me to the Forbidden City this morning? The guide is coming here in an hour.'

'Count me out. Carl can go.'

Violet is not happy. 'But you've been to Beijing six times already and you haven't seen it!' This fact is shocking.

'Make this the seventh.'

'But it's supposed to be magnificent.'

'Not today.'

'You only see the inside of hotel rooms. That can't be fun.'

'I'm not here for fun, Violet. Go with Carl and come back and tell me all about it. I've got a conference call with Bill at nine fifteen.'

Bill. Two days ago Lyle had handed her the telephone saying 'say hello to Bill'. When that creamy Alabaman drawl came down the line, even she knew who it was.

'Well, who is this?' Bill purred.

Violet said her name. 'Mr President,' she added.

'Young lady, from your accent it does not sound like I am *your* President,' he said. A pause while he was waiting for her to say something and then a chuckle, 'You look after Lyle, now. He's a good buddy of mine.' And that's all there was to it.

'We'll wait for you.'

Lyle gives her a quizzical smile. 'You really want me to come with you?'

'Of course.'

'I'm a bore on excursions. Or so people tell me.'

'That's because you won't relax.'

'I can't afford to relax.' He picks up a copy of *Newsweek*. 'You go ahead with Carl.'

'Does that mean you promise to follow?'

He shows a straight line of white porcelain. 'Following is not my style.' And then he is gone to the bathroom, taking the magazine with him.

Violet throws a pillow on the floor in frustration. She can't stand Carl and she's fairly sure the sentiment is mutual, even though he's in constant need of an audience and she is better than no one at all. In the beginning, she made the mistake of laughing faintly at his sour witticisms, which are always made at someone else's cost, usually some poor underling who can't fight back. Now he views her as complicit and even though she tells him point blank when he's gone too far, her discomfort simply goads him on.

She tried to explain this to Lyle one afternoon, but he was unmoved. 'I want you to stick with Carl. He'll take care of you.'

'I don't need a babysitter.'

'That may be so. But you need a chaperone.'

'But—'

'End of conversation.'

During the day, Lyle is often distant with her, like this. She doesn't think it's anything to do with discretion – after all, she is obviously *in situ*, wandering the suite at will, a very definite shape beneath the covers while assistants discuss business strategy. She has her own bedroom but she sleeps in his bed at night. He rarely asks her to make herself scarce, even when the conversation turns confidential. He speaks to his wife on the phone in her presence and always ends the conversation with 'love you too'. Sometimes she feels invisible, or nothing more than an entry in his agenda that needs to be ticked off. In the evening, he rarely dines with her, leaving that privilege to Carl. He doesn't apologise for this. When she asks where he is going, he always replies 'a tedious banquet'.

She comforts herself with the knowledge that coolness is Lyle's default mode. It's a sleight of hand that Violet is only just starting to recognise. Denial is power. He who demands to be pleased finds many, many people willing to give him pleasure, from the tailors who come in to fit his golf clothes to the Saudi prince who sends him trained falcons and the women – other men's wives, divorcées, princesses, social climbers, actresses, newsreaders, game show hostesses, croupiers, models, beauticians, shopgirls, callgirls high and low – who she knows, thanks to Carl, have bent their bodies for him. And the smallest gesture from him in return – a warm handshake, an effusive thank you, a generous tip, a violent orgasm – is treated by the recipient like a prize. Violet has seen the bellhops beam when they open the door of the limo for Lyle, watched porters stumble over each other for the privilege of carrying his luggage. (There is probably some poor drudge, down in the bowels of the hotel's laundry, who feels blessed to wash the semen off his sheets.) But he deals out his approval sparingly, making it all the more precious.

He comes home from the 'banquet' and expects her to be there. He is never interested in what she has done, where she has gone. It irritates her that he assumes she has done nothing worthy of his attention, that her days consist entirely of shopping and eating – which, because Carl has his way, is usually the case. Yesterday, she greeted him wearing a spectacular strand of green-grey South Sea pearls that Carl chose for her from a stall at the Pearl Market. Lyle's comment was offhand. 'They're nice. Did I buy them for you?' Tens of thousands of his dollars around her neck and it hardly raised a heartbeat.

But the sex is different. Although he is sometimes distracted, he is always grateful. This sentiment is unexpected. And flattering. Violet dares to think they have an intimacy that goes beyond this strange arrangement that has been negotiated without words. For she knows *something* has been negotiated, that there are underlying rules governing this relationship. She's not stupid, she can work out most of it. But what is going to happen after Beijing? This worries her more than she cares to admit.

She puts the thought out of her mind. Time to get up. She steps out of bed onto a monogrammed linen mat and wanders to the window to look at the day. Sixteen floors down, a lone speck of a person is practising Tai Chi in the courtyard of an old building that has been partly demolished. The city stretches out before her, a hazy infinity of pale high-rise apartment buildings and red cranes. Somewhere out there is the Gobi Desert – and not too far, judging by the yellow dust that chokes the landscape.

There's a cough and she turns to find the butler waiting silently.

'Yes, thanks, Jun.' That means she's ready for her shower. In Lyle's world you don't ever turn on things – even taps – yourself.

In Lyle's world, there is always someone waiting to give you pleasure.

She finds this quite wonderful.

The guide is a student called Li, who is dressed in jeans and a black and white fur jacket that might be made from baby panda. 'Is that cat, kitten?' Carl asks as he is introduced. He is wearing a Russian-style mink hat, bug-eye sunglasses and a leopard-print poncho thrown over his motorcycle leathers. Violet eyes off her companions and regrets wearing pony skin boots. Standing together in the White Cloud Palace's circular driveway they might be mistaken for a petting zoo.

Carl is in a foul mood. 'Where are we going?' he asks crankily as he slides after her into the back seat of the hotel's Rolls-Royce.

'The Forbidden City.'

'For God's sake, all those miles of cloisonné! Let's go to Liulichang instead and find some gorgeous antique to buy.'

'All we do is shop.'

'You don't mind it when Lyle is paying.'

She turns away and looks out the window. Carl's observation is an arrow that strikes her conscience. She feels guilty for accepting Lyle's extravagance. She thinks of the cost of supporting a child for a year in Namibia: her pearl necklace alone could sustain thousands of lives. And then she pushes the thought away. She can do more for the children as Lyle's mistress than she can do for them stuck in a cubicle in a shabby Melbourne office. When she gets back to the hotel, she will talk him into writing a cheque.

The Forbidden City consists of many palaces and halls. Each hall has its own gate and massive courtyard, which, Li tells them, can hold one hundred thousand people, like a sort of lobby where people await audience with the Emperor. They traipse across courtyards, up grand flights of marble stairs and peer into huge reception rooms with filigree panelled walls, carved and gilded ceilings and lavish thrones entwined with ferocious dragons. From the terrace of the Hall of Supreme Harmony, built high on colossal pillars, Violet looks across the rooftops of hundreds of adjacent buildings – temples, libraries, vaults that stored gold and silks, and living quarters – all with ancient terracotta tiles and peaked roofs that seem to her like the rough scales of a dormant dragon lying in wait for the next tasty political dynasty.

'Eight hundred buildings, nine thousand nine hundred and ninety-nine rooms,' Li explains proudly, noting Violet's amazement. 'Ten thousand rooms in Heaven, so Emperor has one less in this life.'

'So, tell us what's "forbidden" about it,' demands Carl.

'City forbidden to common people for five hundred years. Only for Emperor and court. All of China governed from within these walls. During Cultural Revolution Premier Zhou Enlai save palace from Red Guard. So now all people can enjoy.'

'I don't mean that. Tell us all the *dirty* stuff.'

Li looks puzzled. 'Dirty?'

'Oh, come on, honey. Surely they tell you *something* useful in guide school. Didn't the Emperor have sex with hundreds of concubines?'

'Yes, many wives and consorts,' says Li. 'Also in Ming Dynasty many elephants.'

'He liked sex with animals?'

'No, not for sex.' Li's face is flushed. 'Elephant dung good for concubines' hair.'

'That's a lot of shit for hairdos.'

'Nine thousand handmaidens serving at court in Ming Dynasty. Emperor keeps names of all wives and consorts on jade tablets. When Emperor want particular woman he turn over her name. Eunuch then deliver naked concubine wrapped in gold silk at Emperor's feet.'

'Remind me to tell Lyle about that one,' Carl says to Violet. 'I'll make sure his *next* woman is delivered that way.'

She can't disguise the look of dismay that crosses her face.

'You want to see concubines' rooms?' Li asks, oblivious to the exchange.

Carl gives Violet a snaky smile, cheered up by making such

a direct hit on her emotions. 'My friend over here is *desperate* to. I think she's having a past-life experience.'

As Li leads them towards the low buildings that housed the women of the court, Carl digs his fingers into Violet's upper arm and they drop back. 'You're not expecting he'll take you back to New York, are you?'

'I don't expect anything from him.' Violet extracts his fingers from her flesh.

'Then that's very smart, kitten. He's already supporting a couple of mistresses. Bibi won't tolerate more than two.'

'Why should you care what happens?'

They have stopped in a narrow courtyard. Carl makes a gesture to their escorts to move away from them. He smiles at Violet as if they're chatting about lunch. 'I like to be sure no woman gets too big for her boots. I've seen every type.'

'And what type am I?'

'The innocent, oh-I've-never-done-this-before type.'

'I *have* never done this before.'

'Oh, no? Then why were you with that Báthory character in Vienna? If you're in the company of a well-known gigolo, you're either game or *on* the game, if you know what I mean.'

'Did Florin say something to you?' So she was right, he *had* set her up.

'He said you knew the rules.'

'What rules?'

'Oh, come on, kitten. I'm not born yesterday. And neither is Lyle. You're lucky you were Lyle's type or I'd never have gone near a woman associated with that phoney count.'

'I'm telling you, I'm not "associated" with him. If you really want to know he stole all my money.'

'You wouldn't be the first.'

'You seem to know all about him.'

'I don't know *all*. I know two women who have fucked him and given him money. I've heard the blow-by-blow descriptions. He managed to get himself invited onto Lyle's yacht one summer. And I know about the scandal at Zürs. I'm sure you could fill in the rest of the details.'

'What scandal at Zürs?'

Carl makes the gesture of slashing his wrists.

Some woman killed herself over him? Violet feels sick.

Before she can ask any more Li comes over to them. 'This is house for old concubines. Emperor take care of all of them until they die.'

They peer into dusty rooms, the beds covered with faded embroidery, the side tables laden with ivory combs, jade cups and tarnished bronze inkwells, the walls decorated with watermarked silk and mouldy scrollwork. Violet tries to imagine a time when the rooms would not look so forlorn. But perhaps the women who were confined to them were always forlorn. She thinks again of the unknown woman who has killed herself over Florin and imagines her lying on a faded bed, blood draining from her wrists.

On a cushion on one low divan rests a pair of tiny, pointed slippers in red and black silk.

'In 1912 lotus foot banned,' Li explains. 'In old days, toes broken and bound with cloth to keep foot three inches long. Emperor of Sung dynasty want all women to walk like ballet dancer. These days only very old grandmother still have lotus foot. Factories do not make small shoes any more.'

'Why did the Emperor like the foot to be curved like that?' Violet asks Li.

'Sign of great beauty.'

'That's not what I heard,' Carl interrupts. 'He liked it because he could get more friction when he rubbed his schlong on the soles of his concubines' feet.' He makes an unmistakable gesture. Li blushes crimson.

Violet walks away in disgust. She's had enough. She doesn't know what Lyle sees in Carl. He's neither discreet nor diplomatic. She can no longer bear to be in his company and she no longer cares what Lyle insists.

She wanders into a garden planted with brutally pruned, gnarled trees. As she stands pondering the irony of a sign posted in a square of dirt that reads *Please don't pick the flowers,* Carl catches up with her.

'Counting your blessings?' he asks.

'What do you mean?' She refuses to look at him.

'Lucky for you Lyle isn't a Ming emperor.'

'Lucky for you too,' she responds. 'Didn't you hear? As Lyle's court eunuch, you would've had to carry your balls around your neck in that bag.'

'Touché.'

'And another thing.' Emboldened, she now looks him straight in the eye. 'The Emperor kept his courtesans for life. So don't expect me to be going anywhere soon.'

The Rolls-Royce is waiting for them near the moat at the back of the old city. While Carl is trying in vain to extricate a phone number from the young guard, Violet tells Li she wants to walk back to the hotel. Li is not happy about losing her charge but Violet mollifies her by pretending a knowledge of Beijing's streets that she doesn't have. Li writes in Chinese characters on the back of a business card *Please take me to the White Cloud Palace* and hands it to Violet.

She slips away without Carl noticing. She has a vague idea of direction from the slow limousine ride and an illustrated map of the area from the hotel. She strides out, enjoying the freedom of being alone. People call out to her, wanting to practice their English, but she smiles without stopping and her flat boots leave them in her wake.

In an alleyway, she stops at a little restaurant decorated with flags and points to a bowl of noodle soup. She sits at a formica table and eats. The food is delicious. The waiter, smiling through broken teeth, brings her a plate of dumplings to try. When she gets up to leave, he presents her with a stick of dried cicadas. Is she supposed to eat it? The waiter nods and makes a chomping motion. The cicada legs crunch in her mouth. As soon as the waiter is out of sight, she spits them out into a rubbish bin.

So entranced is she by the sights and smells of the city, only her feet give any indication that she's been walking for hours. She is unaware of the time until the night starts coming down. She consults her map. She has walked in a circle – the hotel is only a few minutes away. But still she doesn't feel the need to hurry. It can't be later than six and Lyle is rarely back before seven. And certainly she's in no hurry to get back to Carl.

Her eye is caught by a tiny café with a window display of wrapped sweets and glazed buns.

As she hesitates, deciding whether to go in, she sees reflected behind her the implacable shapes of two police officers, their faces grey and blank as cement.

'This is outrageous,' Violet says, flinging off her coat. 'Where's Lyle?'

Su'a bends his thick neck in the direction of the gym. It hasn't escaped Violet's notice that he has slipped some folded notes to the police officers at the door.

Lyle is working on one of the exercise machines he had especially delivered to his suite, his arms in straps. When Violet storms into the room, followed by the bodyguard, he doesn't miss a beat in his routine.

'You have no right sending those police to look for me!'

'Half the metropolitan police force, in fact,' Lyle says calmly.

'It's not anyone's business where I am.'

'It's my business. You might have been kidnapped.'

'Don't be ridiculous. I was just doing some sightseeing.'

'You put us all in jeopardy. I can do without the complication of a ransom.'

'No one is going to kidnap me. This is China. Not . . . *Russia.*'

'I'll be the judge of that. I told you to stay with Carl for a reason.'

'Well, he's racist and sexist and I'm simply not going to.'

'That's just Carl. You're too sensitive.' Lyle lets go of the straps and Su'a steps forward to wipe his face with a towel. His tone is now conciliatory. 'You can eat dinner by yourself in the suite tonight if you like. Carl can come with me.'

'You mean, I'm a prisoner?'

'Not at all. But you might like an early night. We have a flight to Hong Kong the first thing in the morning and then we're going to London the day after. Jun is packing for you. So just relax – send out for a pedicure or something you like.'

'Why London?'

'John Major is about to call an election. We need to make sure our interests are taken care of.'

'Am I an interest to be taken care of?' she asks.

She doesn't need an answer.

THE HEAVEN AND EARTH HOTEL
Salisbury Road, Kowloon, Hong Kong

Although Lyle intends to be in Hong Kong for only one night, teams of guards, removalists and interior designers are employed to unload his plane and bring everything – exercise machines, artworks, reference library, trunks of clothing – to the new hotel, where they work all day decorating the twenty-fifth-floor suite to his taste. Lyle is not pleased that the Presidential Suite is occupied that night by an actual president, so the hotel management makes amends by moving the larger suite's baby grand piano into the Harbour Suite on the floor below and sending up a crate of Dom Perignon. Violet thinks the name of the hotel is perfectly apt – Lyle's minions and the hotel staff are moving heaven and earth to keep him happy.

While all this is happening, Lyle goes straight to his meeting, Carl takes a car across to the main island where malls of designer goods beckon and Violet is handed over to the therapists in the hotel's rooftop spa, where she is led away in a white robe like a disturbed child being admitted to a particularly luxurious asylum.

When she returns to the suite Carl is back, supervising the hanging of paintings. He's wearing a ghastly pink vinyl jacket, obviously new. He's clearly expecting her to exclaim over it, but she says nothing.

Her clothes have been unpacked and are hanging in a dressing room off the master bedroom. She chooses a deep blue cocktail dress she has worn twice before. It looks good with the sapphire earrings. She fastens around her neck a triple strand of champagne pearls Carl had chosen for her in Beijing. Then she changes her mind and takes them off. Perhaps Lyle, noticing her bare throat, might buy her the necklace of sapphires and diamonds in the Harry Winston display window in the lobby.

She is learning that the judicious comment, made casually, brings certain rewards. She only needs to express a desire and it is fulfilled. *Within reason* she thinks. And then she banishes the thought. Reason hasn't come into it yet. She'll drop a comment about the necklace into the dinner conversation tonight and it will be on her pillow in the morning.

She is coming to accept that the jewels and clothes are simply part of the bargain. She is making Lyle happy, which is not an easy thing. And the more he responds with lavish gifts, the more she feels her value. She discovers that it is not necessarily a demeaning thing to have a price on your head.

In the harbour-view room, a butler is laying out champagne glasses on a tray. Lyle is hosting cocktails tonight and this time he expects her to be there. She's looking forward to it, in fact. It is her chance to be beautiful and smart for him, to charm his business associates, to have him admire her as a woman of intelligence and style.

In the hairdresser, while fingers caress her hair with Fijian coconut oil, she reads a magazine feature on the handover of Hong Kong to China in less than three months' time. Surely this will be the big topic of conversation over drinks. She wants to dazzle Lyle with her shrewd and witty observations about the socio-economic climate, her innate good sense of politics, her grasp of the implications for the future of international relations. Good practice for the glittering salons of London, she thinks, where Lyle will surely expect her to perform. And for later, when she presides over his yachts and villas and has Madeleine Albright to tea. She sees herself as stepping out of a suburban frame and into a pretty picture of high society. Like a good hostess she plumps a cushion and points out to the butler a silver knife that isn't perfectly polished. She likes to please, the role seems natural to her, having been raised to think of others before herself.

The guests start arriving at seven and Lyle is still not back from his meeting. Violet glides from conversation to conversation easily, a picture of fascinated concentration as names she's never heard of before wash over her . . . DVD, AOL, Amazon-dot-com, Starbucks, Gameboy, SUV, Tony Blair, Taliban, Viagra, Trainspotting, Deep Blue. She is aware that a few of the male guests are hanging on her every word. When she gives a tentative opinion about the handover one civil servant looks at her with so much admiration she feels like Margaret Thatcher. Carl has absented himself from the suite to take a telephone call and so she alone has kept the party running smoothly.

She is pleased with the way she has handled things and when Lyle finally comes in, cool and apologetic, with both Su'a and Carl by his side, she hopes he notices how she holds the centre of the room with a court of besotted admirers. But he looks bleak under his diplomatic smile and barely acknowledges her. Carl, on the other hand, gives her a big wink, which worries her more.

She hardly speaks to Lyle during the party and over dinner at Felix she is placed a few seats away from him, across the table from a diplomat's wife who dominates the conversation at that end with stories about her Thai cook's amorous liaisons. It's only when they're back in the suite that she can ask him what's wrong.

He doesn't look surprised at the question. 'Nothing,' he shrugs. 'Business.'

The servants have retired. She pours a whisky from the sideboard and brings the glass to him. She knows better than to push it. 'I liked your friend from the telecommunications company . . . Kennedy Chan, isn't it? Did you know that they're working on phones that can take photographs?'

Lyle grunts. His black mood hasn't shifted.

'Of course you did,' she says brightly, kicking off her thousand-dollar shoes and curling up on the sofa beside him. 'I suppose you've got the patent on it.'

She's starting to think that he might have been jealous of the young entrepreneur's attention to her, when he says brusquely, 'Let's fuck.'

He puts his glass down and his hand is cold as it slides up her bare leg. 'Get those titties out.'

Not for the first time is she jolted by his crudeness. Sophisticated in every other way, he has the sexual manners of a tenth-grader.

She unzips her dress and does what he asks. Her body has never really been engaged in this. But she likes to see him happy – no, to see that *she* makes him happy. There's a difference.

The eyes of the buildings across the harbour blink back at her as he nuzzles her breasts. She wonders if someone over there has a telescope trained on them, on her open thighs and his hand, gobbed with saliva, fingering her wet. When he enters her she grunts – a sound he likes, echoing his forcefulness – and the neon horizon smudges to a blur. When she opens her eyes again, he's finished.

'It's that damn table-lamp,' he explains as he withdraws. 'It's so fucking ugly.'

She smooths down her dress and pushes her damp nipples back into the bra. 'Do you want another drink? Or shall we go to bed? Do we have to leave for London early?'

He rearranges his shorts and zips up his trousers. 'You're to stay here.'

She doesn't understand. 'What do you mean?'

He sighs, as if it's a chore to explain. 'I won't have time for you in London. Something has come up.'

The news devastates her. 'What has come up?'

'Don't worry about anything. I've arranged for you to stay in this suite the rest of the week. Do whatever you like. I'll take care of it.'

'And then what? Are you coming back?'

'No. I'm back in New York.'

'Will I meet you there?'

'I'll send word.'

'What word?'

'You'll be looked after.'

'I don't need to be *looked after*.'

He stoops to pick up her knickers and hands them to her. It's the first time she has ever seen him pick up anything. 'The sapphires you mentioned – will those make you happy?' It's not a question. It's a signing-off.

He must see the hurt in her eyes because he reaches out and chucks her affectionately under the chin.

'Pity,' he says, shaking his head. 'I could have kept you, Violet.'

'It's Bibi, kitten,' Carl whispers in her ear the next morning before following Lyle out the door. 'She's decided out of the blue to join him in London. She's only protecting her investment, you know. Bibi only puts up with so much. He can do what he likes at this end of the world. But London is too close to home. Don't look so miserable. You've done okay out of it.'

And she has.

She wanders aimlessly through the suite when they're gone, running her fingers over the silk furnishings, idly plucking the petals off roses, flipping through coffee table books, turning the TVs on and off. The walls, the bed, the bathrooms are so efficiently stripped of every sign of Lyle that she doubts even a crime scene technician could find any trace.

What is left, though, is hers.

She opens the cupboard doors and surveys what is there. Does she really own this many things? There are capes with sequins on them, tweedy suits, languid evening dresses, a chubby grey fur – things she would never have imagined herself wearing. While she has chosen a few things for herself, much of it is stuff that Carl has had sent up. She counts nineteen pairs of shoes, dozens of sets of lacy lingerie, Chinese satin nightgowns in every colour, five cashmere sweaters, trousers in every weight, fine silk stockings and pantyhose, ribboned orange boxes of Hermès scarves, a mink hat, a chinchilla cap and a green felt stetson by Philip Treacy, five bikinis, seven handbags, bottles of expensive skin lotions and gold compacts of pressed colour, and silk-lined boxes of pearls, rings, bracelets and earrings, including the blue sapphire ones she received for signing on and the matching necklace she was given this morning for signing off.

Now she sounds like Florin, reducing everything to a transaction.

But it has been a transaction. She estimates she has been paid, in kind, almost half a million dollars for a few sexual acts. If she were Florin, she'd think it reasonable compensation. And, really, how badly has she been harmed? Be honest with yourself, Violet. Lyle dazzled you. It wasn't love. His wife demanded him back, what's unusual about that? In your old life, your old morality, you'd think it was right and just. Maybe you're lucky to get out of it like this, with only a slight dent to your ego. No bruises, no psychological damage. None at all.

The Chinese emperor's concubines were required to have all the little bones broken on their feet. By comparison, she is doing well.

She closes the six wardrobe doors. There's a leather travel envelope sitting on the dressing table. Inside, there's a Cathay voucher and a bundle of $1000 notes. She counts out twenty of them. Lyle has told her to charge everything to the room, so this must be change for tips. Again, she thinks of Florin, and the white dress that was never paid for. How small-minded she has been! Florin was right – rich people do this all the time. And what right have people lower on the food chain – shop assistants, waiters, concierges – to question them?

She wonders where Florin is, the need for him to be there stuck like a needle into a pressure point. She has the desire to show off what she has, to show what a good apprentice she has been.

She takes two of the notes and puts them into her newest handbag, a black quilted Chanel. She might as well explore the city before she gets on a plane and goes back to Melbourne.

Melbourne. She imagines Patrick's face at the airport and how his jaw will drop when he sights the Vuitton trunks and her fur coat and the way her neck and ears are laced with sapphires. (She'll be travelling first class of course.) She will be evasive about it all, brush aside his questions, allow him to think it is Luka who has lavished her with gifts.

But why is she thinking of Patrick? Why should she ever think of him again? There will be other men like Lyle. She has an idea of her value now.

She catches herself in the mirror, one manicured hand on the

Chanel bag, the other clutching a wad of notes. She smiles at the sight – the first big, genuine smile that has crossed her face for a while. Only a few weeks ago she might not have liked this woman. But a few weeks ago she did not like herself. Now she understands how small-minded she has been. There is no shame in being desired by men. And there is no need to fear them.

Bloody hell, Violet, she thinks, *look at you. You're a woman of the world. A glamour puss. A style queen. A sex bomb. Will you ever settle for an ordinary life again?*

The answer, of course, is no.

In the lobby that evening she sits at a small table with a bottle of Crystal in a bucket beside her. She is dressed in black pants and a purple silk shirt, which looks wonderful with her hair. She is wearing little jewellery, not wishing to overdo it. Her high-heeled shoes are new, the bottoms unscuffed. (The size stickers peeled off.) Her nails are pale pink shells, her make-up is minimal. The champagne has given her large eyes a dreamy look.

Why is she there? What is she looking for? Sex? Love? A little companionship?

Men hover, seeking a sign, a way into her heart, an answer to the question.

Even she doesn't know it.

When one of them finally stops and asks, 'Are you waiting for me?' her answer is very simple.

Perhaps.

GRAND HOTEL RIVIERA

Boulevard de la Croisette, Cannes, France

The moment we enter the villa in Haute Cannes, our host, a garrulous British entertainment lawyer, puts his hand familiarly on my rump. I am wearing a sexy blue gown from Yves Saint-Laurent Rive Gauche that Charles has bought me this afternoon and I'm aware of the stir I make as we arrive. But Charles suddenly doesn't want to show me off and excuses himself to speak to the first acquaintance who waves. I suppose he is awkward about being seen in public with a young woman after such a long time.

I am wrong.

At the pre-dinner drinks I get stuck in a corner with two social writers from *Hola!* who mistake me for a starlet with a tarnished reputation. When we sit at our table in the garden, I am placed between a small, intense actor with a knighthood, who promptly turns away from me and spends the whole evening talking to the woman on his right, who is a documentary filmmaker, and a fat, sleepy-eyed American producer who tucks his napkin into his collar, slurps his Puligny Montrachet as if it is Fanta and only addresses the table when the subject of weekend grosses comes up.

Charles sits across from me and hardly looks in my direction. After dessert, I get up from my chair on the pretext of going to the bathroom and stand behind him, with my hands on his shoulders. He reaches up and puts his hand on top of one of mine but continues talking as if I weren't there. I become so angry with him, I don't return to the table but stalk off into the tropical garden, which is all spiky cacti and malevolent blooms, lit by flares.

I follow a path down the hill to the swimming pool and stay there, dangling my feet in the cool water, until a posse of drunken publicists disturbs my peace by stripping off and throwing themselves in. One of them, astonishingly unembarrassed by his pelt of black back-hair, keeps splashing and taunting me in the hope I'll join them. I leave when he finds a pal to threaten to pull me in.

Charles is nowhere to be found when I go back up the hill. The guests have mostly deserted their tables, although the fat American is in residence at ours, eating his second chocolate tart. (Mine.) We've been given red crystal Baccarat hearts as gifts and some of them have been abandoned, glinting in the torchlight like offal on dissecting tables. The waiters are clearing the crockery when an orchestra strikes up on the terrace above the garden. I look up and see Charles steer a woman away from the railing and onto the dance floor. I think I recognise her but, needless to say, she is the wife of a friend or someone with an equally impeccable reputation. We don't want to distress the British peers.

I am thinking up a strategy when a lanky, blond man of about fifty approaches. I avoid eye contact as he makes a beeline towards me but I can't help noticing he's wearing blue jeans and cowboy boots with his white tuxedo and I assume he's Californian. I have already pre-judged him by the time he reaches me and asks, 'How is it a beautiful woman like you is standing here all alone?' His syntax is awkward, but perhaps that's because he is not from LA as I'd assumed, but is a Scandinavian of undetermined nationality. They have a giant cookie-cutter up there which presses out men of an unrelenting sameness, all about six-foot-four, sandy-haired, pink-cheeked and with flat grey eyes onto which everything is projected but nothing transmitted. This one is no different, except that he has a diamond in one ear – of a decent size, I might add – which suggests he is having a mid-life crisis.

I don't answer, so he tries again. 'May I get you a drink?'

'Drink, drink, drink,' I say facetiously, 'Is that all anyone thinks about?'

'You're a teetotaller?' His look is solicitous, as if I'd just announced a terminal illness.

'Not at all,' I say. 'I'd love a big, fat, neat vodka.'

Happily, he goes off to the bar and retrieves one for me.

'Thanks,' I say, taking the squat, cold glass. *'Sköll!'*

Delighted to clink glasses with me, he introduces himself as Mats Göransson.

I tell him my name. 'And what do you, Mats?'

'I have a little film production company. Solar Films, maybe you have heard of it?' He mentions three European films that apparently have been art-house successes.

'I don't keep up with film any more,' I say.

'But you're a friend of Charles?'

'You noticed.' I take another swig of vodka.

'How could I not?'

I empty my glass.

'I'll get you another.'

He returns with another glass, this time twice the size. I clink his again with abandon.

'Charles has told me a little about you,' he says.

'Oh, yes? Like what?' I feel myself becoming belligerent.

'He told me you had been his mistress.'

'That's very indiscreet of him.'

'He emphasised *former.*'

'Did he? The bastard.'

'You're upset by this?'

I look more closely at him. There is an undercurrent of expectation there, something deeper than a handsome Swedish film producer chatting up a glamorous redhead at a party. 'What else did Charles suggest about me?' I am thinking about Jeremy, actor, and the extremely unfortunate six weeks spent with him on location in Valencia eating oranges and dust. 'He didn't mention that I was a good travelling companion by any chance?'

'He thought we would like each other.'

Mats doesn't have to say any more. 'Excuse me for a moment,' I tell him, handing him my glass. 'I'll be right back.'

I find Charles upstairs, brandy balloon in hand, deep in conversation with a film director even I recognise, and the inevitable pump-lipped blonde. He looks a little apprehensive, sheepish, as I approach. But I never make a scene.

'Charles, darling, there you are,' I say brightly in my best impersonation of a British debutante. 'There's someone I'm simply *dying* for you to meet.'

I link my arm in his and draw him away to a quiet part of the balcony.

'Are you fobbing me off on that Swede?' I demand as soon as we are out of earshot.

'I thought you'd enjoy him.' The lights of the old port reflect in his glasses and I can't see his expression. But his tone is edgy.

'You said that when you passed me off on Jeremy.'

'Darling, I didn't "pass you off". I was only thinking of you. You don't want to be tied to an old man like me. There's what? Fifty years between us?'

Ever the gentleman, understating my age. And ever the old bastard, coating everything in sweet concern for others, when the core, the steel, is all about him. I am starting to remember some of the hard little peas of ugliness enfolded in the soft mattress of our two-year-long affair.

'I think I'm capable of making my own decisions about that.

I don't see you as any age.'

'That's lovely of you to say, my dear, but I know it's not true. *I* see my age and it disturbs me.'

'It didn't disturb you this morning.'

'Ah, but there you are wrong. Your kindness was very disturbing. You reminded me who I used to be.'

'I wasn't being kind. I enjoyed myself.'

'Now you're speaking like a sex worker or a nurse. One who performs a charitable service. I can't believe you find my old balls attractive.'

'I did five years ago. Why should I feel any different now?'

He sighs. 'You were as good a liar then as now. But, I was vain enough to go along with you then.'

'And now?'

'I made a mistake. And for that, I'm truly sorry, my dear.'

I don't buy the *mea culpa* business. 'I don't believe a word of this. You're a coward.'

'Perhaps I am.' There it is again, his way of agreeing and not agreeing at all.

'I thought we could travel together for a bit.'

He looks at me cagily. 'That might have been wishful thinking on your part.'

Now I am really mad. 'If you wanted a striptease you could have asked Hervé for the book.' The book of independent contractors, which all concierges will reveal for a palm of notes.

'I'm sorry, Violetta. I've made a mess of this. I don't want you to think that's all I wanted from you.'

'But it's pretty much come down to that, hasn't it? Now you've thrown that Swede at me.'

'Be reasonable. Sammy's coming tomorrow.'

'So you said.'

'It wouldn't do if you're there when she arrives. I know Mats is a nice man. And he's single. You need to look after yourself. This drifting life is not good for a woman your age.'

'You're not my parish priest, so lay off the spiritual advice.'

'If you ever need anything.'

'Now that's a brush-off I've heard before.'

'Many times, I suspect, my dear.'

'That was cruel,' I say calmly.

I don't ever make a scene. I just walk away.

The Swede is waiting for me, as I knew he would be.

'Okay, Mats,' I say, taking my glass. 'Let's get out of here.'

I have been well and truly handed over.

THE HERMITAGE

Avenue Montaigne, Paris, France

World renowned motivational guru Vincent London™ has many tattoos. A bleeding heart stains his chest with red ink, a dragon unfolds across his shoulders, an angel dances on one buttock, a samurai draws his sword across one bicep, a Japanese volcano is covered with pale blue snow on the other. At forty-one, Vince's skin is still taut and smooth as a teenager's and waxed hairless so that the picture book he wears over his torso can be admired in all its deforested splendour. In the first few minutes of his lectures the shirt always comes off, the ropes of his muscles and the dark blue of his pumped veins appearing like more doodles on the canvas of skin. The bleeding heart never fails to incite a collective gasp from his audience, as does the moment when he impishly lowers his pants to expose the dancing angel.

There is one tattoo most of his disciples have not seen (although a series of nudes of him in *Time Out* the year before revealed a goodly percentage). It is a quote from Balzac, inked in script under his navel:

In diving to the bottom of pleasure
We bring up more gravel than pearls.

'Something to read while you're blowing me, yeah?' is what Vincent always says to the women who find themselves in intimate circumstances with him and it is what he says to Violet as he unzips for her the first time.

'That would depend on whether I'm going to find gravel or pearls,' she responds.

He likes that.

Now, whenever he wants her to give him head, he says, 'Time to read the Balzac.'

His sexual vocabulary is so arcane it has taken Violet weeks to understand it. *I think I'll go on a hand diet. Want a facial? Why don't you roll the mink and I'll watch? Let's catch a buzz. I'm up for an old-fashioned. Open the back door. Time for a John Wayne.*

Right now, in the brocade-swagged confines of their Paris hotel bedroom, they are *having lunch*. Or, more correctly, Vince is having lunch and she is receiving it. Her knees lie open, the strings of her thong tangled around one ankle, while Vince laps at her like a feral creature at a honey pot. As soon as the orgasm rattles through her, he jumps astride her, hands compressing her breasts so that the space between them forms a silken chamber where he'll friction his cock like a piston. This is his *Russian* and when he comes he leaves a *necklace of pearls* around her neck.

These are not the only pearls he has given her.

Vincent sits back, panting, still straddling her, and rubs his hands through his damp brown hair, exposing the tortured figures from Dante's Inferno that shriek up the underside of both arms.

'Gawd, look at you,' he says in an east-London accent that waxes and wanes with his mood. 'I still can't get over how fuckin' white you are. Your skin's like bloody marble.'

'But I'm soft,' she protests, reaching for the edge of a sheet to wipe her chest. 'You can feel me if you like.'

'Do I need permission?' He shifts a leg and snakes that hand between her thighs. 'On second thoughts, the bits I like aren't that white at all.'

'If you keep going like that they'll be black and blue.'

'Too rough for you, yeah?'

'No.'

'That's my girl.'

The bedside phone buzzes.

'That will be your guests,' she says lazily. 'I warned you they'd be here on time.'

His hand probes deeper. 'Will we invite them up?'

'No.'

'They might be cute.'

'What if they are?'

'We could triple our pleasure.'

'If I tripled my pleasure I'd explode.'

'I'd like to see that, yeah?' He picks up the phone: 'Send 'em up.'

'Time to get dressed,' she says, moving away from him.

He looks at her body regretfully. 'Yeah, but don't put too much on.'

Violet takes a surreptitious look at the diamond-studded hands of her platinum watch and stifles a yawn. It's 12:15 a.m. Vincent's guests, a French publisher and his novelist girlfriend, look to be settling in for the night. The publisher has slouched into the leather cushions, legs crossed – exposing bright pink socks – his arm loosely around the back of the sofa. His girlfriend is leaning forward, intently emptying a bottle of 1982 Cheval Blanc into her glass, a clove cigarette clamped firmly between her pale, thin lips. She sloshes some of the ruby liquid on a coffee-table book about Versailles and stares at the mess, momentarily puzzled, before lurching back on to the sofa, sticky glass in hand, where she closes her eyes and begins humming to a soundtrack in her mind. She is not entirely sober. Violet thinks she recognises the Macarena by the series of grunts, although this might be because it's still in her head from their brief visit to the Queen nightclub earlier.

She can see Vincent thinks they *are* cute.

He is entertaining them with one of his passionate rants, this time about a new children's book that has just been published in the UK, something about a young wizard and a philosopher's stone. She and Vincent have spent the last two weeks cruising the Mediterranean as guests of the American bond trader who bankrolls Vince's lectures in the United States. While she kept her white skin out of the sun, Vince lay on the daybed on the prow of the yacht and barely said a word until he'd finished the thick volume. Now he is berating his publisher friend for missing out on the French translation rights to the novel, which he pronounces the most brilliant piece of escapism since the Bible.

Violet has heard this monologue several times in the past few days. Vince becomes enamoured with something until he exhausts it. Before this book, he was obsessed with the music of some American guy, Puff Daddy, and before that it was Japanese anime cartoons and before that new British Prime Minister Tony Blair. She can see the publisher is entranced, as everyone who meets Vince is entranced. When he talks, to a publisher and his smashed girlfriend in a hotel room or to a crowd of thousands of people gathered at a wrestling stadium, this slight middle-aged man with the bounce of a teenager has the ability to make every person listening think he is totally focused on *them*. ('Just the gift of the gab, eh?' he will say to anyone who asks.)

Gift of the gab. That's an understatement. His seminars – £3200 a weekend – are revival meeting, rock concert and shopping excursion in one. He can sell anything, it seems – confidence, penitence, videos, books, audio tapes, T-shirts, coffee mugs, posters and thousands of copies of his single, 'Beat Me or Believe Me', which shot to number two on the British charts the year before, just behind The Spice Girls' 'Wannabe'.

Tonight, with his shirt on, he looks feckless, a cocky rogue you might find hanging around a pool hall chatting up the barmaid, out of place in the plush confines of the Belle Époque suite. But on stage he transmogrifies into a half-naked, oil-slicked, sweat-dripping demon, playing to vast stadiums of head-swaying zombies, cleansed of their own free will. Violet has seen him perform, once, in Bangkok, and, standing backstage, she felt the thrill of his language shiver through her body.

He talked her into bed with him obscenely quickly. 'Come on,' he had told her in the Zuk Bar at the Sukhothai, where they met, 'no harm in a little slumming.' She thought he was a bit of a sleaze, a spiv, a con artist, a shyster. (Has she really changed her mind?) And he seemed to encourage the impression. He took her to a cheap noodle bar and she thought he was not the kind of man she was looking for, until he talked her up to one of several suites he had booked in the Oriental Hotel, and then she knew he was.

He's a character all right, this Vince. His past is shady. Ex-crim or incorrigible phoney? In the 'Ring of Fire' speech, which is the centrepiece of his performance (accompanied by the Johnny Cash track), he relates his personal Road to Damascus (a criminal past, an arson gone wrong, a spiritual and psychological awakening while surrounded by leaping flames). A profile in *The Times* magazine failed to shed any light on a police record, although it did uncover two terms spent at the Chelsea College of Art & Design. When Violet first asked him about it – did he *really* set fire to a factory and escape from the flames unscarred (the proof of which necessitates the taking off of his shirt in front of thousands of people)? – he gave her a wink and said, 'What we see depends on what we look for, love,' parroting a pivotal quote in one of his stock speeches.

She watches him now, the way he pokes holes into the air in front of him as he talks. There are blue numbers hacked into three knuckles on each hand: 655 on the right hand and 321 on the other. When she asked him about it, that first night, he said, obliquely, 'It's a prisoner number, love.' She assumed, still assumes, this to be *his* prisoner number, although fans of *A Clockwork Orange* would not be so easily misled.

More than once over the past several weeks, she has asked herself, *What am I doing here?* But she knows the answer. He is greedy. He wants the best. And having paid for it, it bores him. So he wants *more* of the best. And he likes sharing it . . . he *loves* sharing it. He shares it with her.

While Violet has been musing, the subject has turned away from Harry Potter. Vincent has recently become enamoured with a brand of coffee from Seattle. 'Yeah, but it's fuckin brilliant,' he is saying. 'Who'd have ever thought someone would sex-up coffee, right?'

The publisher feels obliged to mount a defence of the French brew against this company called Starbucks.

'Nah, mate,' Vince dismisses him. 'They opened a shop in Japan last year. You mark my words, there'll be one on the Champs-Élysées before the fuckin' millennium.'

Vince's monologue is just warming up, spivvy accent thickening, especially now he has a fully engaged audience of one. (The girlfriend has fallen sideways on the sofa, asleep, like a downed skittle.) In this, he is egalitarian – he doesn't care whether he's addressing a thousand acolytes or a solitary person with an hour or two to spare. She's seen him bail up unsuspecting shopkeepers, porters, flight attendants and panhandlers and bestow on them the wisdom of his latest thought bubble, whether they want it or not. It's equal-opportunity bullying, she thinks. ('Crap,' he replied when she suggested this. 'They'd have to pay for it otherwise. I'm doin them a favour, yeah?')

She's jittery for his attention to be turned to *her.* She wants these French people to go. She could retire to bed, but Vince would only wake her up at 4 or 5 a.m., aroused by the husky cadences of his own voice, and play her until dawn. She hates being woken from sleep.

Restless, she gets up from her chair. The windows are flung open to take in the mild August air. The penthouse's terrace looks towards the Eiffel Tower to the right, across the river Seine. Vince's voice carries to the balcony, but the whoosh of traffic beside the river is like a paintbrush stroking out the sound.

But no sooner has she stepped on to the terrace when a muffled explosion sends sound waves that are almost palpable through the air. She jumps in fright, nearly stumbling into the glass. She steadies herself and steps quickly back into the room.

Vince is still talking as if nothing has happened.

'Didn't you hear that?' she asks him. Her heart feels as if it has flipped over, like a pancake.

He looks up. 'No, love. What didn't I hear?'

'There was an explosion.'

'It is just the Algerians,' says the publisher coolly. 'They are always at it.'

'It sounded like it was only a block away,' she says.

'Probably it is in the Métro.'

'I'm going out to have a look,' she says. She has never been an ambulance chaser, but it's a chance to kill some time. Vincent hasn't even touched on his *other* favourite subject yet – a new TV program called *South Park*.

'Don't be long or we'll worry about ya,' Vincent says and goes back to his conversation.

She finds a light coat to cover her expensive metallic body shirt and satin hipster pants. She doesn't walk city streets much any more, hobbled by high heels and burdened by jewellery that's eminently ripoffable. A car is always on standby. But tonight she wants to make a quick escape if necessary, so she exchanges her heels for flats and ties her hair in a ponytail. Now she looks like an ordinary chic Frenchwoman out for a stroll.

When she arrives in the lobby, it is strangely unpopulated, even by porters or a receptionist. She passes through the revolving glass doors and sees that they are standing on the pavement in a huddle. A police car and an ambulance whine down the avenue. In the distance she can hear the donkeyish braying of the emergency SAMU. Maybe she's imagining it but the night is electric with voyeurism.

The doorman, spotting her, is apologetic for not being at attention. 'Does *mademoiselle* require a taxi?'

'No, I feel like walking. What's happening?'

'An accident at the Pont d'Alma. A car in the tunnel, they are saying. But if you are walking, please do me the favour, *mademoiselle*, of not going too close to the accident. It might still be a bomb.'

She promises to be careful. She pulls some franc notes out of her handbag and passes them to the doorman. The gesture is second nature to her now. He gives her an appraising smile. How easily his admiration can be bought! If she knew this back in March, her life might have been different. If only she had greased that concierge's palm . . . but five months have gone by and she lets it go.

The night air is cooler outside. At first she feels a little bubble of elation walking alone like this, in Paris on different terms – in control of her destiny again, or so she believes, not confused and abandoned as she was before. But soon thoughts of those humiliating few days tug and pinch at her like schoolyard bullies. As the familiar blend of diesel and dog shit assaults her nostrils, a heartstring snaps and she is back in the lobby of the hotel Royal Parc, discarded by Luka, back in that tiny maid's room, molested by the porter, back at the Hotel Quelquechose, fending off Clotaire, and back in the canopied bed in the Pavilion de la Paix, watching Eugen wipe himself with a tissue after their first clumsy attempt at sex.

She wraps her arms around her body, as if they could hold her thoughts in.

Suddenly she feels like her past is stalking her. She gets a fright as a stranger collides with her and makes no apology. Like the other people on the street, he's hurrying towards the scene of the accident. Violet finds herself drifting with them, despite the concierge's warning about explosions, her light-coloured coat awash with the refracted colours of emergency lights.

The Place d'Alma, the bridge and the concourse along the Seine looks like a young boy has upended his box of toy cars. There are vehicles everywhere – police cars, ambulances, motorbikes, trucks with satellites on top – all parked erratically as if they had converged on the spot at once, skidding to a halt at angles to each other. Dozens of people are leaning over the bridge, looking deep into the floodlit tunnel. Violet loathes people who gawk at accidents but something about the scene is transfixing. Maybe it's the number of police or of photographers flashing the night and each other. This is no ordinary accident.

A young photographer is sitting on a grassy traffic island loading a camera. She walks up to him. 'What happened? Why are there so many people here?'

It doesn't even occur to her to speak French, which she can barely do anyway. Luckily he's a Londoner like Vince. 'It's Princess Diana, innit?' he says matter-of-factly.

Violet's nerve ends shirr together like someone has pulled a string through them. 'What do you mean?'

'The boys were following her from the Ritz. The silly bugger drove into the wall.'

'Is she dead?'

'Don't think so. She can't die, yeah? She's too fuckin' famous.'

Violet shivers and nods. She is beginning to understand the world has an order to it, which is nothing to do with nature. The very rich have their own gods to look after them and if the god of privilege looks away for a moment, the gods of money and influence step in. Diana might hurt like anyone else but they won't let her bleed as hard and long. No doubt a team of Nobel-prize-winning medicos have already assembled at the hospital, eager for the transcendent experience of touching her flesh, binding her wounds, collecting her bodily fluids in vials like holy water.

Violet desires this order. The control that money gives. The soft casing of a luxurious hotel suite.

The photographer runs off and Violet stands there, blankly, for many minutes. Princess Diana! Almost ten years ago, Diana had danced with Charles at a ball in Melbourne and seemed so much in love. But maybe she was only in love with the idea of herself with a prince of the realm. A kind of love where the object of desire is yourself. Violet is beginning to know about that.

Gradually more people come out into the night. A girl of about six, dressed in a nightgown, ties a pink ribbon to a tree trunk. A stout matron crosses herself frantically. Finally, it's too much for Violet, who is uncomfortable with public displays of sentiment. She turns back towards the avenue, needing to walk off what she has seen.

As she steps off the traffic island, someone takes hold of her arm. 'Be careful. We don't want two beautiful women to be injured in one night.'

Florin.

He looks unchanged from the night he abandoned her in Vienna – tanned, a little tired, a strand of caramel hair brushing his eyelashes, dishevelled in a way that suggests a few minutes in front of a mirror. If the scent of bergamot didn't accompany him, she would think he was an apparition.

'I'm not a ghost,' he says, acknowledging her disbelief. 'I assure you I am very real.' He grasps her upper arm more tightly to prove it. 'See?'

She shakes her arm loose.

'Aren't you going to say anything?'

Rattled, she blurts out the first thing that comes into her head. 'What are you doing here?'

'Taking some air.'

'And anything else you can lay your hands on.'

'I might say the same about you. Those are expensive earrings you're wearing.'

She lifts her chin and looks him coldly in the eye. 'I happen to be doing very well for myself.'

'I'm pleased to hear it.'

'No thanks to you.'

'Oh? I think many thanks are due to me. Come on, you can buy me a drink.'

His smile does not admit the possibility of rejection.

'Violet, you should take note of this lobby,' Florin says blithely, as if there's no tension between them, pulling out a chair for her in the lounge bar of the Hotel Chardonne. 'It is one of the best in Paris for our purposes. It's very much a businessman's hotel, which is good for you.'

Violet grudgingly sits down and follows his gaze, taking in the crystal tentacles of the chandeliers hanging overhead, the baroque clocks sitting on ivory-inlaid credenzas, the marble-topped side tables sprouting great vases of velvety magnolias, the extravagant tapestries of warriors and angels on the walls. The waiters, who would probably have gone home by now on a normal night, have snapped into action to serve dazed guests stiff drinks. They are not the only ones who have walked in off the street – the hotel is playing host to camera crews, who pile their equipment by the front desk, and shattered locals in need of communal comfort.

'Now, let me look at you properly. That coat is Helmut Lang, no?'

She shrugs, disguising her nervousness and silently willing her pounding pulse to slow down. The beat inside her is wayward, alternating angry and carnal beats. 'I got it in London.'

'And the diamonds in your ears?'

'Beijing.'

'Show me your hands. Where did you get that ring?'

She lays them flat on the table, to conceal the slight tremor in them. 'Hong Kong.'

'And the bracelet?'

'Bangkok.'

'Not bad. You've been circulating.'

'And you haven't?'

'Oh, I've been here and there. Good, here comes a waiter.' Florin engages the old man in a long interrogation in French. He orders without asking Violet what she wants. This time, she thinks, let him leave me with the champagne. I've got plenty of cash.

They remain silent until the waiter returns with two glasses of Armagnac. Florin swirls the golden liquid around in the glass and takes a careful sip. 'Not bad.' He nods towards the glass in front of her. 'Drink up. You won't feel so uptight.'

'I'm not uptight.'

'I think you are. You're disturbed to see me?'

She puts the glass to her mouth. The fumes make her shudder. She throws a mouthful down anyway. Despite his patronising manner, his outrageous assumptions, she reluctantly admits to herself that she feels pleased to see him. She feels her cheeks go crimson and quickly swallows some more Armagnac. 'No, I'm not disturbed by you.'

'Then I will have to try harder.' His smile turns predatory. 'So, who is this man you are with?'

'A man.'

'Well, I would be surprised if it were a woman. Besides, I can smell him on you. That's not a woman's smell.'

His observation makes her uncomfortable. 'What are you, a vampire?'

'Some women call me the Blood Count. Do you want to know why?' His expression conveys humour and yet there is something humourless about him.

'No.'

'Well, I am Transylvanian after all. How much money does he have?'

'I don't know how much money he has.'

'Did you not listen to a word I told you?'

She resents being treated like a child. 'I don't know how much money he has because he has *so much*.' She wants to rub it in. 'He's a motivational speaker. He sells millions of books and videos.'

'What's his name?'

'Vincent London.'

'I have never heard of him. But I must say, he sounds a bit *déclassé*.'

'He's very charismatic.'

'Oh? That sounds even worse. What you want is a nice, uncharismatic man with buckets of money. And a title, if possible.' He sighs a heavy disapproval. 'And where did you meet him?'

'In Bangkok.'

'And how did you get there?'

'Is this Twenty Questions?'

'When I'm finished you can ask me the same.'

'All right. After I'd parted from Lyle, the American you fobbed me off onto—'

'Fobbed off? It was a delicate negotiation.'

'Well, after that I travelled a bit.' No need to tell him everything. 'I've been in Asia mostly. Vince and I spent the summer cruising. Do you know Frank Costello? His yacht is the *Solid Gold.*' She can't quite resist the urge to boast.

Florin says nothing. He opens his cigarette case with one hand, that familiar gesture, extracts a short cigarette and offers her one. She declines, even though she would badly like one. She doesn't want to take anything from him.

The lighter he takes from his pocket is encrusted with clear stones. He notices her looking at it and turns it over in his hand. 'Why does every woman think I want a cigarette lighter? It's so predictable.' He leaves it on the table between them after he lights his cigarette. 'I have to say, Violet, I am very disappointed in you. A mere motivational speaker, when I set you up with one of the richest men in America? A match of such quality doesn't come along very often. Certainly not by chance. My timing was excellent. I made a very clear arrangement.'

'Pity you didn't tell me about it.'

'On the contrary, I explained everything.'

'I wasn't a thing to be sold.'

'Weren't you? I can't remember you saying that. In any case, what are you now? Someone has paid for those clothes.'

'I'm not like you.'

'No? How?'

'I haven't made a profession of it.'

'Funny. I could have sworn you had made the transition from amateur beautifully. As I knew you would.'

'What's wrong with me enjoying myself?'

'I'm all in favour of it. I'm devoted to enjoying myself. We are not charities after all.' He taps his fingers on the table. 'Now tell me more about this magician you're with.'

'Motivational speaker.'

'Do you intend to stay with him?'

'I don't know. I like him.'

'Like, like, like. Is that all you are looking for in a man? He's not good enough for you.'

'You don't know the first thing about him!'

'I know that I don't know him, which is enough.'

'Well, I'm not about to *marry* him.' She is, after all, still married. But she tries not to think about it. She has not phoned Patrick and only sent him one letter. What would she say anyway? *Dear Patrick, having a great time sleeping with rich men, wish you were here?*

Maybe she should.

'Ah! So he's not so attractive to you after all. Very good, Violet. I have hope for you yet.'

'He *is* attractive. That's why I'm with him.'

He laughs. 'So you have discovered the eroticism of wealth. What happened with the American?'

'His wife found out about me.'

'And you didn't expect this? I'm sure she knew about you long before you knew about her.'

'She demanded he dump me. And he did.'

'You didn't fight back?'

'How could I do that?'

'I can think of at least a dozen ways right now. You should have made a fuss. You could have gained an apartment out of it at the very least.'

'I didn't want an apartment. I wanted him.'

'That sounds dangerously adolescent. I'm worried about you, Violet. Are you looking for love?'

'You don't understand anything.'

'I think I understand it very well. You should learn a lesson from this Princess Diana. She divorced the future King of England because she was jealous of his mistress. A very foolish move,

I must say. Especially as she has ended up with a film producer, a bit of a comedown, don't you think? What makes her think she is any better than a courtesan? Because she married him? She should have known what she was. But now she has given everything to this mistress who will bide her time. You have to keep your eye on the prince and not fuss yourself too much about love.'

'You make love sound like a disease.'

'Which it is. Don't look at me with those sad eyes. I am only trying to be your friend.'

'Some friend! You stole my money.'

'Still harping on that? It's very bourgeois of you. Why would I steal your measly few dollars? I didn't need it.'

'That's not true. You didn't have any money yourself.'

'But I had prospects.'

'Prospects at the casino? The race track?'

'You think I spent *our* money on gambling?'

'Didn't you?'

'If you have to know, I spent your small fortune on two tickets to the opera and a bouquet of roses. At such short notice, good seats at the opera come at a premium.'

'You took someone to the opera!'

'Of course I didn't. The seat next to me remained vacant throughout. I paced the foyer for an hour with my roses waiting for her to turn up. Reluctantly, when she didn't show, I took my seat, broken-hearted. There is always some kind woman to take pity on a jilted man. Someone who will invite you to supper with the group . . . to cheer you up, of course.'

'That's a bit of a risk, isn't it? Why didn't you just use the money to buy yourself a good meal at one of those ritzy restaurants where the rich hang out?'

He shrugs. 'It was Vienna. The opera is more stylish. Besides, it was *La Traviata*. It was amusing, having my Violetta in real life and my one on the stage.'

She has been to the opera. She knows what he means. 'You didn't have me. And you left me without anything.'

'It did you more good in my pocket.'

'Meaning?'

'You had to be desperate enough to take the opportunity I presented you.'

'I wasn't desperate. I could have called my parents and had them send money.'

'I knew you wouldn't do that. You are proud, Violet. And this is a good quality for our line of work. Our artistic endeavours.' He stubs out his cigarette and leans back in his chair. 'And so I don't think I did so badly for you after all.'

'My turn with the questions,' she says.

He picks up the cigarette lighter and tosses it in his palm. 'Okay.'

'Where did you get that tan?'

'The Seychelles. A little island with only six bungalows. I'll take you there some time.'

'Who were you with?'

'A woman I have known for a very long time. We sometimes take vacations together.'

'And you're with her in Paris?'

'No. She lives in South Africa.'

'So – who's the woman in Paris? Or is it a man?'

He looks wounded. 'Please, don't be disgusting.'

'This woman then. Who is she?'

'A woman you would not like. She is very French, very snobbish. But in the matter of sex she is frenzied, like a chicken with its head off.'

'I don't want to know about that.'

'You think I am being contemptuous?'

'What do you get out of her?'

'A way to live the life I want.'

He tosses the cigarette lighter again. It's only now she notices that it's engraved with initials that are not Florin's.

She has a flashback to something Carl told her. 'What happened in Zürs?'

He looks at the ceiling. 'Zürs?'

'You had a problem there.' She makes the same wrist-slashing gesture Carl had made.

For the first time he is uncomfortable. 'It wasn't like that.'

'That's not what I heard.'

'Oh, you're listening to gossip now?'

'Is it true?'

'She was very unstable.'

'What did you do?'

'I didn't *do* anything. It was very upsetting for me.'

'For you? It didn't sound like she was too happy either.'

'Look, Violet, you will learn this soon, if you haven't already. Sometimes people think we are their possessions, when we are only loaning ourselves for a while. No matter how careful we are these difficulties may arise. It is very awkward when two women are in love with you. You have to choose one of them.'

'The richest one?'

'Whichever the case, the other gets hurt. I don't like hurting people, but sometimes it can't be helped.'

'She didn't just get hurt, she slashed her wrists.'

'In fact, she hung herself.'

'Oh.' Violet considers the awfulness of it. 'That makes a difference? Whatever she did, she's dead.'

'Some people will end up dead whether they are in love with

me or not. This one would have found another excuse sooner or later. Now, let's not talk any further about this. I find it painful. It almost ruined my reputation.' He gestures for the waiter, who brings the check. 'I'll walk you back to your hotel.'

'I'm leaving for Los Angeles tomorrow.'

'You'll be back. People like us are always in Paris. It's where business and romance intersect. If not, then I will see you in Lugarno or Casablanca or Biarritz. We'll find each other.'

'I won't be looking for you.'

He raises an eyebrow and pushes the check towards her.

When they reach The Hermitage, Florin kisses her on both cheeks. Close, like this, she can smell the faint hint of a woman's oriental perfume on his neck. 'Well, Violet, I'm glad you're looking so well. My risk paid off.'

'Risk?'

'I expect the favour to be returned.'

He is not getting away with this. 'Vincent has a mother. I could arrange for you to meet her. Of course, the negotiations would be very *delicate*.'

'That's enough, Violet. I am expected elsewhere.' He is not offended: shows his gold teeth. When he turns away from her, she puts her hand out to stop him. She looks him directly in the eye and smiles.

'Your risk *did* pay off.'

The doorman, who has been holding the door throughout this exchange, says as she walks through it, 'I hope that gentleman wasn't bothering you, *mademoiselle*.' He gives her a wink.

Cheeky bastard, she thinks. No more tips tonight.

But, yes, the gentleman *is* bothering me.

'What took you so long?' Vincent's mouth is smiling but his voice isn't friendly. He's got his big portable phone to his ear, pacing the room. Surprisingly, the French couple have gone.

'I didn't think you'd be alone.' She takes off her coat.

He puts his hand over the receiver. 'Yeah, well, I've got work to do. The phone's been running hot.'

Of course, she'd forgotten: Vincent was once one of Diana's gurus. *Low self-esteem* is all he's told her.

'Do you think she'll be all right?' Violet asks.

He raises his hand to shush her and points to the receiver. 'I've got the fuckin' *Daily Mail* on the line.' He turns his back on her.

Violet goes into the bedroom, gets undressed and slips between the silky sheets. But her circadian rhythms have deposited her on the other side of sleep. In her mind, she is not in this room but following Florin through the shadowy streets to his lover's building, watching him take the coffin-sized art nouveau elevator up to her apartment, open the heavy wooden door with his key, move across the darkened room to where an old woman is sitting in the window, sucking angrily on a cigarette, balcony doors open, curtains billowing around her. Her shoulders are stiff as he places his hands on them but he kisses her neck and she swoons, dropping her cigarette on the parquetry. He gently raises her to her feet – she's thin as a piece of parchment paper – and carries her to the sofa, where he unbuttons her tweed jacket, lifts the pearls off her neck and unrolls the white stockings down over her bony knees. As he swiftly enters her, she becomes frenzied and spots of blood fly everywhere. Like a chicken with its head cut off.

When Vincent comes to the bedroom an hour later, he wants some Balzac. 'Get ready, princess,' he says. 'There's an unexploded landmine down here.'

She's ready for him.

THE CASA GRANDE

Sunset Boulevard, Beverly Hills, USA

The theme of Vincent London's September US lecture tour is Grab the Stars.

Unhappily for Violet, he takes his own advice literally.

The star in question is a pint-sized diva, one-third of an all-girl singing group, who wears combat pants, earrings the size of dinner plates and six-inch platform boots with silver planets on them.

Violet discovers them in the fourth bathroom of the sprawling Mission-style bungalow, pawing each other in a corner between the bidet and the toilet, while a posse of Vince's new acquaintances – 'gangsta' rappers whose leader is called Notorious – scrawl their tags in purple spray-paint over the bathroom mirrors.

Vincent has brought the gang home after the last lecture of his LA gig. Violet has long since given up on him and has been trying to sleep, but someone has turned up the volume on Tupac's last album and a heavy beat, the thud of a boot repeatedly kicking a wall or an animal or a head, pounds through the stucco walls. Defeated, she pulls on tracksuit pants and a tank top and staggers out of the bedroom barefoot. Expecting to find him on a sofa where she left him, corralled by starry-eyed disciples, instead she finds *this*.

She shrinks against the bathroom door. Why would Vince need to *poke around in another paddock* when he has her? Beautiful, porcelain-skinned her, as he constantly declares?

The woman Vincent is groping is caramel-coloured. So much for that. Violet sees arms and legs and Medusa locks sprawling against the Mexican mosaic tiles. Vincent's jeans are so low he has bared his dancing angel.

Violet is sickened by the mingled fumes of acrylic spray-paint, Versace Man cologne and Jamaican weed. She feels as if someone has filleted all the bones out of her. Her wobbly legs can't take her away, even though she doesn't want a confrontation, now or ever.

But already Vincent is looking over his shoulder, sensing a shift in the room temperature. He is not stupid. He has been caught, but not quite *in flagrante*. He's off the diva in a flash, catching Violet by the arm.

'What's up, love?' he says calmly, pulling her into the shower recess. The yellow rubber duck, given to Vincent by his friend Bono, watches them with wide eyes.

Violet tries to control her voice. 'You were having toilet sex with some Spice Girl.'

'Not Spice Girl, love. PLT. Pretty Little Things. Which also stands for Paula, Lisa and Tashona. Cute, yeah?'

'So you don't deny you were—'

'Getting it off? It was just a bit of fun.'

'You looked pretty serious.'

'You went to bed. What was I supposed to do?'

'You weren't supposed to fuck the guests! You were supposed to get rid of this crowd and come to bed with me!'

He strokes her arms. 'They won't leave, sweetheart. And they'd fuckin' destroy the place if I wasn't awake.'

'Then turn off the booze and drugs.'

'I tried that. Some of these freaks are packing.'

This is not what's stopping him. Vincent loves his tough new crowd. He sucks their brains for gimmicks for his performances. Street talk. Dance moves. Hip-hop beats. His audiences – mainly white, middle-class, middle-management employees going nowhere – lap up all the *yo's* and *bro's*. Just last night, one of the rappers pulled a gun and Vincent's eyes lit like a cat's in the dark.

She calls his bluff. 'You want me to phone the police?'

'No need for that love.' He has recently discovered *bling* and his knuckles are heavy with diamond-encrusted skulls and hearts as he reaches out to touch her hair. 'What if I kick out the rest of them and invite Tashona to stay?'

'What – so I can watch you two go at it?'

'No. So I can watch you.' His expression is perfectly neutral. He has made these suggestions before, but never pushed it. She thought he was just titillating her.

'I don't go to bed with acronyms.'

He blows some air out of his mouth. 'You're a smart girl, love, but you need to loosen up.'

'Really?' Other men have asked her to be 'tolerant'. She knows what that means.

'How loose do you need me to be?'

'Just a little bit flexible, yeah?'

'We're having a good time, aren't we?'

'We're having a fuckin' great time. But let's not get stuck in a rut.'

'We haven't been together long enough to be in a rut.'

'With some chicks you can be in a rut the second time you do it. That's why it's called *rutting*, yeah?'

'I'm not attracted to women.'

'So you don't have to touch her if you don't want to. She can watch us. Or we'll watch *her*. There's a million fuckin'variations.'

'*No.*'

'Maybe we should invite one of the boys.'

'No. I'm not in the mood.'

'Now? Or not ever?'

'I don't know. I'll get back to you.'

'Christ! Who's calling the shots here?'

'What?'

'Who's calling the shots here? Me or you?'

'Both of us.'

'Wrong answer.' His eyes are shining but there's a vein pulsing on his forehead, the sign he is angry. 'You want the stuff, you do the rough.'

'I see,' she says. 'I'm supposed to do everything *you* want?'

'Whose life are you living?'

'What do you mean?'

'Well, it's not your fuckin' hotel room and your fuckin' friends, yeah?'

There's nothing she can say to this. Of course it's his fucking hotel room. She's just been deposited there with the luggage. How could she have lost sight of that?

His rubber duck gawks at her with bright white eyes: *gotcha!*

LA RÉSERVE DE ST-TROPEZ

Route des Plages, St-Tropez, France

Mats has installed me in a villa at La Réserve, a chic little hotel on the hill above St Tropez. There are eight pink-washed villas covered in fiery pink bougainvillea, set in acres of dark green cypress pines.

Each villa is named for a flower. Heliotrope, anemone, lavande, hyacinthe, jasmine, narcisse, muguet. We have found ourselves in villa eglantine, the house of the rambling rose. The two-storey residences form a quadrangle around a small garden planted with perfect symmetry and a square of chlorinated pool in which no one swims. I can sit on our terrace all day and never see another soul, except for a houseboy or maid in starched white linens. The other guests are secluded in their villas behind chalky pink shutters or out doing whatever they do at the film festival, which is a good hour's drive away.

I've heard from the complaining maids that the other occupants include a significant movie star, who has booked the empty villas on either side for privacy and still demands the sheets on the unslept-in beds are changed twice daily, a Parisian department store heiress, who is recuperating from cosmetic surgery done in Tunisia and leaves blood on the pillowcases, and a screenwriter who bangs away all day on an old portable typewriter and clogs up the toilet bowl with rejected carbons. As I curl up under a calico market umbrella, trying to keep the sun off me and concentrate on my book, the only other person I can sense in the place is the entity in villa muguet, directly across the pool, who stands inside the French windows of his bedroom, just out of sight, casting a net of cigarette smoke.

For five days now Mats reluctantly has left at dawn for pre-breakfast and breakfast meetings in Cannes, leaving me with a sloppy kiss, a sticky bed and an empty day. If I had a hundred toes I couldn't count on them the number of days that have begun like this. Mats is no worse than most of them and better than many, although it's hard to forgive him his Beavis and Butthead shorts. It's a contrived goofiness, which is supposed to suggest that he's not past the first (in reality, *second*) flush of youth. I have to constantly reassure him that he's the youngest man – by about two decades – that I've travelled with in quite a while.

Once, in another life, I might have been content with Mats. He's good-looking – *brawny* is the word that is used to suggest someone on the heavy side of muscly – and if he has a scent at all it's the faint and inoffensive chemical smell of drycleaning. When he wants sex it's straight and clean and quick. He thinks it's funny sometimes not to take off his cowboy boots. And really, that *is* funny compared to the other things that men have asked me to do. There's an ex-wife in deep background but he's unencumbered by children, dogs or even a retinue of dogsbodies. The only photo he carries in his wallet is of 'Panther', his black Bell 430 helicopter, which he loves like a baby. He doesn't overeat, drinks modestly and is reading *A Treatise on Human Nature* by David Hume. He is a safe harbour – unimaginative and undemanding.

If people could be caught, he's a good catch. There's nothing wrong with him. But I'm restless already. What's wrong with *me*?

In the beginning I thought – let's see where this life can take me. It will end, sooner or later, with a full stop. I thought that full stop would be a man. But all my relationships have ended in ellipses (. . .) or exclamation marks (!). They fade out or end abruptly. I have long given up on the man who will provide the period.

I think bitterly of my renewed flirtation with Charles. Like all my gentlemen he is just a comma that strings a life together. A little pause before I go on.

But Mats is not playing by the rules. He wants to be that full stop. Already there are little hints. I can see the idea of permanence warming up his grey eyes. He thinks he can keep me to himself in this gilded cage. In five days, we have only twice gone outside these walls as a couple. Once, it was to a small restaurant in the village, where we dined alone, an enormous urn of willow concealing us from the other six tables. On the other occasion, the reception after a big studio film premiere, Mats hardly left my side, pulling me closer whenever one of the smirking ghosts from my past came by to flirt. We didn't stay long (although long enough for Charles to confer another cagey blessing) and in bed later – on the floor, actually – he hammered me as if he were a battering ram trying to break down the door to my heart.

Too late, baby.

I ask for my breakfast to be laid out on the terrace. I watch the young butler smooth out the white linens and polish the knives to a shine that reflects the puffy clouds in the sky. He has a silver link bracelet around a slender wrist that is a gift from someone. I wonder if he demands love of his wife-mistress-boyfriend. The French are usually pragmatic about these things. *L'amour* is more lust than love, an eruption of the body with a little decorative flourish from the heart. Lie down, let it rush over you and you're good as new afterwards. I ask him if he is married. He blushes and says no. I can see I have caught him out in a fantasy about me. If I opened my robe for him now he wouldn't find it necessary to engage his soul before taking me on the stone floor. The soul is not part of this bargain. Why does everyone keep bringing it in?

I hate it when men think they love me. I haven't given them a *me* to love.

The young man asks me if I need anything else. I send him away with twenty euros. Perhaps he has been reading my mind because he looks a little disappointed, despite the tip. But I won't be distracted. I must get down to practical things, given that I'm about to be companionless again soon.

I demolish a croissant, play with the sugar spoon and flip through the daily *Hollywood Reporter*. The windows of villa muguet remain heavily curtained. There's the sound of a door scraping open and I catch my first glimpse of the screenwriter, in striped pyjamas and dust-ball hair, staggering around the terrace of villa narcisse with one of those big French coffee bowls balanced in his hand. He's searching for something, lifting newspapers and magazines off a chair and flinging them on the ground. He looks up, sees me and, startled, scampers back inside like a frightened mouse. I wonder what he's writing and why it is going so wrong he has to clog the toilet with carbons.

After forty-five minutes, another croissant has been worried into crumbs, the coffee is cold in the pot and I've closed the magazine on a gossip item about the young woman 'secreted' in Charles Nathan's Riviera suite. His daughter Samantha, no doubt, unwitting fodder for the parasitic press. I'm sure Charles would be thrilled that he still can command column inches.

I am trying to keep my spirits up but my mood collapses at the thought of Charles. He is the spoon in my soufflé. For a moment I consider the possibility that Mats owes Charles money and I am the old man's revenge on him. Then I reject the idea. It's more fucked-up than that. It's not about Mats. It's about me.

Charles can't . . . *won't* have me but he will not see me happy with anyone else. Oh, how magnanimous he seems on the surface, pushing me at men who are much younger than him and more virile. No sour grapes, my dear, I want the best for you. But he neglects to read me the fine print. Jeremy, famous, bedroom-eyed, with an LA hangar full of Porsches, has about as much personality as the thin white line of powder that goes up his nose every hour or so. Mats, solid, reliable, is like a windowless house built on a swamp of insecurity. These choices are calculated to show an old man in a good light, to remind me – if I need reminding at all – that sex is just a currency that buys you a bed and some sleep. Men like Charles have other goods to barter.

And suddenly, despite everything, I feel again the need for

what Charles can barter. I turned my back on marriage long ago but now my head sinks into the thought of it like it sinks into a soft pillow. To have a life, bookended morning and night by a husband who is yours, and not to fear the bubble bursting when the summer is over or the conference ends or the grinding inevitability of a disgruntled wife at home ends the arrangement. To be *permanent* and acknowledged. Maybe I am not meant to go on forever with this game I started with myself. I read it once . . . Colette perhaps? *Instead of marrying 'at once', it sometimes happens that we marry 'at last'.* Maybe I'm ready for *at last.*

Unexpectedly, a gust of wind scrolls across the table, stripping the single peony in a vase of most of its petals. The pages of *The Hollywood Reporter* ruffle like a cardsharp is dealing them. I move the sugar bowl to hold it down and rearrange the crockery to stop the edges of the tablecloth flapping and when I look up again the windows of villa muguet are flung open as if there has been an exorcism. The curtains twist and flap like dervishes, a maid steps out and pulls the windows closed, and there is nothing.

THE UNION HOTEL

East 17th Street, New York, USA

Violet loves New York.

She loves the fatalism of riding in a limo at night, whooshing down the avenues with the lights of buildings sparkling overhead like a fairy bower, the lanes of traffic streaming and weaving like a roaring river and she carried down it, a tiny, careless petal swept up in something momentous and inexorable, the pulse of the universe.

She loves the view from Windows on the World, the city an electrocardiogram of peaks and lows, shining towers and concrete blocks, the Statue of Liberty small and vulnerable, the narrow streets and vapour trails from planes criss-crossing the island like an ethereal cat's cradle in the sky.

She loves standing in the middle of Sheep Meadow in Central Park and listening to the city breathe, the romantic spires of West Side apartment buildings rising above the treetops. She loves that it's fall, with piercing blue skies overhead and the trees mellowing to gold, cushioning the blow of winter.

She loves the velvet seats of the old Schubert Theatre on Broadway, where she sees the new revival of *Chicago*, and drinking blue cocktails at the Royalton before the show and supper at Balthazar afterwards, where Vincent introduces her to his mates David Bowie and Gary Oldman.

She loves the squirrels in Union Square, near their hotel, which can be coaxed to eat pretzel crumbs out of her hand.

She loves the shoe salesmen at Bergdorf Goodman, who serve her two at a time, one on his knees, the other searching for sizes, encouraging her to try on every pair in the store and complimenting her profusely when she selects the Blahnik over the Ferragamo, as if she had won the Nobel Prize and not merely chosen a kitten heel.

She loves the Chrysler Building, the Woolworth Building and the Empire State, a trio of hypodermics stabbing the sky. She loves the lions on the steps of the Public Library and the national debt ticking over on the electronic billboard near Times Square and the eighteen miles of dusty books at Stand Bookstore on 12th Street.

She loves the cast-iron buildings of SoHo, the boutiques that are minimal as art galleries, the art galleries that are as forbidding as palaces, except to her in her new Gucci coat.

She loves bargaining with the stallholders on Canal Street for a fake Vuitton handbag and then going up to Prince Street to buy the real thing.

She loves the steam that rises wraith-like from manholes at night and the clutter of blue police barricades outside nightclubs and the way refrigerator-sized doormen at Twilo unclick the velvet ropes for her without breaking the rhythm of her steps.

She loves the things people to say to each other on the streets.

She loves the way she can have anything she likes *when* she likes it – a cupcake at midnight, a spa bath at dawn, out-of-season cherries for breakfast, a stroll through MOMA at lunch, a private showing at Calvin Klein in the afternoon, a lychee martini laced with gold leaf for cocktails.

She loves the way everything is for the taking and the people who give it to you smile and say 'Have a nice day'.

'Have a fuckin' nice day. Can't they think of anything else?' Vincent is sick of New York and wants everyone to know it. He has gobbled it up like a starving man for the last six days but now he has indigestion. 'It's not even fuckin' daytime.'

The waiter, caught out in a terse and generic farewell (blaming the individual for the universal, Vincent has been ungenerous with his tip), overhears the complaint and returns. 'Have a fucking nice *night*, sir,' he smiles, slamming a fresh ketchup bottle down on the table.

'Ha. Ha. Ha,' Vincent grimaces, pushing the bottle away. 'That's what I hate about this town. Everyone's a comedian.'

Vincent's New York publicist, a blonde called Ruth with a 'Rachel' haircut and skin pulled smooth as plastic wrap, puts her hand on his arm. 'Come on, Vince baby, let's find somewhere to have a nightcap.' Violet looks at the way she is pawing him with turquoise and pink diamond-studded acrylic nails and winces. Vince calls Ruth 'The Hairdo' behind her back but Violet bets he's spent a few nights in the past hanging on to that hair while the publicist reads the Balzac. Ruth has been attached to Vincent like a spray-tanned tumour ever since they arrived on this the last leg of Vincent's six-city tour (Los Angeles, Las Vegas, Houston, Chicago, Toronto, New York) but has barely spoken a word to Violet, as if Violet is a piece of furniture that opens doors, drinks cocktails and sometimes sits on Vincent's lap. Violet has, in turn, ignored her, but now thinks that maybe she shouldn't have.

There are eight of them around the table and they all stand up and scrape their chairs at once, leaving the small French bistro like bats swarming out of a cave. (They are all wearing black.) In the street, they huddle for a while, arguing about where to go next. The stench from the butchers' warehouses on 13th Street is overwhelming. Violet still has blood on her soles from stepping in a concealed puddle of it when they alighted from their car. She wishes they would hurry up and make a decision. The fashion designer wants to go to Mother but the conceptual artist likes El Teddy's. Vincent's lighting designer has her heart set on The Rainbow Room, where's she never been. Someone suggests Sardis and is mocked. The Hairdo is on her Motorola phoning round the clubs, calling in favours, finding out who's where and where is *happening*.

The only one without an opinion is Vincent. Since his last performance at the Javits Center the night before it's as if the blustery air has been siphoned from him and poisonous gas has been pumped back in its place. She supposes he's exhausted from the tour and experiencing a kind of letdown from it being over.

But as the day has progressed he has become more and more ill humoured. His posse mostly ignore his mood except for the occasional pitying glances they flick at Violet, as if thinking, poor thing, she's got to cope with him alone.

The Hairdo finally establishes that there's a table for them at the Bowery Bar. As the others scramble into two limos, Vincent declares he's not interested, he wants a 'quiet night'. The fake tan drains off his publicist's face. Before she can get past 'But—' he has Violet by the arm, across the cobblestone street and into the third waiting car. He says nothing all the way back to the hotel, his fingers drumming an agitated beat on the smoky window.

In their suite, he wants sex immediately. So this is what it's about, Violet thinks, as he pulls her mouth to his. He's a hungry kisser, he kisses hard and long, like he's trying to find a way to put all of her in his mouth. She likes these moments, for this is when he shuts up and slows down. He has taken to calling her *Ritalin* for her effect on him. She has tried to please him. He who is passionate about everything and bored with it soon after is sometimes hard to read. This has kept her on her toes (and on her back and on her knees.) She wants to be more than a diversion and twelve weeks on she is still diverting him. She knows there have been other diversions, too, but since LA she has learnt to say nothing. The terms of her relationship with him are non-negotiable. They are *having fun, yeah?* On his terms.

But that's okay as long as she gets to shake hands with David Bowie, the velvet ropes unclick for her and the salespeople kneel at her feet. These things are fun. On her terms.

Now, her pulse is captive to the pressure of his lips. She's familiar with his rhythm, ready to go where he wants to go. He pushes her against a wall but instead of allowing her to put her arms around him, crushes them to her side with his strong hands, as tight as if she's wrapped in a shroud. He enters her ferociously, as if he wants a *bit of rough,* but pulls out decisively after only a minute or two.

'What's wrong?'

'No.'

'No?'

'Go get in bed, yeah?' he says, patting her on one buttock. 'I won't be long.'

But he is long. She lies on the big bed, naked, under a fluorescent Keith Haring canvas with a postmodern purple sheet pulled up to her neck. The bedroom gives her the creeps, the startled faces that stare at her from the Fornasetti cabinets, the black walls dotted with yellow and green Pop Art paintings like the heads of festering sores and the twisted brass legs like antler's horns sprouting from under the purple velvet chairs. It's like some psychopath's basement, she thinks, with any view blacked out by big iron shutters like something from a medieval castle. Vincent likes it and knows the Famous Designer who chose the furnishings but she's felt uncomfortable there from the moment they arrived. She keeps scratching her legs on the chairs and stepping in the pods of lighting which sprout like alien spawn from the floor.

After half an hour of lying in anticipation, she gets off the bed and wraps herself in a cotton kimono. Vincent is not in the sitting room. She opens the door of the second bedroom. Immediately she sees that the bathroom light is on. There's the sound of something dripping. *Tap, tap, tap.*

Vincent is sitting in the spa bath with the water up to his waist, knees bent, staring at the wall. The rubber duck Bono gave him stares back from between the copper taps. All Violet can think is that the volcano on his right arm looks ready to explode. But, then so does he: he is holding a gun to his head.

Her brain shifts smoothly into third gear: denial. *It's another of his jokes.* 'Put that stupid toy down,' she tells him sharply. 'You gave me a fright.'

'There's always something else, isn't there, love?' he says casually, pistol still pressed against his temple, like he's talking to her over a cup of tea.

She can't process what he's saying. 'What?'

He doesn't answer.

'Is this some game?' she asks. Vincent has recently been considering doing a live diary on the internet. She wouldn't put it past him not to tell her he had started. She looks around the bathroom. All the lights have been turned up to maximum glare, bouncing off the black marble surfaces. 'Have you put a camera in here?'

'They always want fuckin' more from me.'

His flat tone alarms her. 'Vincent, put the gun down. This is ridiculous.' She takes a step forward and then thinks better of it. The gun doesn't look that much like a toy. It's one of those long-nosed automatic weapons his gangster friends like to brandish. She tries another tack. 'Put the gun down and I'll call Ray.' Vincent's business manager is in the suite downstairs. *What the hell is his room number?* She eyes an intercom on the wall. 'Ray will know what to do.'

'I wouldn't worry about it, love.' Vincent's arm relaxes and she thinks *Thank God, he's going to drop the gun.* But in a swift motion his left hand grabs his right wrist and he turns the gun on her, cop-style. 'Now clear off.'

She seizes up. It's like a bolt has shot through her, pinning her feet to the floor. His arm wavers slightly. She can see that he is shivering, and she realises now the bath is full of cold water. If her legs would take her out of there, she'd run. But she can't move, caught in the crosshairs between heroine and coward. If she stays, he may just shoot her. But if she goes, he'll shoot himself, for sure.

When he finally speaks it feels like she's lived half her life again. 'Have it your own way,' he says.

For the briefest of moments, the gun goes to his temple, but then he straightens his arms in front of him.

And blasts his rubber duck to smithereens.

Violet doesn't see Vincent again.

She is removed to a smaller suite and given a cup of tea, which must contain sedative because she goes unconscious immediately. When she wakes up, it's the next day and Vincent has left the country.

Vincent's manager, Ray, comes to see her. He's doing 'a bit of tidying up', he explains, making inverted commas around his words with his fingers. Vincent, she will be pleased to know, has suffered nothing more serious than a superficial cut on his chin when a porcelain chip from the blasted tub flew at his head. The official line is he cut his chin 'shaving'. Violet needs to understand the importance of keeping Vincent's little 'moment' to herself. It could 'negatively impact' Vincent's career and of course she wouldn't want to see that happen. After all he's 'done' for her? Vincent needs some 'rest' without being disturbed by horrible journalists or hysterical fans. The hotel has taken care of everything. The bath has been repaired already. Now, all that needs to be taken care of is Violet.

Ray doesn't actually say the last thing but it's heavy in the air. You will need some 'travelling money', he tells her. He is there to take care of that. Of course, in return she will need to 'initial' a contract. Nothing alarming, just the promise never to speak a word of this to anyone. I happen to have the contract here, he says, handing her a two-page letter from a New York legal firm. It's very 'straightforward'.

Violet looks at the envelope Ray has handed her. 'It's not enough money.' She is vaguely surprised at her own presence of mind.

Ray capitulates easily on a higher fee. She dispassionately examines the letter. Although it bears today's date she suspects the same letter has been dragged out more than once. It's general rather than specific. No talking to the press about Vincent. *Ever.*

She picks up the pen and signs the letter with her round, child-like hand. Ray tells her it's been a 'pleasure'. And then he asks her to dinner.

'You've got to be "kidding", she says, making an inverted-commas sign around her words.

Once he is gone, Violet sits on the bed and stares at the opposite wall, at a photograph of a roast chicken being torn apart by jewelled hands. She examines her feelings. In a funny kind of way, what she feels is *relief*. Vincent was not one to be controlled. And she doesn't like the thought that she has no control. Even so, she feels like she might have been a little more attached to him than she believed. Her biorhythms had begun to pulse with his. Now they have to be kick-started by themselves.

She looks in the envelope Ray has left her. Fifteen thousand dollars in cash. She has negotiated fifty thousand more, which is promised this afternoon. She deserves it. Vincent did, after all, point a loaded gun at her, frighten her almost to death. As a matter of fact, she is still trembling.

She picks up the phone beside the bed. While she is waiting, she bends down to slip on the shoes that she wore the night before. There is dried animal blood on the soles from where she stepped in a pool of it outside the French bistro. The shoes are Christian Laboutin; they cost $750. She jettisons them across the room. She can buy another pair if she likes.

When the hotel's receptionist answers, she informs him that she expects to stay another week.

And then she goes out to find a bank and a safety deposit box.

Violet's 'compensation', as Ray calls it, arrives that evening when a hotel porter brings up a padded envelope.

She tips generously, handing the porter folded notes, liking the power of it.

She has no plans. She could buy a dress. She could go to Italy.

Something will happen.

But not if she sits alone in her hotel room.

In the lobby bar, she orders a bottle of Roederer. The drink waiter is dressed in black T-shirt and jeans with unlaced Converse sneakers on his feet. This 'hip and casual' theme seems, to her, borderline offensive, especially when the champagne will set her back almost $200. She prefers the formality of the Asian and European hotels, where waiters pour drinks with their eyes downcast. This one asks her 'Any plans for this evening?' as he extracts the cork. She ignores him.

It is not the kind of lobby she has grown to trust. There is no sophistication. She feels like a little girl in a shop full of gigantic toys. The chairs are oversized, modern things with hard backs and long legs, which means she has to stretch her toes for them to touch the floor. Enormous spheres, the colour of bubblegum, hang from the ceiling. The lampshades are the size of crinoline skirts. A blue plastic puppy, big as a pony, sleeps on a plinth in the middle of the room. The waiters carry trays of drinks in glasses shaped like fishbowls, decorated with origami animals.

She could do without the irony. Vincent has given her enough of that. Tomorrow she will move into a hotel uptown, where people take their money seriously.

People like Lyle. She thinks about him. It has crossed her mind, more than once, that this is his town. That she knows where he lives and where he works. That perhaps in the course of an ordinary day, when she's shopping on Madison Avenue or strolling down east 72nd Street, she might come across him stepping into his car and he'll look up and see her and something will ignite in him again . . . and *hang* his wife, he must have her, keep her, set her up in that apartment Florin says is her due.

Florin. He is like a drycleaner's staple stuck to the inside of her dress, needling her. Damn him. And yet, he is right. She deserves better than Vincent. She should not have sold herself so short.

Sold. We are not charities, Florin said. What is wrong if she puts a value on herself?

The champagne tastes like sour lemon on her tongue. She puts the glass down and signals for the check.

After a few moments, a different waiter arrives. His grainy stubble, his sleepy eyes, suggests only a brief separation from the bed sheets. She finds his familiar smile annoying, so she just nods when he places the check on the table beside her. She picks it up and signs it brusquely.

'Anything wrong?' he asks, as she puts the check back on the table, pointedly not handing it to him.

'No, thank you.' She takes her bag and stands up.

'You don't like that vintage of champagne? Let me get you another bottle.'

'I don't want another bottle.'

'Then let me get you a dozen.'

She looks at him more closely now. Full of his own dark-eyed good looks, he is smiling at her impertinently. That demands a response. 'Thanks. Send them up to my room.'

She walks past him, across the lobby and out the doors.

The barman at the Blue Water Grill makes her a martini that is turquoise.

He has dreadlocks to his waist and the juice of the limes he squeezes in his palm runs down his chocolate forearms.

She thinks about what it might be like to follow him home. Vincent has been gone less than twenty-four hours and already she is imagining other hands on her thighs. It is nothing to do with needing the sex. She is not sure who she is without a man needing *her*. When she thinks of herself she is always a column of white marble circled by strong dark arms.

The barman slides the glass across the bar and winks at her. She shivers as if he's run the cold glass down her back. She looks away. She knows that there is more than a bar between them. It's a galaxy between her life and his, as wide as the belt around Saturn. She does not want a handsome man in an ordinary life. She wants a handsome life.

She is taking off her coat in her hotel suite when the doorbell chimes.

A porter stands in the corridor, a carton on a trolley. 'Your champagne,' he says. 'Compliments of the management.'

'Take it back,' she says. 'I'm leaving tomorrow.'

Ten minutes later there is another chime from the doorbell.

Now it is the impertinent dark young waiter standing in the

corridor. He has a grey jacket on now, his hands thrust into the pockets. His face is the picture of concern. 'Is there a problem with your room?'

She's momentarily confused. 'No. Why?'

'You told the porter you were leaving. But we have your reservation for next week.'

'Yes, I am leaving.'

'May I ask – for another hotel?'

'It's none of your business where I'm going, actually.'

'It *is* if you've been unhappy here.'

'I'm not unhappy.' She goes to close the door but the toe of his sneaker has edged into the doorway. 'Do you mind?'

He doesn't take it away. 'I'm sorry about what happened with Vincent,' he says. 'But if we can make your stay more comfortable in any way . . .'

'Vincent?' What does a waiter know about Vincent?

He crosses his arms now. 'I've known Vince for years. He stays in all my hotels. We even planned to open a bar together once.'

She's not getting it.

'Sorry,' he says, holding out a hand. 'I'm Rahul Najara. I own this hotel.'

She takes his strong grip, embarrassed. 'I thought . . .'

'Yeah, I realise. I'm king of this castle and I forget that not everybody knows who I am.' His smile is self-deprecating. 'I've just come back from LA. I missed Vincent while he was here and when you were in LA, I was in Miami. That's why you didn't meet me.'

'You own the Casa Grande too?'

'I own five hotels. This one. The Casa Grande. The Landis in Boston. The Neptune, which is a conversion of a fifties motel in South Beach. And we've just opened the Duane, in an old electrical factory down in Tribeca. We sold most of the condos right off the plan. It's one amazing endless boom right now.'

She has been studying him while he talks. He seems more interesting to her now that he is rich. His stubble is artfully contrived rather than scruffy. His black, ringletty hair looks almost pretty. The swarthy skin has taken on a golden glow. His dark eyes are lit from within. She now sees a beautiful ethnicity in him that she didn't see before. Iranian? Pakistani? She can't place it. She takes a step back into the room. 'Would you like to come in?'

'No, thanks.'

There's a silence. She can tell he's weighing up what to say. Gradually she realises there's a soundtrack running underneath the silence – the muted sounds of a man in the room next door grunting rhythmically. 'Someone is losing his inhibitions,' she smiles.

Now he smiles too. 'It's as if we give them a key, not to a room, but to another life altogether. '

She considers the truth of this.

'So, how long have you known Vincent?' he asks.

'About four months.'

'Where did you meet him?'

'In Bangkok.'

'Ah, yes. Bangkok. One of his favourite stomping grounds. He's quite a guy. Are you a model?'

'God no, I'm too fat for a model!'

'*I* don't think so. But there are other kinds of models.'

The way he says *models* suggests he doesn't mean that profession at all. 'I've never been a model,' she answers, wishing she didn't sound so prickly.

'I meant it as a compliment.'

'Thank you.'

'What *do* you do?'

'I'm travelling.'

'Seeing what the world brings you?' The tone of his voice has changed. The question is not so casual.

'Why not?' No, that doesn't sound so good. 'I mean, I'm not looking—'

'No need to explain. I understand.' His friendliness has shifted down a notch.

'What I mean is – I'm free, I don't have any commitments.'

'And you're beautiful.'

'No, that's not it. It's nothing to do with . . . beauty.' What is coming out of her mouth seems strange even to her. She can see now what he thinks of her. She wonders how many women Vincent has brought to Rahul's hotels over the years. What kind of women. 'I liked Vincent.'

'Of course you did. Vincent's a lovable guy.'

'Not *that* lovable,' she says.

He smiles with teeth that are dazzling white in silk-pink lips. 'It looks to me as if you came out of it okay.'

'There are compensations.' She doesn't know why she says this. It will only confirm what he thinks of her.

'Yeah, there usually are,' he says. After a moment: 'I'm sending the champagne up again.'

'No, really.'

'Yes, really. I want you to open a bottle every night you're here,' he says. 'That should keep you here for another fortnight.'

'I'm not looking for bribes.'

'It's not a bribe. It's a business proposition.'

'Meaning?' She can feel, quite palpably, her heart go beat, skip, beat.

'It's good business to keep our best customers happy,' he says blandly. She feels a wrench of disappointment. He folds his arms across a broad chest. He is not much taller than her, even though she is in bare feet. 'Now, what don't you like about your room? What can we change for you?'

She might as well be honest. 'How about all the furnishings?'

'It's that bad?'

She nods, not quite able to unlock a frown. 'Terrifying.'

'Then I have a better idea,' he says.

GRAND HOTEL RIVIERA

Boulevard de la Croisette, Cannes, France

I don't know why I do what I do next. I tell myself I'm just going to visit a friend for a cup of tea and a chat. I tell myself nothing can be read into it. I tell myself a lot of things and all of them are lies.

The lobby of the Riviera is like a sea with tides of people going in and out. I don't linger: the rip down here is too dangerous for me now. I walk straight into the elevator and press 12. When I step out, the corridor is as quiet as a padded cell. Outside one door, a rolling table is scattered with the debris of a shared breakfast in bed. No one has touched the bread rolls or eaten the bacon but there are two upended bottles of Krug in a silver bucket. Hollywood breakfast. Further along the corridor, a maid's trolley stands abandoned, the little bottles of shampoo and the monogrammed matchboxes there for the taking. I snatch a handful of matches and shove them in my purse. Matchboxes from good hotels never go astray. In a pinch you can start a fire or a conversation with them. And I have done both.

I stand outside Charles' suite and pause for a moment before I press the bell. I have no idea what I'm going to say. But I know that the door between us has to remain open or shut for good.

I am expecting the manservant to appear. If Charles is out, I'll ask to see his daughter Samantha, who I always liked, although the feeling wasn't mutual.

But when the door is finally opened, it's none of these three.

At first I think I have the wrong room and apologise. And then I see the new carpet and furnishings and know I'm at the right place.

'Is Charles in?'

She starts at my feet and then runs her eyes up my body. Her eyes, paler blue than mine, have an arrogant gleam. Right then I know she is not a PA or a film student come to pay homage. 'Who wants to know?' *Who vants to know?* Russian, Czech or Romanian. Knowing my luck, she is Romanian.

'A friend,' I say. To tell her any more would be to acknowledge she has some status in this.

'Vell, he's not in right now.'

We study each other. She has got to be twenty years younger than me and about five inches taller. Her lankiness may be genetic – aided by a pair of gold platforms strapped to her ankles – but everything else is fake. Her breasts, hoisted in a gold mesh crochet bikini top, burst with plastic inserts of saline. Her acrylic fingernails are tipped with opaque white. Her teeth have been stripped by laser beams, her long hair dipped in raven black, the top lip pumped up with collagen, the tip of the nose clipped off by a scalpel, the taut thighs in spray-on hotpants orange with spray-on tan. The whole package is smooth, blemishless and luminous – and strangely 3-D like one of those schlocky postcards depicting perky kittens in a basket. She's a blow-up doll with a pulse.

So Charles has followed my advice and asked Hervé for his 'book'.

I try another tack. 'Is Sammy in then?'

'No.' She's not old enough or bright enough to work me out but she knows I'm some kind of threat. She doesn't want me to impinge on her afternoon delight with Charles, lest she forfeits that big tip.

'So, when will Charles be back?'

She shrugs and pushes the door to close it. These spawn of failed Communist states have no manners.

I step forward and push the door away from me. 'I'll wait.' I'm not entirely sure he's not hiding in the bedroom *in flagrante delicto*.

She doesn't budge. 'Vell, you von't vait in here. I am doing my yoga.'

'In those shoes?'

She looks at her feet as if she's never seen them before. 'My instructor comes in a minute.'

'Look, *Svetlana*,' I insist. 'I am a very close friend of Charles and he won't be happy if he knows I've been turned away.'

'So how vill he know?' she asks brazenly.

'I'll tell him.'

'So, I vill tell him your name. Vat is it?'

'Never mind,' I say.

'Nevermind? Never heard of you.' She gives me a triumphant look and pushes the door but I use my elbow to brace it. She has no real strength in those buffed arms of hers. The muscles are probably injected like the filler in her lips.

I draw myself up to her meet her stare. 'And who are you, I might ask?'

'I am Dina. I am girlfriend of Charles.'

I laugh at her. 'Oh, come on. You've – what? – spent an hour with him?'

She looks offended. 'I haf been living with him in London.'

'Rubbish. How long? How long have you been living with him?'

'Four months.'

'Really? And what's his address?'

She rattles it off, including the postal code. 'And ve haf house in Cotswalds and apartment in Trump Towers.' Her eyes are glimmering with triumph now. 'And ve haf poopydog called Orson. Now, vill you go?'

I don't like the *ve*. I've seen girls like this latch on to dim aristocrats and steal their fortunes. But canny old Charles? I'm still not willing to go there. 'Why didn't Charles mention you then?'

'Maybe you not so much his friend as you think.'

I grit my teeth, but she's right. I can see it now, with cruel clarity. Sammy was never coming. Charles had to fob me off so he could canoodle with this orifice-on-legs, sixty years younger than him. Twenty years younger than me.

These girls, prefabricated, brainless, devoid of personality, wit or charm, they've devalued all of us. Ten years ago they were just desperate teenage whores, found on any Bulgarian roadside, turning tricks for smokes. And now they are trophies, plastic and mute, sitting on Belgravia mantelpieces, requiring nothing but designer clothing, fast cars and money to send home. They don't converse, they don't hostess, they don't facilitate, soothe or run interference. During the Italian Renaissance they might have written novels, published poetry and influenced politics. Now they take it up the ass and read *Cosmopolitan*. They have made their men lazy and cheap and bloated with self-importance.

I am a tight fist of anger, frustration and despair. But try as

I might I can't work up much rage towards her. It's the way of the world now. Everything is immediate, anything can be bought, nothing is worth the trouble. No woman is worth a price above rubies when rubies will do very nicely, thank you.

'Let me give you some advice,' I start to say to her.

'Not necessary,' she says and slams the door.

THE DUANE HOTEL

Hudson Street, New York, USA

The workers who once toiled in the old electrical factory would not be permitted to put their greasy boots on the lacquered floors of the hotel that has risen from its foundations. Everything is white, from the painted plank floorboards to the pooling organza curtains to the rivers of ivory-coloured sofa that curve through the temple-like lobby. A stone buddha crouches in a pond of creamy lotuses. A chandelier of mother-of-pearl cascades from the ceiling, the shells making a faint clacking sound as they shimmer in an artificial breeze. The porters glide around in white T-shirts and wrap-tied yoga pants, pressing their hands together as she passes. It reminds Violet of a place where they lock away delicate people, where every smile is undercut by the fear that it might all come apart.

Her suite is as minimal as a teahouse but she knows it must cost a fortune, with its views through arched windows over a little park, thick-piled cashmere blankets and four different kinds of complimentary water by the bed. The cost is academic, for Rahul Najara insists she stay as his personal guest. She protests, of course, but not too avidly. I won't accept no, he replies. The hotel is in its 'soft opening' stage and he would value her critique. What does she think of the bathrobes? Does the butler come quickly to pour her tea? Is the bed comfortable? Does she like the pillows? The sheets? He knows she has experience with these things. The way he says this suggests he means something else.

She assumes he wants something in return for his generosity. He has a gold ring set with ruby stones on his wedding finger but he has rings on three other fingers too. Does it matter, anyway, whether he's married or not? She should be grateful this soft opening means she has had a soft landing.

So she is disappointed when he doesn't appear to welcome her to the room, although a mass of tuberoses and an impersonal *Compliments of the management* card arrives. When she asks at reception if she can thank him for the flowers, she is told he is out of town.

Now she exists in a strange kind of limbo. Each day, she feels eyes on her as she walks through the lobby. The doorman's smile is always wry, as if he has a secret he is forbidden to impart. She wonders if the porters and maids are keeping tabs on her for their boss, like the servants in a court. Do they note the number of shopping bags she brings back from her excursions? Do they count the hours that she is out? Will they report back to him if she's seen with a man? Or stays away from her room all night?

As the days go on and there is no sign of him, she feels more unsettled. Is she supposed to stay there until he returns? If so, he has made no spoken arrangement. Does he not know she requires an arrangement?

Violet goes shopping.

It is, after all, what she knows how to do. She travels with trunks now; she does not *need* new clothes. But it is a way of making human contact. It was only seven months ago she was frightened into buying those satin shoes in a Paris boutique. Now she has the measure of sales assistants, who fuss over her like a long-lost friend. She enjoys listening to the gossip, the banter about trivial things, fingers tugging at zippers and hems while they prattle on about *Titanic* and murderous British nannies and Backstreet Boys – inane, ill-informed chatter she finds totally seductive. At school, the girls would draw in closer and put their heads together when she passed. She has always been gossiped *about*.

She is not really buying clothes, she is buying the sales assistants' company. She is under no illusion about that.

One afternoon she returns with a dress that has taken three hours, $950 and four fawning sales attendants to buy. She unpacks it, lays it out on the bed and thinks, *Pity I have no one to wear this for.*

But maybe she has.

In the lobby bar she orders a martini.

It's not long before a gentleman pays for the next. He's a surgeon from Philadelphia with an implanted forest of hair, but rich-looking enough. He will do.

She knows the lobby staff is watching her.

The surgeon has to go to a dinner but perhaps she could dine with him tomorrow night?

'Wonderful,' she says and gives him a peck on his microdermabrased cheek.

The next evening, she meets him in the foyer and they walk up to Montrachet. The weather is cool now and she has layered her dress with animal pelts.

Over glazed duck she has to endure his repulsive descriptions of surgical procedures. There is a twinkle in his eye as he watches her squirm.

She drinks too much Chassagne-Montrachet. He observes that one of her breasts is smaller than the other. It would be quite simple to have this repaired. It is just like changing the tyre on a car. And perhaps she might think about other improvements while she's under the anaesthetic? Better to get it done all at once. Body contouring, a tummy tuck? Not that she needs it. But maybe she is unhappy *down there?* You can't be too perfect. He has had all kinds of success with labial reduction *if* that is her problem. Young women these days are so *active*. You can't keep stretching a shoe and not make it sloppy. She looks like she knows what he means. Really, it's a simple procedure to make her as tight as she'd like . . . he is talking about *both* entrances of course.

She wonders, dismally, *so* this *might be my life? Drinking splendid wine in expensive restaurants with appalling men?* She does not feel like dessert. The surgeon takes this for a sign that she is keen to have a consultation. He pays the bill and estimates the tip to the exact cent on a pocket calculator.

They walk back through the lobby together. He has a hand on her plush arm, sure of a conquest. As they enter the elevator, she sees a porter smirk. When he gets off on his floor, she doesn't step out. He turns to see the doors close behind him.

She instructs the operator not to put through any calls.

The evening has been unpleasant and she doesn't sleep well.

But it has the desired effect.

Rahul Najara is back the next day.

He appears at her door in the afternoon, dressed as soberly as if he's going to a funeral. In his arms, he embraces a brown paper cornet of lanky purple flowers. 'I brought these up for you.' He does not say 'Sorry to disturb you', even though she is in her robe. 'I usually forbid any flowers that aren't white . . . but these suit your name.'

'Thanks,' she says and looks for the card.

'There isn't a card.'

She tells him he is thoughtful.

'It's what I've been doing. Thinking about you.' There is nothing flirtatious in his face. He looks like a manager who has been sent up to tell a guest her father has died.

'I'm not making you very happy, then,' she jokes.

A wan smile. 'Not yet.'

'Do you want to come in?'

She thinks he will say yes this time but he shakes his head. 'It's my rule.'

A door opens down the corridor and a guest pushes a breakfast trolley into the hall, closes the door again. The rattling makes her jump, but Rahul does not take his eyes off her. 'I had a dream about you the other night,' he says. 'The night I first saw you in the lobby.'

The way he is looking at her, she is not sure she wants to hear it. 'Did I kill someone?'

He manages a smile. 'Do you want me to tell you?'

'Only if it's not embarrassing.'

'It's embarrassing for me.' He folds his arms, revealing a gold bracelet on one wrist. She recognises it as the kind which can be locked and a lover given the key. She wonders who has the key. 'In my dream you were sitting in the lobby – this one, downstairs. You were dressed very conservatively, a blue suit with heels, your hair up in a formal style, an emerald necklace, earrings, rings. You were sitting on one of our high-backed chairs, knees together, as if you were waiting for an appointment. None of the staff spoke to you. I was driven with an intense need to find out who you were waiting for, why you were there. But a kind of fear stopped me from asking . . . Am I boring you?'

'Will it end badly?'

He looks at her curiously. 'I don't know.'

His gaze is so probing, she averts her eyes.

'So I would walk back and forth across that lobby to catch your attention. And each time you looked me straight in the eye. And do you know what else you'd do? You would take off one item that you were wearing. Slowly, looking at me all the time. First, it was the jewel around your neck. Then it was the earrings. Next, your jacket.You get the idea. Eventually, you had taken your hair down and you were sitting there in just your high-heels and white underwear. Even in my imagination, you weren't as beautiful as you are now. I crossed the lobby and you bent down to unfasten your shoes. The next time I crossed, you were sitting there in just your bikini pants, knees still tightly together. Can you imagine how excited I got, to think that you would be entirely naked the next time? So I start to walk across the lobby. There's a potted palm in the way. And when I reach you . . .'

'Don't tell me.'

'You're dressed again. Except your suit is green this time. And I wake up with a pillow over my head and a very damp sheet.'

Throughout his speech she has felt the blush rise through her body until it sits like a hot collar around her face.

'I *am* embarrassing you,' he says.

'Isn't that what you intended?'

'Maybe. I wanted to see how you react.'

'How else could I have reacted?'

'You could have been offended. The fact that you're not tells me something.'

'And what is that?'

'That you are open to possibilities.'

She tries to laugh it off. 'Do you dream about all your guests?'

'Only when they intrigue me.'

'I'm not so intriguing.'

'I think you are.'

She puts her hand on the door, a gesture that suggests she is about to close it. 'Look, you've got the wrong idea about me.'

'What idea should I have?'

'This room, the champagne. It doesn't give you the right . . .'

'I have no rights. Go on, close the door.' He takes a step backwards into the hall.

She doesn't move. 'Do you hit on all the women who stay in your hotels?'

'I'm just trying to find out what you'll cost me.'

So this is all he wants. 'I thought this was a hotel, not a brothel.'

'I'm not talking about money. I'm thirty-eight years old. Most of my wealth is tied up developing hotels. I work hard. I play hard. I *fall* hard. I don't have time to be messed around. I can give you what I have. But I have to know it's enough.'

His certainty unnerves her. 'You don't know the first thing about me.'

'I know the *first* thing.' Meaning Vincent.

'I'm married.' She doesn't know why she says this except that she wants now to fend him off.

That surprises him. He nods at her left hand where it's clutching the bouquet. 'You're not wearing a ring.'

'Separated.'

'Then that's not married. In the interests of complete disclosure, I've been engaged three times. I just broke up with my girlfriend in California. If you read the gossip columns you'll know all about it.'

'I don't read them.'

'Good. I don't want you to have any preconceptions about me.'

'And what would those be?'

'Read *New York.*'

'So you're going to keep knocking on doors until you find a woman who will take you on the rebound.'

She regrets this as soon as it's out of her mouth. He looks hurt. 'I broke up with my girlfriend because of *you.*'

'Because of a dream?'

'It's enough.'

'And you assumed I . . . ?'

'No, I didn't assume. I am trying to find out. This is what this is about.'

She feels a sense of dismay at his ardour. 'I don't like to be rushed.'

'Sorry about that, but I get the idea I have to be fast with you.' A flicker of humour. 'The minute I turn my back, you're off with another man.'

She doesn't respond to this. The reaction is, after all, what she intended. 'All right. I'll have dinner with you.'

'Fine. I will have dinner with you if food is what you want. Do you require a grand tour of my hotels? A blood test? Or would you rather meet my mother first? Would any of this make any difference? We can either start something now or play games.'

She wants to play games. She is not ready for this weight. The weight of his expectations on her.

'Please,' she says.

'Anything? Just tell me.'

'Don't be so sure of me.'

They do not have dinner.

He takes her to his apartment, in the loft he keeps under the roof of the hotel. It is white as a padded cell, with no sign of masculine disarray. 'The advantage of maids,' he tells her as he brings her to the bed.

If only maids could tidy her feelings.

She knows she should have withheld her favours to give them more value but the force of his passion is like a gale blowing a dancing leaf through empty halls. If he rifles her hair she might snap like a twig. She needs to keep her roots in the ground so as not to be blown over. Or let the wind take her where it will. She is in two minds.

There is texture in the dusk as it falls but the light has no hue. She is cold, even though the heat emanating from his body embraces her as warmly as arms.

'This is not about sex,' he tells her as they stand a fingertip apart. 'In case you're wondering.'

'Do you think it *could* be?' she asks. It would be so much easier.

He leans forward and kisses her on the mouth. He tastes of something that is not meant for mouths, musky and sweet, like perfume. Once she is over the shock of it, she kisses him back hard.

'Slow down,' he says, taking a step backwards. 'It might all be over before we begin.'

She puts out a hand, but he keeps her at a distance.

'Now let me see,' he says to her, not quite smiling.

'What?'

'What you want, Violet.'

He studies her thoughtfully.

'Are you inspecting me?' she asks.

'This is the only time I'm going to see all of you,' he says. 'After this, I won't look at you the same way.'

'What will be different about me?'

'It's what will be different about *me*. I will be in love with you.'

She pretends to herself she hasn't heard. Because underneath it is an unspoken demand: love *me*. And she is not sure, not sure at all, that this is what she wants. In her liaisons with other men she has created a pragmatic Violet to keep herself safe. That Violet is not so easily dispatched.

Rahul comes to her now and his fingers pop the buttons on the front of her dress. She thinks she can hear his quickening pulse, but it is in fact hers, thudding in her ears.

She helps him by pushing the dress off her shoulders, reaches to undo her bra.

'Wait,' he says.

He unclips her bra adeptly. He sighs when she shakes it to the floor. She knows the effect her white skin has. She stands there while the soft pads of his fingers circle every mole. He turns her around and kisses the base of her spine. Then he pulls her against him and slides his hands under the elastic of her knickers.

She pushes his hand deeper in.

'No,' he says, extricating himself. 'Too soon.'

'Then let me touch you.'

He is not much taller than her and when she turns and steps close to him, their nipples graze. She runs her hands inside his

T-shirt, over his thick arms and down his tapered waist. He is fit and hard-muscled, but the flesh that covers him is hairless, smooth and plump, like he has been spoiled by a mother's cooking. His scent, too, is of nurseries, like sweet milk.

Her hands find the gold bracelet on his wrist. 'Who gave you this?' she asks.

'Jealous already?' he whispers.

'Maybe.'

'You're wondering if there's another woman?'

'I am.'

'Don't worry. My mother holds the key.'

She laughs, thinking this is a joke. She snakes her hands inside the waistband of his shorts. He is, of course, already mahogany-hard. The shaft of his cock is rimmed by the thickness of circumcision.

He puts his hand over hers. 'My mother is Hindi and my father is a Sephardic Jew. They argued over whether to circumcise me or not until I was six. I remember it clearly.'

'That's awful.'

'It just makes me extremely sensitive.' He moves her hand away. 'Be careful.'

'What shall I do?'

He places his hand between her thighs. His fingers find her opening and then withdraw again. She watches him turn and find a rattan chair. He brings it back and places it facing the bed. 'Take off your underwear. Sit on the chair.'

She does what he asks.

'Sit more on the edge of it. Now, open your legs.'

He sits on the bed opposite her, very near, but not touching.

'Show me what you do to yourself.'

'I want you to do it to me.'

'Not yet. I want to see.'

She feels exposed in a way that is nothing to do with bare skin. She is used to being looked at nude but it's not her physical nakedness that is on display. As her fingers move she closes her eyes not to see him seeing. The heat between her legs spreads up to her neck. The rash prickles her skin like ants running all over her.

After a while, he asks, 'Do you always close your eyes?'

She opens them again. 'Sometimes.'

'And what do you see when you close them?'

She shuts them tight. 'Me. Sitting here. From my perspective.'

'Not me?'

'If I try.'

'I don't want to be the person you see when you try. I want to be the person you see when you're not trying.'

He places his hands on her thighs. She looks at him. There's a fiery aura around him. It can't be the cold dying sun.

'Close your eyes again,' he says. 'Don't think of any other men.'

Her eyelashes graze her cheek. Behind her lids the veins are red. She touches herself again. But his command has had the opposite effect. She tries to think of other men.

He takes her hand away from her pubic hair and then runs his thumbs along her inner thigh, gently separating her lips. He says to her, 'Do you know what you look like? One of those lilies with petals like a hood, tightly wound . . . I think it's time to open you up.'

He places his hands on her waist and draws her to him. The chair falls backwards with a clunk on the floorboards, echoing a sensation at the pit of her stomach. He kisses her eyebrows, the tip of her nose, her collarbone, her chin, the corners of her lips. The strength of his arms around her and the radiant heat of his body make her feel as if she were something fragile and wilting, like a bruised gardenia too long in the sun. She doesn't give into it. She pulls him harder against her. His cock nudges her legs apart so that the shaft slides against her swollen clitoris. She waits while he rolls on a condom. She can hardly bear the tension now and stretches on one toe, throwing the other leg around his thighs before reaching down to grasp the root of his cock and force the head into her. He obliges by thrusting deeply and then lifting her so she can wrap both arms and legs around him while he moves slowly inside her. He does not quite fill her up, but the ridge around his shaft makes an exquisite friction. When they become unbalanced, he deposits her on the bed without withdrawing and pushes a pillow under her buttocks.

When he comes it is with the roar of a lion. She tries to delicately roll away from under his weight but he clings to her like she's a life raft in a perfect storm. She is content with his pleasure but unsatisfied herself. She thinks he doesn't notice.

'Do you think we're finished?' he whispers from what she thinks is a deep sleep.

Her orgasm is excruciating when it comes, not pleasure or pain, but like an explosion inside her that twists her womb, a cluster bomb of torment and tenderness. She has fought it all the way. She doesn't want to lose control of herself to this man who wants more than she can give.

He pulls her off the sheets so that her thighs are over his knees. His arms encircle her back. Into her neck he whispers urgently, 'Look at me, Violet.' It's quite dark in the room now but his eyes smoulder like the black heads of matches. 'Think about *me*.'

Rahul has held Violet in an embrace for hours, as they lie on the platform bed floating above the street noise of fire trucks screeching through the dark. It's now well and truly night. He has lit a sandalwood candle and the flickering tip of it is the only light in the room. But she can see remarkably well, as if she has become as nocturnal as the owls outside in the trees.

She wants to get off the bed and free herself from him and she wants to stay like this in his arms. It's as if there are two of her, with opposing needs. In her mind he is the perfect man for one of them – and the wrong man for the other. One part of her congratulates herself on making such a catch. The other frets that it is she who has been caught.

The bedside phone purrs, stops, purrs again. He has had all his calls held by reception so this one feels urgent, like a little growling creature angry at them.

'Your wake-up call?' she asks.

'No, my wake-up call is you,' he says. 'Ignore it.'

But it won't be ignored. After the sixth or seventh tone he picks up the receiver and listens. 'Yeah,' he says and puts it down. He sits up and fumbles for the bedside light, then reaches down and finds his shorts, pulls them on. 'I'm needed downstairs. I'll be back.'

'What's wrong?'

'The usual. A guest has been ripped off by a hooker. He's making a fuss. Won't call the cops of course. But he's threatening to sue us.'

'Why?'

'For allowing her to step into the place.'

'He must have called her.'

'Who knows? She might have been sitting in the bar. It's impossible to tell these days who is and who isn't.'

She feels the undercurrent of something unsaid.

He stands up and finds his T-shirt. 'When I'm downstairs I'll get them to send all your luggage up here.'

She studies the exaggerated curve of his spine. She doesn't know what she has been expecting – a nice room for a few months, perhaps, some travelling with him to his other hotels. 'You want me to stay here with you?'

He turns around. 'I want you to *live* with me,' he says, as the T-shirt goes over his head. 'Permanently.'

'But you hardly know me.'

'I know what I need to know.'

'After a few hours?'

'I told you I'm not here for sex, or what you think sex is. It's not only about the body or even the mind. It's not even about the soul. I don't necessarily believe that stuff. It's *character.* The way you respond to me is your character, the way you breathe and sigh and the jokes you make. I don't need to know anything more about you.' He zips up his trousers. 'Unless, of course, you still love your husband.'

How many months has she thought about this? 'I never loved him. It just seemed that I should marry him. I thought that it was the logical conclusion.'

'To what?'

'To having a lot of sex.'

'And was it?'

'Not for him. There were other women.'

'What an idiot. I don't understand men who play around. Especially when they have a *prize* like you.'

She says nothing. Patrick never made her feel like a prize, more like a present in shiny packaging that when opened is not what you want.

He has stopped dressing now. 'So you wouldn't go back to him?'

'I haven't spoken to him since last March.'

'Man, I'd hate to be him. Knowing I was missing out on you.'

He reaches for his key card by the bed. 'I'll get your luggage sent up. But you have to know that your other life stops *now*. I promise I'll never be unfaithful to you. How could I be? But there will be no other men, from the past or the future. I am not someone you play with. Do you understand?'

She has no other life. She nods.

He leans down and kisses her breast. 'Stay safe. I'll be back.'

She winds herself so tightly in the sheet it feels like a straightjacket.

LA RÉSERVE DE ST-TROPEZ

Route des Plages, St-Tropez, France

I start collecting my few things and folding them into the suitcase. Time to make a run for it, vamoose, get out of here, cut my losses, jump ship, haul ass, take a powder, beat a retreat. There are so many ways to say it, more ways than saying 'I'll stay.'

In a pocket of my handbag I still have the bundle of notes given to me by Charles for shopping. It's more than I thought. I have enough money to buy myself a ticket out of here, if I don't go to the ends of the earth. I think about the Hassler in Rome, perched on the Spanish steps, with its seductive salons of velvet plushness. The Ritz in London, where a girl can make afternoon tea last all night. The Peninsula in Hong Kong, playground of the brash and entrepreneurial new Asian rich. The Seiyo Ginza in Tokyo, where an architect hid me for a month. Or the Beaumarchais in Monte Carlo, where . . .

No, time for places where I haven't left a footprint. Dubai, perhaps: seven-star hotels, indoor oceans, oil money, men with cumin-scented skin. Or volatile, dangerous Buenos Aires, where there are gauchos and polo players and parlours festering with snake-hipped tango dancers.

I call down for a car to take me to the airport. I close my suitcase, stash the money in a monogrammed envelope. I am about to tuck it in my pocket when I remember I've left my cigarettes on the balcony.

The maid has arranged the pack on an ashtray with the lid flipped and one cigarette extended, like a still life from an old magazine. I feel a stab of bitter sweetness that I have to leave this ordered life.

I take out the cigarette and turn away from the breeze to light it. The flame sizzles: the cigarette is damp. I turn to find another and almost drop the matches in shock. A figure has appeared on the terrace across the way.

The occupant of villa muguet is angry. She has her bag open on the wrought-iron table and is anxiously rummaging through it while she barks orders in French to a person inside the room, probably a poor maid. She is in a hurry, she will be late, her life will be ruined – these are snatches of monologue that float across the pool to me. She sounds like a fishwife and she may indeed be one – it's impossible to tell because her face is almost completely concealed by flesh-coloured bandages. (Although, unluckily for the maid, not her mouth.) Then I remember being told of the Parisian department store heiress and her Tunisian nip and tuck. The joke is on me. I have been parading myself for a shopgirl dressed like a Halloween mummy. I watch in amused silence as she staggers back into her room, waving a piece of paper – a ticket perhaps – that has been, apparently, 'hidden' from her in the bottom of her bag.

Just as well I am leaving. There is no *next* here. My admirer was nothing more than a wisp of smoke.

I'm congratulating myself for my decision when an altogether different figure appears on the terrace of the villa muguet.

He stands there, one arm across his body, the other holding a cigarette close to his mouth. He is willowy in a white caftan, the cotton plastered to his fine damp torso as if he's just emerged from a bath. He is looking directly at me. This time there is no smokescreen. I recognise the gesture, the set of his shoulders, the tilt of his head. If Jesus himself had have appeared on the balcony I wouldn't have been more shocked.

But he's no saviour of mine.

THE DUANE HOTEL

Hudson Street, New York, USA

The President of the United States is looking angry. 'I want to say one thing to the American people. I want you to listen to me. I'm going to say this again. I did not have sexual relations with that woman, Miss Lewinsky.'

Violet is lying on her stomach on the bed, eating sugared cashews. Like the rest of America she is glued to the television set watching the President's denial. There is a table waiting downstairs at the restaurant for them, but Violet has told Rahul she won't be ready to eat until the televised address is over.

The streets eight storeys below are empty, not unusual for a frigid January night like this. Even the old man who lives in the park with his funny hat and beagle dog is gone, probably, she thinks, down to Broadway to watch TV in an electrical store window. Their condominium hovers above the treetops and from her position on the bed she can look into the other apartments edging the triangular park. Windows are bathed in blue light. In one of the lofts, owned by a famous film actor, Bill Clinton's sandy head flickers from a giant rear projection screen like Big Brother. In another, a party is under way, people crowded around a television set with wine glasses in their hands. She can see into a small room where a family are sitting in front of the screen and she wonders how the parents are going to explain the content of the speech to their two small children. There has been nothing but talk about blowjobs on the television for days.

She has been giving a few of them herself.

Rahul comes out of the bathroom buttoning up a grey shirt. 'What's happening?' he asks, although, unlike everyone else, he is not particularly interested. The only thing he knows – or cares – about politics is the special requirements of the politicians and diplomats who stay in his hotels. He has dined with many of them and he once attended the wedding of a Senator's daughter, but he holds no partisan view. He doesn't even vote, which Violet finds shocking.

'He's denying everything,' Violet says.

Rahul stands to one side of the television, watching. 'I don't believe him. Man, what an idiot.'

'For going on TV to deny it or doing it in the first place?'

'Doing it, of course. That girl looks wacko.'

'I don't think she's a wacko,' Violet says. 'Imagine you're a young girl and the most powerful man in the world flirts with you. He would be hard to resist.'

'She seduced him first.'

'You think so? I don't. I spoke to him once on the phone and he was a terrible flirt.'

Rahul turns to her, suspicion sharpening his eyes. 'When did you do that?'

'Oh, I don't know,' she says evasively.

'Who do you know who knows Bill Clinton?'

She doesn't particularly want to go into it. 'Just some business acquaintance.'

'Come on, not just anyone knows the President.'

'Well, if you have to know, it was Lyle Huntington.'

He turns back to the television set, not looking at her. 'I wish you hadn't told me that.'

'You asked.'

'I know, I should never ask.'

'Look, it was before I met you.'

'I've been to his house.'

'You have?'

'A charity dinner. He's married.'

'Only in name.'

'And he's got at least a couple of mistresses.'

'You see? I wasn't hurting his wife.'

Rahul faces her again. He's angry. 'He's an old guy. Did you do it for money?'

She sits up on the bed. 'You know I didn't.'

'Jewellery, furs maybe?'

She has been circumspect about her jewels, keeping mostly of them in the hotel's safe. But she can't resist wearing a few pieces. Rahul has said nothing about them until now. 'What makes you think a man like Lyle isn't attractive in his own right?'

'Is he attractive?'

'Yes.'

'Was it one night?'

'Of course not. I was his travelling companion for a time.'

'Oh, the travelling thing.'

She holds out her hand. 'Don't be an idiot. You said you never wanted me to talk about the past. I came under his spell, that's all.'

'Like Monica and Bill?'

When he doesn't take her hand, she climbs off the bed and entwines her hands behind his neck. He holds his body like a board. 'He means nothing to me compared to you.'

If she thinks about it, this is not strictly true. She cannot truly say that if both were standing in front of her she would choose one over the other. And she doesn't know how this could be. For Lyle is just a distant memory but Rahul is a dominating presence, who has been put on earth to make her happy, or so he says, and feels a physical pain when he has to leave her, even if it's just to troubleshoot a missing reservation, so he says, and would put a bar code on her, if he could, he says, to stop other men checking her out. These last three months she has been folded conclusively into his life with the loose ends of her past all neatly tied up. Ironically, it is Rahul's flaw, his jealousy, which makes her feel safe, like a baby wrapped tight in the swaddling of his passion. But quite often she finds herself daydreaming about an older, colder man, who would just let her be.

She feels him relax. He surrounds her waist with his arms and whispers in her ear. 'I'm sorry. I can't bear the thought of you with a man like that.'

'I'm not with a man like that.'

And that *is* true. She's not. And that, she decides, is what counts. 'Come on, you were taking me to dinner.'

A hand snakes around to her breast. 'You haven't had my apology yet.'

'I never told anybody to lie, not a single time; never. These allegations are false,' the President is saying.

But Violet isn't listening any more. Even to herself.

The basement of the Duane is occupied by a Japanese restaurant, Sushay, and a bar so fashionable it needs two bouncers and a velvet rope at the door.

Rahul and Violet have their usual corner booth, private enough so that no one can overhear their conversation, but positioned so that Rahul can survey the room and check on the smooth running of the business. Tonight, the two booths beside them, generally reserved for A-listers, have been kept vacant so that the couple can have additional privacy.

As they share a plate of green tea desserts, he slides a black envelope across the table. 'I have something for you.'

He bombards her with witty little fancies constantly – a pair of purple earmuffs he thinks will go with her hair, a tortoiseshell bracelet he spotted in an antique store window, a satin slipper chair for sitting in when she takes off her shoes. Just this morning a complete set of *Eloise* books arrived with the mail.

And then there are the jewels – slowly, piece by piece, little glittering gifts to replace 'that stuff other men have given you', which, he tells her, 'wink gloatingly at me every time you wear them'.

Violet puts her hand on the envelope. It doesn't feel like a jewel.

'Open it,' he says.

Inside is a thick document. When she unfolds it, she finds a hand-drawn chart and pages of script.

'It's in Devanagari. I asked my mother's astrologer to do your chart for you.'

Violet is not sure about Rahul's mother. He keeps a photograph of her by his bed and has long secret phone conversations with her at all hours of the night. But he says very little about her. All Violet knows is that his parents were divorced when he was six and his mother returned to India. His father died in 1996, leaving his share of the business to a young wife who communicates with Rahul only through lawyers. 'My horoscope?' She looks at the circles and lines.

'You told me what time you were born and it was easy from there.' He takes her hand across the table. 'No one in India can get married without an astrologer's approval. The bride and groom's astrological aspects have to be compatible.'

Bride and groom. She has been able to avoid his little hints until now.

'Of course, astrologers can be bribed to give the desired forecast,' he adds, watching her face.

She surveys his. His eyes are the colour of poured coffee, cloudy with hope. 'Did you have to bribe this one?'

'No, I didn't. We're very compatible. We both have Libran moons. The love of harmony and beauty. If only I can tame your air and fire signs, Aquarius and Aries, then we'll have a long life together. But I'm a Cancer with Capricorn rising. So it will work out – water and earth dampen down fire.'

Air, fire, water . . . and earth. She suddenly feels heavy, as if she's trapped in a coffin and someone is shovelling clods of dirt on it. 'I don't believe in astrology,' she says. 'I'd hate to think my destiny was already written out for me.'

'Even if I was in it?'

'Isn't it better to know I'm with you because I want to be,

rather than it being something to do with the planets?'

'No. That makes me feel insecure. People change their minds. Only the stars are consistent.'

'I didn't know you were so traditional.'

'Like most Indians, I'm traditional when it suits me.' He squeezes her hand. 'Okay. Let me convince you. When you broke up with your husband – was it around October 1996?'

'Yes, it was. Did I tell you that?'

'No, you didn't. But according to your chart, the planet Saturn was passing through your horoscope at that exact time. Do you know about the Saturn return?'

She shakes her head.

'Saturn crosses your chart when you are born and every thirty years after that. So it's very auspicious. Whatever you do at the moment will affect you for the next thirty years until Saturn comes back again. So you broke up with your husband and freed yourself completely – for me.'

Violet thinks about this. What she did was free herself for a series of men. Is *this* what she's going to repeat for thirty years? But she doesn't say this to Rahul, who is looking at her intently. 'But he broke up with me. I would have stayed with him.'

'You see? It was the planets. Some force outside yourself.'

In her case, she thinks bitterly, that force was an expensive hooker. 'So what happened on *your* Saturn return?'

'Eight years ago I bought the Union Hotel. Where I met you. See? It works.'

'Only if we spend the next twenty-four years together.'

He smiles and slips his hand from hers. It goes into his trouser pocket and emerges with a tiny, gold drawstring bag. He empties it into his palm. Three fine rings, one platinum, one gold and one rose-gold, glitter in the candlelight. He takes her left hand and slips the gold ring on a finger. 'That's for our first child.' The platinum ring is next. 'That's for our second. And this is for our third.' He slides on the last ring and kisses her palm. 'Do you think three children is enough?'

Violet looks down at her hand and is horrified to find that her eyes well up with tears and overflow down her cheeks. She is not ready for this. And yet, the knowledge that a man wants to have children with her seems overwhelmingly poignant.

Rahul leans across the table to dab her face gently with a linen napkin. He takes her emotion for acquiescence. Violet doesn't know why she won't dissuade him. 'I want to ask you something else. *Vanity Fair* is going to do a feature on us. Is that okay with you?'

'On *us*?'

He shrugs. 'On me, the hotels. They want to photograph us next week at home.'

'But I'm not anybody.'

'You're my fiancée.'

Fiancée. It's touching that he put so much pride in it.

'We need to get a dog,' she says, trying to distract him from the sentimental moment. 'For the photograph.'

He laughs and nods at a waiter, who is hovering. The waiter scurries away. But instead of bringing the check for Rahul to sign he returns with a blazing platter. On it is a pink layer cake, covered in sugared violets, alight with candles set in the shape of a heart and with a plastic bride and groom stuck in the middle of it.

'Congratulations,' the waiter says as he clears a place in the centre of the table for the cake. A waitress brings champagne. She, too, congratulates the couple as she sets the glasses down. The entire restaurant is looking at them. Rahul raises his glass to the room.

'Does *everyone* know about this?' she asks.

'Looks like it.'

There is no way she can tell him she hasn't actually accepted him.

He notices her reticence. 'Is the cake too kitsch for you?'

'No, I love it,' she says.

Does it really matter if I don't love you?

Rahul has given Violet key cards that open the doors to every room in his hotels. She knows that this is his way of trying to unlock her.

He woos her with weekends at his hotel in Miami. When he goes to California, she comes too. They ski in Vermont and look at property in Costa Rica. He flies her up to Boston to spend a few days in the spa. If the slightest frown crosses her brow, a maid or butler appears to smooth it out. When she drops her clothes on the floor, someone is there to pick them up, wash them, press them and put them away. She forgets what it is like to make a cup of tea, fry an egg, paint her own toenails.

'Think of it as having five houses,' Rahul says, 'and all the rooms are yours. I employ nine hundred staff. Every single one of them has been instructed that your needs come first, before any of the guests, before mine. Just tell me if anyone is a problem and I'll get rid of them.'

She finds it ironic that the tables have turned like this, that concierges and porters who might once have looked on her suspiciously are dependent now on her whim, if she chose to exercise it. She has stepped back over some imaginary line that separates those who transgress from those who live socially respectable lives. She knows this line is drawn with chalk, easily smudged.

Sometimes she notices women sitting in the hotel's lobby and surreptitiously watches them to see what they do. Occasionally there is a woman whose provenance is unknown, who checks her watch frequently, and flips through the hotel's coffee-table books as if she were in a doctor's surgery. Then, as quickly as she arrived, she is gone.

One afternoon Violet makes an admiring comment on the shoes of a young woman who is sitting alone in the lobby. Without saying anything, the woman picks up her bag and walks out of the hotel. *I wasn't asking you to move on,* Violet says under her breath, but it's too late.

She knows the concierge desk has a book of fashion models who will spend a night for a price. She has watched beautiful girls slip Polaroids to the doormen. Sometimes the girls are hired in clusters, like balloons, for parties. The doormen must get a cut of the business, she supposes. But she doesn't ask Rahul about it.

It's not a subject she wants brought up.

When the *Vanity Fair* comes out in April, they are part of a feature on fashionable hoteliers. The only mention of her name is in the caption on the photograph.

She looks at it and doesn't recognise herself. She is wearing the Diane von Furstenberg dress of the moment, which appears on models in countless magazine spreads. Her neck is hung with gold chains, which are the stylist's choice. Above these, her face has the hard shine of a pearl, framed in hair that has been teased and sprayed into stiff curls. The way she has been posed, all eyes go to her breasts.

She can see what she looks like to others.

Rahul, on the other hand, is ecstatic about the feature. Like the member of a primitive tribe who thinks that a photograph captures the soul of the sitter, he believes that his soul and Violet's are now fused in the frame.

One night, not long afterwards, they are in Sushay for dinner. The restaurant has been decorated with huge sprays of cherry blossom, so that when they sit in their booth it feels like a bower. The table next to them has been taken over by five long-legged beauties and two young actors, who are in an uproarious state after solidly drinking champagne all night. After a lot of macho posturing, the men start plucking branches of blossom and attacking each other with it like swords.

Rahul subtly signals for the waiters to leave the troublemakers alone. 'If they act up enough it will be in the gossip columns tomorrow.'

'But surely that's not good for business?' Violet asks.

'It's *great* for business. People don't come to our hotels to sleep.' He reaches into his jacket pocket. 'I've got a present for you.'

She sighs. 'I could survive, you know, without a present *every* day.'

'But nature abhors a vacuum. I don't want to leave a hole for someone else to fill.'

She takes the little blue box in her fingers. It is immediately recognisable as a box from Tiffany's. She leans over to kiss him but before her lips touch his, her eyes are pulled towards the centre of the room, where amongst all the chaos there is a vortex of stillness.

Florin is standing there with a group of people, his arm around a young woman. But his eyes are on Violet.

Violet drops the little box in her hand. As she reaches out to pick it up, she knocks a small cup of warm sake all over the cloth.

Florin's group veers away from her, shown to a far table by the maître d.

Rahul, as always, has been watching her. 'What's wrong?'

'Nothing.'

'Do you know that guy?'

'What guy?'

'The one who looked at you as if you were his next meal.'

'Did he?'

'*Do* you know him?'

'Not really.'

'Not *really?* You either know someone or you don't.'

'I met him in Vienna once. He's a . . .' What? Gigolo? ' . . . writer.'

This doesn't make Rahul any happier. 'I have to be worried about writers now.'

'For God's sake, you don't have to be worried about anyone.'

'You don't look at me like that.'

'How don't I look at you?'

'With awe.'

'I didn't look at him with awe.'

'What was it, then? Lust?'

'That's ridiculous,' she says, more to herself than him. 'I'm surprised to see him here, that's all.'

'Why don't you say hello? He still has his eyes on you.'

But she doesn't want to look. Her old enemy, her uncontrollable blush, floods her face.

'I don't feel like eating. I'm going upstairs.' She makes an attempt to push the heavy table away but has to hover, bent over, before a waiter comes and rescues her. She feels like a moth pinned to a board, fluttering to get free.

'Wait for me,' Rahul says.

She walks off without him. She imagines a wall and Florin is on the other side. She doesn't turn to acknowledge him.

As she rides in the elevator alone she is amazed at her own overreaction. She knows she has acted stupidly by making a big deal of something that is not. What is Florin to her? An irritant, at most. But now Rahul thinks he is more than that.

And Florin probably thinks so too.

It makes her a little light-headed.

She's sitting on the edge of the spa bath running water when Rahul gets back to the apartment.

He stands in the bathroom doorway, arms folded. 'Why are you always so distant with me?'

'I'm not distant.' She picks up a bottle of Cote Bastide and absently pours half of it in the bath.

'Yes you are. It's like your heart is anywhere else but with me.'

She turns to him and holds up her left hand. 'What are these rings then?'

He points to her neck. 'What is that diamond? It's something a man you don't care about gave you.'

'Please stop. Everything's good between us. You're jealous of phantoms.'

'But these phantoms have names. What's his name?'

'I haven't got it tattooed across my chest.' She stars unbuttoning her blouse. 'Want to see?'

He looks sadly at her. 'I'm not so easily seduced away from an argument.'

'But why do you want to argue?'

'I want to argue your impassiveness out of you.'

This shocks her. 'I'm not impassive. I'm just different to you. I'm not so demonstrative.'

'Love is a blood sport, Violet. It's not some polite little chat across a table.'

'What does *that* mean?'

'It means it's no good just being *nice* to me.'

'What do you want me to be?'

Disgust crosses his face. 'I'm not a stranger in a hotel room. You don't have to perform to please me.'

'Is that what you think I'm doing?'

'I don't know. You've never said you love me.'

She knows she's been remiss in this. 'I do love you.' It feels clumsy, like a log rolling off her tongue.

She expects him to come to her but he doesn't move. 'Then why don't I feel it?'

'I'm here, aren't I?'

'But you were in hotel rooms with those other men. How do I know it isn't the hotel you love, the things I give you, not me?'

'Then stop giving me things. I'll move out.'

'I don't want you to do that.'

'I'm going to marry you. Isn't that proof enough?'

'When?'

'When my divorce comes through.'

She can see him flinch at the word *divorce*. She knows he hates that she has had a wedding once before. He has a vision of their own, all rose petals and cherubs shooting hearts. 'And when will that be?'

'I'll call Patrick tomorrow.'

'You said you would two weeks ago.'

She knows she has to talk to Patrick but she has been avoiding it. 'He's difficult to reach.'

'You're using him as an excuse.'

It's true. 'Patrick doesn't matter. He can divorce me in

absentia if he can't find me. He might have done it already.'

'Then find out.'

'I will.' The argument frustrates her. It's about nothing. 'You've got to give me time. We've known each other less than a year.'

'If it were me I'd be on the telephone right now and I'd hang on until he answered.'

'But you're not me.'

'I can see that.'

'Why are being so irrational! I'm yours. How many times do I need to say it?'

'Love is irrational.'

'It doesn't have to be.'

'Yes it does. The look on your face when you saw that writer was not rational.'

'I never want to see him again!'

'You see? You feel more passion for him than me.'

'It's not passion. I was a bit surprised, that's all.'

'Are you going to keep running into these little surprises?'

'I'm not jealous of your ex-girlfriends.'

'I wish you were.'

'You'd hate it if I were like that.'

'No, I'd love it. I want you to understand what it's like to be driven crazy by someone. *Me*.'

'I don't want to be driven crazy.'

'I can't separate love and sex, Violet. If you just wanted companionship, you should have told me.'

'You think arguing is passion. Stop trying to drag things out of me. What's the good of it? We've wasted enough of the night.'

'Promise me you won't see that guy if he tries to contact you.'

'He won't try to contact me.' But she is not sure of this at all.

Neither is Rahul. 'If he were me he'd be banging on this door now.'

'Well, he's not you. He doesn't care about me like you do.'

Unexpectedly, he starts to smile.

'What?' she asks sharply.

'Look behind you,' he says.

She turns to see that she is about to be engulfed by a cumulus cloud of white foam rising from the bathtub.

He walks over and turns the taps off and emerges covered in drifts of foam like someone playing a sheep in a nativity play.

She has to laugh too.

'I agree with you,' he says, wiping a blob off his nose and then lifting her away from the bath. 'We've wasted enough of the night.'

The next morning, Rahul tells Violet they are going back down to Miami.

'I know you're hating the cold weather,' he says. 'A few days in the warmth is exactly what you need.'

A few days away from New York, you mean. But she doesn't say this. 'When?'

'How about tomorrow?'

'So soon?'

But, alas for Rahul, not soon enough.

The same afternoon, Violet leaves the hotel to walk a few blocks to Soho, thinking that she might buy a book for the plane.

The squally spring wind lifts the hem of her coat and sand-blasts her face with grit. She ducks her chin deeper into the collar, her eyes on the pavement directly in front of her. Lace-up boots, rubber galoshes, scruffy sneakers approach and skirt around her.

A tangle of small dogs on leads have to be yanked, yelping, out of her way. Stray blue plastic shopping bags puff and contract like jellyfish. A toddler escapes from his nanny and runs at Violet's legs, giggling. She disengages his mittened paws and hands him back to his grateful caretaker.

She looks up into Florin's eyes.

He is standing behind the nanny, arms folded, enjoying her reaction.

She feels a rush of panic.

He closes the gap between them and kisses her gloved hand. 'You didn't say hello the other night. I might have been hurt, except that I could see you had a problem.'

She snatches her hand away. 'I didn't have any problems. Why are you here?'

'I'm doing what I am always doing. And you?'

She looks back at the hotel nervously.

'Oh, I see. He's jealous. Or you're ashamed of me. Or both.'

'I'm not ashamed of you. I don't have any opinion about you.' But she doesn't want to be caught talking to him. 'Excuse me, but I have to go somewhere.'

'I'll come with you.'

'No.'

'Then I'll wait in the hotel lobby until you come back.'

She looks at him. What does he know about her? His expression reveals only innocence.

'Okay,' she says hurriedly. 'But not here. I'll meet you in ten minutes at Bubby's. It's a few blocks north.'

'Very well. Would you feel better if I hid behind a pot plant?'

Violet watches him stroll away as if it were a perfectly sunny day, and then walks in the opposite direction, so that she isn't seen with him. She takes an indirect route back to the diner, skirting along cobbled lanes as if she were trying to shake off a pursuer. When she enters the restaurant, she at first doesn't see him. She feels oddly disappointed. But she walks into the room and there he is, true to his word, huddled discreetly in a nook, with his back to her.

She slides in opposite him, unwinds her scarf and pulls off her mittens. Florin is still wearing all his outdoor clothes, even though the diner is typically too warm. The plush fur collar on his military coat frames his face, which is unseasonably tanned. His gloves, lying on the table between them, are so soft and pristine they look like they have been skinned in utero from the belly of a baby goat. But his hands look cold, pale and bluish-tinged.

'Do you think we will be eighty and still meeting like this?' he asks.

'I hope not.'

'You hope we won't be meeting like this or you hope we won't be meeting at all?'

'Both.'

'I have been thinking of you, wondering when we would next see each other.'

'Why would we see each other at all? We mix in different circles.'

'I don't think so.' His expression is full of irony.

'I've finished with all that.'

'I see.' He reaches across the wooden table and lightly touches the three rings on her finger. His fingers are cold. 'Is that what these mean?'

'They mean I'm engaged to be married.'

'Why three rings?'

'One for each of our children.'

'You don't want children, Violet. They're a burden people like us don't need.'

She pulls her hand away. 'What would you know?'

'I have seen it many times. You'll lose your figure. You'll neglect your husband. And then he will find someone else . . . someone like you, but younger.'

'Rahul won't do that.'

'What makes you so sure? Are you in love?'

'Of course I'm in love.'

'You said that very quickly.'

'How else am I supposed to say it?'

'Not like it's something you want to hide in a drawer. I would expect you to be more gloating.'

'What's there to gloat about?'

'I've never seen a woman about to get married who hasn't had that look of triumph. Like she has managed to get away with something.'

'I'm not getting away with anything.'

'Are you sure you are *in* love? Or just outside looking in?'

'I told you I'm getting married.'

'Marriage and love can be entirely different arrangements.'

'I didn't *arrange* to be in love.'

'Everyone arranges to be in love. This idea of falling is ridiculous. Your heart wouldn't pump the blood if your brain didn't tell it to.'

'My brain hasn't switched off. Anyway, you would approve of Rahul. He owns five hotels.'

'I read *Vanity Fair*, Violet.'

'So it's not such a coincidence you are here?'

'It's a perfect coincidence.'

'What do you want?'

'What do I want? You are sending out a signal like a ship in distress and you wonder what *I* want?'

'I'm not sending out any kind of signal. Except to stay out of my business.'

'Even if I can see what you can't? I think you are making a terrible mistake committing yourself to this innkeeper this early, when life is so full of surprises. In a few years' time perhaps, if you haven't made a more advantageous match, then I suppose he would do. But you'll fritter away your best years with him and what will happen? You will get bored with him or he will get bored with you. And then you'll find that you're too old for another man.'

'Then I'll be the perfect age for someone like you.'

'I suppose, if you play your cards right, that's true.'

She hates the way he is smiling blithely, making a joke out of her. 'Am I rich enough for you *now?*'

He opens his palms on the table. 'I don't know. I don't know how much money you have. Are you propositioning me?'

'I have my own man, thanks.'

The waitress interrupts at this moment to take their order. As usual, Florin orders up big. Fresh orange juice, steak and eggs, an extra side of bread, coffee.

His espresso comes quickly and he tosses it down.

'Been out all night?' she asks.

He grunts and pushes the cup away.

'Were you with that girl from the other night?'

'No. She was just someone I met in a bar.'

That surprises her. 'That's not like you.'

'No, it's not. And unfortunately this creates complications.'

'Like what?'

'You don't need to know. The upshot of this is that I'm going back to Europe tomorrow.'

He pounces on his juice when it arrives and swallows it in three gulps. He tears at the bread, butters it and sprinkles salt on top. Violet watches him. She looks at her own glass of juice disinterestedly. She feels suddenly squeamish. But she sips it anyway.

'So, your travelling companion threw you out.'

He shrugs. 'She behaved appallingly. Screeching so badly hotel security was called.'

'I thought you had these old women under control.'

'One day you will be old too, Violet. Besides, this woman is not old. We are talking about forty-five, fifty, sixty perhaps. My relationships are not hindered by age or looks. I prefer women older, frankly.'

'Why?'

'Because after a certain age women are less demanding. And they are at a point in their lives when money means nothing. They would give it all away for a few more years of feeling young. Besides, I get pleasure from making them feel good.'

'I don't believe that. It sounds like a line you feed them.'

'You don't think an older woman can give *me* pleasure?'

'You know, I can't imagine you having pleasure at all. That's why you hate the idea of Rahul and me.'

He puts his fork down. 'It's the body that experiences pleasure. I guarantee I could please you. And you wouldn't have to be in love with me.'

She grasps her bag. 'I have to go. I'm going to Miami tomorrow and I have shopping to do.'

'Do you sometimes wonder what it would be like, you and me?'

'No,' she lies.

'Then you are not very curious. I think about you.'

She pushes her chair back.

He reaches across the table and puts a hand on her arm. 'I have a favour to ask you.'

'What is it?'

His expression is abashed. 'I'm temporarily embarrassed. I wondered if you would lend me twenty thousand dollars. Just for a week or two, of course.'

She pushes his hand away. So this is it. 'Twenty *thousand* dollars!'

He shrugs as if it's nothing. 'Fifteen thousand, then. It's for a debt.'

'Do you think I'm an idiot? Ask one of your rich women.'

'What does fifteen thousand dollars matter to you?'

'It's a matter of principle.'

'And what principle is that?'

'The principle that you only want money from me.'

'That is far from the truth. But you have some now and I need it. It is only small change. I am sure you can earn it back from that innkeeper of yours in a few hours.'

Offended, she rises from her chair, as regally as she can manage.

'Don't go,' he says. 'I can pay you back in kind.'

'What sort of kind?'

If his eyes were hands they'd peel her clothes from her skin.

'I need to go to the bathroom. I would be really happy if you weren't here when I get back.'

In the bathroom she washes her hands and leans against the sink to defuse. She has deliberately left her handbag sitting on the table between them. In it is the wad of hundred dollar notes she always carries around.

If he takes it, then I know for sure what he wants from me.

When she returns to the table, as she has demanded, Florin has gone. When she looks in her wallet she discovers that all her money is still there.

Florin has a price and it is not a few hundred dollars. And although she knows the cost is more than money, she wishes – not for the first time, she realises – that she were free to pay it.

LA RÉSERVE DE ST-TROPEZ

Route des Plages, St-Tropez, France

Panicked, I gather up the last of my things. I fold the envelope of Charles' money and stash it in the inside pocket of my jacket, where my passport should be. But it is not. I dump the contents of my handbag on the bed, in a frantic search for it. With it tumbles out the silky toe of a stocking in which I have knotted three fine rings, one gold, one platinum and one rose-gold, dull souvenirs from another woman's life, like the mementos murderers keep, or the hair of a dead person caught in a locket. I should have tossed them long ago for they give me little comfort. And yet I keep them, to remind me that what is lying in my palm is one choice and I once made another.

No time to reflect on them. I shove the stocking deep into the bag and flee, leaving the suitcase for the porter. If my car hasn't arrived I'm going to stand in the driveway and wait for it. I need to get out of here.

The lower level of each villa opens onto a flagstone corridor, dank with old age, which is charming in its way but treacherous when you're running in spindly heels. I have to go carefully, lest I break my neck. The hotel's small reception is roughly halfway between villa eglantine and villa muguet and when I round the corner he has beaten me there.

I stop, trapped. 'No way,' I hiss at him. 'No fucking way.'

His smile is so smug I want to punch it through his head to the other side. 'Tsk, tsk Violet, I didn't teach you to swear.'

'You didn't teach me anything. And it's Violetta. Remember? You named me that.'

'Oh, yes. You left Violet behind.'

I do not want this. I do not want any of this. I am not going backwards. I am *not*.

'Let me pass. I don't know you.'

'I think you do.'

I raise my palm and it makes contact with his cheekbone. It's a limp gesture: my traitorous mind won't let me hurt him, despite having desired for years to take a knife and carve out his heart. He grabs my wrist and kisses the back of it. His lips are dry as they have always been. I jerk my hand away. 'My car is here. I'm going to the airport.' I try to move around him. But he is more agile than me in his bare feet. He has always been more agile. He pins my elbows to my side and pulls me into a service alcove. So far, there's no one around, but he has more to lose than me if we're discovered like this. 'Okay,' I say, shaking my arms free. 'You have one minute.'

He hasn't stopped smiling. 'Why are you in a hurry to escape? That big blond of yours is treating you badly?'

'None of your business.'

'I think it is.'

'Then what about that victim you're scamming? Won't she be looking for you?'

'She has, in fact, this very minute left for Tunis to have her bandages removed.'

'And she hasn't invited you along?'

'I am not interested in the results. Besides, her husband is meeting her there to inspect what he has paid for. And, might I add, *Violetta*, I am not "scamming" her, as you say. I am merely ministering to her.'

'Like a nurse?'

'That is exactly what I am.'

'So that's what you've been doing for almost seven years? Medical school?'

'I don't need to go to school for what I do. And I am pleased you remember how long it is since we have seen each other.'

I remember all right. How could I forget? But I'm not letting him know that. 'Well, nice to see you,' I say. 'Now if I may go—'

'*Nice?* Well, I am disappointed you see our meeting as merely *nice*. "Fortuitous" would be a better word, don't you think?'

'For you, maybe.'

'Yes, for me.' He drops the smile. I can almost believe the tender look that fills his hazel eyes. Almost. 'Don't go. If you must leave him, come to my villa.'

'It's *your* villa, is it?'

'I have one more night. We are both at loose ends once again. Why not tie the knot together?'

I remember the one night we almost spent together in Vienna. 'I'm not at loose ends. I'm going to Dubai.'

He raises his eyebrows. 'Please don't insult yourself. You are too good for Dubai. And, without being offensive, too old.'

'I'm glad you've still got my interests at heart.'

'Don't be so cynical, Violet. I will always look out for you.'

'Like you did the last time.'

He runs his eyes up and down my body. 'You only look slightly the worse for wear.'

'And you're not?'

'Oh, I am very much the worse for wear.' He takes my hand. 'Come. Let me tell you about it.'

'Florin . . .' I don't mean to hesitate. I am just composing my words. Weighing up whether to launch a tirade of abuse or just walk away.

But she who hesitates is lost.

THE UNION HOTEL

East 17th Street, New York, USA

There is a large Fedex envelope waiting for Violet when she returns with Rahul from Miami.

'What is it?' Rahul asks, flipping through his own mail at the front desk.

She is shocked to see a sticker with Patrick's Australian address. 'Documents.'

Rahul looks up from his mail hopefully. 'What we've been waiting for?'

The receptionist seems a bit edgy. 'I don't want to trouble you as soon as you arrive, sir, but they need to speak to you over at the Union. There's a problem.'

'It can't wait?' Rahul says testily.

'No, sir.' He casts a sideways glance at Violet.

Rahul picks this up, frowns. 'All right. I'll call them from the penthouse.'

Violet goes ahead with a porter while Rahul chats to the concierge. As soon as she's inside the door, she tears open the envelope.

The letter is curt:

Thank you, Violet, for letting me know where you are. I had to pick up Vanity Fair *to find you. As I wish to sell the house to reinvest in the business I think it's best we get the divorce over and done with. Here are the papers. I would appreciate their return post-haste. Sincerely, Patrick.*

She has expected to feel relief at this moment but she experiences the cut of his anger like a lash. She tears up the letter and signs the papers quickly without reading any of it – *there, I'm done with him* – then shoves them in a drawer.

Rahul is back five minutes later. He pours himself a drink before picking up the bedroom phone. Violet busies herself unpacking but she's listening.

'I'll ask her,' Rahul says and puts down the phone. His expression is blank. 'There's someone over at the Union claiming to be a friend of yours.'

What he's saying doesn't register at first. 'I don't have any friends.' And then her heart sinks. 'What's the problem?' she asks as if there possibly couldn't be one.

'Let's go over and find out.'

'*Now*? We just got off the plane.'

'They're insisting. Or they'll call the police.'

'Police?'

Violet's face says it all. Rahul is watching her closely. 'Don't you even want to know the person's name?'

'Yes, of course,' she says weakly, knowing he has caught her out.

'Then you'll have to wait,' he says curtly. 'I forgot to ask.'

When Violet and Rahul follow Alfonso, the hotel's head of security, into the suite, Florin is standing at the window with his back to them. He doesn't immediately turn around.

'Sir,' says Alfonso, clearing his throat.

Florin turns, looks mildly surprised, and says 'I see', as if this were his hotel and Violet and Rahul were the interlopers. He saunters over and lifts Violet's right hand to his lips. 'There you are, Violet. I am sure you can sort this out.'

She has wanted to deny he's anything other than the merest acquaintance but his greeting is too familiar for the lie to work. 'Florin,' is all she allows herself to say. She knows she sounds too neutral, not angry or surprised enough.

Rahul watches them. His voice is matter-of-fact. 'What happened, Alfonso?'

'He's been staying in the hotel all week, Mr Rahul. Different rooms. One of the maids, Maria, reported him to us. He says that Miss Violet gave him a key.'

'Did you?' Rahul's eyes bore into Violet's.

Florin speaks first. 'Violet is probably a little embarrassed because it was my idea. She offered me your penthouse while you were away but I wouldn't accept it. It's slow now in the hotel business, no? So *I* suggested that there might be a room for me in this hotel, which is only at half capacity. Violet thought it an excellent idea. But perhaps she forgot to tell you in her excitement about going away?'

'Is this true, Violet?'

She knows he knows it's not. She never forgets anything. Florin looks at her with one eyebrow cocked, as if he is daring her *not* to lie. The impertinence makes her furious. Oh, how she would love to see Rahul throw him out! She is about to shake her head, *It's not true,* when she stops. Florin is using his good hand to straighten the cuff above his crippled one and something in his feigned nonchalance undoes her. He is threatening everything she holds dear. (But what does she hold dear? Rahul or Rahul's life?

The uncertainty is so fleeting it's not much more than a shiver through her nervous system, hardly a thought.)

She says to Rahul, 'I did forget to tell you.'

Rahul's face betrays no sentiment. 'Alfonso, could you leave us alone for a moment?'

The security chief nods and backs out of the room.

As soon as he is gone, Rahul stabs an angry finger in Violet's direction. 'Why didn't you make a formal booking with the desk? Why did you feel the need to hide this from me? Who is this guy anyway?'

'Florin Esterházy de Bathory.' Florin bows and clicks his heels.

Rahul looks at him with total contempt. But Violet can smell his fear. The fear of what Florin means to her. She tries to assuage it.

'I told you I was in Paris for a while. I knew Florin there. He . . .' She tries to make the circumstances sound less intimate. 'I'm a friend of his girlfriend.'

'Violetta sends her love,' Florin says. He says to Rahul pleasantly, 'They are very close. They share the same name.'

Rahul is no fool. He knows he is being provoked. Violet could kill Florin for being so flippant. She has never understood him and she fails to understand him now. He seems to be deliberately trying to nettle Rahul. Given his circumstances it seems a foolhardy game to be playing. And then she realises that Florin knows now she will lie for him. She has been indecently quick to corroborate his story, in an attempt to protect Rahul. Florin thinks she has thrown her lot in with him.

She can see Rahul thinks this too. She takes Rahul's elbow in her hand but he unhooks it and moves slightly away. 'He's just a guy I knew in Paris,' she reassures him. 'I was trying to help him out. I gave him my master key and told him I'd fix things up. But then I forgot. We did talk about the hotel being half-empty at this time of year. Look, I'm sorry. It's a misunderstanding.'

'Violet, I know what type he is. You don't have to protect him.'

'I'm not, okay? Let's just forget it.'

'You don't want to call the police? You're sure he's not taking advantage of you?'

'No, please don't call them. Just let him go.'

Rahul turns to Florin. 'You could be arrested for this.'

'And embarrass your fiancée?'

By the way Rahul's chest expands, Violet thinks he is going to hit him. Even Florin seems to be expecting it. But he pushes his nails into his palms and says with chilling calm. 'He can go.'

Violet hopes he doesn't hear her sigh of relief. She looks at Florin and then flicks her eyes to the door. *Go on.*

But Florin doesn't move. He crosses his arms in front of him. 'That's all very well, but I have nowhere to go.'

'Why should I give a shit?' Rahul goes to the bedside table and picks up the telephone receiver.

'Because your security man has just accused me of staying here under false pretences and kept me in this room against my will.'

Rahul puts down the receiver and glares at him. 'Meaning?'

'Meaning it would nice of you to make amends.'

Violet has had enough. 'Florin, for God's sake!'

'You are the one who got me into this mess, Violet.'

Rahul looks back and forth between them.

'Rahul, let me talk to him,' Violet implores. 'He'll go.'

'And what will you say to make him do that?' Rahul's voice is so heavy with cynicism it could break tiles.

'Rahul, *please.*'

He gazes at her so intently she has time for a blush to slowly rise from her fingertips to her cheeks. But she doesn't avert her eyes. 'Okay,' he says. 'You know where I'll be.'

'I won't be long—' But the door has already closed behind him.

Florin does not admit relief at this. 'I should know better than to trust maids,' he says. 'I gave her a very big tip too.'

She tries to be as controlled as Rahul. 'What do you think you're doing?'

'It is just survival, Violet. It's not personal. I had to stay somewhere. What harm has it done anyone?'

'It's done harm to *me*. You'll screw up my relationship with Rahul.'

'If *I* could screw it up, it is a very flimsy relationship.'

'Why didn't you just ask me for a room?'

'Because you would have said no.'

'And so you steal from me? I didn't even realise my master key was missing.'

'I didn't intend to cause you trouble, Violet. I did ask you for money. Perhaps if you had given it to me I would not be here.' There is no trace of irony in his voice. His eyes reflect utmost sincerity.

She sees now that he is speaking his own truth. He simply cannot comprehend that she would not do what he asks. 'I won't be blackmailed, Florin.' She wishes she could sound tougher.

'Do you think that badly of me?'

'I don't know what I think of you.' She turns and studies a Keith Haring baby on the wall. There's a thought bubble coming out of the crawling baby's mouth. It's blank. 'I can't keep up with you.'

'You could.'

'I could what?'

'Keep up with me.'

She turns back to him. Her turn to say something but she can't find the words.

'I was waiting for you to return, you know. That is why I took an unacceptable risk.'

She shakes her head. 'I don't know why you did. I can't give you what you want.' She knows they are not solely talking about money now.

Florin doesn't argue for once. Instead, he changes the subject. 'Your innkeeper is very handsome.'

'Yes, he is.'

'And very possessive, I think.'

'He happens to love me.'

'But I was right. You're already tired of him.'

'Of course not! I'm *content* with him. I can trust him. Not that it's your business.'

'If you are content now, imagine how bored you will be in a year or two. I know you, Violet, you left that bourgeois little life behind in Vienna.'

'You have no right coming here and saying that. You, who have no feeling for anyone.'

'I think you will find that that's not true. I have feelings for you, for instance. But I don't act on them.'

'What's holding you back, then?'

'I am a little afraid of you.'

This is not the answer she expected. 'What are you afraid of?'

'I can't predict what will happen between us.'

'Nothing is going to happen between us.'

'Perhaps. But, Violet, I think that you are a little afraid of me too.'

'That's nonsense.'

'And this makes me fascinating to you. I think you would come with me if I asked you.'

If his expression is an open book, then he has just flipped to another chapter.

'That's outrageous,' she says. She has to make a conscious attempt to relax her hands so that her nails don't shred her palms.

'No. I've been thinking about this while you were away. And I have come to this conclusion.'

'Why would I leave Rahul for you? Where would we go? To a homeless shelter? You're contradicting your own philosophy. You want me to be with a rich man.'

'I'm as surprised as you by what is happening.'

'Nothing is going to happen.'

'No? You lied to him to protect me. What does this tell me?'

'I was protecting *him*.'

'Then you would have not hesitated for a second to have him call the police. Ever since I've known you, Violet, you have professed to want to get rid of me. Don't think I am not sensitive to that. But when you have the chance to do it, you do not.'

'I felt sorry for you, all right?'

His pride is unshakable. 'I don't think so. I'm not the sort of man you feel sorry for.'

He draws himself up straighter as he says this and suddenly she wants to laugh.

'Don't you see how ridiculous this is? All we do is argue. It just goes round and round in circles. You're supposed to be the great lover but we skipped that bit, if you recall.' She is surprised at the lingering bitterness in her words. 'It's like we've been married for years and can't stop bickering. If there were any feeling between us we wouldn't be talking now, we'd be fucking.'

As soon as she says this she knows she has stepped off a cliff.

Florin doesn't move from where he's standing a few feet away. 'For once we agree,' he nods, with the formality of a supervisor conferring with an underling. Then he says, with much less assurance, 'What are we going to do about it?'

'We can't do anything.'

He takes a step towards her now. 'But you want to, I think?'

'No.' But she takes a step towards him.

He is close now, his eyes on her mouth. He lowers his face towards hers.

She pulls back. 'A kiss is not going to work this time,' she says crossly.

He reaches out and touches her under the chin.

'I know,' he says.

Part Three
Violetta

THE OCCIDENTAL HOTEL

Pearl Street, New York, New York, USA

I felt strangely exhilarated making the worst decision of my life.

Present tense, Violetta. Nothing painful is ever past.

We walk out of the Union Hotel and onto 17th Street and keep walking.

Downtown, I say to myself, we must keep going down.

I am going down in the world with Florin in more ways than one. I know leaving Rahul is a bad thing to do. He deserves an explanation at least. But there is no explanation that I can make that would help him to understand. I can't explain it to myself in any rational way. All I know is that Florin has made me what I am and he has called me and I have left my good sense behind.

We look like an ordinary couple out for a stroll on a brisk afternoon. Or a pair walking to the gallows. Florin saunters beside me, saying little, except to warn me once or twice about stepping into the path of traffic. I don't ask where we are going or voice any preference. He will have to make the decision. Where. Which room, which lodging, which bed.

We have almost walked ourselves off the bottom of the island when he finds the place that will do: a small hostel, as charmless as a chain hotel, with a soft-drink vending machine in the lobby and a pegboard sign on the desk warning *daily and weekly rates only*. The desk clerk, hemmed in by a pink vase of dead grasses on one side and a display of Big Apple Bus Tour brochures on the other, doesn't seem to notice that we don't have any luggage. There would be no one to help with it anyway.

I am not surprised at Florin's choice. I understand the message. If we are to have each other it will be in a cheap hotel. I will not be like his other women. He will not be like my other men.

In my handbag are the things I have carried on the plane from Miami – my passport, enough cash for a few nights at a dump like this, a few pieces of jewellery in a roll, my journal, and credit cards. I am not poor, even though I have left behind my clothes, all the gifts from Rahul and my most expensive jewels in the hotel safe. Vincent's money is untouched in my bank account. We will get by for a while at least. I open my purse, but Florin puts a hand on mine.

'I intend to pay my way, Violet,' he says and counts out all the money from the clip in his pocket. When I look at him in astonishment, he says, 'I don't want there to be any doubt about that.'

Our room is on the second floor at the back of the building with a view across an alley of metal dump bins to a wall of aluminium window frames and airconditioners covered in soot. Luckily, there are discoloured vertical blinds to close over the scene. There is a small kitchenette containing an electric kettle with a frayed cord and no cups, a bathroom with a salmon-pink toilet, pastel blue bath and a mirror with a starburst of disintegrating foil trapped under the glass. The vaguely disco theme is carried through to the bedroom, which is wallpapered in grey and pink stripes. The padded bedspread is a tempest of dark grey and turquoise clouds. Over the bed, a Hockney print of an azure Californian swimming pool threatens to draw us, Alice-in-Wonderland style, back to a more familiar world.

I throw my handbag on the lumpy bed like a gauntlet.

I should be ragged with emotion, shattered, terrified, at the very least torn with confusion, but the finality of what I've done gives me the clear head of a Tibetan monk meditating on a mountain top. The part of me that is screaming, *Turn around, walk out of there and go back to Rahul, there will be no harm done if you go back now,* has been locked in that hotel room and the key thrown away. I can hear her banging on the door but she will not be released. The choice I have made is irreversible. I am going down these new corridors with Florin, wherever he may lead me. And I feel the freedom of it, as if the material world I lived in had the heaviness of so many layers of mink coat, now thrown off.

I am shivering, but it's only my body. The room is freezing.

Florin inspects the heater and kicks it. He thrusts his hands in his pockets and hunches his shoulders.

'If we survive this, we can survive anything,' I say.

I expect Florin to make a joke but he has that concentrated look on his face, the one he gets when he doesn't understand what I'm saying or approve of it. 'I wish we were in the Cipriani in Venice with a blizzard raging outside.'

'Instead of a blizzard raging *inside?'* I smile.

'What is raging in me is not a blizzard,' he says, in that way he has of misunderstanding me but understanding me perfectly.

Despite my coat and scarf and hat I feel so light I could float to the ceiling. But Florin seems weighted down. 'Let's take off our coats,' I suggest.

Instead, he walks a few steps to the window and fiddles with the blinds until they are closed. He stands there for a while, looking through a grimy slat at the dark coming down. As usual, we are standing so far apart even the radiant warmths of our bodies do not touch. He is not coming to me, so I at last go to him. I reach up to unwind the soft cashmere of his scarf. He takes a hand out of his pocket and places it firmly on my arm. 'Leave our clothes on,' he says. 'I want us to be in Vienna seeing each other in the street for the first time. I should have taken you into an alleyway then.' He gives me a wan smile. 'Before it became too complicated.'

'It's not too complicated.'

'I am afraid it is.' His hand goes in my hair and his lips brush my eyelashes. 'But at this moment I do not care.'

Lyle. Vincent. Rahul. Through the whole sorry mess of it I have only been trying to please Florin. And I want so badly to please him now. But I am afraid I will disappoint him. I am afraid this experience will not transcend all the other experiences he has had with many women. And there is something else. I'm afraid of his potency. I am afraid that he will turn me inside out like a glove and I will never be able to pull myself through again. I'm afraid of this but I desire it too. I have wrapped my arms tightly around myself for too long.

I want badly to please Florin so I do what I know I do well. I push my hands under his soft coat and find the buckle of his belt. As my fingertips run over his hipbones I am shocked at the furnace heat of his skin. Or maybe it is the fever that arcs through me like a current looking for its ground. Under my touch I can feel the hum of his body through the nerve endings and the stirring of the blood familiar from many men. But Florin does not press himself on me or push his fingers into my flesh or guide my head to where my hand is now. He stands with his fingers lightly on my forearms, looking down. Between us is the source of something so profound a young woman may take her own life because of the lack of it.

Florin says, 'I think there is an extra inch for you.'

And I say, lightly, 'I bet you say that to all the girls,' but I don't mean it lightly because I'm sure that's what he does.

And I have the tiniest moment of doubt before I bend my neck and slide down his length and engage my lips in worshipful communion with his silky and magnificent prick.

'Violet,' he whispers after a while, lifting my head from his belly. 'You don't have to show off.'

'But I want to surprise you,' I hear myself say thickly as he brushes my hair away from my face.

'I don't want you to surprise me. I want you to be exactly as I imagined.'

'Which is?' I ask, resting a cheek in one of his hands.

'Unspoiled. I am tired of all these games.'

Somewhere in my body a little plum of hope thuds to the ground. 'It's too late. I *am* spoiled. I'm spoiled to death.'

'Then I will have to un-spoil you again,' he says with such certainty that my heart swells in my chest and I don't stop to wonder what he means.

I do not know what I expected from Florin, distant, amused, infuriating Florin, but it is not this tenderness.

Our clothes eventually come off. Delicately, without tearing or clawing at each other. We are being unspoiled, no tricks of the trade, simple as teenagers on a riverbank, which we have never been. At first we are nervous, clumsy, imperfect, out of sync.

I know Florin could correct this. He could turn me over, hoist my legs, play me with his fingers and mouth, press his thumb on pulses that would turn me on like a toy – I am sure that he has a dance card of movements that his women can tick off one by one.

But he doesn't practise them on me. He is straight and true as a youth and I am deeply touched.

Unlike a youth, he is in no hurry. He lays me on the bed and gently raises my arms above my head. The fingers of his good hand stroke me like a vet calming down a frightened animal. I find the wall with my palms and press against it, raising a knee so that I am tense, elongated, my muscles rawhide straps that bind me to his pleasure. Even where his hand is dead it draws more spark from my skin than that of any man before. I have time to think of the wonder of this as his lips, polished like a stone in the sea by hundreds of other lips, slowly blow rippling waves of air in the dimples under my arms, in the hollow of my navel, and on the thin inner skin of my thighs. I am all tide, all wetness, and salty tears.

I am a string on which he keeps threading lovely beads. I will be a mile long before he is finished and I think I could keep going until I wrapped around the moon.

His eyes are closed, as if how I look might disturb the communion he is having with the taste and scent of me. He is not like Rahul, watching, watching, wanting to rip my soul out with his eyes so that I have to look away, even from myself. He is unconcerned with his own satisfaction as he spends a year kissing my mouth, pressing my arms against the pillows so that I cannot distract myself by touching him. But our ribs are fused together more closely than Adam and Eve's and he swells where I dip, making us one organ, one pleasure, indistinguishable. I am a membrane of nerve endings stretched under his and only when he pierces me do I sense the shock of otherness, that we are not twins, sharing one river of blood. They call these moments 'trysts' and yet I am not fighting him in any way, but rather like a true believer allowing a faith healer to plunder her body for cancer, I am open to the miracle.

When the first orgasm ripples through me I think how like the death rattle it is.

I feel like the only woman he has bedded or ever will.

And it is very, very easy to believe that love and sex are one and the same.

In the morning, there is blood on the sheet. My hormones have surged, delivering an early period.

I go to the bathroom and when I return, Florin is awake, sitting up in the bed with the top sheet twisted around him and a thin pillow folded behind his back. The damp patch on the bed is the shape of an overblown rose.

'If you were a gypsy bride we would have to display this sheet in the village,' he smiles.

'I'm sorry. I didn't expect it.'

'Why are you sorry?'

'I want you inside me again.'

'Then there's no problem,' he says, reaching out for me to come back to the bed. 'I am not known as the Blood Count for nothing.'

The heating comes on in the middle of the second night and suddenly the frigid little box is like a furnace. We throw off all the bedcovers, toss and turn for a while, finally turn on the dim bedside lights and lie apart, facing each other, the touch of our eyes as pleasurable as any touch of the hand. The room smells of the Chinese food we called in for dinner and the heater and the back of a solitary chair are hung with underwear I've washed out in the hand basin. Florin has surprised me by making no comment about our squalid circumstances. But the novelty has worn off for me.

'Let's get out of here,' I am suddenly inspired to say. 'I don't want to be in New York any more.'

'Now?'

'Tomorrow. Let's go to one of those places you talked about – the hotel with lemur-skin canopies or the one carved out of rock?'

'For that we need money.'

'I've got money.'

He sits up on his knees and pulls me gently towards him. For a moment I wonder if he is as graceful with all those other women, and then I push the thought away. *Was* graceful, I think. He can stop now. We both can stop.

I don't ask myself *how* we are going to stop. Can I see Florin going off to work every day with a brown bag? Or me working illegally in some dingy Lexington Avenue office? Rushing home to be together in front of the television for a few hours before he goes out to gamble away what we earn at a club and I slump off to bed to flip listlessly through celebrity magazines? I don't ask myself how we will stop because, in the back of my mind, I expect that we will *work this out.* I conveniently forget that the devil is in the detail. And that detail is usually, always, money.

But Florin is kissing the small of my neck with his warm, dry lips and any misgivings rush out of my head like a flock of butterflies. He whispers in my ear, 'Where would you like to go, Violet? Venice? Istanbul? Budapest?' He pulls back, brushes my hair from my shoulders, takes my ears in his hands and looks at me with that familiar amused expression. 'Of course, we can avoid the Ottoman empire altogether if you like.'

'Take me to Bucharest.'

'Absolutely not. You would hate it.'

'Why?'

'Because it's full of unhappy people.'

'Are you hiding something from me?'

'Of course not.'

'All right. I have never been to Venice,' I suggest. 'Or Marrakesh.'

'Or St-Tropez?'

'No.'

'Then we shall go to all these places. But let's leave our first destination to fate.'

He takes his hands away from me, turns, and opens the small drawer in the bedside table. His broad back and tapering waist are like a Renaissance sketch of the ideal man; his buttery skin has no blemish, no gypsy scar, no mark of love or violence. I have to stop myself from throwing my arms around him and drawing him back to the bed. Plenty of time for that.

'What are you looking for?' I ask.

'Paper and a pencil.'

'I've got it.' I slip off the bed and go to my bag. I pull out my wallet of business cards. When I turn he is lying back against the pillows studying my naked body. I sit on the bed next to him and show him one of my cards. 'Will these do? They're useless to me now.'

He takes the card and looks at it. 'No. We should keep them.'

We settle on toilet paper and my Tiffany pen. Florin tears off sheets and scrawls the name of a destination on each one. Places, he says, where he knows hotels I will like. I look over his shoulder as he writes. *St Vincent. Mahajanga. Aswan. Cadiz. Kyoto. Biarritz. Oslo. Prague.* Some places I have heard of and others I have not. The sheets go in the tin waste-paper bin and Florin holds it above my head. 'You choose.'

Biarritz.

He seems pleased. 'It will be cold but you can practise your French.'

'And what will we do there?'

'I'm sure we will think of something.'

LA CHANT DE SIRÈNE

Perspective de la Côte des Basques, Biarritz, France

The Siren's Song is a vertiginous little house with whitewashed turrets and blue doors, perched on rocks above the Côte Basque.

'How strange,' I say, when we are shown to our third-floor room and I open the old casement window to let in the sea air. 'The wind does sound like a woman singing.'

Pity I don't know that the siren sings for him.

Florin puts our case on the bed. I have bought us some clothes in New York, so now we are real travellers with real luggage. He insists that I buy a first-class case to go with our first-class tickets and it looks handsome on the white damask coverlet in the yellow-painted room, like an advertisement for the things in life that are priceless. This is a modest hotel and yet expensive, one that is very chic, according to my companion, who has not slept here before (he claims) but knows of it through some anonymous gigolo bush telegraph.

There, I have said it. Gigolo. Biarritz is a gigolo town. Florin admits he has 'summered' here twice. 'Naturally, I stayed at the Hotel du Palais,' he explains in the car from the airport. 'But I think, Violet, in the circumstances, you might no longer be happy in such a place.'

In the circumstances. It makes me quite delirious to hear him say this. I like the idea of 'circumstances'. Our own special fate. Our own little bubble that no one can burst. I don't think of the alternative, that 'circumstances' may mean something out of the usual, a thing that is passing, finite, troublesome and in need of being conquered.

We have been sitting side-by-side, fully clothed, for hours, on planes, in cars and in airport lounges, and I want badly to strip off and slide against his skin. But he is restless – anxious, he says, to get out of there. 'I am famished. And the sea air is making me hungry.' It is true we have barely eaten for two days. And so we wind our scarves around our necks again and set off.

The Bay of Biscay is the colour of a teal silk dress I have left far behind. The wind is brisk as we follow the road around a rocky peninsula, past nineteenth-century villas and apartment buildings in the art deco style. A white cat pads along with us for a while and then disappears between the bars of a wrought iron gate. From the top of a hill we can see clear to the lighthouse at the end of the *Grande Plage*, a long stretch of beach that surprises me with its silvery beauty. There are even a few surfers riding curls of white water into the shore. The natural melancholy of the weather does little to suppress an air of jauntiness that infuses the town like droplets of sea spray.

Or maybe it's just me who is jaunty.

Florin points out the Hotel du Palais, built by Napoleon II for his empress Eugénie, and the Bellevue and Municipal casinos.

'*Two* casinos?'

Florin laughs and pulls me closer. 'Don't worry. I'm not here for the casinos.'

We walk through gardens of scrubby conifers down to the old fishing port. Nestled in the cove are several fishermen's shacks that have been converted to cafés. The one Florin chooses is hung with fishing nets, with heavy wooden tables and hand-painted tiles fixed into the walls. As usual, he orders for both of us. We work our way through a platter of *jambon de Bayonne* and olives, a fish soup called *ttoro* and salted cod with pimento. The red wine, decanted into a plain jug, is sweet as cordial, but it could be gasoline and I wouldn't complain. In this mood, I would obligingly drink hemlock if Florin administered it himself. I am a spineless jellyfish of love floating on gentle seas.

I'm drugged with too much happiness to eat my share but I watch Florin devour every spoonful of his. I wonder briefly who has watched him eat here before and again I push such thoughts away. I can't think like this.

'I want to buy you a new coat,' I say, suddenly inspired. 'That New York coat is too heavy for Biarritz.'

'I don't want you to buy me anything, Violet. Buy yourself one first. Did you know Coco Chanel opened her first boutique here?'

He changes the subject adeptly and I realise I have made a *faux pas*. He doesn't want me to buy him things, I reason, because then our relationship would become like all his others. He is proud. He has accepted, to a degree, that I am paying for everything for the moment. He did not protest when I bought the airline tickets or told him I didn't care how much the hotel cost. But I'm afraid that if we talk too much of money he will feel obliged to contribute in the only way he knows how.

And so I have avoided discussion of how we will live. Florin knows I have money in my New York bank account but he has not enquired how much. I do not have a fortune, we will need to curtail extravagances to make the money last – but that would require sensible acts that deny the senses . . . I do not want to be sensible, to tally up the cost of everything as we spend it, least of all what I have just done.

It suddenly comes into my head that I don't want the burden of Vincent's money that I have saved, three thousand dollars of which are stashed in the bag on my lap. I have brought a roll of jewellery with me – not the sapphires from Lyle, which are still in the hotel vault, lost to me forever, nor little of what Rahul has given me, which has been left behind in the apartment, but everything else I carried back from Miami – a strand of black pearls, a pair of diamond drop earrings, the triple rings from Rahul that I tied in a stocking; stuff of some value but no longer of any consequence to me. The cash, the jewellery, all seem tarnished, bad omens, the wages of guilt if not the wages of sin.

And then it occurs to me. I could hand it all over to Florin. *All* of it. In this way, I will have no more to give. I will not be like his other women and it will no longer be a thing between us.

'I want you to sell my pearls,' I tell him as he is finishing his *bakalao*.

He barely raises an eyebrow. 'No. This is Biarritz. A woman needs jewels.'

'I don't want to wear them. They're ugly. I want you to cash them in and look after the money for us.'

Now he looks surprised. 'What has brought this on, Violet? You, who are always fretting about money?'

'I want you to know I trust you.'

'Aren't you afraid I will gamble it all away at the casino?'

I shrug. 'If you do, that's your decision.'

He shakes his head and pours me some more cabernet. 'No. I will buy you some myself, one day soon – how about rubies the colour of this wine? Only then can you get rid of the pearls.'

And I am happy with this because he has had his chance to take my money and he doesn't want it.

Happiness is an illusion, of course. It is a verb, not a noun. You can *be* happy for a finite moment in time, but it is not a continual state of being. How can it be, when its very existence depends on you experiencing misery, fear, torment or loss in order to recognise it?

But I skate along the thin ice of happiness for a little while.

We start out doing all the simple things you do when you are an ordinary couple *en vacances*. Most mornings, we walk down to the town to have *café et tartines* at a little place near the cathedral. Sometimes Florin gets up with the pale morning light and comes back with bread and cheese from *les halles* and we stay in bed for breakfast, lunch and longer, enjoying the crumbs between the sheets and the smile on the maid's face when we crack the door to tell her she can't come in. When we do go out it's to visit touristy places like *le Musée de la Mer* to giggle at the moray eels and to sit in the rotunda in the public gardens and watch French teenagers pretend to be Californian ones with their baggy pants and skateboards. We dangle our legs on the sea wall and throw baguettes to the gulls and then walk out to the grotto where the Virgin Mary stands on a rock, guiding the fishing boats into the shore. We sample marzipan and macaroons and warm our faces on the steam from hot tea in rooms where the waitresses wear starched caps. We hold hands looking in dress shop windows but when we do buy things, they're amusing little souvenirs like snow domes or Basque berets or a pair of yellow straw espadrilles for me.

And Florin – what a perfectly beautiful lover he makes, intuitive of my every need, opening doors for me, lighting my cigarettes, choosing my lipstick colour, finding sweet treats he thinks I'll enjoy, translating the morning paper while he feeds me morsels of croissant, whispering how beautiful my breasts, the inside of my thighs, my long toes are, kissing the back of my knees, draping my shoulders in his coat when the wind whips up, shaking the sand out of my shoes, lifting me to dry safety when the tide unexpectedly rushes in, lighting a nightly shrine of votives around our bed, drawing my bath, washing my hair, touching me, touching me constantly as if he is making up for all those hours when we sat facing each other across tables. Oh, the very busyness of love, how tireless he is in his textbook romance, the callow sweetness of our New York hotel room replaced, so carefully I don't notice it, by an altogether lovely and nuanced performance of complete devotion to another human being.

And I reciprocate with extravagant praise, which pleases him, with drawn-out sighs, which please him more, and with caresses so fervent he sometimes has to laughingly untangle me, like I'm a child leaping on a father who has just walked in the door bearing gifts.

Mon petit amour fou, he calls me on these occasions and my French is good enough to know what that means: Little mad love. His affection delights me but I don't see that he is being descriptive, too.

I have not quite gone mad. But it has started. And I know it and I don't mind. Because love is madness, is it not?

Each morning, I slip folded-up francs into his pockets so that he is the one who pays for our coffees and deals out the notes onto the bill after dinner.

And soon it is easier to hand over my debit card to him and have him extract the money from the cash machine while I sit in a bar sipping the Pernod he has ordered for me – after all, it is dark outside and the bank is several blocks away and I am tired from a day of walking.

You might think you know where I'm going with this.

One afternoon, as we are taking a walk back from the lighthouse, we pass the terrace of the casino, as we usually do. Florin has said little about it since we've been here and I suddenly feel like rewarding him. 'Will you take me gambling tonight?' I ask. 'You were going to take me in Vienna and you never did.'

'You're not going on about that again, Violet? I did what I had to do to help you. And it was a good investment, no?'

'I'm not talking about that,' I reassure him. 'It's just that I've never been to a casino before and I want you to show me.'

He seems reluctant. 'I'm not sure you will like it. Contrary to what the cinema would have you think, casinos can be rather dull.'

'I don't mind if it's dull as long as you're there. We could always leave.'

'All right.' But he says it grudgingly.

I squeeze his arm. 'I'm excited. What will we play?'

'We will buy coins for the poker machines and see if we can make our fortune.'

'No. I want to watch you do what you usually do.'

'That will require at least three thousand dollars, Violet. I won't turn up to the gaming tables with less. Let's stick to the slot machines.'

'We have the money.'

'We might *have* it. But you only gamble what you can afford to lose.'

'We won't lose. You told me in Vienna you were lucky. *Please*.'

Does it occur to me that I have just offered a sober alcoholic a drink? Looking back on it now, I can see that I am goading him.

'If you insist. But if I lose, you can put it on my account. I will pay you back.'

'Do you think I'm tallying up an account in my head? Anything I have is yours.' Even as I'm saying this, I am amazed at how reckless I am sounding – reckless with my money and reckless with my affections. I believe one is not possible without the other, at least where Florin is concerned. And foolishly, very foolishly, I don't care about the consequences. In fact, I *embrace* the consequences.

Florin seems to look right into me. 'One day you will tally it up, Violet,' he says.

He is subdued as we dress for our night out. He has bought a dinner suit in New York because he says he feels insecure travelling without one on hand. I put on one of two new gowns I have brought with me, a silken black thing that pours like crude oil from one shoulder and has a high slit up the side. I think it's sophisticated but he takes one look at me in it and says critically, 'I suppose it's suitable if you want to be mistaken for a croupier.'

And he is right. The female croupiers wear black dresses and I am glad I agreed to change into something blue. And he is right about another thing – on this cold spring night, out of season, the casino is is a kind of upmarket shopping mall populated by dazed tourists, clutching buckets of coins, and fusty old locals who look rusted on to their chairs in resigned familiarity. Although everyone is wearing evening clothes, I still feel overdressed.

The games room is a curvaceous art-deco boudoir with huge swagged windows, which give on to the promenade by the sea, and walls of pink faux marble, the furnishings and carpets predominantly red and pink, like the lining in a velvet box where we are the jewels. When we enter, people look up from their tables and stare – and why would they not? Florin, in his black tuxedo with satin lapels and white scarf, his hair an inch too long for his collar, has the raffish air of an Edwardian conjurer and I am displaying flesh worthy of a Bond girl. I suppose we are culturally confusing, to say the least.

Florin's mood lifts now that he is being admired. And I have to admit to enjoying the stir we are causing. We have had our few days of sensible clothes and hibernation – now it's time to show each other off.

'What do we do now?' I whisper as we reach the bottom of the staircase and everyone goes back to his game.

'It depends how quickly you want me to lose your money,' he says.

'Fast,' I tease, basking in my new recklessness. 'It's always better fast.' But I don't really mean it.

'I wish you had told me that before.' He kisses my fingertips and he sits me at a bar table. He orders champagne ('predictable but obligatory') before leaving me for a few moments while he changes some cash at the teller.

I look around the room. There is a pianist playing popular classics behind me. A dapper old gentleman at another table raises his glass when his wife is not looking. For a moment I panic, thinking Florin has set me up again, but he's back, thank God, with a roll of notes and a big smile.

French roulette is Florin's game of choice.

He makes me sit at the table and stands behind me. 'What colour would you like?'

'I'm not playing!' I say in fright, turning to him.

'Of course you are. I think blue to match your dress, don't you? . . . *Bleu, mademoiselle.*'

The croupier passes him some blue chips in return for a few large notes. I pretend I don't notice what denomination they are. He leans over my shoulder and arranges the pile in front of me. 'All right, Violet, let us see. We can play this dangerously or we can play it safely. We can make a straight-up bet on one number, which is the most risky. We can bet on one of two, three or four numbers, which rather improves our odds. Or we can bet on *rouge* or *noir*, we can bet on even or odd, we can bet on low or high, we can bet on the outside column – these are the combinations with the most chance of success. How do you feel about 50-50 odds?'

'That sounds good.'

'The problem is that it's rather boring. If we take the straight-up bet, our odds are thirty-seven to one. Which is far more profitable. But, of course, the single number rarely comes up.'

'Can I try a single number? Just once? For fun?'

He kisses me on the neck. 'Good girl, Violet. I knew you would. What number would you like?'

'Eleven.'

'Why?'

'I don't know.'

'That's the best reason. Follow your instincts. *Onze* it is.' One blue chip goes on the eleven.

Eleven doesn't come up.

'Now, Violet, this is where it gets interesting. What system shall we play? We could change numbers and try something else. We could play it safe for a while and take a twelve-number *douzaine*—'

'No, let's stick to the eleven for a while. It feels right. And I like the way you pronounce it.'

He places two more chips on the eleven.

Eighteen comes up. A woman who has placed a number of yellow chips between the seventeen and eighteen is delighted.

'That's a *cheval*. A two-number split. The odds are seventeen to one.'

The woman exchanges her chips for numbered ones and leaves the table.

Florin places more chips on eleven. 'What are you doing?' I ask. 'I think eleven is a dud. Let's try something else.'

'No. I have a system. I increase my bet every time I lose. Eventually our number will come up. And we will get everything back plus our winnings.'

'Are you sure?'

'Eleven will come up one day.'

'One *day*?'

'The only problem is the house will put a limit on what we can bet. But don't worry. We are nowhere near it yet.'

It takes about eleven more minutes for the eleven to suck up the last of our chips. 'Do you want me to bet more?' he asks.

'No,' I say, suddenly tired of watching a ball go round and round.

'But the eleven might well be next.'

'I don't care. Let's try Blackjack or something.'

'I only play roulette.'

'Why?'

'Because it is illogical and therefore much more satisfying. Now, hurry up . . . the croupier's about to call it. Shall we try the eleven again?'

'How much have we lost so far?'

'About seven thousand dollars.'

'*What?*' I almost fall off my chair.

'You did say you wanted me to lose your money fast.'

I turn around and look up at him. His eyes have a gleam of mischief in them I haven't seen since he abandoned me in that Vienna lobby. I realise now he has *wilfully* lost it. He is teaching me some kind of lesson, but I don't know what it is.

'That was just small change,' he says. 'You need to have less respect for it. Sometimes it's necessary to spill a little blood when you operate on the heart.'

Heart, money. Why is it always so damned mixed up with him?

I know he is testing me. 'All right, ' I say, as calmly as I can. 'You can get me another champagne when you go to the bank.'

'No, Violet. I think we will go.'

'What if I want to stay?'

He laughs now. 'You see? Losing is as much a thrill as winning. That's why we have to know when to stop.'

He has led me into this and now I am being scolded for going along with him. 'I am only trying to be more like you,' I protest. 'To throw everything to the wind. To take risks. Isn't that what you want?'

'My dear, bourgeois Violet. How ever did you get the idea I was like that?'

After that, something is different. I don't know why. I still don't know why. Maybe it was just that the wind changed.

The next afternoon I am dancing around on the cold, wet sand with my shoes in my hand and Florin is trailing behind, bending to pick up stones and then throwing them into the sea. I don't notice that he's in any kind of a mood until I turn around and see that he is now standing quite still, staring out across the Atlantic as if there is more there than a small fishing vessel and a flock of cormorants bobbing on a wave.

I walk back towards him. 'Let's get some hot chocolate!' My voice is gathered up by the wind and sent out to sea with his thoughts. I throw my arms around his neck.

His eyes have taken on the pumice colour of the rocks. 'If you like,' he says tolerantly.

The café that we like is almost empty. We take a seat by an arched window overlooking the ocean. These days, we sit side by side, touching.

Florin doesn't say anything until our *chocolat* comes. I smile at him as I scoop froth from the top of the cup and put it in my mouth.

He doesn't smile. 'Enough, Violet.'

I put the spoon down, confused by his stern tone. 'Enough of what?'

'Enough of this childishness.'

'I'm not childish,' I protest and I feel my chin start to tremble, like a schoolgirl's, as if it were confirming what he has just said.

'*We* are,' he insists. 'We are playing this silly little game of being in love, dancing on the beach, buying foolish trinkets, having the wind in our hair. As if any of this is enough.'

This outrages me. 'It *is* enough for me.'

He shakes his head. 'And for how long? You think we can live on hot chocolate and rock climbing forever?'

'We've only been here a week. Why do we have to think about the future now?'

'Because we need to plan if we are going to have a better life than this.'

'I can't imagine having a better life than this.'

He taps the table impatiently. 'Violet, please come to your senses. Anyone can have this hearts-and-flowers idea of love, but you know we are different. Common domestic arrangements won't do for us. I remember very clearly that you said you wanted to come with me to St-Tropez, Madagascar, Morocco. Have you changed your mind?'

'No. I want to. Of course I do.'

'Then we need all the resources we can get. I am going to take the TGV up to Paris tomorrow. I am owed money there. And I have some clothing in storage. The weather is changing, and I could do with it.'

Florin leaving me? Is that what he is saying? My head is a grotto, crumbling into the sea. 'There's no need to go, Florin. We didn't lose that much last night. We still have enough for . . . months, if we're careful.'

'I told you I was going to pay my way.'

But that's exactly what I don't want him to do. I don't want him to pay his way with another woman's money. 'I'll come too,' I say quickly. 'We could stay wherever you like. The Chardonne or somewhere small and romantic.'

'No. I'm only going to be away for one night, two perhaps, depending on the train schedules.' I'm tapping the side of my cup with the spoon now, quite agitated. He reaches across my lap and stops my hand. 'I am only retrieving what is owed to me. It's no more than that.'

'Who owes you money?'

'It's a very old debt.'

'Some woman I suppose. Some chicken carcass.'

He snorts. 'Do you think I am going to Paris to sleep with a woman for money?'

The directness of the question embarrasses me, even though this is exactly what I am thinking. I shrug. I can feel my mouth twist into an unattractive knot.

'Because I do not do that. And if ever such a thing had been proposed to me in the past, I wouldn't do it now. Now that I have you.' My hand goes to his lips and is held there.

'I don't see why you have to go now.' I wish I didn't sound so whiny.

He kisses me lightly on the forehead now. 'I'm coming back, Violet.'

How can I be sure of that? He hasn't before. I let him out of my sight and he disappears. 'If you don't, I'll track you down,' I say.

He laughs, thinking I am joking. 'When I come back we'll go to San Sebastián, perhaps? It's only an hour away and it's more exciting than here. Would you like that?'

'What am I going to do while you're gone?'

'I don't mind, Violet, as long as you don't go sitting in any hotel lobbies without me.'

Everything seems lustreless without him. I mope in our room, I slope down the hill to a café and console myself with *callisons d'Aix*, sticky marzipan sweets to which I've become addicted, I go to the cinema and watch a film I don't understand, I walk the cliff like a sea captain's widow. I imagine people are looking at me pityingly – the hobbling old waitress in our café who makes the point of removing the second setting with a sigh, the female concierge in our hotel whose face falls when I say I don't know his plans, the maid who changes my tear-damp pillowcase each morning.

True to his word, he does return.

But he is away four nights, not two.

'These things can't be so quickly arranged,' is as much explanation as I get when he arrives in new clothes with a large suitcase in tow.

But I am so overjoyed he is back I'm not interested in conducting any sort of interrogation.

And he embraces me as if he has been away for months. 'I have presents for you,' he says, opening his case and taking out several glossy shopping bags from good stores.

I unwrap the tissue lining of the first, while Florin sits back in a chair smoking a cigarette that I notice is Romanian. It's a grey cashmere dress, not quite my style, but very expensive-looking nevertheless. The second package is a Scottish twinset, the third a blouse and skirt, the fourth a silk scarf, the sixth a camisole top. The seventh is a ring set with a modest emerald.

I look at him. He helps me slip it on. 'It's not good enough for you,' he says, 'And a little large. But it's quite pretty, I think.'

Now he takes it off my ring finger and pushes it on to my index finger. 'That's better,' he says. 'We don't want anyone to think you're engaged.'

I feel a bit hurt. He looks at me with amusement. 'If we *were* engaged you'd have a much more spectacular ring than this. Now try on the dress.'

Feeling mollified, I do what he asks. Florin watches me from the bed while I slip out of my things and tie the dress at my waist. Something inside it scratches me and I find a piece of paper stapled to the label. It's a drycleaning tag. I show him. 'Someone has worn this before.'

'Didn't I say? I bought it from Didier Loudot, the vintage boutique at Palais Royal.'

No, you didn't say. Doubt starts creeping in. The clothes Florin has bought for me are very conservative. Do they belong to someone else?

He must see the look on my face. 'I've bought the wrong things, haven't I? I can see now that they're not sexy enough for you. Are you offended?'

'Where have you been, Florin?'

'I've been trying to solve all our problems. Now, let's get rid of that dress and pick up where we left off.'

I didn't think we had problems.

For the rest of the night he convinces me he doesn't think so either.

HOTEL ROMÁNTICA

Zubieta Kalea, San Sebastián, Spain

I intend to go with Florin to the ends of the earth, but we only get as far as San Sebastián before the axle on our little gypsy caravan starts to wobble again.

Florin insists we are driven across the border from Biarritz to Spain because he thinks it is inconvenient that we will have to change trains at the Spanish border town of Hendaye. (Where, my guide book tells me, Hitler got off the train and shook hands with Franco in 1940.) The dark Mercedes speeds along the ocean cliffs and plunges into the velvet green valleys as if it is carrying contraband and when the authorities stop us at the border to check the trunk for bombs I can't help feeling guilty, as if we are getting away with something.

When I confide this to Florin he says, 'Life is always better when you feel you are stealing from it.'

San Sebastián is only thirty miles from Biarritz but we are in a different country, in more ways than I know. The austere, slightly dismal, elegance of Biarritz has gone, and we enter a city that looks like it has been designed by a hedonist, someone who has put in place curvaceous beaches of white sand, cobbled streets bursting with exuberant bars, boulevards of spiky palm trees, immaculate public gardens and fountains, gracious nineteenth-century buildings with iron balconies, lush craggy mountains and, hedging his bets, a statue of Christ on an isthmus that embraces it all.

Our hotel is a grand old dame with four stars of Belle Epoque character and our suite has two little wrought-iron balconies, barely big enough for both of us to stand there at once, that look out over the *bahia de la Concha,* the beautiful main beach that curls in the shape of a conch shell. I open the doors on to it as soon as the porter has left and lean for a long while with my arms on the railings, letting my hair rifle in the honeyed breeze.

'It's like Venice with surfers,' Florin says, bringing me bottled water from the mini-bar. 'I thought so the last time I was here.' He leans on the railings next to me.

'How long ago was that?'

'A few years ago. It was September, when the film festival was screening.'

'I won't ask you who you were with.'

'In fact, I was with some friends from school. One of them had an idea he wanted to be a film director.'

'You're a dark horse, Florin. Why don't you ever talk about that?'

'Why should I? There's nothing special about it.'

'Not everything you do has to be special.'

'But there you are wrong. Despite what the priests will tell you, we only have one life. It's depressing but it is true. And who knows how long it will be? To reach thirty is an achievement where I come from. Every day is a bonus so you are obliged to make it special.'

'But for someone with your background to go to school in England *was* special.'

'Well, it was boring, so I dropped out, if you really wish to know. To be bored or boring is unforgivable. There's no God to give us a reward for being dull and good.'

'I thought we were supposed to get that reward on earth.'

'And who is going to give it to you? You have to take it.'

'But some things can't be forced. They happen by chance. I met you by chance, didn't I?'

'That may be so but I might not have asked you for a drink or gone to find you in your hotel room. I have put a lot of effort into taking you, Violet.'

I do feel like I've been stolen, I tell him, smiling.

'You know what they say about the Roma. At the Crucifixion a gypsy stole the nail that was supposed to be driven through Jesus' heart. God was so grateful he gave the gypsies the right to steal whatever they wish in perpetuity.'

'You don't believe in God.'

'But it's an excellent excuse, no?'

'You have no morality, Florin.' I say it lightly, and touch his cheek.

'It obviously doesn't bother you or you wouldn't be here with me.'

'So you admit it.' I kiss that lovely Roman nose.

He pulls away from me. 'I am a very moral person, in fact. I have very strict rules of conduct for myself. But I have to do what I have to do. And I never worry about what people call me or think of me. I don't intend to spend a day of my life being concerned about that. So you can call me amoral, if you like, but they are your words. '

'I was only joking.'

'But sometimes, I think, you jump to these conclusions.'

'I told you I trust you.'

'You shouldn't put so much value on this question of trust. In the end even you, Violet, can't be trusted. Don't protest. I don't care if I trust you or not. Because I assume I can't trust you – and it makes no difference. We all do what we do and there is no changing it.'

'But you *can* trust me,' I say limply. 'I've given up everything for you.'

And I realise that's the wrong thing to say. He glares at me. 'I would have thought you made that decision because I offered something better.'

'I'm sorry. Of course you do.'

'Then you know what you are doing. And it proves what I am saying. We only do what we need to do.' I think he realises he is sounding harsh, because he puts his hands on my ears and tilts my face towards his. 'You will always want to believe the worst of me, Violet. But you must know that whatever happens I am thinking of you.'

Whatever happens. I hear him say it. I have been warned. But I choose to tuck it away behind my thoughts while he kisses me. And then it is gone.

San Sebastián has its own microclimate and we have our own microclimate within that. The May afternoons are warm and our room is a hothouse where we rootless organisms can bloom. Sometimes it is after 9 p.m. before we pluck ourselves out of bed to wander onto the streets in search of food. They call the tapas *pintxos* there and we might sit at a bar for hours, drinking fizzy rosé and eating fist-sized plates of anchovies, stuffed red pimentos, tiger mussels and plump potato omelettes, under a roof of suspended hams dripping acorn oil into little umbrellas of paper. If we are out late enough we go to a club, stay awake until it's morning and walk back to the hotel through the historical quarter, the *Area Romántica*, where we sit on a park bench watching the sun come up. Sometimes, in the middle of the night, we get up and go down to the beach, which is lit by huge street lamps like candelabras dripping wax, and sit in the cool sand breathing with the tide. In the day, when everyone else is having a siesta and the shops are closed, we might go into a cathedral, where Florin lights candles dutifully, even though he doesn't believe in God. ('It's what one does in a church.')

One afternoon we take the funicular railway up Mount Igueldo to visit the old funfair and I drive a yellow dodgem car until I am sick with laughter. While I'm recovering on a bench seat, two little children run up to us and play tag around our legs. Florin asks permission of their parents to buy them ice-cream and treats them with such gentleness, I find my mind naturally straying to thoughts of Florin with his own children, with children by *me*. I think about what he told me in New York, that children are a burden for people like us. But we are not people like that any more. We are in love and the sex we have stirs our hormones into such frenzied activity that I take all my pills carefully, at the same time each day, fearing the one slip that might implant in me what neither of us wants. But now I see that he might want it after all, that his denial might have been bravado all along, and my body is suddenly filled with the recklessness that has fuelled my heart and mind in these past few weeks and I become woozy with the notion of bearing him a child . . . a little blonde girl in a red coat, like the one whose chin he is wiping now.

I smile at him and he comes back to sit on the bench with me.

'You'd make a good father,' I venture, certain he will like the compliment.

He stares straight ahead, expressionless. 'Don't get ideas, Violet. We are not having children.'

'I don't mean now, but—'

'Never.'

'But . . . what if I want to?'

'Then you need to find another man.'

'You would give me up like that?'

'Let's not talk about unpleasant things.'

Unpleasant? I pull my jacket tight to me even though it is not at all cold. Has his childhood been so bad that he mistrusts his own instincts with a child? I decide this is the reason and feel slightly cheered. The subject is not dead between us. I put it away for another day.

We continue the life of pleasant things. We buy each other summer clothes and books and occasionally eat wondrous food – raw thistle leaves or sea anemone – at Michelin-hatted restaurants. I like to walk down to the *talasoterapia* some days and wrinkle my skin in the marine steam bath, while Florin sits on the beach with a newspaper. We don't want for anything except a schedule and I think it would be wonderful if we could go on like this forever.

'I like this better than any place I've been,' I tell him one afternoon as we're drinking 'breakfast', a milky espresso called *cortado,* in a café in a square. 'I think I'd like to stay.'

I expect Florin to indulge me but his expression is severe. 'And how would you do that?'

Now I'm nervous to suggest what I've been thinking about for days. 'We could find an apartment.'

'And do what?'

'Do what we're doing.'

'I thought you were coming with me.'

'We haven't spoken about going anywhere yet.'

'Not yet. But I have been thinking we should leave soon.'

'I thought you liked it here.'

'It's not wise to get attached to any place. We are not European, we don't belong.'

'I could learn Spanish. I could learn the Basque language. They speak English, anyway.'

'That's not what I am saying. Eventually you need papers. There are complications. We would have to show our bank account, references, residential visas to get an apartment for the long term.'

'We could get a tourist apartment.'

'No, Violet. It's better to stay in a hotel where we don't need credentials.'

'Why?'

'I don't believe in anyone knowing my business. When you have grown up like I have you prefer to live under the wire.'

'Under the wire. Is that how we're living?'

I mean to be frivolous but Florin is in a philosophical mood. 'Or perhaps walking along it?' he asks.

I laugh and he smiles at last. But his smile goes all around the room and not on me.

It doesn't take me too long to find out what he means.

We are asleep one morning when I am awoken by the sound of an envelope being slipped under the door. I get out of bed and retrieve it. Florin, usually a light sleeper, doesn't stir. Between us, we disposed of three bottles of Belondrade a few hours before.

The envelope contains a printout of our hotel bill. We have been there eight days and spent more than twelve thousand dollars. This doesn't particularly shock me. It's modest compared to the sort of money Vincent threw around. But Florin, supposedly flush with money from Paris, has told me he has taken care of it. I start to feel a bubble of apprehension but then I tamp it down. If Florin hasn't paid it, I have plenty of money of my own.

But – and I am sure you are well ahead of me – I have not.

The unpaid bill niggles at me. I decide to leave Florin sleeping and go to the bank. He has been buying me clothes and paying for our meals and so completely looking after me that I haven't needed to touch a cent. In fact, I have to go his wallet to find the bank debit card I handed over in Biarritz.

My American bank has a branch in a street behind the hotel. The teller seems very pleased to help me but returns with a long face. He is sorry, but there is not an amount in the account to cover what I need. As everyone does in these circumstances, I tell him there must be a mistake. I show him my passport to prove I am who I say I am and he returns with a printout. Amounts of four thousand nine hundred dollars, just under my daily limit of five thousand, have been taken out in eight lumps. And fifteen thousand in total has been withdrawn, two weeks ago, from a Parisian branch.

I feel a strange satisfaction. I had – hadn't I? – told Florin he could have all my money.

When I return to the hotel I pay the account with my credit card.

I don't say anything to Florin. When he awakes, we go out for *cortados*, as usual. Then we go for a stroll to the historical quarter to look at the shops. In a bookshop, Florin discovers he is short of pesetas and leaves me there while he goes to a cash machine.

When he returns to the shop he looks unperturbed to find the card missing but says nothing. He knows that I know.

When we are back in our room, Florin continues to pretend nothing has happened. I can't stand it for long. I take the hotel bill out of my bag and wave it at him. 'That's how I found out. It was slipped under the door this morning. I went to the bank to arrange to withdraw enough money to pay it.'

'It doesn't need to be paid,' he says casually.

'We are supposed to pay in advance. It was overdue. So I paid it with a credit card.'

Now he is angry. 'You shouldn't have done that.'

'Why not? Did you expect us to sneak out of here without paying our bill?'

'Yes, of course.' He is looking at me as if I am half-witted.

'And how were we supposed to do that?'

'It's easy, Violet. Even someone as honest as you could do it.'

'That's not the point.'

'The point is, we have been living very luxuriously and you have been happy for me to take care of it.'

'Not *this* luxuriously! How could we have spent fifty-five thousand dollars? There's less than ten left.'

'Do you think those fine restaurants we dine at cost nothing? Those clothes you are wearing? You are sounding like a fishwife, Violet, adding up her piece of paper. Money means nothing. It's easy enough to get more.'

Now *I'm* angry. 'What happened to the money you were owed in Paris? You were so insistent on paying your way.'

'As it happens I couldn't collect. People are not always honourable. I didn't want to disappoint you, Violet, so I continued as if I had, knowing money would come to me eventually. And if you hadn't gone to the bank this morning, you never would have known and you would not be angry with me.'

'You think it's *my* fault?'

'You would be much happier if you didn't put a bourgeois value on everything. I have tried to explain this to you countless times.'

'How are we supposed to live from now on?'

'We are not by any means poor. We have some cash. We have your credit cards.'

'They're not going to do us much good. I don't have any money to pay the bills when they come in.'

'You don't need to pay the bills. You don't live in America any longer. They can't chase you here. You have good credit, I assume, and unlimited balances? The cards are in your name, not your boyfriend's?'

I nod reluctantly.

'You have two cards. I would have preferred that you waited to use the first so we could delay the debt, but in any case we can happily use the first for a few weeks until the account is overdue and they block it. Then we can start using the other. And, beyond that, there are other things you can do to muddy the waters, as you call it, like contacting the credit company and claiming your cards have been stolen. In any case, we have two months of unlimited card use, at least. Of course, if you have a moral problem with this . . . '

'What if I do?'

'Then you should go home. How do you think the rich live? Don't you think they play games with credit? The real thieves in this world are the banks and financial institutions. I don't lose a moment of sleep that they are sponsoring my lifestyle. And you shouldn't either.'

He knows I don't want to go home. He knows that my moral compass is a wildly fluctuating thing that he needs to reset every now and again.

And I am so easily reset. 'What happens after the cards don't work?' I ask. My tone is no longer confrontational. I want him to tell me we can keep on going on.

'There will be other cards to play,' he says and I know he is not talking about plastic ones now.

I also know that Florin has avoided my silent questions. If he didn't get the money he was owed in Paris, then did he pay for the gifts he brought me out of my bank account? And I am not stupid with figures. We have not spent the amount missing on meals.

I assume he has gambled it away somehow, in the few hours we have had apart. But it's very easy to tell myself I forgive him. He is only doing it for us.

My mental calculations must be written across my face because Florin gives me his most encouraging smile. 'Now, what you need to do is call American Express and inform them that you are on a round-the-world tour for a few weeks and you will be charging a considerable amount to your card. That way, no alarm bells will ring when we really start to live it up.'

HOTEL BILITIS

Rue des Ramparts, St-Tropez, France

My second card is declined in June when I present it to buy Florin a silver cigarette lighter in the village of St-Tropez.

Florin has been right about the card. We have had almost two months of uninterrupted credit, as we spend the spring tracing the Mediterranean coast of Spain and France like blind people reading Braille. San Sebastián to Madrid to Alicante, then Valencia, Barcelona, Montpellier, Marseille, Toulon and now St-Tropez. We have stopped for a few days in the fishermen's village on our way to Cannes, Monte Carlo, Menton and Italy, where we are going to follow the coast down to Sicily, then across the water to Tunisia. At least, I think this is where we are going. This is as much of a plan as we have had, or wanted, as Florin is always uneasy on the question of where or how. He remains in a good mood as long as I don't prompt him about the future. And so I have kept quiet about the inevitable and crossed my fingers every time the card is plopped on a restaurant bill or passed across a reception desk to be run through a hotel's accounting machine.

God knows, we have spent some money. Money that we have no intention of paying back. If I thought too hard about it, it might astound me – *me*, who has always paid my bills on time. We are travelling light, so as the season changes we have simply ditched our winter clothes and replaced them with summer things. Using our reserves of cash, we have tipped like millionaires and in turn we have been treated like angels come down from the sky. We are fawned over by shopkeepers and saluted by concierges and slipped little extras wherever we go (free drinks, complimentary desserts, *marron glacé* from the *chocolatier*) because we are so damn beautiful and charming and everyone wants to share in the joy of a young couple in love – or so the patron of a restaurant in Toulon tells us when he refuses to accept payment for a meal.

Whenever Florin is not looking, I find myself scrutinising his profile to see what love looks like. What is it that other people see? I suppose it must be the pulling out of chairs and the shawls wrapped tenderly around my shoulders so that I will not get cold, or the way he sometimes takes a strand of my hair and gently pushes it behind my ears. Or perhaps it is the attentive, patient waiting while I try on a new pair of shoes or his habit of stopping me mid-sentence and placing a kiss upon my mouth. Whatever the look of love is, it must be there if shopkeepers and waiters see it. But I know what they don't know – that everything he does for me he has done for someone he cares nothing about. And it eats at me, it eats at me.

The saleswoman in the tobacconist is very sorry but my card has been declined. I tell her I will take the cigarettes and the lighter anyway and pay her with some of the cash we have left. Before she wraps it, she asks me if I would like it engraved with some *sentiment*. I don't want to be reduced to a meaningless greeting on a worthless piece of metal tossed in a drawer with all his other lighters. I shake my head. *Non, merci*. And then I ask myself, what makes me fear, in the midst of this extravagant expression of love, that I will be so readily tossed aside and forgotten?

I am a tug of war. The two directions: it will all be all right, it will all go wrong.

It will be all right, I think today. It would take a great effort to think otherwise on a beautiful day like this one. I walk down the hill to our *auberge*, which is situated above a little bay and among a jumble of fishermen's houses. It is not yet the height of the tourist season and Florin always manages to find us rooms in the prettiest hotels and inns. We avoid altogether the big hotels. We have never discussed this but there is no need. We both know why.

I take the second key to the room from reception, thinking I won't knock and disturb Florin, who has been taking some morning sun on our rooftop garden amongst the terracotta tiles and chimney pots. He is scrupulous about his tan, a vanity I find endearing. ('I thought Transylvanians were afraid of the sun' is one variation on my standard, limp joke.) But when I climb the wooden ladder from our attic to the roof, and stick my head through the open window, there are pigeons and a stalking tabby cat, but no sign of Florin.

The other key is on a provincial wooden table by the door. I look at it and think, it's okay, he has just forgotten it. I go to the armoire anyway to make sure his clothes are still there. As soon as I open the antique, battered door I feel ashamed of myself. His shirts and jackets are hanging undisturbed. The wallet that holds his passport is tucked under a pile of folded sweaters. I extract the passport and smooth out the title page. I have seen it before, when he has flashed it at airports and border controls. Once

I grabbed it from him and teased him about his photo, which looks like it has been posed for a fragrance advertisement. I know from it he is a year younger than me and that he was born in Brasov, as he professed. The stamps on the stiff, creamy pages are further validations. He has been where he says.

I slide the passport back into the soft leather wallet, wondering who might have bought it for him. As I do, I notice that the other side of the wallet contains something bulky. I pull out a small glassine envelope. In it, I count three short locks of hair, secured by elastic bands. I hold them up to the light. The shades of hair range from corn yellow to dirty brown.

I shove the envelope back in the wallet. *How sick*, I think, to keep souvenirs like this. I wonder if the women willingly gave up their hair for him or whether he stole it from them when they were sleeping. Did he take the locks at the beginning of the relationships or at the end? It's not something I imagine Florin doing and yet the evidence is there. I am not going to ask him about it.

There is no strand of red hair.

I close the armoire. The room is stuffy, so I open a small casement window to let in some air. There is a view of the citadel across red-tiled roofs. A famous French actress of the 1960s liked to stay in this room, according to the old porter who brought up our bags. It's deceptively simple with its bluebell-sprigged wallpaper and hand-stitched lace curtains but the prospect that the writer Guy de Maupassant may have debauched himself in this very attic means that the tariff is high. We are not going to be able to afford places like this much longer. I have to think of a gentle way to tell Florin.

I have brought back with me a bag of the almond pastries he likes. I sit on the bed and turn the television on with the remote, and then watch the BBC while pulling sticky almonds off the top of a *brioche*. I hardly know what is happening in the world. Florin doesn't even read me the morning newspaper any more. The world of trouble and conflict exists beyond the edges of our frame.

Near San Sebastián a terrorist bomb has killed a politician. It is too close to home and I am about to change the channel when there is a knock on the door.

Florin has a towel over his shoulder but his hair is not wet. He kisses me on the forehead as he comes in. 'The water is too cold for swimming.' He throws the towel on the bed and picks up the remote, turns the television off. 'Why are you watching this?'

'A bomb went off in San Sebastián.'

'I never trouble myself with unpleasant things.'

He goes into the bathroom and closes the door, when usually he leaves it open, so I think he is cross with me. The shower runs for long minutes. When he emerges, a white towel slung low on his hips, I can see he is ready for sex. I start to unbutton my blouse automatically and then I remember the gift.

I hand him the brown paper package. He raises an eyebrow and unwraps it with amusement. The heavy silver lighter rests in his hand.

'I didn't want to be the only woman in your life who never gave you a cigarette lighter.'

'How extravagant of you,' he smiles.

He is in a good mood. I will tell him.

'It is more extravagant than you think. The credit card doesn't work any more.'

He closes his palm over the lighter. I can see the veins in his arms as his fingers flex. 'Are you sure?' he asks neutrally.

'Of course I'm sure. The woman ran it through twice. But we were expecting this, weren't we?'

'Don't sound so pleased about it. I think you want us to be poor.'

'I don't care if we're poor or rich.'

'I do. I am not going back to living like a pauper.'

'You don't have to. I've thought about it. You wouldn't let me sell my jewellery in Biarritz. But we really need the money now.'

'Absolutely not.'

'None of it means anything to me. In fact, it just reminds me of things I'd rather forget.'

'You may not care for them but we need your jewels. They open doors for us. Do you think we would have been given the best room in this hotel if you weren't wearing those pearls when we arrived?'

'Then *I'll* go out and sell them.'

'You will get the wrong price.'

'I'll get a job, then. I probably could earn a decent wage.'

It is a provocative thing to suggest. I know how he will react. He throws the cigarette lighter down on the bed and glares at me. 'Why do you want to keep pulling me into this dreary life of wages and work? I might as well have stayed in Bucharest!'

'What do you mean?'

'I thought you were different.'

'Different from whom?'

He doesn't answer.

So there is a *whom*.

'Don't worry, I will not allow lack of resources to get in the way of our pleasure.' His tone is hard and arrogant. 'I promised you this.'

I fight back with cynicism. 'I suppose you're going to tell me you have to go to Paris now, to "raise" some money – like you did so successfully before.'

'And tolerate your jealous moods?'

'I wouldn't be jealous if you didn't give me reason to be.'

'Don't send me away. I might not come back.'

'Is that a threat?

'No. It is my worst fear.'

I am about to fling off a wisecrack when I see how terribly serious he is. A thousand goosebumps pop through my skin. I feel every one of them. 'Who else has got a claim on you, Florin?' I wrestle my words into a steady sequence. It is not a question I want to ask.

He manages a faint smile. 'It does not matter, Violet. You are winning.'

I wind and wind my long red hair around the shaft of his penis.

'You are bad, Violet,' he whispers. 'The Roma would call you *chovexani*, a witch. A witch with hair the colour of the sunset.'

'I am very bad,' I say. 'I have been practising for you.' I move up his body to kiss him on the mouth. He is staring at the ceiling, which slopes down over the bed like a lid half-shut. But his lips are smiling.

'You know, soon it will be the season. I should be elsewhere making my fortune. You are ruining my career by taking me out of circulation. You have stolen me from my life.'

'*I* have stolen you? I thought you were the thief.'

'I am just the apprentice. I have never stolen what you have.'

'And what is that?' Heart? Soul? I am waiting for him to say it.

'My certainty.'

Florin sells the pearls. He goes out the next afternoon and returns with a bundle of cash.

I don't make any comment.

'It is enough to tide us over,' he says.

I don't ask him 'until what'?

Every day takes us a few steps closer to it.

HOTEL BEAUMARCHAIS

Avenue Princesse Alice, Monte Carlo, Principality of Monaco

Through the cavernous lobby of the Hotel Beaumarchais stagger Monte Carlo's Walking Dead, as Florin calls them, ancient Monégasque citizens on their way to dine, as they do every night, in the hotel's esteemed three-Michelin-starred restaurant. The women are all dressed to the nines, and look too frail to carry the weight of the rocks around their necks and the stiff brocade of their gowns. Their male companions wear dinner suits and bow ties with a crumpled resignation, as if they would rather be at home in front of the TV.

'They only live here because of the tax.' Florin lights a cigarette, as we sit side-by-side on a velvet sofa waiting for our drinks. 'And so they are miserable. They live in high-rise apartments with a view of the sea, they have every comfort, perhaps even a yacht, but they are stuck with each other and the sour memories of what they had to do to get here.'

That raises an eyebrow. 'I thought you were full of admiration for rich people.'

'I don't like rich people who never spend their money.'

'On you.'

'I have observed that you don't mind it so much yourself,' he says, a bit sharply.

We haven't touched on this subject for weeks. We have been pretending, very beautifully, that we are young and innocent and independently wealthy – independent of everything else but each other, in fact. Florin has stepped very lightly on the earth since St-Tropez . There have been few mood shifts, no unexplained disappearances and only rare moments when he seems out of sorts. It is as if the moon that ruled him had ceased to wax and wane. And yet, there is something else, a thing I did not admit to even the tiny part of myself that still kept aloof from him. Where he had been sometimes brittle, he now is smooth as the Cristofle spoons we dine with, but the silveriness has been dulled in some way. Although he still dictates where we are going and how our days are shaped, although he still tells me what lipstick and clothing to wear and he is the one who strides into hotels and shops and demands what we need, there is a new passiveness about him, something desultory, fatalistic, which I read as a sign that he feels that at last everything is right, that I am the right woman and there is no longer any need to 'take' me, or look elsewhere, and that our rambling is evidence of the naturalness we feel together, because we have our own structure aside from anything the world might impose and I am quite stupidly complimented by that.

So when Florin sounds a little ill-humoured, I say nothing. I wonder what has happened to him in Monte Carlo in the past that causes him to view it with such distaste but I know the chances of me finding out are next to nothing. After all these months I still know very little about him and he is excellent at deflecting my questions so that they end up being about me. If I ask him 'Don't you miss your family?' he might answer, 'Do you? It's the same for me, Violet.' And I am so busy thinking, *do I miss my family?* that I forget that he hasn't told me about his.

He seems to sense I am wary of his mood, because he makes

an effort to be his usual companionable self. 'We haven't sat together, like this, in a hotel lobby for a long time,' he smiles, as our bottle of Mumm arrives.

It's true. We have mostly stayed in chic little hotels where the guests' comings and goings are discreet. The grand scale of this hotel makes it an unusual choice for us but we still have some cash from those pricey black pearls. He has bought me a new dress to wear to dinner and insisted I wear my diamond drop earrings with it. 'I suppose we will have to sell these next, so you might as well enjoy them,' he says as he helps me loop them through my ears, and although he smiles, I know he is serious.

Florin takes charge of the bottle and sends the waiter away. 'The lobby is beautiful, I think. The art nouveau style is about controlling nature in the face of the industrial revolution.' He sounds like a guide in a museum. I nod and say it might be the most gorgeous lobby I've ever been in. Above our heads floats a glass dome with a rosette centre like a huge iris, supported by decorative iron columns that grow out of the floor below like rampant weeds. Persian rugs covered with knots of unruly flowers cover the marble floors and vines sprouting pink trumpets climb all over the walls and dark wood doors, which are set with many mirrors so that the effect is like being in a hothouse of exotics that haven't been tended for years.

Florin passes me a glass of champagne. As I accept it, I notice his hand is unsteady. He looks at the wristwatch I have bought him in Cannes and says, 'Perhaps we can go into dinner a little early.'

I look around the lobby. All I can see are clutches of old people drinking aperitifs from tiny glasses and some Americans, with the weathered faces of yachtsmen, quite unsuitably attired in bright polo shirts and jeans. 'You've seen someone you know.'

He brushes my observation aside. 'No, no one. I always feel is if something is going to happen when I am in a lobby. And sometimes it is a pleasant feeling and sometimes it is not.' He touches my glass with the rim of his. '*Nuroc.* To a wonderful evening.' But his knee continues to betray his attempt at nonchalance by jittering against my thigh.

We are just finishing the bottle, and I'm feeling a bit tipsy I admit, when a couple ask if they might take the two armchairs opposite where we are sitting. Florin ignores them, which surprises me, so I overcompensate by saying brightly, of course, we are just leaving, and the man responds, please do not on our account and insists we share a glass of champagne with them. The man and woman are about a decade, or more, older than us and she is extravagantly overdressed, if that is possible in a place like this. They are Greek, I find out, and sailing the Mediterranean on their 'boat' before they take it down to the Maldives for winter. So I am surprised when Florin continues to be haughty with them and barely touches the champagne they have ordered. I am halfway through explaining where we have been travelling when Florin suddenly jerks my elbow and nudges me to my feet and says, rather curtly, that we are late for our dinner reservation and thank you for the drink.

'What was that about?' I ask angrily as he guides me across the foyer to the restaurant. 'Why were you rude to them? They were your type. Rich.'

'We shouldn't appear to be too enthusiastic.'

'What do you mean?'

'They are trying to pick us up.'

I feel myself blushing. 'Did they think I was flirting with them?'

'You were sounding that way.'

I stop him before we reach the maître d. '*You* thought I wanted to go with them!'

'I thought you understood these things.'

I can't help smiling now. It's funny. 'You were jealous.'

He looks at me sadly. 'No, Violet, I was not jealous.'

I don't believe him and I barely taste the three hundred dollars of food and wine I consume nor notice that the shepherdesses on the frescoed ceiling above our heads are suckling tiny fat pigs or that a British movie star is dining at a corner table because I am so pleased with the idea that Florin is jealous.

And perhaps he *is* jealous, a little, because he is subdued over dinner, and barely praises the food, which even I recognise as sublime. It is such a natural step for me to make this assumption, for in my limited experience a jealous man is a quietly seething one, like Rahul, and something in Florin's mind is clicking over, if not exactly seething, as we eat.

But Florin is not very jealous, as it turns out.

Although he professes to dislike Monte Carlo, Florin unexpectedly decides in the morning that we might stay for a day or two more. And that suits me. I want to visit the Palace and go swimming at the Beach Club and lie on a sun lounge on our terrace overlooking the sea. I am getting a little colour and my hair is in need of a cut but I like this new feral me, although Florin is unhappy that I am sullying my white skin – 'jaundiced', as he calls it. He keeps pointing out freckles and blemishes that he says are appearing on my skin, as if I were a piece of fruit overripening.

Which I am.

One afternoon, returning from the Beach Club, where I have swum and sunned myself alone, I stop on my way to our suite at the concierge's desk, to see if there are any tickets to the Opera. I remember that Florin likes the Opera and think I might surprise him. But the concierge tells me the season does not begin for a few weeks. I ask him if there is anything else he recommends and he passes me a few brochures of cultural attractions. I'm aware that there is someone standing behind me waiting to speak to the concierge and I can see that the concierge is anxious for me to move aside so that he can help this person, so I pick up the brochures and turn to take them away.

'May I recommend the *Uncle Vanya?*' It is the British actor who had been dining in the restaurant a few nights before. He has a white straw hat on, as a disguise, I expect. At this point in his life I suppose he is about forty and so often seen in period films that his slightly old-fashioned clothing seems to me not odd at all.

'Oh – hello,' is all I can think to say.

'It's in Russian, of course,' he goes on. 'But in my humble opinion it is not to be missed.'

'Thank you. My . . . *friend* speaks Russian.' What do I call Florin? When people mistakenly refer to him as my husband, I never correct them.

'Then you're a fortunate woman. He can interpret.'

He no longer seems the slightest bit interested in the concierge. He offers a hand and introduces himself. I know from the photos in *Madame Figaro* that this actor is living with a woman older than himself and therefore his sexuality is not in question – and yet his hand feels feminine and limp in mine. But there is no doubt from his eyes what his interest is in me. I feel flattered. How could I not?

I tell him my name is Violet and he remarks that, of course, he can see why.

I say that my eyes aren't really purple. It's just a trick of the light inside.

In that case, he says, you should stand under this glass dome forever.

I don't fancy being a statue, I joke.

And we banter lightly like this for a while, until he looks at his watch and says he must go and suggests perhaps we can have a drink some time – that is, if I am staying here for a few days?

And I say, that would be nice.

I do take Florin to the play and, even though I don't really understand all of it, I join in the mass hysteria and shed a few tears along with the rest of the audience. Florin, who remains dry-eyed, thinks this is amusing. When I accuse him of not being moved by anything he says, 'But it's not real. It's only playacting. How can it be sad?'

As we are walking through the hotel lobby afterwards, the British actor comes out of the bar and says 'Good evening, Violet' as we pass him.

Florin's reaction takes me by surprise. 'How do you know *him*?' he asks when we are alone in the elevator.

'I met him yesterday at the concierge's desk. He was the one who recommended the play.'

'I see. I thought it was odd you had a sudden urge for Chekov.'

In our suite, he throws his jacket on a chair and pours himself a slivovitz without asking me if I'd like anything. I'm taking off my clothes when he comes into the dressing room, drink in hand. He stands behind me so that I have to talk to his reflection in the mirror.

'Do you want to sleep with him?'

'*What?*' I know who he's talking about but I'm stunned at the question.

'Do you want to sleep with that actor?'

'Of course not!'

'Because if you do, I will not stand in your way.'

I stop unbuttoning my blouse. The tiny pearl buttons suddenly feel like boulders. 'I want you, not him.'

'But you're attracted to him?'

I try to be calm. This might all be academic. 'Well, if you really want to know, I'm attracted to the him I see on the screen. But in real life, I don't know. He has a girlfriend anyway.'

'As if that matters in this world, Violet.'

'This world?'

'The world we live in. The world of the privileged. He can do what he likes.'

'He can't sling me over his shoulder and run away with me if I don't want it.'

'But if I were not here, you might want it?' He is leaning against the wardrobe door, shaking the ice around in his glass.

'How do I know that? You *are* here.'

'I am not always going to be here in the way you want.'

This is the first I've heard of it. There is a rush of blood to my head. I slump on to the stool in front of the mirror, facing him now. 'What do you mean?' I ask shakily.

'I am not leaving you, Violet. I am just saying that perhaps it is time to rethink our plans.'

'I wasn't aware we had any plans.'

'I have always had plans. I told you back in Biarritz we cannot go on like this forever – without a strategy. I can sell your diamonds but the money will soon run out. Besides, I don't like doing it. You should have diamonds if you want them.'

'But you're the one who is spending big. This hotel room – it must cost several hundred dollars a night.'

'Sixteen hundred, actually.'

'You see! We could have rented a nice apartment for a month for that.'

'I told you I cannot live that way.'

'It's normal.'

'I am not normal.'

'You were the one who said "Money means nothing. It's easy to get more".'

'And it is. Nothing has changed.'

'Yes it has. Why are you talking like this all of a sudden?'

'When I saw you with that actor I realised that I am being selfish. I am holding you back. I am preventing you from fulfilling your potential.'

'You didn't seem to mind stopping me fulfilling my potential with Rahul.'

'I can see now that you are bitter about that. I'm sorry, Violet. It was selfish of me to want you so badly.'

I look at him sceptically. This humility is not typical. And yet, I can't discount it. He is talking slowly and I can see the cogs turning over in his mind, as if all this has truly just occurred to him.

You know what I think now? I think that when I ran out of resources – money and jewellery he could flog – I stopped being useful to him. That is the cruel truth of it. But I cling to the hope that he is speaking out of a misguided sense of duty to me. 'We have been together half of this year, Florin. And I'm happier than I've ever been. Does it have to stop because we can't be certain what is happening next? I know we have been buying time – but we have to be buying time for a reason. That reason is that we want to be together.' Something bleak occurs to me. 'Unless, of course, you are tired of me.'

'I am not tired of you, Violet, how could I be?'

'Well, God knows, Florin, I'm never going to be tired of you if you keep on like this.' I am trying to make a joke of it. I want to distract him away from saying anything further that might damage us.

'I cannot provide for you in the way you would like. You need someone like that actor who can.'

'No I don't. I don't care if you can't *support* me financially—'

He interrupts. 'You do not understand. I can support you. You can support me. It is the way we can support each other that we need to discuss.'

It suddenly falls into place. 'This is not about me and that actor, is it? It's about you and some woman.'

'Believe me, there is no woman. I am just being practical. If we can't provide for each other, and we want to be together, then we need others to provide it for us.'

He is looking at me as if he has just suggested the most reasonable thing in the world.

'You would let me sleep with him? For money?'

'I am not suggesting that. I am suggesting that you might like to live it up for a while.'

'I *am* living it up.'

'He can give you things I can't.'

'And where will you be when I'm with him?'

'I will be waiting for you.'

'Here?'

'Not necessarily.'

'You're pimping me!'

'No, I am not. I am, of course, prepared to do the same.'

'I bet you are!' I stand up now, propelled by rage and confusion. I pull off my blouse and skirt and almost tear my earrings out of my ears, slamming them down on the dressing table. I tie the belt of my bathrobe, as if I were jerking a rope around his neck, all the while avoiding looking at his reflection in the mirror. But

I catch it briefly and his features, reversed, make it seem as if a stranger has inhabited the familiar form.

He doesn't move. 'Violet.'

'No,' I say, fiercely pulling a brush through my hair.

'Violet,' he says again. He steps towards me now and puts his hand over mine on the brush, taking it from me. He stands close behind me and drapes his arms lightly around my collarbone. I stay perfectly, frigidly, still. 'This is about keeping us together,' he whispers, kissing my throat.

'There are other ways,' I say cruelly. 'If you had done something with your life, learnt a profession, instead of wandering around the world like some young prince, we wouldn't be talking like this.'

I feel him go rigid. 'I do have a profession. I have never pretended otherwise.' He slides his hands down to my elbows and pulls me roughly around to face him.

'You're hurting me,' I say dully.

He loosens his grip. 'This is the only way I know how to keep you, Violet.'

'You mean it's the only way I can keep *you.*'

I break away from him and walk towards the bedroom but I don't want to go there. I take the other door instead, into the bathroom. Florin follows me – or several Florins. This time, he is refracted in five different mirrors. I want to escape them all. I go to the basin and turn on the taps. I pretend to wash my hands.

'I am only suggesting something we have both done a hundred times before,' he says.

'Maybe you've done it a hundred times.'

He sighs. 'I accept that this is unorthodox for you. I know you want an *amour fou* and I have tried to give it to you. But we are serious about each other now and what we once did selfishly we can now do for each other.'

'And do you suggest we do it in shifts? One week for me, one week for you?'

'It is more organic than that. Who knows what will happen? I am just proposing that we are open to the possibilities. Do you want me to return to stealing to keep a roof over our heads? Because you only need say the word and I will do it.'

We have joked about him being a thief so often I am astounded that at last he admits to it. I shake my head. 'I don't want you to do that.'

'I think it is more respectable, is it not, to make an arrangement with another consenting adult?'

'I can't share you.'

'You won't be sharing me. Come now, Violet, was it really you with those men you have told me about? Do you think it is really me with these women?'

Five Florins look at me. If I can't resist one of them, what hope do I have with five?

MAJAFUSHI PRIVATE RESORT

Faafu Atoll, The Republic of the Maldives

There are eleven hundred and ninety coral islands in the Maldives, in a double chain of atolls that touch the equator. Eighty percent of the country is less than one metre above the high tide. If the sea levels permanently rise even as high as a man's knee, whole villages would disappear.

This is where I finally drown Violet.

It starts in Monte Carlo, in our suite, one afternoon when I have just returned from the pool. Florin is restless and soon I find out why. He sits me on the bed and takes my hand, as if he is about to propose marriage (a little fluttering of my heart) and instead outlines another kind of proposition altogether – delicately, rationally, like a groom putting blinkers on a horse that is easily spooked.

'The Greek couple we met the other night, the ones you flirted with, they have asked us to come cruising with them to the Maldives. There will be the occasional other guest joining us but mostly it will be the four of us – and twenty-seven staff. You'll like the Maldives, Violet, the islands are exquisite.'

He has taken me entirely unawares. He had been so dismissive of this couple before. He'd even made a joke, a little bit obscene, about her long nails. 'Really? When did you speak to them? You weren't very friendly the other night.'

'Today, at lunch. When you were at the pool.'

He is being far too gentle with me. This arouses my suspicion. 'They're not a charity. What do they expect in return?'

'As far as I know, Violet, just our company.'

'I find it hard to believe *that.*'

'Why do you always assign an unpleasant motive to things? They are people who like to be surrounded by beauty. We're not pretending anything. They know we are together. We don't have to sneak around below deck like rats. They are happy if we appear to be in love with each other. It sets the tone for their own relationship.'

'*Appear* to be in love with each other?'

'What I mean is this – we can be as openly together as we like. I am not pretending that this is all there is to it. But it is a fluid situation, Violet. You are not obliged to do anything you don't want. But I hope you will want to do a lot of it with me. Cruising can be an erotic pastime, especially when we are in the lap of luxury. If you are not happy you can always get off.'

'And if I say no?'

'Then we will stay here. I am not forcing you. I am only trying to keep our little family together.'

Our little family.

If you are not happy you can always get off. How reasonable that seems! I don't believe that we are going on a jolly cruise for weeks with a couple who want us around simply because they enjoyed our sunny dispositions, but if I don't like it, we could always get off. Notice my use of the plural. Notice Florin's use of the singular.

Do I agree to the voyage? I suppose I must have. I remember arguing with him. I remember saying no. But it must have been an equivocal kind of no because we are on deck on the handsome, black-hulled, 205-foot motor yacht, the *Hedonia,* the next afternoon.

Florin has been in excellent spirits ever since we sailed off from Port Hercule. He's like a man who, having been unemployed for months, finds himself at last going out to earn a living and put food on his family's table. It's as if all those weeks spent drifting along the Mediterranean coast with me were just a way of marking time – a lovely way to be sure – until the real career opportunity, ingratiating himself with the very rich, came along.

He warned me enough times. But I am stubborn, arrogant, wilful, like the young woman who, faced with a suitor who insists he never wants to have children, sets out immediately to make herself pregnant by him. I wanted to push Florin to the edge of the cliff to see which way he would jump, and now I have my answer.

Observing him in company, for the first time, I see how he comes alive with an audience. How *glowing* he is since we've been on deck, how sweet he is to everyone, how pretty his manners are, how knowledgeable he is on every subject! He is like a circuit without a break – he creates the sexual charge and then plugs right into it himself. Half the male crew members are in love with him, and he teases them mercilessly, smiling ambiguously when he holds a glass up to be filled or dropping his towel for them to pick up when he enters the pool. Anything to keep the friction crackling around him like a halo.

When I accuse him of enjoying the tension he creates, he doesn't deny it.

'This is a *bad* thing? Do you want me to be miserable? At last we have found our gravy boat, so we might as well get pleasure from it.'

I suppose he means *gravy train* but the mistake is understandable. There is plenty of gravy: eight staterooms; twenty-seven crew, including three chefs, seven French maids, two personal trainers and two masseuses; six decks; four bars; a cellar with 2000 bottles of wine and 500 bottles of ouzo; a beauty parlour; a mini-golf course; an outdoor spa; a lapis and marble frescoed pool; a movie theatre; a helicopter; a Bentley in the garage; sixty television screens; nineteen video phones and an egg-shaped dining room that our host, Constantine, has frescoed with Bacchanalian scenes of his naked wife romping with various creatures from mythology. Our stateroom, 'Nairobi,' has walls lined with zebrahide, a Swarovski crystal ceiling that sparkles like the night sky over the veldt (according to the Guest Directory) and twenty different fragrances on the bathroom shelves.

In private, Florin calls our hosts Ari and Maria because they are Greek and ostentatiously wealthy. But this is where the similarity to that other, legendary Greek couple ends. She, Anastasia, is not a tempestuous, trilling brunette but a golden-blonde, former aerobics instructress with no singing voice whatsoever, if the onboard karaoke is anything to go by, and he, Constantine, is not a dwarfish shipping magnate but a medium-sized, rather shambolic, mid-fiftyish software mogul, who is increasing his fortune by reprogramming computers that might go haywire at one second past midnight on 1 January 2000, which is more than a year away. ('Think of that!' a starry-eyed Florin whispers to me one night as Constantine is explaining 'Y2K strategies' over cigar smoke after dinner. 'The new millennium has not yet begun and already people are making money out of it!')

I am wary of our hosts but all the while we are at sea they are charming to me. Anastasia loans me her jewellery at dinner and sends her favourite masseur to our cabin every morning. When I express a desire for those little French marzipans I like, the helicopter is sent a hundred kilometres back to Menton to do the shopping. At every port along our route to the Arabian Sea, a flunkey comes on board with a library of the latest books and magazines for me to read. We are scooped up by limousines and taken on guided tours of monuments and antiquities, followed by a few hours in the best boutiques, where Anastasia buys me anything I admire. She is only a few years older than me but she is quite maternal, always advising me on this and that, and I feel sometimes like a waif who has been taken in by a kindly but bossy aunt.

It is she who chooses the menus, confers with the bodyguards about security, inspects that the Meissen china is laid out on the table correctly, decides where the latest art acquisition should hang, designs and constantly tweaks the interiors, and orders ailing crew members to bed with bowls of *fassolatha*. Constantine takes little interest in any of this, spending long hours locked away in his off-limits 'control' room, from where he runs his company, only appearing during the day for a listless jog or a bout of boxing with his trainer and for cocktails and dinner in the evening.

On the occasions when they are together with us, she dominates him too. Even when we are all by the pool, ostensibly relaxing, she is constantly running interference, making sure the ice is topped up in his ouzo and Coke, applying sunscreen to his chest and back, lecturing him about such-and-such business associate who is untrustworthy, chiding him about his thickening waistline, rejecting towels until the fluffiest one is found.

I find the clash of personal styles fascinating. Anastasia never emerges from her stateroom until midday, needing, she confides to me, 'at least three hours' to get prepared for the day. That would probably include, by the look of it, her sinewy body being massaged with oil, those long fingernails freshly painted, her yellow hair washed, dried, and styled into a twist (and the dark roots – for she is no blonde – regularly doused with peroxide), various stray hairs waxed off, and a mask of make-up, with plasticated lips and winged eyebrows, contrived to look as unnatural as possible and applied with a deft hand. I find myself casting surreptitious looks her way as we lie by the pool. We are a similar height, but where I am soft and fine and pale, she is muscular, toned and so expertly bronzed that the delicate skin under her arms is the same colour as the skin stretched over her enhanced D-cup breasts. How perfect she is, gleaming, metallic, poised – and I see where that term *trophy wife* comes from. You could put her on a mantlepiece and she would oblige by raising her skirt. I see in her what I might have become if I had stayed with Rahul and it disturbs me to think that this woman is in me.

Constantine, on the other hand, is careless with his personal appearance, apart from Anastasia's tweaking. He looks like a man who sits at computers all day, although his tan, under the grizzled fur that covers his body, is a perfect match for hers. His posture is slightly slumped and he has belly that spreads over his swim trunks. He only works out with the personal trainer under threat from his wife and would smoke and drink to his heart's content if she did not limit it. He couldn't care less which china they use at dinner and most of his guests – not me – are bores. He doesn't like being away from Athens so much and misses his three children by his first marriage.

He tells me all this one afternoon as he is showing me his art studio, where he is working on several awful paintings at once, most of them strange nudes done in swirling abstracts in the generic style of the airbrushed designs tradesmen paint on the side of their vans.

'I am an artist, Violet,' he tells me earnestly. 'The way I make money is nothing to do with my soul. I can see you are a woman who understands that.'

When I tell Florin about this conversation, he laughs. 'Next he will ask to paint you, you'll see.'

'Great,' I say unenthusiastically.

'It's up to you, Violet, but I wouldn't say no. He hasn't asked anything else of you.'

'And what has Anastasia asked of you?'

'You have spent more time with her than I have.'

'Don't be evasive.'

'She has asked nothing of me. Do you want me to tell you if she does?'

I look into that blithe, doe-eyed, I-would-never-hurt-you expression and shake my head.

Would it have made any difference if I had known precisely

when he started with her? Perhaps. Perhaps I might have faced what was happening and taken defensive action. But, in truth, the moment I stepped foot on that yacht it was too late. I was all at sea.

Now that I tell Florin I don't want to know, I desperately want to know. In my head I start carrying a map of where he is and where she is in case the coordinates intersect for any damning period of time. From behind my dark glasses I watch their body language carefully and listen for hints in what they say to each other and try to work out if there is any discernible shift in her attitude to me, but she continues to seek out my company and he is scrupulously flirtatious with everyone, and they behave perfectly politely with each other, like dinner guests who tolerate one another for the sake of their partners.

And I cannot say he is neglecting me. Quite, quite the opposite. I am someone to be stroked and fondled and nibbled – and not just privately but as a public broadcast to the entire ship, as we lounge by the pool or share a hammock on a lower deck or sit side-by-side at dinner, where his immobile hand lies perpetually between my thighs. In the afternoons, while everyone else is having a siesta, he always leads me to our bed, but not with the intention of sleeping. Under the Swarovski sky he is tireless, a symphony of different instruments – no, more like an opera, full of passion, comedy and glass-shattering crescendos. When I close my eyes, all the colours of the proscenium lights play under my lids.

Why should I resist? I like the attention and I like it most of all because if he is with me he cannot be with anyone else. And this is where I become unstuck because I begin to crave the proof of his fidelity more than I crave his love.

'You are very lucky to have a man who loves you so much,'

Anastasia says to me one day by the pool as Florin, who is concerned about me getting sunburnt, detangles himself from my body and saunters away towards our cabin to retrieve one of my hats. It has not gone unnoticed by either of us, as he stands to tie his sarong, that his erection is so strong it strains the waistband of his swimming briefs. I am embarrassed by this and say something inconsequential but she says, 'No, really, he has told me how much he adores you. It is very sweet,' and instead of basking in this I immediately think, *When? When did you have such an intimate conversation?*

And I see in Florin's fussing over me how alike he and Anastasia are. It's as if they're having a competition to prove who can best satisfy their partner. In my eyes they are only doing it for each other, like a feverish kind of foreplay.

I try to tease out of him some kind of reaction to her but it's always something neutral like 'Anastasia has done well for herself' or 'Perfect bodies can be acquired'.

One night, in port at Tripoli, a group of Tuareg women come on board to play their *anzads* for us. As we all stand around on deck watching the performance, Florin gradually moves me to the rear of the crowd, where he embraces me from behind and thrusts a busy hand up my skirt. I close my eyelids, expecting him to be outrageous and enter me then and there, and when he doesn't, I open my lids again and see that Anastasia's eyes, across the crowd, are on us – on *him* – and I know that his eyes are on her and I know it has started.

I throw myself into a kind of despair, which is all the more bitter because it's of my own making. I have been acquiescent in this.

And so I cast around for a way to hit back.

Constantine.

I can't say I haven't been thinking about him. Many times I have watched him and wondered *Could I?*, knowing that the answer is yes. Of course, *could* and *want to* are different propositions. Until now, I haven't wanted to and I've been glad his little chats to me have all been about art. He seems to think I understand him in some mystical way, which I do not, and he has an intensity when we are alone together that isn't altogether sexless – and yet he has not once laid a hand on me, even to guide me from a room. I wonder if he has no interest in sex, spending all those hours with his computers. Perhaps the industrious Anastasia satisfies all his urges and he is simply too empty to contemplate commingling with me. But there is a slow burn between us and now it's time to spark it.

It is brutally easy. Florin would be proud of me.

One morning, as I am coming from the pool, I ask Constantine how his painting is progressing.

He asks me to come to his studio before lunch.

It is built under the lower deck with skylights so occasionally the shadows of people walking overhead pass over the room.

He shows me an incomplete nude of a pink woman with a purple vagina. I admire it even though it is anatomically incorrect.

'I've never been painted before,' I say.

'Then I would be very honoured if you would pose for me.'

'Of course,' I smile. 'How lovely. When?'

'What are you doing now?'

'I am completely at your disposal.'

And I am.

He is nervous setting up his easel. He frets over the colours he will use. He places a stool for me and changes its position several times. Then he fiddles with his brushes.

'Do you want me to take my clothes off?'

He looks up from the bench, where he is squeezing a tube. 'Perhaps your top?' He goes back to his work.

I unhook my bikini bra. 'Will I sit on the stool?'

He looks up again. His eyes flash with interest. 'But you are much paler than I thought. It will be difficult to match the colour of your skin correctly.'

I sit on the stool while he mixes paint on a palette. Then he brings his palette to me and stands in front of me, brush poised. 'The skin on your breasts is like pearls. Would you permit me to apply some pigment to get an exact colour match?'

When I nod he dabs the sable point of the brush into a daub of paint and then delicately runs the tip of it from the top of my breast down to the nipple, making a fine line of ochre. 'Too yellow,' he mutters to himself. He does some more mixing, then applies a stripe to my other breast, swirling the colour around the nipple.

'Too pink?' I suggest.

He smiles at me, his collaborator. 'This might take quite some time,' he says.

The nipples have to be colour-matched exactly too. And then he finds a faint bruise on my arm that requires a squeeze of purple and green. I untie my sarong so that he can examine the tint of my belly, which is the pink that redheads go in the sun. He is using a thicker brush now and the broad head of it slides momentarily under the fabric of my bikini bottom. 'Ah, hair,' he exclaims, delighted. 'My wife rids herself of hers. And see – it is exactly the same hue as the hairs on this brush.'

Without him asking, I slip my bikini off. I close my eyes. I am disgusted – and aroused. There is nothing attractive about the hirsute Constantine and his eager stink of sweat, but it is the touch of his brush that is making love to me.

I open my thighs for him. He crouches and nudges my labia apart with his brush, as delicately as an archaeologist uncovering a fossil. 'Look at that colour! Crimson – and flamingo!' he dashes away and busies himself with his paint. When he returns, his palette is slashed with violent reds, purples and pinks, as if it has been in a war.

I slide forward on the stool so I am better presented for him. I close my eyes again. I am surprised at the shudder that seizes me almost as soon as the wet brush daintily touches my clitoris. As orgasms go it is just a weak little tremor but it is significant in that I could have it at all.

When Constantine finishes, he brings me a damp cloth to wipe myself down. But the pigment in the crimson leaves an indelible stain. And I don't mind because I want Florin to know.

Florin, who misses nothing, remarks on it that afternoon.

'Constantine has been painting me,' I say, as casually as I can.

'Literally, I see,' Florin replies. He stops what he is doing to me and gets up on his knees. I raise myself on my elbows and we look at each other. I am pleased to see he is not smiling.

'I thought you expected it,' I say.

'In fact I did not expect it of *you*.'

'You told me to be cooperative.'

'Since when do you do what I say?'

The springbok rug is bristly against my skin. I sit up. 'I was only being *fluid*,' I say, reminding him of his own words. 'Besides, why is it all right for you to fuck Anastasia but not okay for me to fuck her husband?'

'I am not fucking Anastasia.'

'Yes you are. I've seen you two look at each other.'

'We might look at each other but we have never been alone.'

'I don't believe you.'

'Why would I lie? I have admitted the possibility. But it looks like you have rushed the gun.'

'*Jumped* the gun,' I correct him. 'Why have I jumped it?'

'Because whatever may or may not happen between Anastasia and myself, you have now made it easier for her to do it.'

Easier for you to do it, I think, miserable at the irony of it. He is angry with me and now I know why. Despite everything he has said he would have felt guilty sleeping with her . . . and perhaps this is why he hasn't leapt into her arms. Now I have unwittingly given him permission.

And maybe he doesn't want it.

I see how unhappy he looks and I think, despite what he professes, he has misgivings about what he is doing, about this kind of life, and he would, after all, rather be living alone and uncomplicated with me.

'Let's ask to get off at the next port,' I urge him. 'We don't have to be with these people.'

'It's too late for that.'

'No it's not. You said we could get off at any time. We're not prisoners.'

'Don't you want to go to the Maldives?' His face is now full of consternation.

'They're just islands.'

'I think they will be good for us.'

'It's at least another week until we get there.'

He stands up and looks out the porthole. 'Constantine will need that time to get his portrait finished.'

I get up too. 'So you don't care after all if I go to his studio?'

He shakes his head. 'It's not you who fucks him.'

'Yes it is.' The truth is, Constantine has only touched me with his brush, but this is no time to admit to that. 'Whose body do you think this is?'

He turns to face me. 'Did you give your heart to Constantine? If you did, forgive me, but I think not. You can separate sex from love as well as I can. Which is fortunate, is it not?'

'Are we ever going to get off this ship, Florin?' As soon as I say it, I realise that I am speaking metaphorically. This ship of duplicity.

I think he knows this. The yacht suddenly lists and he pulls me towards him, a safe harbour for a moment. 'We will get off, I promise you.'

I assume that he means together.

By the time we drop anchor off the tiny island of Majafushi, Florin is disappearing for hours at a time to visit Anastasia. They are, I suppose, discreet about it. But it's hardly a secret. As I roam the yacht, at my wit's end, I see what everyone else on board sees. Trays of food delivered to her stateroom. The two masseurs summoned at once. A waiter, with a bottle of the Romanian plum spirit, *tuica,* which only Florin can bear, knocking on her door. I find myself skulking like an assassin under the staircase or making up excuses in my mind for having to return to our room, which requires passing hers on the way.

'Having fun?' I ask him one afternoon when he returns to our cabin after an absence of a couple of hours. I am lying on the bed looking at an Egyptian fashion magazine. Sometimes I am deliberately not here when he comes back from her but today I am sick of the pretence.

Florin looks squeaky clean, his hair wet, his skin glowing, a faint blush of rash on his bare chest, as if he has been scrubbed in a bath. I suppose he has. He casts me an irritated glance. 'It's only a transaction, Violet.'

I'm in the mood for an argument. 'What exactly is changing hands?'

He is on his way to the bathroom, but he stops and comes to the bed, where he sits beside me and puts a reassuring hand on my thigh. 'Anastasia is talking about loaning me her villa at Oia. Wouldn't you like to visit Santorini? All the buildings are white and we could eat at a little *taverna* every night.'

'How lovely. I'm not sure she'd approve of me being there.'

'Of course she would! She knows you are with me.'

'And what would we live on? Perhaps you should ask her for some money as well.'

'I don't do that.'

'Oh, I forgot. Perhaps, then, I should ask Constantine for it.'

He digs his fingers into my arm. 'Do not do that. You will ruin everything.'

'Everything?'

'Do you think they would have us here for one moment if they thought we needed money?'

'I haven't pretended to be rich.'

'They don't think we are *rich.* I am a count, a little impoverished in the typical Eastern European way, and you are a well-to-do Australian divorcée. They met us in the most expensive hotel in Monte Carlo, after all, and you still have your diamonds.'

'But you're as much a count as I am.'

'I am enough of a count to appeal to Anastasia. She was an aerobics instructress if you recall.'

'But she is always buying me things.'

'She is just reminding you she is richer than you.'

'I thought she recognised you . . . *us* for what we are.'

'And what is that?'

'Desperate? Desperate enough to come on board their stupid yacht and fuck them?'

He shakes my arm again. 'The only thing I am desperate about is keeping you. Why don't you understand this? It is a delicate proposition. I am balancing many needs.'

'I can see that. Yours first.'

He drops my arm and stands up. He looks down at me coldly. 'We will finish this cruise and we will go to Santorini. *Then* you will see.'

Majafushi is little more than a sandbar in the Arabian Sea. On it, there are ten bungalows made of banyan-tree wood and thatched coconut fronds, all built along the lagoon. Each bungalow has its own 65-foot *dhoni,* or traditional fishing boat, with a four-man crew of lithe, barefoot Maldivian boys, a mirrored bedroom and a refrigerator full of Krug. Although the whole island is not much longer than the *Hedonia* and barely as wide, between the yacht, the *dhonis*, the bungalows, the spa, the sunset yoga, the beach bar and the restaurant, it is very difficult to keep track of Florin.

Constantine has rented the entire island for a week – so we don't have to share it with any Russians, he says. His painting of me is not yet finished and he has turned one of the bungalows into an art studio. He goes back and forth to the *Hedonia* to work on his computers and spends the rest of his time in the studio, appearing often late for dinner in the main hut, barefooted and dishevelled. Anastasia seems to mind this less and less. She spends much of her time in her bungalow or reclining on the daybed on the prow of a *dhoni*, sailing around the lagoon like Cleopatra on her barge. She seems to have stopped interfering in the day-to-day running of everyone and barely raises a protest the night our tuna is over-cooked. She is still friendly to me, in a patronising way, and has bought me resort clothes from the island's little shop, but I can see all is not well in paradise.

When I ask Florin about it, he says, 'Maybe she is ill. It's very hot here,' and that's as much of an answer as I get from him.

The monsoon has almost ended but some days are so humid I feel like I am breathing under water. The rain comes down heavy as a velvet curtain and then lifts to expose a sun so violent the sweat on my skin sizzles like oil on a hotplate. My joints feel glued together. I can barely raise enough energy to walk the island in search of Florin. But I still find myself doing it, listlessly, repeatedly, round and round, because what I need to know is that he is still there.

I feel like the Arab sailors who, on the spice route to India and Asia, were forced to sit out the monsoon on these islands for months until the prevailing winds changed. I too want the winds to change and blow us out of here.

Constantine summons me to pose every other day and I have taught myself not to dread it. I have long ceased getting any kind of unwelcome thrill from this arrangement but I find my own escape by becoming a tourist in my head and sailing off somewhere else. Sometimes I'm so disconnected from myself I get down from the stool and walk out of his bungalow still streaked with paint and it's only later when Florin observes it that I'm even aware of what I have done.

The *thakarus,* the young men in sarongs who are our butlers, give me their dazzling smiles and giggle furiously at the wild white woman, half-naked and smeared with tribal colours (Constantine is experimenting) who walks the island and lurks among the palm fronds, always watching for something.

And Florin? There is something out of sorts with him, too. It's not just the monsoon that is sapping his strength. Anastasia demands his attention from midday until dinner and late at night we fall on our beds like a married couple who have been drained of the passion for each other. He would do pornographic acts with me if I asked him but I don't and he just kisses me and says, 'Don't be unhappy, Violet, we have only a few more days to go.'

I become friends with Mousa, the young man who rakes the sand on the beach outside our bungalow. Every time I make a footprint he appears, to smooth it over. We laugh at this and soon he is my lifeline, telling me stories of the islands while I help correct his broken English.

He has beautiful burnished brown skin and palms that are pink as the inside of a shell. He tells me that long ago those Arab sailors, stalled by the monsoon, married local women, the *dhivedin*, to bide their time and then divorced them when the monsoon ended and they finally could sail for home. The result of these intermarriages – plus a little bit of canoodling with African slaves – created a people of extraordinary beauty and grace. I wonder about these boys on the islands, how devoutly Muslim they might be, or whether the constant exposure to semi-naked, decadent westerners corrupts them. Mousa recounts the story of Miriam Kabaafaanu, a slave girl who 'three hundreds of years ago' gave birth to the Sultan's son and then, when he was poisoned by enemies, seized power herself and ruled the kingdom 'in a very depraved manner'. When the next Sultan ascended, he forced strict adherence to the Islamic code, which has been followed to this day.

'A woman's instincts must be restrained, Miss Violet.'

'How true,' I say.

But Mousa doesn't seem to mind my bikini and more than

once I am tempted to ask him if some of the boys earn money in other ways, but I know he will misconstrue it. And maybe I want him to.

On our fourth night there Anastasia makes a comment that spoils everything, as it is intended to. We are having cocktails in the bar before dinner, as usual, and Mousa is on duty tonight serving us our drinks. Once he has delivered them, and is padding back across the sandy floor to the bar, which is an upturned dinghy, Anastasia follows him with her eyes and says, 'That is a very darling boy.' Then she flashes a smug look at me. 'Violet thinks so too.'

I hadn't been aware that she had been paying any attention to me, so wrapped up has she been with Florin, but she must have spies. 'I feel sorry for him,' I say, trying to keep the conversation abstract. 'He has a wife and child at home and only sees them once every few months.'

'You know,' Anastasia says, sipping her Negroni, 'if any one of these boys so much as lays a finger on any of the guests, they are instantly dismissed. And sometimes they are sent home to face shari'a law. We Western women are filthy they say. By the sound of it, the women guests – and perhaps some of the men, yes? – think they are fair game.'

'You seem to know a lot about it,' I say, not disguising my anger all that well.

'When I saw how friendly you were becoming with this boy, I asked.'

I glance at the others. Constantine is reading the wine list and doesn't appear to have registered the conversation. Florin has not been his usual talkative self tonight but now he looks quite pale, as if some total stranger has come up to him, slapped him across the face and then walked away. I am astounded by his reaction.

Does he really think I've had sex with the boy? And why would he be so upset? I try to catch his eye but when I do he looks right past me.

'I'm just friends with Mousa,' I tell him when we are at last alone after a dinner, a Maldivian feast of many curried dishes, that seems to have dragged on forever. 'You don't think I'm trying to seduce him, do you?'

He seems uninterested. 'I wouldn't blame you if you did.'

'As a matter of fact, I wouldn't blame me either, things as they are. But I'm not risking getting him fired.'

He doesn't comment.

'Why do you think Anastasia was so mean to me?'

'Mean?' he asks. 'I didn't notice. But it's only to be expected. She is in competition with you.'

That's all I get out of him as the sheets fall over us. He turns away from me and I am left lying there in the deep dark without even a moon to illuminate my thoughts. The ceiling fan overhead churns as if the moist air is thick as butter. When I do sleep, it is fitful. I can sense that Florin is lying next to me with his eyes open. He gets out of bed at one point and I fall back to sleep, thinking he has gone to the bathroom. But I awake again, an unknown period of time later, to hear him returning to the room. I pull the sheet over my head, not wanting to think about it.

The next afternoon, when Florin is occupied with Anastasia, or so I imagine, and Constantine is on the *Hedonia* solving some kind of technical meltdown, I retreat to my bungalow, where I have a bottle of 1988 Krug delivered, thinking that I have not taken nearly enough advantage of our hosts. The *thakaru* leaves it on ice for me and I am just about to pour my third glass when there is a knock and the door, which is never locked anyway, opens a fraction. I think it is the housekeeper, come to decorate my bed with frangipani blossoms, the way she does every day, but then I hear a voice, surprisingly like Anastasia's. 'Violet?'

Anastasia enters the bungalow, looking almost sheepish. She is wearing a white cotton kimono over her bikini. She no longer looks grand, expensive, but like a beauty therapist. 'Am I disturbing you?' she asks hesitantly.

If I'm surprised to see her during her Florin Time, I have no intention of showing it. 'Not at all. I'm just drinking your champagne. Do you want some?'

She looks at the bottle as if I just offered her floor polish. 'I didn't know you drank alone, Violet.'

'Only when I have something to celebrate.'

'And what is that?'

'Let's see – you being with *me* this time of day?'

'That is what I want to talk to you about.' She closes the door behind her as if there is an army of spies outside.

I curl up on a rattan chair, taking the half-empty bottle of Krug with me. To hell with glasses. I'm sufficiently sozzled already to find this very amusing. Anastasia takes the chair next to me, her legs crossed. She fiddles with her charm bracelet for a while before looking at me with cow-brown eyes and saying 'Let me not beat about the bush. I want you to give him up'.

I think she means Constantine. I shrug. 'All right. The portrait's finished anyway.'

'I do not mean my husband.'

Oh. 'I thought I *had* given Florin up.'

'He doesn't seem to think so. Look . . . do you have cigarette?'

She taps her long nails on the rattan chair arm while I dig out a packet of Florin's *Carpati*. He has been savouring this packet for weeks – there is only one cigarette left. I hand it to her with the matches. Let her light it herself. She takes a couple of puffs and looks at the cigarette in her hand in disgust. 'Unfiltered,' she says, rolling her tongue.

'Have an ashtray.' I hand her a conch shell.

She stubs out the cigarette and then holds it between her fingers. 'You know, even this cigarette is dear to me because it is one of his.'

I'm not in the mood for any of this. 'You can smell his clothes if you like.'

She flashes me an acid look. 'This is not funny.'

'No. I suppose it isn't. What did he do to you?'

'He touched my soul.'

The thought of Anastasia with a soul is beyond me. 'For God's sake,' I explode. 'He touched your pocket.'

I know I shouldn't have said that, but it goes over her head. 'I'm going to leave Constantine for him.'

I try not to sound shocked. 'Does Florin know this?'

'Yes.'

'And what did he say?'

'He said we have to be careful not to hurt *you*.'

Do not react, Violet, I say to myself. 'What about Constantine? Don't you care about him?'

'He can't be hurt.'

I tell her that's not true. I think he can.

She makes a dismissive gesture. 'He has his computers. He has his art. And that sick pornography of his . . .'

'What pornography?' I suppose she means the paintings.

She looks at me with an eyebrow raised. 'My dear, you have provided it.' She waves a hand so heavy with rocks it's a wonder her fine wrist can raise it. 'Anyway, we are not talking about him. We are talking about Florin and I. You have to speak to him and tell him you set him free.'

Does she spend all her time – when she's not fucking Florin or applying make-up – watching appalling Greek soap operas on television? 'So buying him doesn't work?' I ask, taking a swig from the bottle.

'I don't know what you mean,' she says haughtily. 'You have to face the fact that he is tired of you. But he is a gentleman and he feels responsible for you.'

'Is that what he said?'

'Yes.'

'Why would you give up all *this* for him?'

'Ah, you see, you don't love him. He said you wouldn't understand. That you are only with him for the sex.'

'Oh, did he? And you're not?'

'No I am not.' She tugs so hard at the diamond dangling on a fine chain around her neck that she pulls it off. She looks at the stone in her hand and then throws it on the floor. I watch where it rolls, under the chair. 'Listen to me, Violet. I have never been in love before. I am tired of looking after men. I want a man to look after me. And Florin . . .'

Her bottom lip is trembling. Her eyes fill with tears. I sober up quickly now, aware that this is not a performance, a diva running through the repertoire to get whatever she wants. Florin has made her love him. I know how, but I don't know why.

'You think Florin is the one to do that?' I ask more gently.

She nods.

'You realise he doesn't have any money? What are you going to live on?'

'I have my own money. I have a villa in Santorini.' Ah, yes, the villa. 'I am not poor. Besides, he has a castle that is tied up in a family dispute but will be his eventually.'

By now I can't disguise the astonishment on my face. I have

been wrong about Anastasia. I thought she was a hard nut, sophisticated, jaded, avaricious, cunning, a woman who has planned out her life, succeeded brilliantly and is in total control of her destiny – the sort of woman Florin wanted me to be. Instead I can see that she is naïve, stupid even, and willing to believe anything if it delivers her the kind of transcendent experience of love she has read about in books.

Like me.

She stands up now. 'It drives me crazy to think of you with him. I am going to tell Constantine tonight. And then Florin can move in with me.' She has tossed her beach bag on the bed and now she goes to it. She takes out a thick yellow envelope and hands it to me. 'You don't want him. You are only on the rebound from your husband. And so I feel sorry for you. Florin says you will need something to make you feel better. Here it is.'

And she leaves.

I don't need to open the envelope. By the feel of it I suppose it is a lot of money. I don't intend to accept it, of course.

Because the deal isn't done.

She can't have him.

When Florin comes back to the bungalow to change for dinner, I am waiting for him. A little drunk, to be sure, so I am ready for a fight.

He takes one look at me and says, 'Anastasia.' Not a question. He knows.

I am sitting on the edge of the bed, crushing today's frangipani blooms under the weight of my wretchedness. He lifts me off it and embraces me. 'I'm sorry, Violet. She is not easy to control.'

I nudge him away. 'What have you done to her?'

'I? Nothing.'

'Nothing? She has fallen in love with you.'

'And that is my fault?'

'You might have had something to do with that.'

'She is a highly paid whore. She should know better.'

I'm stunned by his cruel words. I find myself defending her. 'What right have you to call her that?'

'There are rules and she is stepping outside them.'

'What rules? Who made them up?'

'I made it very plain, Violet, that I was with you.'

'While you were with her.'

'Stop it. You know the arrangement as well as she does. I wish you women would keep to it.'

'*You* women? Am I the same as her?'

He closes his eyes and when he opens them I see they are red like they've been aggravated by pollen. He suddenly looks very tired. 'I'm sorry, Violet. I don't mean you.' He wraps warm arms around my neck and I smell the coconut oil that clings to his hairs. He speaks to the back of my head. 'I am frustrated, that is all, and I am being pulled in many directions.'

'Let's leave then. We have money now. She left me an envelope.'

I can feel his muscles tense. 'She did?'

I pull back from him. 'Don't act surprised. You told her to. You told her I needed something to make me feel better.'

His hands are on my shoulders now. 'Yes. But I didn't think she'd fall for it.'

'*Fall* for it?'

'You know I was never going to leave you for her.' He winds a length of my hair around a finger.

'Then you're conning her out of money. I thought you never accepted payment.'

'I didn't say that. I said I never *ask* for money. If they wish to give it to me spontaneously, then who am I to insult them by not accepting it? In any case, the money is yours.'

'Well, maybe I should give it back.'

'Why on earth would you do that?'

'Because it was payment for leaving you. And I'm not going to do that.'

'How much is it?'

'I didn't look. But quite lot, I think. Unless it's cut paper.'

'Where is the envelope?'

I show him. Why hide it from him? I know he will take it anyway. He shakes the contents of the envelope onto the bed. Four neat bundles of crisp bills, each secured by an elastic band. He picks them up, rifles them, and makes his estimate. 'Fifty thousand dollars.'

'God, I thought it might have been a few thousand.'

'It's only small change for her. She has bundles of cash lying around in her bungalow with nothing to spend it on here. The safe on the yacht probably contains considerably more.'

'If I don't give it back, can we leave? Now? Tonight?'

'It's not very much money, Violet.'

'But it's enough, isn't it?'

'It might be,' he says.

It is cruel of Florin to make love to me like he means it that night. No performance now, just a circle of tenderness tinged with something sad and far away.

In his arms, I fall into the deepest sleep I have had for months. It's strange the way it comes over me, as if all my fears have been thrown into a sack and buried. I dream of bat's wings beating and lying under a roof woven from thousand-dollar notes and an African child in a sling that smiles at me with a mouth of gold teeth. I hear a small animal, perhaps a rat, rustling around in the room and the sound of an outboard motor puttering away in the still night.

It is raining hard when I wake. I look at the bedside clock and it's eight a.m.

Florin is not beside me.

I drag myself off the bed. I know what else will be gone.

The diamonds are missing.

The yellow envelope sits against the mirror by the bathroom vanity. He has the grace to leave me a little, although it will be reclaimed by Anastasia when she accuses me of being a thief's accomplice.

In the middle of the night, in the dark, he has scrawled my name on it. The writing is shaky but I get the message.

Violetta.

Anastasia turns her fury on me. She threatens to call the National Security Service, to have me thrown in jail where, she says, they will flog me and only chop off one hand if I'm lucky. It is shari'a law there, she has pleasure in pointing out, a slut like me won't be believed. A woman's testimony is worth only half that of a man's in any case. There are no jury trials and it's impossible to find a lawyer because lawyers are often jailed with their clients. I can rot in that hellhole of a prison forever for all she cares. And if I am repeatedly raped by guards, by other prisoners – well, that will be something to keep me entertained, won't it?

Luckily, Constantine takes pity on me – I am his muse after all – and arranges a speedboat to take me under the cloak of darkness to the airport at Malé, where a first-class ticket to Paris is waiting for me. Constantine, I am sure, does not arrange for me to travel in style out of the goodness of his heart – he simply doesn't understand that there is any other way to do it. As I am packing, I remember the diamond Anastasia dropped the afternoon before. It is still under the bed – because of the hysteria, the housekeepers have kept their distance. I hold it in my palm, and estimate that it weighs between one and a half and two carats. I am becoming expert in this. At this rate, I will soon be able to bite pearls to know their value.

A few days later, I will sell the diamond in a shop on the Quai Voltaire for almost six thousand dollars. But it is not nearly payment enough.

I lie in the shallows of the lagoon, parrotfish nibbling at my toes. I am floating in the shape of a cross, my white muslin caftan drifting around me like a net around a silver tuna fish.

Like the coral islands I am waiting for the tide to flow over me.

'I give in,' I say softly to the sky.

This moment is a baptism . . . and a drowning.

I hereby drown Violet, who has done me no good.

Part Four
Violet and Violetta

THE HOTEL REGRET

Strada Mattei Millo, Bucharest, Romania

'Why Romania?' the dispirited immigration official asks me as I present my passport at Bucharest airport. 'There is nothing for beautiful young woman here.'

In the taxi, as I transfer my passport from my pocket to my bag, a slip of paper falls out. After studying it for a while I realise it is the official's phone number. *Mugur 021 313 4038.*

We are all looking for the unattainable in Bucharest.

The back seat of the taxi has no springs in it and I feel as if the hard bone of my coccyx is being scraped along the road. The driver jams an old cassette into the player and a woman starts caterwauling, out of sync with the percussion instruments accompanying her. 'You like?' he asks me, watching me blearily through the rear-vision mirror, which is strung with tangled wooden rosaries.

'Gypsy music?' I ask him.

He makes a hawking sound and spits out the window, as if he has a gob of poison stuck in his throat. 'Not gypsy. Is Romanian. Iona Radu.'

I nod and turn my head to look out the window, not having the energy for a conversation in broken English.

The once-tender leaves of summer hang like shrivelled grey bats from the trees stationed along the boulevards. There's something almost painful about it, as if nature is strangling itself in disgust at the ugliness of the man-made landscape. The roads are cratered with pot-holes and congested with old Russian cars, vans with mismatched panels, trucks belching diesel, meandering bicycles, slow-moving horse carts, crawling, smoky-windowed limousines, and the occasional pig being walked home. Down the very middle of the highway limp amputees on a variety of apparatus – crutches, canes, makeshift frames – with their hands out, begging for pale notes of almost worthless *lei*. Children run in and out of the traffic, selling woven straw. At a traffic light, a group of infants not old enough for school, their bony faces like skulls, thrust primitively carved figurines of Vlad the Impaler, the local folk hero, through the window at me. I don't have the heart to wind up the window, so I distribute 10,000 *lei* notes. By my reckoning each note is only worth fifty cents, but the children become frenzied, thudding their little bodies against the door and reaching into the car to grasp my hair, their waving arms like fine, sticky tentacles. The driver yells out *'Idite!'* and floors the accelerator a moment before the light turns green. 'Do not do,' he chastises me as we bump away. *'Tiganii.'*

Welcome to Romania, I say silently to myself, home of orphans, vampires, dictators, gymnasts, gypsies, prostitutes and black-hearted souls.

Everything is strange. We pass monuments, sports complexes and a model of the Arc de Triomphe but also small oil wells, vineyards, squat factories, and yards populated with garden gnomes. One stretch of boulevard is lined with heartbreakingly neglected mansions, many of them boarded-up, the copper roofs stained with verdigris and the gingerbread windows smashed in. The next moment we are in the city proper, dwarfed by implacable high-rise apartment buildings, grey, prefabricated Communist blocks showing the cracks and strains of age, the narrow balconies strung with shabby underwear, the facades scarred with billboards and, around the Piata Revolutiei, stray bullets from the 1989 revolution. The taxi driver points to a wall strafed by mortar shells. Next to it, a black-gowned priest, heavily bearded, stands in the doorway of a

Romanesque basilica, as if an eruption in time had thrown up a scene from three centuries past. The driver crosses himself and I don't know whether it's because of the priest, the memory of the revolution, or as protection against the infamous vampire, whose cartoonish figure is plastered everywhere on posters for the 1998 Dracula Congress to be held this month.

I have been given the name of a cheap hotel by a woman on the information desk at the airport. The driver wants to take me somewhere else, where he'll get a kickback no doubt, but I am not going to start trusting Romanian men now. He shakes his head when we pull up outside an old building with stiff fringed curtains in the window and a tarnished copper plaque with the hotel name boasting one lonely star. He sourly takes my suitcase from the passenger's seat and drops it none too carefully on the pavement, which is so cracked it looks like a smashed grey meringue. The suitcase lists and falls while the driver demands an exorbitant fee from me, almost two million *lei,* and then takes his kickback – at my suitcase – when I tell him there's no tip.

I have to politely fight off two men who run from opposite ends of the street to help me carry my case through the hotel doorway. They each want a gratuity anyway, and I wave them off but not before the younger of them – and he has lost most of his teeth – offers to escort me around the town.

'*Da,*' says the woman behind a glass window, like the kind they have in banks, when I ask her if there are any rooms available. 'No bath, six hundred thousand *lei.* Is all.'

She extracts my money, hands me a key attached to a heavy brass weight and points me to the elevator, a black cage which lies beyond a parlour crammed with gloomy furniture and dusty vases of artificial mauve roses. The elevator takes minutes to come and when it does, I can barely fit both my suitcase and myself in it.

I sit on the case and the contraption lurches to the fourth floor, where it stops with a groan and the doors refuse to open until I rattle them furiously. My room, down a corridor with the carpet half pulled up and damp, as if a bath has overflowed, is a nun's cell containing a narrow bed, a washbasin, a rickety cupboard and lace curtains, creeping with mould, which flap at the brick wall next door. There is a metal reading lamp stuck in the wall over the bed and a naked bulb hanging from a cord in the ceiling. The towel is threadbare, the soap a doll's-sized scentless thing that still bears a black pubic hair from the previous guest and, when I wander the labyrinth to find the toilet, it has no lock and no paper and an ancient cistern that drops rusty water on my head.

The bed sags under my weight like a horse slouching towards the knacker's yard. I have chosen a miserable, degrading place. And yet, I feel certain that everything is as it should be. I am like a sleeping assassin, suddenly activated, who arises from her bed in a trance, and goes out to seek her target, not sure until the last few seconds of life who that target might be. And like a good little sleeper I am patient, stubborn, prepared to wait months if necessary. Some time, sooner or later, Florin will be here, in this city that he wants to keep hidden from me. I don't know what draws him back here but I know this is where he comes – his supply of Romanian cigarettes, not found anywhere else, give him away. If I have to sit in every lobby, knock on every door or stalk every park, alley or café in this city, I will find him, eventually, one day. And then I will . . . I don't know what. Make him apologise for the many ways he has humiliated me?

Kill him sounds better.

In the middle of the night, or so it seems, my neighbour next door receives guests. Through the cardboard walls I hear grunting and giggling and even a drawn-out trumpet of flatulence. Hours later, after someone noisily heaves out the window, the door slams and the guests depart and my neighbour falls into a snoring stupor on his bed, his open mouth pressed precisely against the part of the wall where my pillow lies. The intimacy of it is unsettling and reminds me of other, more beautiful rooms, and softer beds, and the men who have lain with me on them. And yet, perversely, I am more comfortable here in a room I have paid for myself.

The morning light comes in like porridge off a spoon, wan and gluggy. Soon my rest is infiltrated by the sounds of the morning rush hour, that long, drawn-out string of car horns and wet tires that always sounds so futile to my ears. There is creaking in the hallways as other guests negotiate the mouldy carpet in search of the shower. I decide to wash myself in the basin – a wise move, as it turns out, because later I find out the stream of water from my tap is Niagara Falls compared to the meagre drips that tumble from the calcified shower rose. My hand towel almost does the job of drying me and I struggle to pull warm clothes over my damp skin. When I'm dressed, I hang up my clothes and find a hiding place for my cash and traveller's cheques. There are not many options in this tiny cell so I shove them in a pair of boots for the time being.

In the breakfast nook downstairs, an old waiter in a crinkly bolero jacket that looks like he has rolled it up and used it for a pillow (and perhaps this is the case if he has a room in this hotel) offers me a plasticised menu with three breakfast choices, Plan A, B and C. Only Plan B permits coffee. I discover the only turn-down service this hotel offers is the turning down of milk to go with it.

I have no plan myself. Florin has told me almost nothing of this place. I don't know where he stays when he comes here, or with whom, or whether any of the men I pass in the streets – some of whom look remarkably like him with their high, strong noses and violent cheekbones – share a genetic relationship with him. I don't know if he still has family here and whether those brothers, uncles and nephews can be found in any of those towering concrete slabs that pass for human habitats. I don't know whether he has a favourite café or bar, or if he takes taxis or the trolley bus, or whether he likes to walk in the gardens or browse the roadside bookseller stalls. I don't know where to find him but I hope that if I walk round and round enough my spiral will become a vortex that draws him in.

There are always the casinos. On every corner, as my taxi driver said, there is 'one casino and one church'. Surely, one night, one month, one year he will be there.

I leave the hotel in search of real coffee. It is still early, Bucharest rush hour, and cold enough for me to be glad I bought a heavy woollen coat. I become aware as I walk that I am attracting attention. Although I am dressed modestly and in subdued colours, befitting the clandestine nature of my operation, my clothing sets me apart. My fashionable bag and boots and the cut of my coat is unusual on these streets, where the men look like they have just come from soccer training and the women, even the young girls, dress in neat but very old-fashioned combinations of things, like court shoes with long floral skirts or secretarial suits with white stockings. The women seem to have taken care with their appearance – their faces are carefully made-up, their hair rigidly styled – but they remind me of the conservative way another generation dressed before the advent of jeans. I look altogether vixenish with my pointed toes and fur cuffs and people stare, not in an unfriendly way, as if I had been jettisoned from a plane on its way to the Paris couture.

Like this, I am a target for beggars, most of them children who should be at school, but who congregate in doorways and surge aggressively, sometimes with sticks, when a potential mark, like me, ventures into their territory. They clutch at my hem and my cuffs, launch themselves at my bag, and cannot be shaken off unless I walk into a hotel or a department store, where the doorman shoos them away, or take a seat in the back of a café where they boldly wait outside for me to finish. I feel sorry for them at first, thinking of scab-encrusted children tied to orphanage beds and gypsies being sold as slaves to profiteers, and carry rolls of 10,000 *lei* bills in my pocket but the more money I give the more children appear and soon I tire of the physical and emotional burden of lugging them all around with me.

On this first, cold morning, I run into a scrappy street fight between rival gangs of children in an alleyway beside a Pizza Hut and I am quite terrified by the malevolent expressions on their faces, as if they were gargoyles who had stepped off the plinth of some church to continue an ancient war. When I walk past, they stop their battle and come after me, instantly transformed into angels of need, smiling, cooing and reciting a few snatches of English, such as 'pretty missus' and 'sweet lady please.' I dash into a passage, which is beautiful and dilapidated, with a high arched glass roof and the remnants of old, painted, soft-drink signs peeling from the walls, and find a café, where I retreat inside and order my coffee. The children hover for a while, and then start fighting again, at which point a waiter beats them off with a broom.

The coffee is Turkish, good and dark, and it comes with bread and jam. When I ask for butter and a paper napkin there is none. Tucked away in the back of the café like this I can watch the locals read their papers and scan their faces for any sign of Florin, undetected. I'm reasonably sure he would not be up at this hour and so I'm more relaxed than I will be as the day progresses, when every blond head, every Roman profile, every waft of *Carpati* brand cigarettes becomes evidence of him.

When I leave the café, lingering street urchins pursue me for another block or so. As I shake them off by walking into a shop selling peasant blouses, the irony of gypsy children chasing me while I'm chasing my own gypsy, is not lost.

I go to my first casino that night, after sitting uneventfully in the lobby of the Intercontinental for an hour. The casino is a soup of excreting sweat glands and cabbage breath. Hands slide all over me as I fight my way to the bar. Everywhere, there is the sound of creaking as men in vinyl pants adjust themselves to greet me. I am out of there after five minutes, to the consternation of the big security guy on the door, who pulls a gun from under his jacket and shows it to me, to make me feel safer I suppose, and then hands me a photograph of a man he says is his brother, who can come in ten minutes if I need 'gentleman company'.

I hop a taxi and go back to the hotel where no one has made my crumpled bed and someone with a key opens my door in the middle of the night and then closes it again, like a parent looking in on a sleeping child.

In the morning, I find a bakery a block away and eat a hot pastry that has a whiff of apple in it. At the end of the street are the gates to the Cismigu Gardens, which, according to my guidebook, is a popular place for assignations. The gardens are well kept, with wide paths that meander around a large lake that is fringed with weeping willows. On one side the gardens back on to old mansion flats, faded, beautiful, like Tuscan villas, with climbing roses dead on the vine and colonnades of twisted wisteria branches. It's a bit windy and rather quiet at this hour of the morning and after a circuit of the lake I find a table at a tavern by the water and have my coffee. But even here, in this bucolic place, I am harassed by the inevitable swarm of children who wait for me on the path outside, with pinching little hands that find my pockets and fiddle with the lock on my handbag. The children follow me right to the gates of the park, where the presence of the *politia* makes them shrink back into the bushes, like little ghouls caught out of their coffins as daylight breaks.

Some days I feel like the only visitor in the city, for there are very few tourists. It's obvious why. Eleven years on from communism, the people are suspicious and opportunistic; the language, which is like Italian with a Balkan bent, is impenetrable; English is rarely spoken; the progeny of animals made homeless during the revolution, roam the streets, snarling, hungry; toilets are stinking holes in the ground and there is no paper; rubbish bins overflow; some buildings are in such a state of ruin that people are forced to walk on the roads in case the facades shed brick and mortar, which they often do; and the 'number one Bucharest tourist attraction', is not something uplifting like an opera house or a palace a maharaja has built for his love, but the horrifying Palace of the Parliament, dictator Nicolae Ceausescu's great folly, a twelve-storey wedding cake of megalomaniac ambition with 1100 rooms, for which whole neighbourhoods were razed, known to everyone as 'the madman's house'.

And yet at night you can turn a corner and come across a plaza where dozens of couples are dancing to a small orchestra, so light on their feet and in their hearts that you are transported to a time between Vlad Tepes (the 'Impaler') and Ceausescu, between successive invasions of Turks, Goths, Austrians, Nazis and Russians, when this city might indeed have been the Paris of the east, as Florin called it.

I suppose it is a burden to live with a history like this – the most violent warlord in history as your national hero, the most corrupt and indulgent of the Eastern European dictators as your ruler for four decades, and much of your national identity based on a bloodsucking count who is the invention of an Englishman.

I return to the hotel late one afternoon, to find that I have been moved to another room. A busload of Moldovan tourists have arrived and they all want to stay on the same floor. Esma, one of the two women who run the reception, hands me a new key without apology.

The tiny foyer is overwhelmed with suitcases. As the elevator can only take one or two at a time, this is going to be a long night for the new arrivals. The tour guide, an anxious, unhealthy-looking young man in the ubiquitous vinyl jacket, grimaces at me and says, 'I am apologising for this.'

I tell him it's okay.

I walk up to the third floor and unlock the door on a room that is the mirror image of my other one, except it has a small television on a chest of drawers. I watch a game show with a man in a chicken costume running on a treadmill and a rock video with girls in bikinis soaping a naked pig. I fall asleep and it's dark when I wake up. I put my coat back on to go out on the usually thankless mission of finding edible food. But Florin has to eat sometime too.

It's quiet in the lobby downstairs. The tour guide is sitting in the parlour on a plastic-covered lounge chair, legs crossed, poking the sole of one shoe. I stop in front of him and say *'Buna'. Hello.*

He looks up, startled. He really is quite ill, his skin jaundiced, his stubble blue. 'They are going to bed now,' he says.

'You are tired?' I say in that tortured English I have adopted since I've been here.

'No,' he insists. 'I am making sure they are asleep.' His forehead has broken out in sweat, like someone has sprayed a wax statue.

'Are you sure you aren't sick?'

'No. I am just going home.'

He stands up awkwardly.

'Don't go,' I say.

He hardly knows where to look. He takes my hand in thin fingers that feel as cold as metal skewers and presses it to his mouth. *'Sarut Mana.' I kiss your hand.* He releases it delicately, like he's placing a robin's egg in cotton wool.

I tell him my name.

'I am Florin.'

There must be thousands of Romanian men called Florin – I have read that the king of the gypsies is named Florin Cioabu – and yet the name bounces around in my skull painfully.

I must make a face because he looks uncomfortable.

'I'm sorry. Please sit down,' I tell him.

He does what I say. When he crosses his legs again, I see that there is a hole in his shoe, and that he has packed it with cardboard.

I am lonely. And his name is Florin. Maybe there is some destiny here. 'Look, may I sit with you for a minute?'

He doesn't look very happy about it. He nods and hugs the arm of the sofa as if it were a flotation device and he was in the middle of the ocean.

I plunge into a plastic-covered chair. 'How long have you been a guide?' I ask.

'One year. I am being student at Suceava.'

'Where is that?'

'Moldavia. Border of Moldova.'

'What do you study?'

'Didacticism.'

'Bucharest is a long way from there.'

'I have vacation.'

'And you are trying to earn extra money?'

'Yes. Even students must eat.' He smiles now, with an old man's yellow teeth.

'I have an idea,' I say, enunciating what has been forming in my mind. 'Are you free tonight?'

He blinks at me. He goes paler, if that is possible. I realise why. He thinks I want sex. 'You are lonely?' he asks carefully.

'No. I'm not lonely. Look, I just wanted to ask if I could pay you to show me around.'

'For what? What are you wanting to see?'

'I thought we could go to some casinos.' When he looks dubious, I quickly add, noticing how hungry he looks. 'But first we could go somewhere to eat. Do you know a good restaurant? I will pay for everything, of course.'

He still looks uncertain. 'For how many hours?'

I check my watch. 'It's nine o'clock now. Four hours?'

'And you will be paying me one hundred thousand *lei* for one hour?'

That's only five dollars. 'I will be paying you three hundred thousand *lei* for one hour.'

His eyes open wide. Then he tries to disguise his pleasure. 'That would be suitable,' he says tersely. 'Paying in cash?'

He takes me to Burebista on the Calea Mosilor, a traditional restaurant that is expensive by local standards. He says he has never been here before but that he has always wanted to go. We are shown a table under a stuffed goat head. I tell him it's okay for him to order the local delicacy, bear paw, but I stick to cabbage rolls with pork knuckle. I don't realise how hungry I am and we order pancakes with rose preserves to follow. It's all unusually delicious and Florin blushes when I praise the meal effusively.

I watch him devour his pancakes like I watched another Florin in Vienna long ago. I am still trying to find connections between them.

Florin shows me a nightlife guide and asks me where I want to go. As it turns out, he has never been to a Bucharest casino and it's obvious his lack of funds is the reason why. He asks a taxi driver and soon we are in the MGM Casino International, watching a hand of poker. I'm becoming nervous and Florin picks it up. 'You are looking for someone?'

'Yes,' I admit.

'He is gambling?'

'Sometimes.'

'He is owing you money?'

'Yes.'

Florin now becomes energised by the concept of someone owing me money. He speaks to a group of men who have been ogling me but have kept their distance. When he returns he is a compendium of information about all the casinos.

We try two more places before I become sick of it. He accompanies me in a taxi back to the hotel and then I pay the driver to take him to where he is staying. I hand Florin more money and he waves as he is driven off, tipsy from the glasses of *tuica* he has consumed during the night.

The next evening, we go to the Actor's Café near the national theatre, where Florin tells me most of young Bucharest hangs out. We try more casinos but I have lost interest. When I pay him and see him off in a taxi, he admits that he is staying in a hostel that costs 20,000 *lei*, or one dollar, a night. But, he adds brightly, he would be sleeping at the railway station if it were not for me.

On the third night, Florin says to me, 'We are leaving to Targoviste tomorrow.'

'Oh,' I say, disappointed. I have quite enjoyed the company of my anxious student. But he has not led me to my Florin.

'But I am having friend Nicolae coming to Bucharest. You would like.'

'No. It's okay.'

'Nicolae is knowing about money and where to get it.'

'I don't need money.'

Florin shrugs. '*I* am coming back if you like?'

'Give me your address. I'll write.'

'You would be bringing me to Australia. Maybe?'

'I'm not going to Australia.'

'Why not? Is rich country.'

'It's not that interesting,' I say dismissively and then I immediately regret it. How can I explain to someone whose idea of luxury is a one-dollar hostel room what 'interesting' is? Florin has told me the train trip from Suceava is thirteen hours and he has to save for a year to find the fare. Most weeks he lives on bread and pork dripping. He has never been on an airplane. He does not have a telephone or access to a computer. If he wants to watch soccer on television he has to go to a sports bar. He has worn the same pair of shoes every day for four years.

He looks deflated. I know he doesn't believe me. 'Give me your address,' I say again.

'You will not be writing,' he says sadly.

I return to sitting in hotel lobbies.

Men approach me, as usual. This country has, after all, the reputation of supplying the world's 'best' whores. 'Best' meaning the most beautiful, desperate and anxious to please. I am not anxious to please any of these men. I need nothing from them – not sex or money or even their compliments. There is only one man I am looking for.

There are men who don't like being rejected, although I am as polite and condescending as a queen meeting minor heads of state. Sometimes this overflows into drama, but my defenders are on hand. One of the doormen at the Capsa becomes a veritable Prince Galahad, throwing an insistent predator right onto his nose on Strada Edgar Quinet. The cocoon of hotel security is spun around me. I speak English, I dress well, and my resemblance to that actress doesn't do me any harm. In this town, where everyone is on the make, a woman who appears not to want anything is a curiosity, not to be offended. I walk into a hotel lobby and I am treated like a VIP.

Only I know how risky this act is. VIP. Violetta in Peril.

And then I see him.

Just like that.

The telephones in the old Wallachia Palace Hotel are free of bugging devices in the year 2000 but once the old hotel was a hotbed of Cold War intrigue, with the bellboys and concierge on the payroll of the Communist Securitate and every ashtray wired for sound. In those days the housekeeping staff used to routinely photograph documents in guest's rooms while they were out. Intellectuals and artists were planted in the bars to pick up indiscreet conversations. The hotel was so widely known to be bugged that one visiting Frenchwoman, upon checking in, enquired if it were possible to be given a room without a listening device.

But renovation has wiped out any remnants of Cold War charm. The hotel is efficient and businesslike. The racy Westminster Bar where during the Second World War you could find members of British Intelligence, the Gestapo and spies of King Carol all rubbing shoulders, is now a sedate parlour of overstuffed furniture and hunting scenes on the walls. As soon as I walk into it, I feel the imprint of Florin here. He loves this kind of conservative Britishness. And so I haunt the Westminster Bar more frequently than any other establishment, sitting on a gin and tonic for hours at a time.

But in my haunting I feel my bodily presence getting fainter with every visit, like a ghost who fails to make contact with her unbelieving loved ones left behind in the physical world. Soon I feel no more than lip print on a glass, an outline, a vibration who occupies a striped chair with a pink gin in front of her. When I talk to people my conversation is just ectoplasm wobbling in the air, disconnected from my thoughts.

One night I am having this kind of conversation, my mouth moving but not my brain, about Romania joining the European Union, with a Croatian bureaucrat who thinks, like all men do, that he has a chance with me, when I see, beyond the door of the bar, Florin walk through the lobby.

I leap up immediately, without apology and rush to the door, clumsily knocking a waitress on my way through. I know everyone is looking at me but what do I care about them? Florin is nowhere in sight but he has been walking towards the elevator bank, rather than in the direction of the street, so I round the corner expecting to see him – *wanting* to see him, not afraid of this – but he is not there. I think perhaps he has gone into the restroom, so I wait, but none of the men who come out of that door are him. There is nowhere else he could go unless he took the fire stairs and they are alarmed. I track back to reception, the cigar store, to the street outside. No sign.

It *was* him, definitely him, not a doppelganger or some Romanian who shares his DNA. There is no doubt. Why I am so sure I do not know, except no other creature on earth holds its body like that, the sauntering gait with the curled, dead hand and the cigarette poised in the other like it's a delicate flower with a heady perfume that must be savoured.

I find a seat in the lobby and sit heavily on it. I know he can't escape me here. If he has gone to a woman's room – well, he must eventually come down. Even if he stays the night I will be waiting for him.

But, of course, I can't sit here for hours because I attract attention. I know I am wringing my hands like Lady Macbeth but I can no sooner stop it than get up off this chair. Men, women, porters can't take their eyes off me, the madwoman in the hall. I have only been there an hour – it's about ten o'clock – when a concierge approaches me and asks me if he can assist in any way. He is polite but formidable, protecting his own stable of girls, who provide his *baksheesh,* against this clear interloper. I tell him the truth – I have caught a glimpse of a friend walking by and am waiting for him to return. The concierge tilts his head solicitously. Is he a guest? he asks, and if that is the case, have you enquired at reception? No, he is a local, I reply. And then I think – how foolish of me. The concierge is waiting for something and I know what it is. I reach into my bag, pull out a large note, which he palms with a nod. Perhaps you can help me find him, I say, I believe there is a directory.

And there is. The concierge brings me to his desk. From a drawer he pulls out a photo album and places it casually on one side. I come around to look at it surreptitiously, while he turns his back to me, answering the phone.

I flip through the polaroids of men in seductive poses. Many of them are in their underwear, pouting as aggressively at the camera as the escort girls in the nightlife guides. They are not all young and they are not all beautiful – far from it. In fact, a few are middle-aged, hairy, spread-bellied, like farmers come to town to sell their pigs. But, in this world, there is no accounting for taste. I look at one young man, just a boy, barely more than sixteen, I guess, and the S-bend curve of his skinny body speaks of a hunger that is nothing to do with sex. 'Mihai' is the name scrawled under his image. I take out the polaroid from the plastic and turn it over and study his phone number and some other scrawlings – *bi, coupé, français.* I am tempted to slip the polaroid into my bag and free him from this servitude but who am I to make this judgement? Am I any different because I demand the most rather than accept the least? He might be supporting a family of ten with his earnings. It might be a better life than jail or being forced to sell himself in truck stops on the highways leading out of here. It might be a better life than . . . not better perhaps, there is no 'better', but a way of staying alive. And then I think how strong the life force must be for boys like this and I wonder at it, me who now questions every morning why she should get up.

I put the photo back and close the book. Florin is not among them. He always claimed that he doesn't ply this trade but there would have been a grim satisfaction in finding him out. I slip the concierge another 500,000 *lei* and take my seat again. But Florin doesn't come.

And not the next evening either. I am sitting on one half of a sofa, smoking a cigarette, when I am harassed by a man, Russian or Czech, who comes and sits almost on top of me so I am forced to wriggle a small space between us. When I get up and move to another sofa, he follows, bringing with him the stale smell of butted cigarettes.

'What do you want?' I say loudly, looking for the concierge, whom I have tipped generously, to rescue me. But he is occupied elsewhere.

This bully doesn't appear to speak English. Instead, he removes the gold cufflinks from one of his sleeves and pushes the fabric up to his elbows. Discreetly he shows me his arm, which is scarred with the burns from dozens of cigarettes. He points to my cigarette and his little eyes glint beckoningly.

I reach over to the coffee table in front of us and slowly stub out my cigarette in an ashtray. He lets out a sob of frustration and I get up, walk away, gaining some pleasure in leaving him so cruelly unsatisfied.

Back in my tiny cell I watch the TV news from a world that seems as if it has nothing to do with me. A Kurdish militant hijacks a Turkish Airlines plane. A British poet dies. A disco in Sweden is burnt down and 63 people, mostly the children of refugees, die. John Glenn blasts into space on the shuttle *Discovery*. A New Jersey teenager pleads guilty to killing her baby in the toilets at her senior prom, moments after delivering him. Something about the Romanian soccer team. And then, a report from the Dracula Congress, where a daffy American professor in a cape says something incomprehensible about 'bloodletting existentialism'.

I fall asleep in the flickering blue light. Dracula takes me in a kiss of death. He is John Glenn in a cape. A little dead New Jersey baby floats above the bed, with the marks of my nails on his wrists, holding the concierge's photo album in his tiny, outstretched hands.

I sleep in on Sunday and miss out on Plan A and Plan B for breakfast. I have become quite fond of Radu, the old man who will never bend the rules. He tells me he is named after Radu the Handsome, Vlad the Impaler's brother. Radu is sweeping the dining room as I go past and surprises me by giving me an orange. *'Ai grija,'* he says without a smile. *Take care.*

Does he know something?

It's a gorgeous day, cold and clear. The birds are singing their lungs out, as if trying to coax the last leaves off the trees. I walk down to the Cismigiu Gardens and stroll around the lake, with the rest of Bucharest, men pushing prams, women wiping chocolate off babies' faces, couples hand in hand, old people in wheelchairs, children kicking balls. A fountain in the middle of the lake spouts feathers of water joyously. Even the gypsy children are giggling, chasing each other around the paths and wrestling under the bushes. People look upon them more kindly today and I even see a local man give a scabby boy a few *lei*.

One of these children, a little girl with corn-yellow hair, comes up to me with her hand out. She looks so sweet in her ruffled smock that I reach into my bag and give her the orange. She's delighted with it, tossing it between her palms like a ball. I hear a woman calling 'Elena!' and the little girl swings around and runs up the path towards her mother, a dark beauty dressed in a blouse too thin for the season and a long skirt, wearing the headscarf of the Roma. The woman crouches down to take her child in her arms and, as she does so, she catches my eye and her look is so full of hatred I take a step back. What have I done? I think for a minute the child must be forbidden oranges and then I see the woman swing the child into her arms and pass her to a man who has been walking slightly ahead of her. I haven't noticed him. God knows why. Because as he turns to face her and accept the child I see who it is.

Florin.

I shrink back into a bush but he hasn't seen me. The child climbs on to his back and throws her arms around his neck. The woman calls and two more children race up – boys. The smaller boy takes his mother's hand. The older one, who must be about ten, takes Florin's.

It's his sister, I say to myself. His sister. His sister who is as dark as he is fair.

I follow them, at a distance. I have no choice.

They stroll out the northern gates, past the National Museum and across to the Piata Revolutioni, to the tangle of back streets where the houses and apartment buildings still retain a Turkish character. It's easy to keep up with them as the children are slow. The woman has a serene way of walking as if she is carrying a bowl on her head. Florin's arm touches her shoulder from time to time. I am as tangled as the streets with bitter jealousy.

Occasionally they stop to tie a shoelace or call a child back from chasing a cat. Luckily, they don't turn. And yet I have a feeling the woman knows I am there. It's almost as if she is deliberately keeping Florin facing forward, engaged in what is ahead. The little girl turns at one point and, spotting me, waves her orange and I slip through the gates of a deserted old house for a minute before the coast becomes clear.

Eventually, they stop at an old *vila* on the Strada Calderon, with a tiled roof like a Turkish warrior's helmet. Under the eaves there are balconies strung with washing but the building is handsome, if dilapidated. I watch from behind a pillar as Florin puts the little girl down and punches a code into the door. Then I study the balconies to see if they appear. After several minutes, there is no sign of them. I take a deep breath and walk across the road to the front door. There is a directory – five names on slips of paper that are yellowed with age and mostly illegible. I suppose I could press all the bells and see who appears . . . but I am not ready for this.

At the next corner is a little bar café. There's only one small table and it is positioned inside the window. I take it and order *cafea* and *mitieia*, little meat pastries. I am ravenously hungry and dry in the throat, as if everything I'd eaten in the past two weeks had gone through my ghost body without touching the sides. The guy behind the counter has a handlebar moustache and fingers that are scarred along the tips. I don't ask about them but when he brings me coffee and pastry, he volunteers, quite cheerily, that they were burnt off constructing homemade bombs during the 1989 revolution.

'One bomb goes over the wall of the Central Committee,' he grins, giving me a thumb's up. 'And it kills one of the dictator's guard.'

His English is good. Romanian is a romance language and it's usually easier to converse in French. But Bogdan, hero of the revolution, is a former stage manager from the National Theatre and has learnt his English from touring companies. '*King Lear* and *Waiting for Godot*,' he says, clasping his hands together in a gesture of adoration. 'When they do *The Tempest,* Ceausescu is in fury because he thinks it is about him.'

I ask Bogdan if he lives in this neighbourhood.

'All my life,' he says proudly.

'Maybe you can help me.'

'Anything, young lady,' he says. He goes away to serve a customer but quickly returns, sensing intrigue, I suppose. He pulls up a chair. 'You shoot.'

'I'm looking for a friend.'

'Yes?'

I point down the street. 'That white building. I think he lives there.'

He looks at me cagily. 'Then you are not looking for him?'

'Well, I'm not sure he lives there. But I saw him go into it yesterday.'

'You didn't knock?' Decades of Communist rule have made him suspicious of other's motives.

I try a different tack. 'Well, you see, he was with a woman.'

'Aha!' He sits back in his chair and slaps his hands on his thighs. 'You think maybe he is being unfaithful?'

'Yes.' I look at my plate, coquettishly. It always works, this helpless act. Men expect women to be jealous, irrational. And they like it.

'You think I know this man?'

'You must have seen him, *if* he lives here. He's tall, long fair hair, very handsome – a gypsy. Roma.'

'Roma? You should not be knowing Roma.'

'I didn't know he was when I met him.'

He looks at me sadly. 'And you are having his child?'

'No! Not at all.'

He runs a finger along his moustache. 'Let me see.' A couple more customers come into the shop. He jumps up from his seat to serve them and then returns. 'You say he is handsome? But all Romanian men are handsome!'

'Yes, I know,' I lie. 'Look, the woman with him is a gypsy – she is very beautiful.'

'Like *all* Romanian women.'

'Yes, like all Romanian women. And there are three children. Two little boys and a girl.'

'Aha!' he says again, waving a mutilated finger. 'I know this family. But you are mistaken. He is not Roma.'

'He isn't?'

'No, no. Everyone knows this scandal. He is the son of General Stanescu of the Securitate.' Here, he spits on the floor. 'This man is now a millionaire. But his son married a Roma girl and he was disinherit. Now the son lives with wife and all her family. They no good.'

Married . . . wife . . . family. I hear the words but they don't make sense. If Florin is married then it's a funny kind of a marriage. He is barely ever in Romania. 'Are you sure? I don't mean the son – maybe my friend is her brother?'

'You say he is fair? She has many brothers but all are dark and fat. The general's son comes here to buy cigarettes. I know him.'

'My friend has a crippled hand.'

'Yes. Hand. He hurt it falling from pony.' He gets up again to serve a customer. 'You wait,' he says. 'I will bring another *cafea*.'

This is too much for me. Florin the son of a rich general, and not a gypsy? So even these stories are lies – his sister being killed, his father teaching him to steal, his hand being crushed so that he could better make money begging. And yet, when I first met him in Vienna, he told the truth, he said he hurt his hand falling off his pony. Why did he change his story? Did he think I'd be more impressed by a gypsy than a Communist's son? And of course, that is the answer. He has spun a romantic tale of a cruel father and a dead sister and a life on the streets of Bucharest because it sounds, perversely, glamorous. He has embroidered it with tales of the Blood Count and the Blood Countess for good measure.

I am the sucker in this vampire story.

In the time I have been here I have kept my eyes on Florin's building. It is Monday and the street is clogged with impatient cars but no one has come in or out of his doorway. I stand up and count out some money for Bogdan. He comes from behind the counter with my coffee.

'No, thanks,' I tell him. 'I need to go.'

Bogdan is disappointed. 'Come back this afternoon. He will be here some time.'

'Maybe.' I pick up my bag.

'I will tell him you were here?'

'No,' I say and then I change my mind. 'Yes. You do that. Tell him Violetta was here.'

'You are not going to try to get him back?' Bogdan is clearly looking forward to another chapter in the ongoing neighbourhood soap opera.

I shake my head. 'I never had him.'

It is no use dwelling on this. I cry. I cry until blood vessels burst behind my eyes and stain my eyeballs red. I cry until my lungs are squeezed of all air and my body feels like a horse is trapped inside me, kicking to get out. I cry until the guests in the next room thud on the walls to shut me up.

And then I don't cry any more.

The three pieces of hair Florin carries with him do not belong to the women he has loved.

They belong to his children.

He has what I have never had, what he dissuaded me from.

I haven't the heart to kill the father of three children. I haven't the heart to touch him at all.

It's better all round not to have any kind of heart.

LA RÉSERVE DE ST-TROPEZ

Route des Plages, St-Tropez, France

In the intervening several years, in all those lobbies in all those distant places – Berlin, Istanbul, Moscow, Cape Town, Shanghai, The Hague – I did not see Florin once. I saw other men like him, lighting women's cigarettes and carrying their glossy shopping bags and staring into their hopeful eyes in dim bars where pianos delicately tinkled. And, really, on the surface of it, they were *quite* like him, some of them more handsome, others less refined, all of them with well-rehearsed stories about being students or models or poets . . . or counts. If they all had one quality in common, it was the burning need to be gazed upon with desire, as if erotically charged air alone contained nutrients that sustained them. Over the years, I travelled parallel paths with men like these, even found myself in stolen embraces with one or two when the options were limited and there was nothing else with which to amuse ourselves, but in the end, at close range, none of them were Florin, not at all, even though I dearly wished him to be a *type,* as the French colloquially call it, a formula, nothing special, a regular, everyday, garden brand of gigolo, prostitute, hustler, stud – I don't care for any of these words but they will do.

When I didn't see him in Paris, not in a dozen visits, nor Vienna nor Verbier, his regular haunts, I told myself he was already dead, that someone or something had stolen my last satisfaction from me. The world was different and newly treacherous. There were so many ways Florin could die. Every time I picked up the

International Herald Tribune or flicked past CNN in the hotel room, there was a fresh possibility. He became a casualty of every world disaster – a fire on a train in Egypt, a plane crash in Kenya, the Concorde going down in Paris, an earthquake in Morocco, a suicide bomber in Cairo, a cluster bomb in Baghdad. For a long while I was convinced he had gone down with the World Trade Center – until I convinced myself he'd died in a terrorist attack in Bali. I thought it a sure thing that he had contracted HIV or developed a spiralling coke habit or been infected with the bird flu on a jaunt to Vietnam. There were floods, mud slides, ice storms, avalanches, volcanic eruptions, heatwaves, hurricanes, bushfires, soccer riots, restaurant shootings, kidnappings, theatre sieges, sinking ferries, civil wars, assassinations, military invasions, SARS, Ebola, foot and mouth, mad cow, nuclear meltdowns, Basque separatists, Chechen rebels, Islamic insurgents, Tamil Tigers, Jemaah Islamiah and Al Qaeda terrorists in every cabbage patch. I thought a jealous husband might have taken a shotgun to him or a distraught lover might have poisoned his tea. So many ways a person could die in this world suddenly gone mad.

'I thought you were dead,' I say to Florin as he closes the door of villa muguet, and the rest of the world, behind us.

And maybe, as I walk into the room and see him in the light that cascades in from big windows, he *is* dead, in his white caftan, with skin paler than I've seen it before and a hand that feels as if it has lost the flesh on it when it takes mine. His hair is darker and his beard is unshaven and my first reaction is – *good*, something or someone is making him suffer.

'If that is the case, then I have just been resurrected,' he says. He walks over to the window and draws the chintz curtains, for privacy, I suppose. Or maybe he doesn't like my scrutiny of his depleted state.

My heart seizes a little at the gesture. 'I am only here for five minutes,' I tell him, gathering my resolve. 'My car is waiting.'

He saunters over to the round glass dining table and picks up a packet of those wretched Romanian cigarettes. He offers me one. I shake my head. He lights the cigarette and opens his palm to show me the silver art deco lighter in it. 'Do you remember when we here the last time? That small *auberge* in the town? You bought me this. I really should give up smoking, but it would mean giving up this lighter.'

'What do you want, Florin?'

I am still standing near enough to the door to make a speedy escape. My arms are crossed in front of me and I'm aware it looks rather schoolmarmish but I don't know what else to do with them. My body, so adept at obeying my mind, is hardening into a shell around the soft parts within, so I feel stiff, jagged, graceless, like a cricket or a cockroach waiting for a foot to stomp on it. But I am no longer Violet and he can do me no harm.

'It's perfect, really, that we are in villa muguet,' he says, inhaling deeply. The bitter Carpathian smoke mingles with the medicinal smell of the room – lavender and lemon, formaldehyde and seeping wounds. His voice is strangely wafting too. 'Do you know what the meaning is for lily-of-the-valley? The return of love.'

Almost seven years and still this ruse about love? He's like an actor who once made a great success of *Hamlet* and now sits in his room alone and unwatched repeating the lines. It's easy to find cruel words.

'Are you *that* desperate that you have to fall back on me?' I say with as much scorn as I can muster. 'I have nothing but this suitcase. I haven't had anything for a long while. And I like it that way.

It makes me less vulnerable to blood-suckers like you.'

'Do you really think that badly of me?'

'Yes.'

'I don't think badly of you.'

There it is again. This way of seeing everything through a prism of himself. But it doesn't eat at me now. 'Now that we've established that, I can leave.'

'Aren't you curious?'

'About what?'

'What I have done for seven years.'

'No. I know what you have done. What you've always done. I've wasted enough of my life worrying about what you're doing.'

'Never a day has gone by without me wondering what happened to you.'

'Thank you for your concern.'

'I saw you in London,' he says unexpectedly.

'When?'

'A few years ago. 2000 perhaps. You were with that old man at the Ritz. I asked about you. And I found out that you were living with him.'

'How nice. Why didn't you come up and say a friendly hello?'

'Because I didn't want to upset your plans.'

'You didn't mind upsetting my plans with Rahul.' Rahul . . . I almost cannot get the name past my tongue. It's like a dry, furry pill stuck to the roof of my mouth, the ugly medicine I have still not quite learnt to swallow.

'That is because he was wrong for you.'

'He was wrong for me because he was in love with me.' I have had seven years to think about this. 'And you couldn't bear that. In your mind I was your protégée. And you wanted me rootless and heartless like you.'

'Are you heartless, Violetta?'

'Yes I am. You succeeded. Although it can't be said that I lead men into believing I love them, I *have* learnt many things from you. How to play roulette. Where to sell jewellery. The way to occupy a hotel room without paying. And certain sexual acts that guarantee expensive rewards. Given how little time we have actually spent together, I have learnt a lot.'

'But still, you are angry with me.'

My suitcase is standing beside me. I reach down to pick it up. 'Am I still a joke to you?'

Before I can close my hands around the handle he has my wrist. 'Don't go.'

I look him straight in the eye. 'If you want me to stay in this room with you, you have to give me something in return. It's all I'd ask of any man.'

'Look around you, Violet, you can see I have very little. I only have the things I have always had. Is that what you want?'

'That's all we ever had. It wasn't enough for you.'

He reaches out to me again, but this time I am faster. I jerk my hand behind my back. 'I intended to find you one day,' he says. 'Where did you go? I always wondered where you would choose.'

'Paris,' I answer. 'Where else?'

'And then?'

'And then I survived how I could. Very well, in fact.'

'But you haven't married well, as I expected. What happened to that old man?'

'I don't want to talk about him.'

'I thought you would go home. We were halfway there.'

'Home is a hotel room, preferably a luxury suite. But sometimes just a room will do.'

'What happened to you, Violet?'

'*Violetta*. You were there.'

'You have always known that when I am with you there is only you.'

I'm not falling for that again. But I can't bring myself to say the thing I know about him. 'And this department store heiress? I suppose this last week, when you were with *her*, there was only her?'

'In fact, Violet, there was only you. I have been watching you every day.'

'Well, I hope you got a good look. It's your last.'

I am doing well. I am feeling strong. I am leaving now. I pick up the suitcase.

Violetta is not going to make the same mistake Violet did.

I have my suitcase in my hand. I turn my back on Florin and grasp the door handle.

His voice, behind me, is hard now. 'You need to turn the handle up, not down. It's a peculiarity of this room.'

Now I swing around. I can't help it. It's as if someone has put their hands on me and yanked me round to face him. My fists are rolled into balls. I struggle to find the words. I have so many grievances against him. *Abandon. Steal. Betrayal. Wife. Children.*

But *children* is the worst.

'Did you tell your wife about me?'

'I didn't have to. She knows these things.'

'Let me see – is that because she actually *is* a gypsy? Unlike you, the general's son. Everything you have told me is a lie. Your parents, your dead sister, even your poor hand.'

He shrugs, as if we are just talking about what the weather will do. 'My wife is not important.'

'Telling me you had a wife was not important?'

'I married Romica when I was twenty, Violet. I came back from school in England after the Revolution and met her in the gardens. She was sixteen and selling herself to men for a few *lei*. I had to rescue her. My family cut me off. Her family didn't like me, either – I was a *gadjo*, a stranger. But they like me when I provide for them.'

'So, you want me to think you are a hero?'

'No, I was selfish. I admit this. I was young and spoiled and very attracted to her life. I didn't know what I was getting myself into. But I had to have her.'

'And you had to have every other woman who came across your path too.'

'You know who I am, Violet. I told you I wasn't free. I have always made it clear that my life is complicated.'

'You were free enough to spend a summer gallivanting with me.'

'I always spend the summers gallivanting with someone.'

'You bastard.'

He sighs. 'Why do you always make me say things in the wrong way? There are no jobs in Romania. It is a very desperate situation. Many men are forced to travel abroad to support their families.' His tone is the very essence of reasonableness.

'Yes – working in mines or kitchens.'

'And you think the worse of me because I do my work in the bedroom?'

I don't want to rake over old coals – or diamonds. I want to go out this door and be free of him. But I cannot control my need to know the answers. I cannot go on with my life, what is left of it, without the truth. 'Does your wife know how you earn your money?'

'We do not discuss the details. But she knows.'

'And she accepts this?'

'If I worked in a kitchen I would not bring her such pretty things. I would not be able to support her entire family. We would have to live in the *mahala*. Our children would beg on the streets. And she would have to earn her living another way.'

'So you are doing it for her?'

'It is easier for me. A woman can be exploited.'

'You are a hypocrite. You want to protect your precious wife from selling her body but all along you have encouraged me to sell mine?'

'I don't believe that is what I have done at all. There is a very great difference between being a rich man's mistress and giving blowjobs for American dollars in a Bucharest alley.'

'Is there?'

'Only you can answer that, Violet.'

He turns away from me and goes to the round table, picks up his cigarettes and lights one. Then he sits in the chair again, his legs crossed nonchalantly. 'Sit down.'

'I'm leaving.'

'We both know you are not.'

'I'd rather stand.'

'Suit yourself.'

'You know, this is all just lies,' I say. 'You're educated. You don't have to do this. You could work as a translator or something. There are many ways for a man like you to earn money in your own country. You *enjoy* this life. You have told me as much before. You like luxury. You despise poverty. This is your choice. I think you want to have it both ways and you have manipulated it all brilliantly.'

'Then we are very similar, no? What is wrong with having it both ways? *Shuk tski khalpe la royasa.* You cannot eat beauty with a spoon.' There is no smugness in his voice. He sounds weary.

I notice again the drawn muscles of his face and the way his skin is tight over his cheekbones. The hand that holds his cigarette is twitching. I wonder for a moment if he is ill. And I think immediately of the worst: AIDS, tuberculosis, anthrax. Maybe the dangerous world has caught up with him after all.

'What is wrong with you?' I ask this without much compassion. Whatever is wrong with him he has brought upon himself.

'You are right. I made my choice.'

'And you chose your wife.'

'No. I chose you.'

The lie is outrageous. 'It might have helped if you had told me.'

'You have every right to be angry. You will be pleased to know I have paid for it.'

'What – your wife put a curse on you?'

He doesn't say anything. My teeth, my muscles, all my connective tissues twist into a single sheet of anger. It must show in my face because he becomes very still. 'So you chose me. But you weren't prepared to leave your wife.'

'I did leave her. I left her the moment I walked out of that hotel in New York with you.'

I shake my head until my common sense rattles back into place. I don't want to go here, it is another country. But I can't help myself. 'You were just on your annual scavenger hunt.'

'That is not it at all.'

'No? You played around with me until the money ran out and then you launched a plan to scavenge off those Greeks. Was it profitable in the end? Did your wife enjoy my diamonds?'

He rubs one shoulder, a liar's gesture. 'I did not launch a plan. Anastasia fell in love with me. It was unacceptable. I hoped I would see you again one day and explain. But I can see now we have gone past that.'

'You got your money and you didn't care what happened to me.'

'Violet, I'm not innocent of stealing but I am innocent of intending to hurt you.' He stubs out his cigarette and stands up now. He walks towards me. I feel the door against my back.

'Don't come any closer or I *will* go.'

He stops. 'Why are you so afraid of me?'

'You're the Blood Count. You've bitten me twice. The third time might be fatal.'

He laughs at my sour joke but the sound is as hollow as if it has been piped all the way from Transylvania. 'It's I who have always been afraid of you.'

'Why would you be afraid of *me*? Look at me.'

'I am looking at you, Violet. I have wondered for many years how you bewitched me. I have been watching you from this window, trying to work it out. But now that you are here I feel the force of you again.'

There is a plaintive look in his eyes that almost sinks me. Damn that sentimental Violet, she is still clinging to me, a dead weight, pulling me down. I fight her off. 'So I'm some kind of witch? That's your excuse?'

'You are not entirely innocent, Violet. You know men cannot take their eyes off you. Beauty is power, as you well know.'

'Tell that to your beautiful Romanian prostitutes. Power is power.'

'Nevertheless, you are a beautiful package that powerful men would give everything to unwrap. Do you not realise in that moment of distraction what influence you have?'

'That's all I am, a distraction. Once unwrapped I am discarded.'

'I think you discard yourself.'

'Well, I never got the chance with you. You jettisoned me first.'

'And don't you think you had some responsibility in this? You saw in me a chance to escape something – an idea of yourself you didn't like, perhaps? And this was like a call to arms for me. I knew there was a danger with you. I tried to keep you distant. But you were wilful. You demanded something of me I told you I could not give.'

'You could have stopped. You didn't have to lead me on.'

'It is true I could have stopped. When I left you in Biarritz and went to Bucharest I was trying to stop it.'

'You told me you were in Paris.'

'I went to Paris *and* Bucharest.'

'Where you gambled away our money.'

'I did not gamble with it. My family needed money. Did you want me to return to them empty-handed?'

There. He has made it clear. There is something more precious to him than me. There always was. His family. My disgust at myself is only marginally stronger than my disgust for him.

'We've had six years of this century, Florin. Do you realise how many innocent people have died in terrorist attacks and hurricanes and plane crashes since I saw you last? Why couldn't one of them have been you?'

'You are heartless, Violet. And I made you like this.'

'Don't give yourself all the credit. There have been other bastards.'

'I'm sorry to hear that.'

'No, you're not. When I walk out of here you'll go back to Bucharest and forget all about me again.'

He starts pacing. 'All right. I will tell you another truth. I loathe Bucharest, my wife, her stupid brothers, all the poverty, the terrible food, the ugliness, the complaining about the Communists, the limited imagination, the way everyone lies down and lets the bureaucracy trample over them . . . you have seen it. And many times I have wished to walk away from it, from the very beginning in fact, but Romica kept having babies —'

'And that's not your fault?'

'Please, Violet. So it became convenient for me to have another life. The life I would have had if I had not met her in the park. And I liked this life, as you know. And Romica liked it too. She liked the gifts I would bring her. She liked those things better than she liked me as a husband.'

'*My wife doesn't understand me.* Do you know how many times I have heard that from men?'

'But she does understand me. She understands me very well. And she understands why I am here. A cash cow, as you say. This is very fortunate for me because it clears my conscience when I am not with her.'

'I thought you didn't have a conscience.'

'But, on the other hand, if I wish to be entirely free of her . . . it is impossible.'

'Don't you care about your children?'

'They have a better life than most Romanian children. They go to school, they have new clothes, they are well fed.'

'That's not what I asked. Don't you love them?' I think about the three locks of hair in his wallet.

'I wanted to be with you, not them. Does that answer your question?'

'I had my chance to have children. And you took me away from it.'

'I didn't take you away from anything. Like me, you chose. You chose me.'

'It was the wrong choice.'

I remember the night I met him, in Vienna, when he fought those gypsy children away from me. I should have seen it as a sign.

'You are not too old bear children, Violet.'

I don't respond. Even if I could bear children, I can no longer bear the thought. 'And now?' I ask him. 'Who do you chose now?'

'Now it doesn't matter.'

He is expert at saying things that sound like they come from the heart when there is no heart for them to come from. I am not so much a fool that I feel sorry for him. 'Are you going back to your wife?'

'I don't have the requisite gifts yet. Stephanie was disappointingly ungenerous.'

'You have been cruel to me,' I say as calmly as I can. 'Bringing me into this.'

'I have been punished for it.'

'And so have I. I have been punishing myself for six years.'

As soon as my words fill my ears I am undone by the truth of what I have said.

I *have* been punishing myself.

I have drifted from man to man, refusing offers of marriage or permanent liaisons. I have been indifferent to their extravagant gifts, taking only what I need and giving the rest away. I have for the most part, accepted men who do not attract me or cannot satisfy me or have obligations elsewhere and when any of these men proves to be wholesome and sweet and honourable, like poor Mats, I have taught myself to be quickly bored by him. And Charles – I hitched myself to Charles because I could see from across a hotel lobby what kind of rogue he would be. And, yes, he was a *great* man and a *respected* one and could tell a thousand tales at the dinner table to make people love him. But in truth

I was in it for the degradation, the gleam in his eye as I masturbated for him, the patronising dismissal of my views on anything, the negotiating of my talents for other men – what a perfect couple we made, the courtesan and the old bastard.

I punished myself because I didn't want Florin to be right about me. I didn't want to be seduced into dependency on a man like Lyle Huntington, who would shower me in jewels and finery, set me up in my own apartment, keep me in the style I was accustomed to until I became too accustomed to it and was ditched like a portfolio of underperforming shares. And it wasn't because I didn't want the *things* this man could give me but precisely because I wanted them too much. I wanted luxurious sheets and real diamonds and the respect of hotel concierges and the chauffeurs who opened doors. I had begun to love the life but it was not *my* life, it was something I borrowed in the way that men borrowed me.

We are only loaning ourselves, Violet.

If Florin saw every relationship as a commercial arrangement then I would go against this. I would make arrangements but they would not be commercial. I would take or leave everything – companionship, sex, expensive handbags, embroidered sheets. If Florin wouldn't love me then I would show him one day what that lack of love had done to me. I would meet him in a lobby somewhere and I would say, *Look at me. I am Violetta. I only have one suitcase. And I am free of you.*

But, of course, in wanting Florin to be wrong, in wanting not to be the woman he made me, I have only wronged myself.

And I am not free of him.

There's nothing more to say.

'I'm leaving.'

He nods. He has confessed all he wants to confess. 'Where are you going this time?'

'I told you I was going to Dubai. There is no reason to change my mind.'

'The gypsy life.'

'I'm more of a gypsy than you.'

He smiles. 'I think that is true.'

He walks me to the door. He opens it for me, pushing the handle up this time, and takes my suitcase out into the courtyard. It stands between us while he takes my hand and presses it to his lips. 'Perhaps we will see each other again one day. There are thousands of hotels where we have not been. We never did go to Madagascar.'

'If you see me in one of them I want you to pass me by.'

'If you wish.'

I take my hand away. 'Goodbye, Florin.'

'Violet?'

'Yes?'

'I tried to give you what pleased you. I did please you, didn't I?'

I don't say anything. He knows the answer.

He gives me a faint smile and goes back into the villa.

I stare at the door as it clicks shut. The room service card floats to the ground. I pick it up and slip it back over the handle.

Ne pas déranger.

AL ABU FALASA
Dubai, United Arab Emirates

Violet sits in the lobby of the Al Abu Falasa hotel, feeling like a tiny fish that has been swallowed by a monstrous, gilded whale. Gold-leafed ribs soar overhead, ten storeys high, encaging the lobby in a blubber-soft plushness of red and turquoise furnishings, with Persian carpets the size of small lakes and bronze palm trees bent to an invisible breeze. A series of fountains shooting single spurts of water tumble between floors, forming the scaly body of an enormous, enamelled sea bass. The glass dome that hovers above is patterned from palace tiles and sends showers of coloured light down on the white *dishdashas* of the Arab guests moving below. Violet half expects that the giant hand of Allah will come down from the heavens and grasp the dome, turning it like a kaleidoscope so that the colours and patterns change.

She is dressed, very plainly, in a black frock, and although the label is expensively Italian, the long sleeves and high neck suggest a visitor who is sensitive to the prevailing religious codes. (But, really, sensitivity is not necessary in this Wild West of a town. Seated in this very same lobby are women whose attire would not look out of place on the podium in a pole-dancing club.) Her earlobes are bare of diamonds and her fingers of rings. She knows some men would see a challenge in that, so she keeps her hands entwined in her lap, shakes her head so that her hair falls in waves over her ears. She does not want to draw undue attention to herself. But, of course, that is an impossibility. Three months shy of her fortieth birthday she is still a beauty of some reckoning.

A waiter has poured her a sparkling rosé and the glass sits in front of her on the low marble table, untouched. She is nervous sitting here, more nervous than she has felt in a hotel lobby for a long time. She has to go back ten years, to Melbourne, to the night she waited for Patrick, or to Paris, to the night she waited for Luka, to arouse the same level of anxiety. And again she is waiting, waiting for a man, but this time it is an active waiting of her own bidding, not the passive waiting of years gone by.

She has been looking for him for thirteenth months and, having found him, the slow exchange of letters and short, awkward phone calls from obscure locations delayed this moment even further. She is not even sure that he will be here, that their history won't defeat him, that he won't in the end decide she is untrustworthy, erratic, or compromised.

As the time lengthens beyond their appointed hour, she worries that the choice of hotel was a mistake. She thought they would not stand out in this hub of races and cultures, this *garam masala* of Arab women wearing black *abayas*, Africans in their mud-print gowns, Pakistanis in *kameez* and *shalwar*, Buddhist monks in saffron robes, Chinese in zip-up jackets, Moroccans wearing *fez*, British soldiers on leave from Iraq in their khakis and oil men in their tight, dark business suits. She thought it might be easier for him to meet her somewhere that is entertaining, where there are always things to talk about outside themselves, but she worries now that it really is too much, that the extravagance of gold and fountains and carpets will overwhelm him and scare him off. Perhaps the airport, his suggestion, might have been more neutral after all. A hotel lobby is only a short elevator ride from the bedrooms upstairs.

She smooths her skirt over her knees and pointedly ignores the admiring glances of a man, seated near her, who smiles approvingly from beneath his checked *gutra*. She has noticed the sizeable gold watches on each wrist and the bodyguards standing discreetly aside while three Westerners in suits make some kind of pitch for his business. Once she would have responded to his smile, accepted a drink, encouraged an approach, engineered an arrangement. She feels the familiar twinge of curiosity. Who is he? Where might he take her? What is his body like under those robes? But then she checks herself. There is only one kind of arrangement she wants now.

She has been bad and she has to become good again.

Her large handbag, on the sofa beside her, is as costly as a small car. In preparation for what is to come, she has rid herself of the last of her valuable things. But she can't quite put on the sackcloth and ashes. Time enough for that. In the small monogrammed suitcase she has left with the porter, there is a cocktail dress from Balenciaga and a winter coat from Lanvin. They will be useless where she is going and yet she can't quite bear to divest herself of them. They are sentimental remnants of another life.

She flips open the latch on her handbag and rummages for the little travelling clock she carries now that the Cartier watch has gone. The small emerald in the ring on her index finger is her only ornamentation. In the bag, there are other sentimental things. Her old passport, scarred with the stamps of a hundred ports of entry. A cigarette lighter, although she no longer smokes. A few business cards from The Union Hotel. Tucked into a side pocket, a folded piece of bathroom tissue with *Biarritz* scrawled on it. And in the bottom, the book she is writing, a shabby thing now, the spine coming away and some loose pages out of order, tear-stained and tea-stained and undisturbed since the last entry,

Ne pas déranger.

She can't bear to read it. Many times she has wanted to throw it away. Once or twice she has deliberately left it behind – in a café, in an airport lounge – but each time some misguided soul has pursued her to return it. She has poised on bridges, contemplating dropping it like a heavy stone tablet into the water and lit matches in bathrooms, intending to make a furnace of it. But, in the end, she recognises that abandoning it would be abandoning part of herself. Violetta *is* Violet, and she is not a page that can be torn out or discarded but something written on the skin, indelible. She is like the flowery tattoo, demanded in a moment of drunkenness, that leaves you shaking your head that you could ever mark yourself in this way, and yet remains, months and years later, curiously beautiful.

Violet tucks a loose page back between the hard covers and retrieves her small clock. She looks at it and puts it away, closing the bag. He is now fifty minutes late. She tries to calm herself. Lateness is not, in itself, too troublesome. Perhaps it is to be expected. His plane might have been delayed. He may not have accounted for the lines to get out of the airport, which are impossible. And then, there are the roads, which are often in gridlock. A dozen excuses, which will do for the moment. She won't panic, she won't think about what happens if he doesn't come. There are other ways she can save herself . . .

At first she doesn't recognise him. He has grown a beard that crawls all over his cheeks and down over his throat like black mould. He is unexpectedly heavy, given that he has been living for years in a country rent by drought and plague. When she stands up to give him a peck on the cheek he is shorter than she remembered. His smooth hands are now rough. She can feel a wedding band on one swollen finger. The only thing that remains the same is his round wire glasses. She is sure they are the same ones he wore all those years ago.

'Daniel,' she says, not letting go of his hand.

He rolls his shoulders awkwardly as if he doesn't know what to do with his bulk. 'You don't look any different,' he says quietly, a faint African lilt colouring his words.

'But *you* do. I thought they would have starved you.'

'It's all the starch,' he says, unsmiling. 'Bananas and corn. And the drugs. My malaria keeps recurring.'

'That's terrible,' she says, extracting her hand now. 'Do you mind sitting here?'

'Looks good to me. I've been flying around Africa for a day.'

'I thought the hotel would be easy to find.'

He nods thoughtfully. He waits for her to sit before taking the other side of the sofa. He looks uncomfortable with his legs together, not quite facing her, his satchel resting between his calves. Ten years have passed and he seems like another man altogether, no longer the sweet, funny lad who brought her silly presents to cheer her up, but someone stolid, middle-aged and wary. But why wouldn't he be wary of her, appearing like this after all these years and demanding to be part of his life, when she was barely in it before? They had worked together for less than a year. He had developed a terrible crush on her and she had done everything she could to discourage him. This hardly counted as a relationship or even a friendship, she thinks guiltily. And yet I am now expecting him to behave like the truest friend.

He looks stunned by the surroundings. 'You've been here before?'

'Once. A couple of years ago.'

'What was it like?'

'Ridiculously extravagant. The suites are on two levels, and there is one butler to each guest.'

'You've had quite a life,' he says. A pause. 'What happened to that tennis player?'

'That was a long while ago.'

He looks directly at her now. 'Sorry. That was the last thing I should have asked. I was just curious. A lot of people were upset when you left like that.'

'Was it bad of me?'

'I left too.'

'That's not the same thing. You went to Mozambique and helped people.'

'And look at me. Still there.' There's a scar she hasn't noticed before on the corner of his mouth and it lifts the side of his face in a half-smile. He tugs at a pocket on the thigh of his cargo pants. 'I bet you've been a few places.'

'I've seen enough.'

He studies her now, taking in her prim dress and pearly nails. He seems on the edge of saying something. But a waiter interrupts and takes his drink order.

'Coca-Cola?' she asks when the waiter has gone.

'I can't drink any more. My liver is shot.'

'I remember you used to like your whisky.'

'It's not that. I've had amoebic infestations, meningitis, hepatitis A, C, you name it.'

'I'm sorry.'

'Nothing's going to get me now.' He adds wryly, 'Unless it's a gang armed with AK47s.'

'Is it that bad?'

'Not really. The economy is growing. There's massive foreign investment. The politics are relatively stable. But there's the inevitable corruption. And millions of refugees still to be repatriated. Every year, hundreds of people are still blown up by live landmines. The children pick them up, thinking they're toys. We see a lot of that in Mocuba.' His green eyes behind the glasses are now blazing with a cool fire. She recognises what she'd found attractive about him before, a spark of young man's fervour.

'From what they said, you're living in some kind of refugee camp there?'

'Yes, in an old hotel.'

'And you're married?' Her eyes go to his wedding band.

'Yes. She's Dutch. Anika. She runs a school in the refuge. I met her four years ago. When I was just about to give up, in fact. It's funny how things happen.'

'Any children?'

He shakes his head. Another silence. 'I tried to find your Eliniphao, you know.'

'You did?'

'According to the World Care profile, she lived with her aunt in a village near Nampula. I went there once, but there wasn't any trace of her.'

Violet feels the colour rush to her cheeks. 'Oh . . .'

'Don't worry, she probably moved away. The drought. She'd be a young woman now, anyway. Married. Taken care of.'

Taken care of. Violet thinks of girls marrying at thirteen, slaves to older husbands. And herself at thirteen, confused and ashamed. 'I left money for her. I didn't want to abandon her.'

'I'm sure she's all right.'

'Are you?'

He slips a finger under the wire of one lens and rubs his eye. Then he looks at her seriously. 'Violet, I don't know if you're ready for this.'

'I've got my visa.'

'That's not what I mean.'

'You have my ticket?'

'Yes. The money came through.'

'And we're still leaving tonight?'

He nods. 'The flight is at 10 p.m.'

'Then I'm ready.'

'Violet . . . I don't think you understand what it's like there.'

'Describe it, then.'

'All right.' He turns his body to square with hers and rests a sandalled foot on one knee. His fingers pick at the buckle while he talks. 'The Excelsior was once the grandest hotel on the African continent. I've seen photographs of it, in the old days. There were marble bathrooms and enormous chandeliers, gardens, blue water in the swimming pool, things you can't imagine now. The richest people in Europe came to stay there. Frank Sinatra gave a concert in the ballroom. But during the war of independence in the 1970s it became a refugee camp. About three thousand people lived there for more than a decade. Looters stripped everything out of the hotel – the wooden flooring, the furnishings, the marble tiles, even the bath plugs. At the end of the civil war, in the 1990s, it was home to more than one thousand squatters. There's more now. New babies, orphans that have been abandoned, children dumped there because they've been crippled by landmines and their families can no longer look after them. Everyone is taken in, even though there is nothing for anyone. We don't even have clean water – we rely on aid for that. You should see it—' He stops, realising the invitation implicit in the sentence. 'Well, everyone does their washing in what water is left in the swimming pool, dozens of families sleep under the grand staircase, when there is corn it is stored in the baths. Whole chunks of ceiling have fallen in, floors have collapsed and the roots of trees have grown around the pillars of the lobby. There have been floods, earthquakes and war. The squalor is unimaginable – and yet these people love it like it's a palace.'

'I'm ready for any squalor you can throw at me.'

He sighs. 'Are you, Violet? I don't know anything about your life but you look like you've been pampered. It's distressing there. You have to develop a hide like an elephant. You will probably get sick with something serious, and more than once. There's a lot of crime. A woman like you is sure to attract attention. You have to guard against kidnapping. It's not enough to have a good heart, you know.'

'I don't have a good heart,' she says simply.

His knee stops jiggling. The furrows between his brows deepen to ravines. 'What happened to you?'

She brushes off the question. 'People are always saying a woman like me shouldn't do this or should do that. What kind of woman do you think I am?'

'I don't know. But your hands are soft. I haven't seen a woman with soft hands for a long while.'

'I don't mind getting dirty. Don't judge me by this dress, these shoes. I have work clothes in my suitcase.'

'It's not just the clothes.'

'Then what?'

It's his turn to avoid the question. 'Why did you think of me? No one has heard from you in years. I asked about you . . . once or twice.'

'I always wondered where you were.'

'Did you?'

'I never meant to hurt you, Daniel. You knew I was married.'

'That didn't seem to matter with the tennis player, did it? Sorry.' Appalled at his outburst, Daniel looks down. A refraction of coloured light from the dome makes a wine stain on his cheek.

They don't say anything for a while. The waiter brings his Coca Cola and places it on the table. Daniel stares at the foggy glass for a while before picking it up and sipping it. When he puts it down, he turns to her, and rubs his eye nervously again. 'Violet, I can't take you. I can't be responsible for you.'

She reaches across the sofa and puts a hand on his knee. It tenses under her touch. 'You don't have to be,' she says. 'I can look after myself. Just get me there. Or give me the ticket and I'll get there myself.'

He moves her hand off his knee. She blushes, thinking that he has misinterpreted her gesture. 'It doesn't work like that. You'd be part of a team. In fact, if you were anyone else you'd have to go through a series of interviews.'

'Interview me, then. I don't want special treatment.'

'But you are special. I wouldn't have flown from Moputo to Johannesberg to some godforsaken North African outpost to here if you weren't.' There's an edge in his voice now. Bitterness, she thinks. Where did that come from? Not a ten-year-long unrequited love, surely? Is her beauty working against her again?

'Daniel—'

He cuts her off. His face is concentrated. 'This is a kind of interview, anyway. I'm not making a decision until you explain everything.'

'What do you want me to explain?'

'Why you want to work in Africa *now*. You're not running away from someone, are you? Mocuba is not a place to run to.'

'No, I'm not running away. I've always wanted to do this. I just got . . . distracted.'

'Distracted by what?'

'Possibilities that weren't fulfilled.'

'When you wrote to me you said you didn't have any children. Is that what is making you feel unfulfilled? Because if that's the case we can't take you. We've had problems before. Women who fall in love with children in their charge and want to take them away.'

'I wouldn't do that.'

'Are you sure, Violet? You mentioned children specifically in your letter.'

'I want to *save* children. I don't want to give birth to them.'

'But we don't save most of them. That's the truth. You'll end up being bitterly disappointed. Like me.'

'Saving one would be enough.'

He looks hard into her eyes now. 'We're not missionaries, you know.'

'I know.'

'It's not a way of saving yourself. Of making amends . . .'

But it is.

He appraises her for another moment and then hoists his satchel on to his lap. He takes out a folder and shows it to her. 'Here are your tickets. Maybe you can exchange them for another destination.'

'And where would I go?' She bites her lip to stop it trembling.

'If you really want to help children, don't come to Mozambique. It's too dangerous. Go to China, where they toss little girls into the garbage, but the society is relatively safe. Or to Romania. I read a briefing about it yesterday. The government is closing down the orphanages but now the country has joined the European Union it's worse than ever. Parents are abandoning their children to go off to Britain, France and Germany to earn a living. You could do a lot of good work there and it's not as risky as Africa.'

Romania.

He misinterprets her snort of derision. 'It's not as bad there as you think. I believe it's really beautiful.'

'You've made up your mind about me, haven't you?'

'Yes. It's not safe for you in Mocuba.'

'It's safe enough for your wife.'

'She's not like you, Violet.'

The way he looks at her now, gravely, his eyes watery with the poignant realisation of lost opportunity, she knows she will never fit in. He has a wife, a life, and he is fearful her presence will disturb or even destroy what it has taken years to build.

She takes the folder of tickets out of his hand. 'Thank you for coming all this way to meet me.'

'Not a problem,' he lies. 'I do a lot of recruiting.'

'Hopefully you find people who are more suitable than me.' She smiles to show him there are no hard feelings. But there are.

'I didn't say you weren't suitable. The country isn't suitable for *you*. I could put you in touch . . .'

'No, it's okay. I know people.'

'Good. That's good.'

'There are a few hours to kill before your flight. Do you want to have dinner?'

He looks uncomfortable. 'No, no. I think I might go to the airport early. I need to write a report.' He points to his satchel.

'About me?'

'No. No one knows I'm here.' He blushes at the admission. He clutches his satchel under his arm, poised to stand up. 'You don't need any money, do you?'

'No, I've got plenty,' she lies.

'I thought so,' he says. 'I'm glad life has been good to you.'

'Daniel, do you really want to know what I've been doing all these years?'

'No, I don't,' he says, looking alarmed. 'It doesn't matter to me what you've been doing.'

So, there have been rumours, she thinks. 'I've been travelling,' she says.

He looks relieved. 'A bit of a gypsy, then?'

'Exactly,' she says.

He stands up and so does she. He leans over and gives her a peck on the cheek. He pats his pocket. 'I'll leave some money for the drink.'

'No, you won't. It's taken care of.'

'Thanks.' He rolls his shoulders awkwardly again. 'What will you do?'

'I might take your advice.'

'Great,' he says. 'That's great.' He turns and walks away, turns back once and waves.

She takes her seat again.

As soon as she does, a waiter pounces. 'The gentleman over there would like to send you a bottle of champagne. Will you accept?'

Will she accept? There is more than a bottle of champagne on offer. In her head, she should pick up the life she left long ago, back in Melbourne, Patrick's life, her parent's life, the life of family, community, responsibility, routine, the comforting mundanity of it all. In her conscience she should go where Daniel sends her, Romania or China, to make amends. In her heart she is still in Biarritz, running along the wet beach with shoes in her hand.

But these are other people's lives and she is only borrowing them.

She is a lobby, a glittering shell, a place of expectations, where people come and go.

She doesn't even look in the direction the waiter is indicating.

'I'll accept it,' she says.

I am sitting in the lobby of the Al Abu Falasa. It's the devil's hour, cocktail hour, when gentlemen are known to stray from their intended paths.

Sooner or later, one of them will stray my way.